I0685934

Praise for J. Daniel Stone

Praise for
Stations of Shadow
by J. Daniel Stone

"Wildly inventive and dazzlingly transgressive, Stone's writing is imbued with a unique, otherworldly fire that will have you both terrified and mesmerized during those revelations."
—Rue Morgue

"Stations of Shadow is Stone's most personal work to date and features some of his darkest, most daring imagery."
—Ink Heist

"Stone's writing style continues to be just as lavish and dark and evocative as ever. There are few people more qualified to deliver jet black poetic tales from the shadowy streets of the Big Apple."
—This is Horror

"There's a sepulchral feel to Stations of Shadow. Strange, bold, and perversely beautiful {as the book} strips away the outer skin, revealing the bones and sinew beneath each performer."
—Deliciously Dark Romance

"Stations of Shadow is not your regular cliche supernatural horror story. It has a lot more depth to it which needs you to be focused and concentrating on the events happening. The vivid scenes make the story comes alive before your eyes. Sometimes this can be scary because of the amount of darkness some of the scenes have. The dark horror and the complex LGBTQ characters combined made this a wonderful reading experience."

—*Rainbow Reviews*

Praise for
Lovebites & Razorlines
by J. Daniel Stone

"Vibrant and harrowing, Lovebites & Razorlines features 13 fascinating, powerful distillations of dark prowess, covering an insanely diverse thematic and atmospheric range."
—*Rue Morgue*

"Stone has delivered a collection of stories as horrific as they are thought-provoking. Everything about this collection screams quality. His lyrical and poetic style make the words come to life and dance right off the page and into your head."
—*This is Horror*

"J. Daniel Stone crafts potent descriptions of characters and settings. It's rare for most artists and especially rare in writers."
—*Drunk in a Graveyard*

"Every time you pick up a book by J. Daniel Stone, you are at risk of transformation."
—Donna Fox, author of *Dark Tales from the Den*

Praise for
Blood Kiss
by J. Daniel Stone

"*Blood Kiss* is a powerful book that sticks with you. Raw and subversive, it presents horrific imagery in a stark, unflinching manner that keeps us turning the pages. It's a nihilistic romp through the underground art world [that] captures the outsider energy that attracted so many of us to not just watch and read horror, but make it a lifestyle."
—Rue Morgue

"Stone's writing does not skimp on the poetic flourishes, deep philosophical ruminations, or not-so-subtextual subtexts. There is deviance and intoxication and unshakable imagery and cataclysms and no shortage of haunting moments. A welcome respite from the mania for utilitarianism currently plaguing genre writing. This is challenging work from an author clearly chomping at the bit to screw with convention and preconceptions. Even at its most brutal—and *Blood Kiss* will goddamn bloody well disturb you at times—it is a paradoxically lovely read."
—Fangoria

"So many fierce images, so immediate and propulsive! There's huge energy in *Blood Kiss*—the energy of a performance, when the audience and the people on stage feed from one another, push each other past all boundaries, together."
—**Kathe Koja, author of *The Cipher* and *Christopher Wild***

"It's the art-scene, it's the death-scene, the sex-scene . . . the shadows, the madness, the mania. Nightmare, but mostly bone-wide awake. Stone makes it feel like you are the characters . . . in all those scenes. And it's tempting to say, 'Keep an eye on this guy.' Because he's young. Because this is only his second book. But you'd only say something like that to mean one day he's gonna do something great. The thing is, he already has. It's right here. Blood Kiss is refreshing as hell. In a field where most are trying to out-thrill one another, Stone is riffing, philosophizing, writing . . . out loud."
—**Josh Malerman, author of *Bird Box* and *Black Mad Wheel***

"Be warned, J. Daniel Stone writes with a razor blade and he aims to cut you on the very first page. Blood Kiss explores interwoven themes of lust and inspiration in the lives of struggling artists in New York City. Haunting, visceral and equal parts poetic prose and madness."
—**John C. Foster, author of *Mister White***

"Like Poppy Z. Brite, dark and sensuous and filled with artsy characters on the fringes of society. Like Clive Barker, even darker and viscerally sexual, where blood and love come together to paint a disturbing picture. But even more, *entirely* J. Daniel Stone, with a voice like no other new writer I've read. He drips this novel, *Blood Kiss*, with a bleak, disturbing sensuousness that oozes from the pages. Stone makes you feel the pain that goes into art—whether music or painting—and the pain that art causes. He'll make you believe that art has a life of its own—dark and dreadful. And love . . . oh love hurts."
—Bram Stoker-Nominated Author John F.D. Taff

"J. Daniel Stone's *Blood Kiss* is a chilling marriage of Clive Barker's vision and Kathy Acker's style. Stone writes with a wicked carnality that is frightening and frighteningly sensual. *Blood Kiss* will be in your head long after you've finished reading it."
—Bracken MacLeod, author of *Mountain Home* and *Stranded*

"*Blood Kiss* is more an experience than a book. By some kind of sleight-of writer's-hand, Stone does more than simply create a world, he leads us from earth to dark "other sides" and back with ease, as if it were all a simple matter of taking the G train between Manhattan and Brooklyn. And when Stone gets you to the end, well, let me just say that *Blood Kiss* may give you that elusive bookgasm you didn't know was possible."
—Erik T. Johnson, author of *Yes Trespassing*

"Blood Kiss is a memorable novel bursting with vivid prose, incredible and original characters and enough darkness to cause an eclipse. At times I was unable to put this book down as Stone dragged me deeper and deeper into a New York art scene where the merging of two different art forms creates something totally new, unique, exciting and sexy. It's an immersive reading experience, and one of the most original dark fiction books I have come across in recent time."
—**Beavis the BookHead**

"Everything J. Daniel Stone publishes breaks new ground, but *Blood Kiss* leaves gigantic furrows of earth in its wake. It would sit comfortably on the shelf between Barker and Kiernan, and it should definitely be on your shelf."
—***Ginger Nuts of Horror***

"J. Daniel Stone's writing possesses a mesmerizing, silken music. He's one of those rare storytellers who can draw you along irresistibly and thrill you with his artistry at the same time. His scrutiny of love and desire is fearless. *Blood Kiss* is a haunting journey through the dark labyrinth of the wounded heart, where obsession can fuel both creativity and destruction. Terrifying, beautiful and utterly unique, it will leave you hungry for more from this brilliant young author."
—**Stephen T. Vessels, Thriller Award-nominated author of *The Mountain & The Vortex***

Praise for
The Absence of Light
by J. Daniel Stone

"*The Absence of Light* is lush and lyrical...a jangled and disturbing book that seeks to transcend through rituals and incantations. This book is highly recommended for anyone who wants dark prose that seeks to transgress boundaries though not designed to appeal to people who want streamlined plots, transparent prose, or simple stories. First novels are often ragbags where writers try to explain life, so Stone has clearly come across more dark wisdom than most people."
—Hellnotes

"J. Daniel Stone is a gifted young writer, capable of some of the most beautiful sentences about the most horrid things. [*The Absence of Light*] combines horror, the art world, the music world, the paranormal world, the young, displaced hipster world...and combines it all into a heady, trippy story that is sad at times, powerfully dark at others. I didn't just enjoy the book; I enjoyed the act of reading it."
—John F.D. Taff, Bram Stoker-nominated author of
The End in All Beginnings

"From the first few pages I was swept into a dark punky world of nightclubs, Jägermeister, craft beer, ghosts, and music. [Stone knows] what it feels like to grow up "different" – different being, queer, goth, fat, loser, outcast, whatever you want to call it. To me [*The Absence of Light*] became instantly important because it represents the power of so-called "outsider" fiction and it is with this power that this book will call its' readers home."
—*Drunk in a Graveyard*

"*The Absence of Light* manages to walk the fine line between the suffocatingly eerie and tear jerking beautiful. J. Daniel Stone gives his characters life in a bleak world resonating with song…which you will never want to leave."
—Jonathan Moon, author of *Heinous* and *Stories To Poke Your Eyes Out To*

". . . one part ghost story, one-part alternative lifestyle exploration that explores the themes of identity, loss, and the power of art through poetic language."
—Fanboy Comics

ALSO BY
J. DANIEL STONE

THE ABSENCE OF LIGHT

BLOOD KISS

I CAN TASTE THE BLOOD

LOVEBITES & RAZORLINES

STATIONS OF SHADOW

Daubed in Darkness

J. Daniel Stone

For Frankie Maddox Rex,
gifted musician and my rockstar

You were the one person
who always understood my books
from the inside out, and looking back,
you're the only one that mattered

I miss your creativity, your passion,
your voice, your music, and most of all,
our lifelong friendship

RIP

Daubed in Darkness

J. Daniel Stone

Part 1

Macabre Musings

"We make our world significant by the courage of our questions."

—Carl Sagan

1

Rust. Skeleton key. A box of gilt and gold.

I stare at these nightmare relics, transfixed that someone once loved them far beyond my comprehension. Antiques tell stories of horror and adventure, like works of fiction in physical form. When they are passed from hand to greedy hand, tainted by haunts and time, they take with them parts of the people they once were owned by. I can't help but wonder how many ghosts they hold.

I've always been fascinated by the plight of artists. They disturb common notions, dare people to think. The muse is a mystery, and we will never understand why it comes and goes. If you were to transpose yourself into the head of any artist, you'll draw the same conclusion. Ache, fill a void, and then ache again. It's the creative circle of life. But art has drastically changed.

Long gone is the idea of chasing your own dream. We now live in a technological collective. To be relevant today, one needs to insert themselves into the world with a social media presence. There once was a time when an artist could communicate with their finished product; now we are mired in self-promotion and silly online posts that are doomed to drown within the endless static ocean of the internet, or are simply passed over by the ever-shrinking attention span.

When I created @MiniMonstrosities on Twitter and Instagram, I had to come up with a catchy bio and take pics of myself before I could even show my art. After days of pulling my hair out I settled on *The Kooky Creations of Atticus Atlas* so the alt, e-boy, goth/ punk/metal, hipster, queer, and questioning culture knows where to find me. All it takes is a vampire face to draw them in.

I post the secret ways of sculpting and sketching. Sometimes I do this shirtless or scantily clothed, just to cater to various crowds. Social media is greedy and fleeting and you never know who will be looking at you. Thus, we are trapped in a sick computer game of cat and mouse, just to hopefully catch the eye of an intermittent beholder. Covering all bases is key. Hashtags ensure that my posts trend, and engaging with my audience satisfies their need for validation. All of this effort to build an avatar family.

I would have once considered the internet a safe space before social media. But supportive online communities have been replaced by cell phone silos and tiny remote despots that use the shield of their keyboards to bring others down. I don't recognize the world anymore. I am still not even sure if I want to be part of it. And art is not the only thing that's changed.

For the first time in fifty years, New York has gone dark. More people are moving out than moving in. The buildings are stiller than ever. No longer do I see them sway, and somehow, I've become completely apathetic to the sawtooth skyline that at one time or another gave me life. I've never seen so many windows without light, so many businesses shut down and so much looting. Graffiti has risen from the abyss and homelessness is running rampant. It's bedlam.

Since quarantine began, life has become a newfound solitary confinement. Not in the way I used to enjoy. I find myself pissing time away by trying to top my own social posts or reading about random things that turn my brain into oatmeal without even knowing it. That's another secret of the internet: It chooses for us, despite having free education at our fingertips.

Now that social media has become the only means of connecting to the greater world, our resident electronic germ might possibly destroy any sense of culture left in this city. All people want to do (and this was even before the pandemic) is view the world through the lens of a cell phone, rather than creating bonds with actual people. It's a common technological entitlement.

The mystery surrounding artistic process died when we sold our souls to social media. And my own art has seen better days. My newest miscreation is called *Garden Gob*. A jade bust that puts the image of Cthulhu into my head if it were covered in kudzu and wore a Gothic dress. Porous to keep it lightweight and textured with pieces from the urban gardens of New York. A tiny crown of pebbles rests upon its head, and a sewer rat coat of fur that beguiles its lengthy tongue; the glint of glass gives its eyes life.

Sometimes I trick myself into thinking it's alive. Maybe that's because I live in one of the last Italian strongholds on Mulberry Street. Surely a handful of people have died inside my apartment over the decades, be it old age, a slip, trip and fall, or a Mafia hit. Though the supernatural always comes to mind, these days there are less places for ghosts to go as non-believers have outnumbered the believers. Even if there were a ghost, someone would just get it on video and post it online, and it'd be forgotten three days later. Another mystery hyped into ruins.

My abstract busts and sculptures are usually commissioned by obscenely rich people, but those snobs are buying less these days. Yet here I am, acquiring another burn, callous and scab just to claim my creativity, rather than succumbing completely to the internet.

I was born sometime between the release of Guns n' Roses' *Appetite for Destruction* and Nine Inch Nails' *Pretty Hate Machine*. Classic millennial and gestational metal head. It was the late 1980s, a simpler time, but it was also one of great divide. Not just culturally or socially. Technology was at the precipice for society's next mutation. Video games and the internet were the crux of my formative years, whereas cell phones and social media were the bane of my adolescence.

Luckily, modern hypnotization didn't indoctrinate me immediately. My safe space was not indulging the lights of a cell phone screen, but inside my own head. I had no need for human interaction given the general desensitization of intelligence. I practiced social distancing before it became society's law of pandemics and quarantines. Thus, my life was a series of unfortunate events due to my inherent weirdness.

I was picked on at school for being scrawny and feminine, as well as the fact that I have two different colored eyes. *Devil*, they would call me. *Faggot!* The rejection that might have driven the normal child to suicide, I turned into inspiration. My fascination to break rules set me apart from the rest. Straw was spun to gold. It was in my Aries nature to do this. The more people made fun of me, the more I took it as incentive to do something that would have them hate me with a greater vigor.

If I was too skinny, I ate less; if too spooky, I became darker. Someone once called me "a fucking fem-boy", so I made sure to polish my nails and brighten my lips. We don't think deeply enough about the mechanics of our minds. It's a tidal wave of immense opportunity. If we took more time to explore our limitations, toy with every particle and sensible magic of human potential, we might be happier creatures.

That's when I realized that making art was more than just a hobby. It was emotional resonance. It started with breaking things down, and then rebuilding them. Destroy to create. I started with cut-ups. My literary hero, William S. Burroughs, had done this with his books by collecting pieces of prose and cutting them into triangles and squares, circles and oblong shapes, which then were pieced back together like a quilt to create some of the most elaborate texts I've ever read. Burroughs taught me that words could be used as a weapon, much like art.

I remember ripping the legs off a doll and shoving them into the body of a stuffed animal that made no biological sense. Sphinx or centaur, part man, part beast. Silly Putty helped me discover that I could use my hands to mold; Play-Doh was when I discovered I could dry these monstrosities and form embodiments of plague.

But what is incarnation without a face? I used a sewing needle to create elongated teeth, sunken eyes and gaping jaws; wings, talons and tongues that could reach into the body and slurp out vital organs. When I graduated to hot glue, clay and resin, I began to reshape my way of thought. These new materials brought about a range of possibilities. The paths I could take seemed endless.

I've always had a soft spot for darkness. It is the original temptation and the answer to our mortal existence. Darkness is the grim reaper *and* the grand giver, for life always begins, and ends, in darkness

Today, a message request came through on my Instagram. A rush of adrenaline besieged me. Internet-junky verified. The account was blank, save for a few craftily placed images of shadows and inkblots. Things we give into and question; things that sometimes look back at us if we look hard enough. I clicked into the message. *U cAnT hIde* written over and over and over. I counted three hundred and forty-seven times before I looked away. Somebody wanted my attention. Knowing the kind of people that I deal with, they were going to get it from me one way or another.

When I was seventeen, I dropped out of high school and ran away. The thought of one more day stuck in a droning classroom being told what to learn, what to read, how to act, how to think, was going to drive me to suicide. I also took this time to accept my sexuality. I shouldn't have been that surprised about it as life has always thrown curve balls my way, but it was still one of the hardest things to accept. I knew I wasn't straight even before I hit puberty. *Faggitus Faglas*, they called me in school, a play on my name. Kids can be so cruel.

But not as cruel as a neglectful mother.

Having been raised in an alcoholic home, I grew up far too quickly. My mother was once what we call a "babe" before she had me. However, the embarrassment she suffered from opening her legs to the only man she ever loved, and losing him, turned her haggard. In the eighties, teenage pregnancies were still the cause of much gossip. My family was Catholic, as were all the Italian stock that flooded the five boroughs. Abortion was immoral in the culture of the working class. Alas, I was a bastard child.

My mother never recovered from my father leaving her. I've deduced in my adult life that people aren't good at saying goodbye . . . in any form. Be it death or a breakup, this means things must change. People hate change. As a child I never understood my mother's mind, the utter selfishness of a woman so involved with her loneliness that she forgot her offspring desperately needed her. But now as an adult I have found the strength to simply feel sorry for her.

Since my mother saw a lot of my father in me, our relationship suffered for it. She rejected her only son, just couldn't bear the constant reminder. We were never close; she never wanted it. Subsequently, I could never find those feelings a child should have for their mother. No affection, no reason to equate her to a safety blanket.

Dismay in the home changes the human brain, and this ancestral trauma has followed me into adulthood. The home is supposed to be where one is safeguarded from all bad things. But when the home reverts into hell, its occupants are reshaped. They delve, unwillingly, into depression and anxiety. This is especially apparent at the time of puberty, when our bodies undergo that special dynamic shift: emotions exponentially sensitive, heightened awareness of our flaws and dealing with the graduation from childhood to the rest of our life.

We become sickeningly aware of our own mortality.

The problem with society is that we don't recognize our brief lifespan. Why are we here? Where did we come from? Why are the stars already dead by the time their light touches the night sky? Ignorance is the real virus, and apathy the manifestation. Introspection becomes impossible to avoid. How can I not be curious about existence? Is it here to serve some greater purpose? Is the construct of time a scientific fallacy? Is consciousness limited to just us Earthlings, and can we rocket ourselves out of this dimension and be something more? We're all a product of the stars, yet so obsessed with pretending that we are not.

I spent a year wandering through my own darkness. Headspace dangling between real life and the one of my dreams, conscious and unconscious, awake and not. I had art to create, boys to meet, and a laundry list of experimental platforms that I wanted to showcase. I was ridden with every primordial want and need you could imagine, no matter how much I tried to fight it. I could only dull my hormones for so long by my own hand. The touch of another was something I craved.

Humans, whether we like to admit it or not, are creatures of cohabitation.

So I consulted the internet, the greatest tool of my teenage life, putting myself out there in hopes to gain friendships and romances with only keyboard characters and the trust that the person on the other end of the screen wasn't going to kill me. Due to my insane mother, I was almost convinced that all humans were of that crazy archetype. Still, I had hope.

With the click of a button, I was able to locate people who were just like me: a little lost, a little queer, and passionately creative. The internet sucked me into its digital black hole of information and community. As a graduate of the Class of the Socially Awkward, this was my only chance to molt and find out exactly who I was to become. A lot of these so-called weird kids convened on the other side of Queens where I was born and raised. It was a place where strippers, pimps and the Mafia still had a presence.

Drugs were the town's lifeblood; death lurked and lurched on every corner. The avenues wobbled unsteadily, and the sidewalks sagged under the weight of your shoes. You could see the parts of the ground where the land was slipping away from the foundations of the buildings. And Manhattan was close enough to touch; at night it tattooed the sky with bright bars of luminescence so that no stars could be seen.

But in the places that the light didn't touch lived so many transients and those who thrived in hypodermic hypnosis.

Warehouses were strewn across a forgotten strip, soaring out of the concrete as if fungi made of brick and glass. It made sense that society's outcasts careened here. They called them *Saferwaters*, *Road to Nowhere* and *Fascination Street*, three songs that gave each dwelling an allegorical meaning.

Inside, the black walls seemed to absorb all light, and the ceilings were interlaced with a hex here and wicked insignia there. Plastic furniture met your body like jutting bones; scrungy couches were filled with bed bugs. There was always a honey-colored glow that emanated from unknown sources, but it soothed my nerves to have that kind of gloomy light touch my pale skin.

Every artist, queer, weirdo and in-between prospered here. It was a community that I had never known existed, even when the 5Pointz graffiti mural used to haunt this part of town. Sadly, in 2015 the building was sold to modern developers and torn down. But not before a daring graffito stamped his revenge on the newly painted white facade. ART MURDER slathered in red as deep and rich as the blood that artists spilled for 5Pointz. It's a sight I will never forget.

Anyway, this place was the hangout of all hangouts. Shut out from the world that never allowed us to express ourselves without being judged, we sought to bring our inner havoc to life, driven by shadow and loneliness and being misunderstood. Painters, poets, drag queens; authors, dancers, musicians; pain-seekers, lunatics, funzies; goths, emos and metalheads, all mingling and exchanging brilliant ideas.

Gatherings became routine, so much so that I crossed into many sects, hierarchies, and social circles. The warehouses were so big it was not uncommon to see a new face, hear about a new form of art, or catch the ectoplasmic gleam of a ghost. At one point I wanted to drop everything and move in with my new family all together, start a brand-new life, maybe obtain a new identity . . . until the day the absolute love of my life showed up.

He was the human form of anthracite and peridot; the most unique creature I had ever seen. An aura emanated about him, bright blue and shimmering, which made my eyes do a double take being he was so tiny. His getup was so loud my ears perked toward it. Wallet chain, ripped black jeans to reveal moony skin; a crop top that said *EAT ME* in a drippy font; thumb ring, a ring in his lip.

All things changed.

I was baffled and mesmerized all at once as a golden tendril reached into my hormones. Blood suffused every part of my sexual identity. My jeans became infuriating, restrictive shackles. I had to meet this radiating boy; he exuded life's tenebrous side. Not to mention, his smile was about as sharp and dangerous as a razor blade.

"Hi," I said shakily.

He winked. "Hello."

I knew immediately that I wanted to kiss him, but just didn't know how to go about it. Once again, the awkwardness that dominated my free will was getting in the way—but the red-hot temptation that drizzled over my hormones was pressuring me to reject hesitation and embrace nature. After I collected myself, after my heart went back to a normal rate and my smoker's breath stopped racing, I talked to him again.

"That thing in your hand."

"What about it?" The boy turned the music down from his headphones, "Blue and Yellow" by The Used.

He twirled the object so that I saw he'd painted each fingernail a different color, which reminded me of a mood ring. The item looked like the accidental melding of a spider and serpent that had more teeth than could fit in its horrible little mouth. The boy smiled at me, lips as pink as a newborn's gums, then flipped a fabulous wave of blue hair away from his eyes. The dark static that he gave off seeped into my bones; I could feel a snapping and cracking inside of me. He was almost too alive in a time when people like us were considered zombies of pop culture.

"You wanna hold it?"

Gum slapped between his tongue and teeth. For a moment my misophonia went nuclear, but I dared not let it control me in the presence of this devil-angel. I could smell the cigarette he'd just smoked, which was expertly covered up by the wintergreen flavor of the gum. Once again, my hormones were feral. I wanted to rip into him or have him rip into me in any way he would have me. Dead, alive, sweat-soaked and gleaming; desperate, muscles tensing, lips tied together, tongues at war. Eyes locked, pulses racing.

Instead of making a move on this prince of darkness, my hand instinctively reached for the thing he held. All six senses zeroed in on the object. I profoundly remember its weight, no more than a paperback book but its outer metal shell so thick and shining that a hammer couldn't have made a nick in it. Then its legs somehow *moved*, as if I'd taken some illicit hallucinogen. I saw flowering shapes and earthly darkness bloom as the toothy mouth clamped on my thumb ring; if not for that it surely would have drawn blood.

The boy laughed. I dropped the object on the floor, saw it scurry into a small crowd of squatters. Nobody batted an eye, probably mistook it for a rat. But the image of its snake-like face and octopus teeth swirled behind my eyes, nightmarish mini Sarlacc. The boy didn't move, almost as if he was testing me, and it was in the garish light of the room that I noticed he had two different colored eyes.

"The fuck was that?"

I must have sounded quite vanilla because he started to laugh.

"It's from my collection."

"What kind of collection?"

The boy lit a Marlboro. "A weird one," he said, blowing rings of smoke into my face.

"May I get one of those?"

"Yes, you can. But if you wanna get my name you'll have to sit with me."

We sat on a fire escape, dangling our legs and entwining our feet, a perfect fit like two spoons in a drawer. The experience was organic. As I cradled him, his head rested on my collar bone. I could smell his hair, the lush mixture of the dye and his natural oils. I was falling in love. There was something cosmically insane about the entire situation. For the rest of the night, we drank beer and talked. When the sun came up, I saw waves of heat drift across the city skyline, erasing the luscious night and welcoming a new chance at misadventure.

2

The boy with the blue hair was holed up in one of the shittiest neighborhoods Queens had to offer. A rotting, swampy excuse of traffic lights and incandescent shadows. Local artists dubbed this place "The Abyss" as it seemed nowhere else in the world could an amalgamation of smoke, silence and disdain mix so unkindly. Graffiti wriggled across dissolving facades, DEPORT TRUMP and STEAL AWAY THE NIGHT, followed by mocking caricatures and brooding cityscapes.

The town sprawled darkly off the 7 line and stood like some prehistoric fossil. You could feel the unease the moment your shoes met its shaky concrete. Passerby beware. Enter if you Dare. The machinations of Manhattan didn't live here. Its tenements wound back the hands of time in the way they slouched, exposing cracked foundations and crumbling fire escapes. Warehouses were found strewn across the last of the cobblestone roads, and its occupants were as sinewy and strange as house centipedes.

You could be born here and never leave.

This was the way it always went.

That kind of destiny was too frightening for Zephyr. To be stuck in some sick, looping time warp where life repeated itself, was a nightmare reality. Though he'd been raised somewhat a transient, the need to run away was ingrained into his DNA. But sometimes it was nice to call a place home, even if that place was a shithole.

Zephyr was not native to New York City, but he'd been here more than half his life and he now thought of himself as native. The memory of moving here was a bone-white blur, and Zephyr often tricked himself into believing it was a good one. He was too young to truly understand why his parents fled the Golden Coast for smog, sulfur, and swamp. It was one of those things where you were told to pack your stuff, keep your head down and don't talk until you got there.

They arrived two years before 9/11. Zephyr was twelve years old and on the verge of puberty. Hormones out of control, new hairs growing in places he didn't want them. Worst of all, his mezzo-soprano voice took a nosedive. As if it wasn't already bad enough feeling like an outsider in one of the biggest cities in the world—socially awkward, pale and two eyes that didn't match—everything Zephyr once knew about safety had cracked in two.

Fourteen years old, and the first day of his wretched high school stint—where over three thousand loud-mouthed ingrates brought immaturity to new levels—was halted the moment everyone saw black smoke billowing into the sky. Fiery debris and jetties of flame spit from various windows. Metal melted faster than he could have imagined. Before Zephyr could process what was going on, the buildings crumbled, and a plume of nuclear-smelling smoke engulfed lower Manhattan. And he could do nothing about it.

It was this moment he knew what death was: an instant and infinite nothingness.

In his adult life he'd occasionally watch videos on YouTube about 9/11. Zephyr liked to do this thing where he injected himself into the minds of the people who were stuck on the floors above where the planes hit. It was a way to vicariously see what they saw, feel what they felt. You either burned alive or jumped out. He didn't know what he'd do if he were in their position. He didn't think he was that brave.

Zephyr was an only child of parents who believed in a world where there was no heaven, hell or anything to divide people, as

John Lennon instructed through his music. A wayward belief that didn't work in the real world. His mother was a soft-featured, red-haired goddess of Irish stock, while his father was a dark-skinned, aquiline-nosed Roman god. Psychedelia was their religion. Quaaludes, LSD and psilocybin. It was the only way to stay in touch with their souls, star energy, and the gray zone that guards the other side of existence.

Procreation wasn't in his parent's plan. The first rule of enlightened hippies is to not have kids. Being privy to the fact that the world is doomed was one of the many reasons they didn't want children. Adding another mouth-breather would only deplete its resources faster. The child would most likely do no good with its life, and then pass on its corrupt DNA to create more emotionally unhealthy humans. But out came Zephyr either way, a premature mewling with one green eye and one brown.

Perhaps it was the hormones, or the empathy that enlightened people must suffer, but Zephyr's mother decided early into her pregnancy to not cut him out of her, nor put him up for adoption after birth. She raised him the "right" way, whatever that meant, although she lacked the classic gusto and pride of a typical mother. She was never overcome with that "calling" most women feel, and she didn't require a child to justify her existence. She was much better off doing her own thing.

A child equaled emotional and social prison. It always needed you to look out for it, do things for it. Children take over your entire life. However, Zephyr was nourished, given books to read; the only thing he was never given was attention. Rather, he was let loose on the warm California streets to do as children would do at a certain age. Zephyr often recalled his mother sitting at the kitchen window neither smiling nor frowning, shrouded in spicy green smoke until her eyes burned red through the haze.

She never developed that special glow a mother historically feels for her offspring. In fact, it was almost as if Zephyr's mother purposely rejected it. This wasn't a case of apathy or mental illness. It was simply a case of no need. There was always a strong disconnect in his mother's face when it came to family time. She just didn't know what to do with herself, couldn't put on that tired-but-supportive smile like mothers have done for centuries.

Zephyr was never encouraged to excel in school or do anything productive for himself. It seemed his parents wanted him to become another lazy hippie. They never explained the real world to him, how money, class and sexual orientation were going to define him until the day he died; or how the world deals in absolutes and does not pick up the pieces of anyone's personal disaster. It leaves you behind without afterthought. He had to figure this out on his own, and it was a rude awakening when he did.

His father, much like his mother, was also caught up in existential laziness and abstract spiritual jargon. Marijuana kept his mind in a softened state. He claimed that it helped with a back injury, despite Zephyr never seeing his parents ever have a job. Government checks were the only way they kept a roof over their heads. The only thing that differentiated Zephyr's mother and father was that his father was a talker.

"In the Occident, people think that the world revolves around them," Zephyr's father once said. "But I believe in a collective. We're all in this together, as they would say in the Orient."

Zephyr had no clue what *occident* or *orient* meant at that time. He was only seven years old, so it fell on deaf ears. But no matter how much his father talked, no matter how "involved" he tried to be, there was no making up for the longing a young boy feels to be connected to his mother. It's built into our mammalian nature to be attached to the thing that gave birth to us. There was a hole in Zephyr's core that became impossible to fill. Thus, childhood was lonely.

When you don't have a safety net, you can't truly build a foundation. This bothered Zephyr for as long as he could recall. Perhaps that was why he had severe trust issues. When you come from a life where every home you lived in was shabbier than the one before, you develop a wall within yourself, to protect yourself.

By the time he was thirteen, Zephyr became hyper aware of his abnormal upbringing. Knowing other kids had it better toyed with his self-loathing. Seeing other mothers picking up their kids happily while he had to walk home alone was salt in an invisible wound. He wasn't the type to make friends, so there was no taking his mind off the constant rejection. But perhaps this was the strongest trait she'd passed on: the loner gene.

This was when a light went off in his brain. He picked up a hobby: accumulating things. It started with a journal to consolidate thoughts. Then he began smoking, an easy hobby to acquire when your parents do it. Cigarette butts grew into piles, followed by wine corks and beer bottles with funny labels. CDs and cassettes of various hair metal, industrial and rock bands; DVDs of horror and dark fantasy; mountains of Legos, nail polish and books.

It all clicked from there.

After a few months his bedroom transformed into an unorganized museum. You couldn't see the floor or out the window because there was so much stuff. But he finally had come to like his lonely life with his things. Humans were mostly mean and always wanted something from you, even if you had nothing. So why not create your own friends? It wasn't that he believed his collection was actually sentient, but there was a voice inside of Zephyr that told him it *could* be. It was his way of communicating with himself and his inner goddess. He would be king of his own castle, even if that castle lived only inside his head.

"A garden of horrors," his mother once said after finishing up a crystal healing class. "I really wish you had a better outlet."

"Fuck you."

Zephyr had never mouthed off to his mother before, no more than a standard pubescent teenager, but he couldn't hold his tongue. At the end of the day, he was going to do what he wanted. If he'd learned anything from being stuck in his head more hours in the day than he dared to admit, it was that he was the ruler of his destiny, despite what the stars said. Occident Descendant.

"Don't curse."

His father had a fat joint in his mouth as he stood in the doorway, face blocked out by shadow. And then he went into another one of his blabbering, philosophical rants. What would the world be without its obsessors? The act of collecting could very well be what saved cultural history. Collectors document the past. But for Zephyr this was never about creating some sort of cultural archive. He was simply looking for escape.

He went on expeditions to find the odd and macabre item, heirlooms that brought with them haunted histories rather than ones of opulence and royalty. A glass goblet with copper trim that he imagined was used for blood drinking; an Yggdrasil amulet once worn on the neck of one of the world's first serial killers.

This is what attracted Zephyr.

He wasn't a sensitive or medium by any means, but sometimes a feeling welled up inside of him. Strange energies, a clairsentience he never really understood. But what this meant to him was that these things bore an importance the naked eye didn't see; he could feel the past, present and future as they lay in his grip, dusting his fingertips in ancient secrets and ludicrous philosophies. Their energy gathered darkly around him. They had a story to tell; a piece to a mysterious puzzle that he could put together on his own.

But the world post-9/11 was one of myth debunking. The unexplained became an underappreciated cult phenomenon thanks to Earthly science. Physics and chemistry solved poltergeist theories, as did modern psychiatry when it came to possession, seeing ghosts and outer body experiences. They called it *schizophrenia* and *dissociative identity disorder*. But does modern science never consider that the science we abide by here could be unfathomable to minds in other galaxies?

There was still so much more to do in terms of figuring out the universe. Aliens or Gods? We see the remains of these old beliefs in obelisks and at altars where ancient civilizations once worshiped. Petroglyphs and hieroglyphs, cave walls filled with star people who just might have given them intelligence. We see it in the ruins of Egypt, Mesopotamia and Sumer, and the Annunaki shrines left behind on Easter Island.

Our forefathers of collecting.

When Zephyr moved out, it was no surprise his parents didn't even bat an eye. The space he occupied wasn't legal; it was a squatter paradise. He'd come full circle, falling headlong into the life he always tried to avoid. It was on the far edge of Queens where the warehouses remained untouched from the city's gentrification projects. The only way to get in was to climb a rickety fire escape, which was what drew Zephyr unwillingly to the building in the first place. It reminded him of the former tenement he lived in.

It was always a spectacle entering and exiting, a feat that he secretly loved. The people who lived here were very much like him: quiet and awkward, artistic; a mix of addicts, thinkers and queers who had run away from unsupportive families; society's "rejects" that shared no place with common folk who. Following the leader was not their way. Gazing into the television or a cell phone screen did not excite them.

It was in this slimy shithole where Zephyr began to make friends. Conversations, while at first timid and cautious, grew into fabulous understandings once they greased the hinges of each other's minds. A collective levy opened into shared world possibilities. Judgment never set foot here, only curiosity, patience, and learning to cope with other people's madness so as to hone one's own.

There had been a missing link in Zephyr's life that he'd not realized until he started talking to people and caring about them: a human connection. One of those new friends was a shadowy boy. He had a green bridge piercing and a blue industrial in his left ear, obscure tattoos and a suave voice that seemed to be full of gold dust and tiny diamonds.

This boy did not live in the squatter warehouse. He was a friend of a friend who sold marijuana. When they smoked together, he would rant about sculpting and Zephyr would blab about the narratives he created with his collection. It had grown so big he could barely fit it within the basement that it currently occupied.

The energy that surrounded this boy was double that of Zephyr's, and he was slightly taller, which Zephyr also liked. The sharp nest of bones jutting from his pale skin spoke of the classic emo diet of one meal per day. His clothes were always a bit too tight and specked in what looked like clay, or paint, and his t-shirts had niche prints on them; just the type of boy Zephyr was into emotionally and sexually. The frantic artist.

"Your eyes," the boy said one night as they smoked a pack of Pall Malls on a fire escape. "They're two different colors."

"I've never met anyone with the same condition as me."

"Condition?" The boy blew smoke in Zephyr's face. "Each eye is its own organ."

Zephyr's intuition was aflame. Was this boy a metaphysical trick? Or was he real? It was one of those weird, random moments when all feelings just clicked. *Good chemistry*, they call it. He knew then that he needed this for the rest of his life. Boyflesh, black Converses and flower-petal lips that he wanted to tear off the face and keep in his pocket.

"I'm Atticus," the boy said. "Atticus Atlas."

"What kind of a name is that?"

"My name," Atticus smirked.

"What's yours?"

"Zephyr. Like a morning breeze."

"What kind of name is that?"

"Gee, I guess you're right. Hippie parent problems."

"You got a last name, wind boy?"

"No, just Zephyr. Like *Madonna*, or *Cher*."

That was the basis of their initial conversation, which naturally grew into bigger and better things. After a few weeks of running into one another, they went from talking to kissing as if it was normal for two boys to do. Atticus' lips sent little spikes of electric through every pore in Zephyr's skin. They exchanged the ancient language of lust through sticky saliva, cigarette breath and IPA bitters. A wet weight crawled into Zephyr's mouth, Atticus' tongue, and while it felt completely alien and new, it tasted rich and sanguine. His first French kiss with the boy of his dreams.

"You want a beer?"

Atticus showed Zephyr two different bottles. One was a Broo Doo ale by Three Floyd, which had a pine sap and flowery bite; the other was a rare Celest-jewel-ale from Dogfish Head, which was fermented with lunar meteorites. Zephyr chose the one with meteorites, and when Atticus passed it over their fingers brushed together. In that moment Zephyr felt their hearts beat as one.

Atticus went for it then, buried his face into Zephyr's neck, licking the delicate skin there. At first Zephyr was horrified by this act, being a virgin and so confused by this powerful attraction, but soon learned it was the most romantic thing a boy could do, to be the center of their attention. This made Zephyr's insides go into a knot.

Here were two boys trying to escape a fevered past, doing their best to hide the unified lunatic within, but somehow finding solace in one another. It was all so organic, almost magical. Nobody batted an eye within these walls, but outside them, they knew, it would be a whole new ball game. But there was no denying how powerful Zephyr felt when he was in Atticus' arms, while at the same time so completely vulnerable. He quickly learned that relationships are a two-way street. You both must give up something to meet in the middle. If one fails in doing that, so does the relationship.

They knew how one another ticked.

They knew how to get under each other's skin.

It frightened them both to think about what they would accomplish, together.

3

Zephyr stood 5'8" in his vegan lace-up Doc Martens, a dark red that resembled occluded blood. He'd been up all night, but nothing strange about that; Zephyr had dreams to figure out. By 5 a.m. he was sick of sitting around and put the rest of his clothes on. Darth Vader crop top, thumb ring, gemstone bracelet of the solar system and ripped black shorts. You had to stand out in the environment of stale fashion; make a statement before someone else made one for you.

He hit Mulberry Street like a shooting star. It was filthy and smelled like compost. Garbage hadn't been picked up in days, which made rats surge out of the sewers and feast even in broad daylight. Zephyr, like everyone else, was forced to ride out the pandemic, which left him too much time to think. He didn't recognize the city he'd lived in for more than half his life. It was emptier, stranger; it brimmed with abandonment and an almost unforgiving anger. The early-nineties ghosts of graffiti and boom-boxes made a disastrous comeback.

The sun was just beginning to rise. Even though it brightened the sky, in this part of town it was hard to compete with the LED signs and technicolor awnings. During the day one could navigate New York's streets with ease, but at night it could be an entirely different place. It had a distinct hallucinatory quality that has always bugged Zephyr. Superficially it played the part of any metropolis, but within it was a labyrinth that began at its tallest skyscraper, winding down into a whorled underground.

Zephyr took Mulberry south, then turned right on Canal and walked through a watery red shadow. Here, the avenues split like a pitchfork. Three different roads to nowhere. There was the miniature red, white and green heart of Little Italy, the air thick with the enticing smells of bubbling red sauce, espresso and fresh bread; then there was the gaudy yellow pagoda that marked Chinatown, and the scorching memory of Beatnik poetry that once dominated The Bowery, now gentrified and available to only those who could afford it.

As he approached the dilapidated strip of the Bowery, Zephyr realized that he was famished and in need of coffee to wake up, but chose a diet soda instead. He bought a bodega donut as well. The night before he'd been on a Voodoo Ranger IPA binge, and bitter hops still haunted his tongue, taunted his loins. The soda had just enough caffeine to reset his body. He depended on that to find focus.

After wading through hobos and drug addicts, Zephyr saw that half of the businesses on this strip were shut down. Boarded windows assaulted the landscape, neon barely flickered. On top of the city forcing shutdowns on all business aside from essentials, a lot of these stores were unable to pay the rent for reasons beyond the pandemic. The material world was shrinking.

No idea how time had gone so fast, but his phone now said 11 a.m. The lock screen was two silhouettes that could only be told apart by their opposing body types. One skinny boy wrapped in the arms of another with a swimmer's build. It was already seventy degrees outside, and the humidity was so thick you could inhale it like smoke. Indian summers were becoming a thing in New York. The white scorch of July lasted as far as October, and the frigid prison of February could be felt well into June.

Zephyr hated heat, hated how tiny beads of sweat burgeoned on his skin, hated to see kohl eyeliner stream down his cheeks and have his clothes feel like a wet condom on his body. He raked his hands through his hair. The humidity made it do crazy things. Cowlicks formed ugly little corkscrews that bounced across his brow; frizz owned one side of his head, and whatever didn't surrender to the heat came over his eyes like rain. The blue dye had a nasty smell on a day like this.

But within his social circle, this look was uniquely his own. Everybody knew him when he walked into a room, the boy with the blue hair. The boy who kept the sides shaved down so that the black serpent tattoo ear-to-ear could be shown off. The rest of his tattoos were petite but conveyed a strong message. Snakes, spirals, prophetic lyrics and ancient images. All placed in areas of his body that made untrained eyes quiver.

His headphones felt glued to his ears from the heat, classic black wraparound blasting Holst's *The Planets*. With the fancy noise-canceling function it was as if he was at a real symphony, which dredged up memories of the times when people did those things, when people were allowed to be in crowds. He missed those times, missed the scene, missed hanging out. The virus had changed everything.

He took the headphones off, put them in his bookbag. In there he kept many things. A journal, cigarettes and gum; multiple face masks, a paperback copy of *The Dark Eidolon*, pins and patches and random ephemera. Never leave home without a piece of yourself or the world will do everything in its power to erase you. Carry your comfort. *Keep Calm and Carrion*, said one of the patches.

Zephyr turned down Bowery and eyed the filthy storefront window for a long time, rubbed his finger into the grit that was black as his nail polish. There's no dirt like that of New York City. It is maleficent, unabashed, and not afraid to brand your clothes, hair, teeth and skin. It will cling to your cells like stepping on hot gum. But that's part of the city's charm. It gets its claws into you whether you like it or not.

Two Parliaments later and a piece of peppermint gum to cover up the smell, and Zephyr was ready to browse. **CLOSING SALE** in huge black letters stamped over the original **HEIRLOOMS - VINTAGE & VICIOUS**. Sandwiched on the Bowery between Bleecker and East Houston, the shoppe was a lone wolf in a city that no longer enjoyed this kind of antiquity. The scratch and sway of the tin sign that hung outside the door rang in a time of mourning. Another store about to be killed off by the pandemic. These kinds of stores lay suppressed in the shadows of all the big business that has changed the landscape of Manhattan from a unique cultural experience to the stale solution of major retailers and pharmacy chains.

Although Heirlooms was very dark inside, Zephyr could see various bodies shrouded in interestingly weaved ponchos, fashionable eyeglasses, shawls, and opulent jewelry. The fashions of the forgotten. Ghoulish faces illuminated like gas lamps beneath a single-filament light bulb. You needed low light for the keepsakes. That much was understood. They were like fine wine: the darker the storage chamber, the better preserved.

While it was sad to see another store shutting down, the upside was that it was a chance for Zephyr to buy stuff at affordable prices. He watched the parabolic handles of a gaudy grandfather clock turn, saw little dunes of dust on the faces of zombie dolls; heard the creak and squeak of an ancient bear trap; danced to the eerie prongs of a music box that was meant to instill fear in children.

"You should be wearing a mask."

Zephyr almost jumped out of his skin. "I have one," digging into his backpack to remove a Ouija board patterned mask. "See?"

"Fancy."

"Did you follow me?"

"If I don't know where to find you by this point in our relationship, then I oughta quit."

Atticus was many shades darker than he appeared in the window's reflection. His facemask was etched with trippy tarot and neon cobweb, which highlighted his sardonic demeanor and expertly covered up the boyish face that still got him carded for alcohol, despite being over thirty years old. Even with a mask on, Atticus' heterochromatic eyes gave him away.

"You have my location."

"But I don't spy. And you know I don't enjoy technology as much as you," Atticus said.

"Unless it gets you attention."

"Touché."

On a clear day like this, Atticus stood out sorely. His hair was a strong auburn at the roots, but the rest dyed black. It laid calmly over his brown eye, and it needed no product to be contained. His clothes seemed to be picked out of random rummage, barring the carefully placed classic high-top Chuck Taylors on his feet and the faded King Crimson crop top. But the way it stuck to Atticus' torso made it so everyone could see the outline of his chest, abs and sharp hips. It's what got him half his social media following.

Unlike Atticus, Zephyr was usually subjected to some disdain from passersby, due to his outré way of dress. It wasn't anything New York hadn't seen, but it's always the people who look strange on the outside that get judged the quickest, and the people who are deemed perfect from the outside that eventually reveal true ugliness. Beauty is transitory, but hideousness is a demon that latches forevermore.

"Your eyes pop today," Atticus said.

"It's the sun.

"One brown eye, one green."

"I hate when you say that."

"Been saying it for a decade by now," Atticus winked.

"I must be a masochist to put up with you." Zephyr stuck out his tongue.

Atticus put his hand on the store window, as if taking in its energy. Too bright against the dirty surface. The reddish tint in his nails, Zephyr knew, was not polish. It was as if the antiques spoke to him; whatever tongue they originated from didn't matter. Zephyr saw a fly-specked mirror that cast unforeseen reflections; a vinyl record player and tape deck; a Cthulhu sculpture no bigger than a fingernail, hectic in its myriad-armed stance. The call was inside those who believed in it.

Zephyr lined his lips with bee venom chapstick, kissed Atticus and then took the cigarette he kept behind his ear. They smoked it together, and when they were done Atticus wisped past Zephyr to go inside. They were welcomed by uncomely stares from the store clerk and overtly guarded customers. But the only type of quack to be attracted to these kinds of places was both kooky and superstitious as they were, so it didn't bother them.

The first thing Zephyr noticed was the smell, the kind that spoke of antiquity and archaism, like that of a freshly unearthed fossil. How time would smell if one could bottle it up. The aisles were slim but brimmed with stuff. Matryoshka dolls, crystal deities, ammolite gods and monsters evoked right out of the Necronomicon; vinyls and VHS; books bound in strange coverings; a Dybbuk box encrusted with mirror shards and gnarled twigs. Any idiot could satisfy the *You Break it, You Buy it* rule by brushing against something too carelessly.

Within this random litter of oddments, Atticus and Zephyr stopped at a table and both eyed something deep within the recesses of a forgotten past. The thing gleamed if you looked at it from one angle, and then was completely dull from another. Its surface was opaque but somehow light was trapped within. Atticus held it up, wrinkled brow confirming that there was no way to tell the secrets of this alternating illumination.

"No fucking way," Zephyr said.

"Is that . . . how did it end up here?"

"How am I supposed to know, Atticus?"

"I was thinking out loud."

Atticus moved closer, brushed his fingers against Zephyr's exposed belly. The little thing receded into the dust that polluted the table, as if not wanting Atticus to touch it. Its spider-like legs began to wiggle; its crystalline paunch shuddered, as did the rows of sharp teeth. The thing looked like it wanted to scream, or attack. It was difficult to define the little inanimate soul.

"I've thought about this thing for the last ten years," Atticus said.

"It was my most treasured antique, until you let it go."

"You forget that it nicked me."

"Your thumb ring." Zephyr winked, then leaned in close, dangly spike earring clanking on the smooth surface. "It hasn't changed at all."

Atticus went down on one knee, exposing his pale thigh and the *Ad Astra* tattoo in Cyrillic, eyes at the same level as the table.

"I wanna hold it."

"Are you sure?"

In the low light, Zephyr saw Atticus' eyes latch onto his *Luctor Et Emergo* tattoo that branded his forearm. Both sayings had deep meanings to Atticus and Zephyr. It was another one of those strange reasons why you find yourself loving someone, sometimes more than you knew was safe to, sometimes more than you were willing to admit.

"Yes. Give it to me."

Zephyr handed Atticus the little thing, but Atticus threw it back onto the table in no less than a second. *It's hot,* he whispered. Zephyr picked up the outlandish statue for a closer inspection, closed his eyes and tried to find the memory of where he acquired it, but came up empty. That memory was lost long ago, as it had been more than a decade since he last saw this wrong thing. Time, as it does with anything else, aided in the fading of that memory.

Being that nothing happened—no heat, no movement—Zephyr put it back on the table, face down about old-school rock magazines. *It likes me,* Atticus chuckled. Then Zephyr moved along, maneuvering through each aisle with practiced precision. They both knew this type of place better than they knew their own homes. Even the shadows took on the scent of wasted years, those same shadows somehow rearranged, as if this place was its own world with its own laws of physics and alchemy, dampened by ghoulish light.

"Should I buy it back?" Zephyr said.

Then from behind. "I can confirm that it was done by hand."

The voice dropped like a guillotine, echoing powerfully over the cluster of items and water-rot ceiling. Zephyr went straight into panic mode, but then was suddenly besieged by horniness. Atticus turned his head so fast his neck made a snap, crackle and pop. The shape soared, scarecrow bones and elongated young face covered in a gnarly mask, bringing with it a chaotic aura. Zephyr tilted his head and lowered his Ouija board mask; Atticus slid two fingers into Zephyr's belt loop and pulled him close.

"And who are you?" Zephyr said curtly.

The shape moved itself into the low light. "I'm Dexter."

Nobody said anything for a full minute. There was only peaked interest, rising heart rates and the faint sounds of rapid breath. One of the things that stuck out to Zephyr was Dexter's face. This boy was no different than those that already infiltrated his spooky social circle, and he gave them no reason to be this nervous— except for the fact that Zephyr had never seen a face so devoid of wrinkles, even though he had to be at least thirty.

"I'm Zephyr. And this is Atticus. What do you know about that statue."

"It's not a statue," Dexter whispered. "It's a sculpture."

"No sculpture is that perfect," Atticus said. "I would know. I'm a sculptor."

Dexter eyed Atticus strongly. "Well, I hate to burst your bubble, but I made it." Dexter's disposition was inflected with an artistic confidence.

Atticus let go of Zephyr's waste. "*Made* it?"

"Yes."

"Doesn't seem possible . . . given how–"

"How trained is your eye?"

Dexter removed his cyberpunk facemask to show off a tiny not-smile, all teeth and lips that begged to be kissed. Something was different about this boy, the gut never lied. But that didn't mean Zephyr didn't want to find out. How could he not, given the attractive getup? Skintight Glassjaw tank top, vintage black jeans that looked like they'd been through a tree chipper; all-black Converses, black pinky ring and nails painted various colors.

"My eye . . . is fine," Atticus sounded a bit jarred, which was not uncommon when he was challenged.

"Anything is possible . . . if you put your mind to it."

Dexter tilted his face towards Atticus, sharp nose donned with sharp glasses, eyes glowing a rich purple. It reminded Zephyr of flowers. He was enthralled by Dexter's skeletal beauty, so full of angles that it looked he'd been drawn by several different artists and stained by youth, chance and circumstance. Three of his tattoos illuminated. Flaming Eye on the right biceps, *Cthulhu Fntagn* on his left forearm, and a Krueger knife glove on his neck.

"MiniMonstrosities, isn't it?" Dexter smirked.

Atticus' dark eyebrows raised. "You know me?"

"Yes." Dexter's tone was swift and flirtatious. "I admire your work."

"Thank you?" Atticus was perplexed, as was apparent from the tone of his voice.

Then some customers cut through. With them came the vanilla spice of clove cigarettes and searing licorice of Jägermeister. Three males, one female, and a macabre drag queen, all looking like they belonged in a heavy metal circus. The girl's hair was a pink and black tarantula, while the three males could barely be seen, their clothes were so dark the macabre drag queen was head to toe in cephalopod glamor. Three had eyes of green and blue; the drag queen's eyes were onyx stones, as were the male's who had acrylic paint smeared on his Slipknot t-shirt.

"I don't like them." Dexter turned away.

"You know who they are?" Zephyr interjected.

"Insufferables. So full of themselves."

"Isn't that what every creative type is?"

After agreeing, Atticus and Dexter began to converse about sculpting, but Zephyr's attention went right to the throb of his penis, since Dexter was so dangerously attractive. But that could wait until later. He watched the boys carefully. Dexter revealed that this store owner would every so often purchase his work and sell it. Various sculptures, all made of gemstone, which often sounded like marbles in a bag when examined in their hands.

"If given the chance, artists love to babble. We selfishly take up anyone's time so that we can blow smoke up our own asses to try and sound clever."

"But what we don't recognize is that sometimes we wind up coming off as elitists," Atticus said.

Dexter nodded. "Come, let me show you something."

They were on the opposite side of the store now. Here the wall was lined with glass cabinets polluted with fingerprints and sticky clumps of dust. Through the dirty panes Zephyr saw a kaleidoscope of interesting items, skeleton keys and stained glass that covered his body with colorful reflections. He caressed a wrought iron candelabra, the clawed feet of a Bohemian table lamp; curled his finger around the cold metal until a fleeting static image bulldozed his vision.

At his feet was a beat-up paperback book. He picked it up, which filled his nostrils with dust and lignin. That always put Zephyr in a safe place. Books held the power to transport one away from this new world of pandemics and gentrification. He eyed the spine, the dog-eared pages, but could not find its title. He put it back down, and at his feet saw a pair of pince-nez, as well as crumbling puppets with freakish faces and a skull that had an elongated cranium.

But Zephyr wasn't done. He reached past clotted dust and insect carcasses, into the void that beckoned, arm disappearing up to the elbow. He expected a vacuum sensation, like the kind in stories of deep space that could slowly pull an unprotected human body apart. But what he felt left him at a loss for words, as if his skin had absorbed an anomaly that lived beyond the reaches of our understanding.

Something slid across his hand. Tiny spines, like that of a cat's tongue. A sound burst in the middle of his brain as panic spread, and a fat worm of blood dripped out of his ear. When he pulled his hand out, he saw that it was slathered in acrylic paint. He'd gripped a small canvas tightly, without even knowing it. When he slowly unwound his fingers, the painted thing he saw was the absolute incarnation of beauty and rage.

The backdrop was a writhing black haze, blacker than the smoke that haunted his dreams since 9/11. The longer Zephyr stared, the more he saw it *change*. It was as if the art was *bleeding*. Fear trumped any reaction his biology should have initiated, as the horrible shape in the center slowly transitioned into a phosphorescent serpent.

But Zephyr knew this trick, had seen it all over Brooklyn and Queens, in secret galleries and underground art exhibits; at local shows where New York City's most popular underground band, Electric Orchid, used their music to create a hallucinatory reality. But something else was to be said about this painting: it was not new enough for the paint to still be wet.

"Blood."

Dexter was behind Zephyr, little hand digging into his shoulder, mouth so close he thought for a moment Dexter might lick the blood straight out of his ear canal. Atticus was in front of them staring. It was strangely erotic, as if the three of them were aligned in this moment of mitigated violence and strange illusions.

"Isn't that the Hydra?" Atticus said.

"Mythical monster or the drag queen?"

"Drag queen," Dexter said as he opened the cabinet near the floor and dug his hand into the sparkly basket. "Look, gemstones."

"I can see that," Atticus returned.

"But can you actually? This serpent is made from tiger's-eye which is for strength," Dexter whispered. "This claw is made from bloodstone, and it's for creativity." Atticus clenched his mouth so that a huge vein throbbed at his left temple. "This one is called *Stone of Tears: Terrifying Tentacle Terrorizer*," Dexter continued. It was the one Atticus had just seen on a different table. Zephyr watched envy take shape on Atticus' face, followed by that unique inquisitiveness that meant a bond was forming. More than friendship, less than lovers. That risky gray zone of new interest.

"Are those yours?"

"Indeed, they are."

"And how'd that one get here?"

"This one is special."

The stone of tears monster was in Dexter's hand. Now that Zephyr was able to see it at this angle, and under this wan lighting scheme, he thought it almost looked like a bat, but with a tarantula's eight legs and drippy fangs. It seemed that the little thing reshaped itself when it was in the hands of its creator. No drug could have allowed Zephyr to see that. This was as real as the hand in front of his face.

"Let me hold it," Atticus said.

Colors within the Cthulhu-esque structure coalesced, then split apart in a burst of polychromatic blooming. It was reacting to Atticus' touch. A mesmerizing pattern of deep green and speckles of red. And then its proboscis wrapped about Atticus' finger. Dexter stepped back; Zephyr caught one of the mysterious customers looking their way, the one with the paint on his clothes. And then the oblong body quivered, tiny mouth ringed in uneven teeth making an indescribable sound that weaved into their eardrums.

One of its apparitional eyes locked onto Atticus—

Viperfish teeth gripped the soft skin between his thumb and index finger.

When he pulled it away, there was no blood, only darkness.

4

Atticus and Dexter drifted beneath an old-fashioned light bulb, twin shadows blending and extricating from reality all the same. They posed for a social media post; Atticus brought Dexter close to take the selfie, their cheeks touching and hair covering the other's eyes. After, Atticus shined his cell phone light on the small suppurating wound.

"Doesn't hurt."

"Why would it?" Dexter whispered. "And don't forget to tag me. *TheEventualDevil* "

Zephyr was halfway out the door, slightly impatient but exalted. The two boys were magnetized; a certain alchemy flowed. He knew this type of attraction, hot and white as a live wire. Zephyr could not break that chain even if he pulled their physical bodies apart.

"You guys ready?"

"Already has five hundred views," Atticus squealed.

A moment's jealousy sizzled in Zephyr's blood, but the wind was warm against his face, wrapped about his body like a huge maw. As the sun plateaued, hot light reflected from the surrounding windows, forcing people to shield their eyes; it set pigeons to the air, and pushed bums out of their wet cardboard mansions. Zephyr lit a cigarette beneath the shadow of a tree that was bare as bone. Here, the temperature dropped significantly, seemed to crawl down the back of his neck with spindly legs. One of its last yellow leaves fell gently on his shoulder.

"That's good luck," Dexter said.

"Is it?" Zephyr exhaled heavy smoke in Dexter's direction.

It was time to get on with his day. But how? Was Dexter now going to accompany them? Zephyr knew if he sent Dexter away, Atticus would get upset, so he bit his lip and just went with it. He pocketed the yellow leaf, keepsake of the last dying morsel of summer 2020, one of the worst he ever experienced thanks to the pandemic. Dexter then took out his own cigarette from a steampunk fanny pack and daubed the filter in white powder.

"Ketamine."

"Drug of choice for the gays."

Atticus took a drag of Dexter's cigarette. Zephyr saw little bits of powder in the corner of Atticus' mouth before his precious tongue swept it away. For some reason that made Zephyr want to scream; he felt his chest get heavy and his heart drop into his stomach. It wasn't a terrible thing that Atticus was into Dexter; he was used to flings and one-time sexual partners, but it was insanely irritating that Atticus would not even look in Zephyr's direction. He had eyes only for Dexter right now.

"Tingles," Atticus said.

"Tastes bitter to me," Dexter said.

Zephyr's throat clicked dryly; he couldn't speak.

"You want?"

Dexter lolled the cigarette between his fingers. Zephyr accepted the offer, and the moment his fingers touched Dexter's, he wished he hadn't done so. The boy's skin was soft, almost infantile. It was as if he hadn't done a hard day's work his entire life, the kind of clammy, velvety skin Zephyr very much enjoyed touching, smelling, and licking. Atticus' hands were burned, calloused; they were the hands of someone who breaks things down and puts them back together. This was a stark difference.

"People usually dip their bogeys in coke," Zephyr said.

"That bores me."

"You ever do bumps?"

"You mean snort it? Never."

"Why not?"

"Don't enjoy going into a K-hole."

"That sounds silly." Zephyr took out his snuff bullet and did a bump. "It's an experience you can't explain through words. Best lived."

"Put your masks on before someone gives you a dirty look," Atticus interrupted. "Cases are rising again. A dark winter is coming."

"But we're outside."

"Do you wanna get canceled?"

Everyone scrambled for their masks, finished their smoke, and threw the butts on the sidewalk. Given the amount of detritus that lined the streets, the cigarettes blended right in.

"Isn't it ironic how social media tries to control us?" Dexter said, a bit muffled with his cell phone at eye level. "This little rectangle, created from child labor, injects itself into everyone's personal life because we've allowed ourselves to surrender to it."

"I remember a time when the online world was an actual community," Atticus said. "But now, social media has rewired our minds into this evil clique culture."

"*Exclusivity guised as inclusivity.* It's the Gen Z motto"

"Millennials have finally aged out, huh?"

"Not to worry," Zephyr said. "Gen Z won't last long either."

"I don't want to know what comes after them."

That's when Zephyr began to feel the ketamine. It made him feel mushy inside, almost dreamy. His mind lightly detached from his body, ushering in dissociation golden and slow as honey. It had been a while since he'd done drugs during the day, so the experience was kind of like visiting an old friend. But when Dexter and Atticus went back to yapping about sculptures and sketches, Zephyr once again felt like the insolent third wheel that nobody wanted around.

This made him think way too hard. He saw his life ten years ago, the times when it was just him and Atticus against the world, before they allowed sexual toxicity into their lives. Those were simpler times. Realizing this made him feel old, knowing that he was at the point where he could say "in my day" when referring to people and places from yesteryear. He also realized that these memories surfacing were likely rooted in his jealousy.

Had it finally happened that the sacred connection he thought only Atticus and himself shared—that perfect union of contrary circumstances—was wilting? There was no denying the way Dexter and Atticus looked at one another. Blushing grins, glowing eyes and wet lips. The first signs of attraction. To see this happening in front of his face was not only insulting, but straight up rude. It made Zephyr want to scream. But why was he finding himself oddly turned on?

Atticus and Zephyr planted the seed of an open relationship years ago, but the first sapling of experience sprouted only in the last two. Neither he nor Atticus were particularly fond of monogamy, but in the beginning it was safe and practical; it's what we are taught to do. However, after so many years together, people change, as do their needs; fantasies start getting in the way of real life.

At that time they were in their late twenties and still considered aesthetically desirable, so nothing was going to stop the male ego from getting what it wanted. Sex was usually how it was stroked. Most men feel the best about themselves when they have sex, but more than that, when they are *wanted* by others. In this culture of social media and online personas, validation is sought from random people more than ever.

Back then, they both felt time was whittling away; every second they hesitated a new wrinkle formed in skin, hairlines threatened to recede, abs started to fade. Each passing day meant that person gets older than the one before it, and a little less alluring. Wracking himself with guilt wasn't going to get Zephyr anywhere, and hiding it from Atticus would only poison him slowly. Zephyr came to realize that it was quite natural to be curious about exploring the flesh of another. Like our taste buds, interests change over time.

It always fascinated Zephyr to know that most people force themselves to partner sexually with one person until the day they die. Not every relationship in your life must be serious. They can be playful, sexual; they can be fleeting. Still, one gets jealous. Still, one can't help but to bat an eye when a new boy catches the attention of your partner so quickly it feels as if you don't even exist. Insecurity plays mind games on you. It makes you wonder if what you have is even worth fighting for.

Every couple goes through hard times. Happiness isn't achieved by never knowing sadness. There's always bound to be some resistance, defiance, annoyance. Over this last decade, Zephyr realized how hard it is to keep a true romantic relationship going strong. Conscious effort is key. Not once a week when it's convenient. Not once a month because you've become disgustingly comfortable. Not solely on an anniversary because you know your partner isn't going anywhere. Every. Single. Day. The minute you don't water your flower, it begins to die.

But sexual exploration is ingrained into our curious nature, so it felt natural to move in the direction of an open relationship. Zephyr acted on those feelings first. It was with a boy in a metal band. After taking back four Hearts of Darkness, the most diabolical stout Magic Hat had to offer, there was no resisting temptation. The kiss was wild and alien; it had been so long since he'd touched another boy. The sex was quick and rough, but the rush made it something to remember.

After Atticus freaked out, he admitted that the thought of Zephyr being with someone else turned him on. They finally agreed that they both could sleep with others, but that they'd communicate rather than doing it behind the other's back. Despite the rush they both received from this new definition of a relationship, that didn't mean it didn't come with a host of problems.

Jealousy and envy can plague even the strongest of open relationships. If your partner gets more attention than you, it's easy to succumb to insecurity and self-doubt. And the same could be said if you're the one getting more attention on the sexual market. One of the most interesting facets of the human mind is that even when we have it all, we simply want more. And those laces are wound tightly into our mechanics.

Zephyr envisioned a slow buildup to being non-monogamous, something organic, like meeting in a dive bar or dance club and hitting it off. But Atticus took "open" to another level. Notoriously impatient, he fell headlong into gay hookup apps (an offshoot to his social media addiction), which allowed him to collect boys like Zephyr did morbid antiques. Their taste in the male specimen almost never matched, so it was difficult to find a suitable third. They were at their best when they played apart. It saved the drama of trying to please all parties sexually.

These thoughts tore vehemently at Zephyr. After being certain that he'd solved all the microscopic mysteries of human emotion and long-term relationships, here he was now being tested. Were throuples the paradigm shift of gay culture? If we're all on this planet to shape its evolution, culturally and biologically, it made sense that the next step for romantic couples was to invite in a third. He'd been around plenty of throuples to know that they do sometimes work, at the end of the day he found them mesmerizing. How was it that three people could make something successful when most can't even survive two?

The K came back for a second round. It crawled bitterly down his throat, sliding into his cells and splicing his consciousness as if he was a man of multiple personalities. The street swayed and extended far beyond the city limits into a place he didn't want to go. The world was gray, left only were the silhouettes of Atticus, Dexter and himself set upon this pathway. But when their voices hit into his tympanic membrane, he was pulled out of the trance.

"Let's sit a minute," Dexter said. "I wanna show you something."

"Not more sculptures," Zephyr said before he could stop himself.

"Something better." Dexter winked.

Hester Street playground was sad and empty, save for some stray cats. Zephyr had no clue how they'd gotten this far south. There was no pain in his feet, no soreness in his knees. Normally after a long walk he'd be ridden with complaining bones and muscles, but right now he felt fine, as if he'd been carried. Dexter and Atticus were on either side of Zephyr, and all three boys had their shoes placed in a shape that reminded Zephyr of a pentagram. They removed their masks and busied themselves with their phones for the next few minutes.

"Three thousand views now," Atticus said.

"I got a bunch of new followers!" Dexter's grin was all teeth so that it almost looked wrong.

"What artists do you follow on Instagram?" Atticus leaned toward Dexter, hair tickling the top of Zephyr's nose.

"All kinds. Are you on Twitter as well?"

"Same handle."

"Let's post and retweet."

"Twitter gays are out of their mind."

"But so is everyone in the artistic community. We can't escape it.

"Most people on social media are crazy."

"Keyboard warriors."

"It's true. Technology has empowered the stupid."

Zephyr found himself falling deeper into the accessibility that is ketamine, knowing very well that one can get lost in strange thought, then easily slip into the k-hole; a mawkish, terrorizing state of mind for some, and a dissociative paradise for others. He felt a slight paranoia well inside him. If someone were to walk by, the three of them could easily be mistaken for gay transients.

"I think the people who attack on social media do it because they're too afraid of in-person confrontation."

"That's part of the problem," Atticus said. "It used to be that people would get together and have discussions, find resolve. Now we've been forced to argue on all these apps, and we misconstrue tone since we can't decipher exactly who's behind the screen."

"So much time is spent arguing on social media because we've cut out empathy. Everyone's become so brash."

"However, the ones stirring up the most trouble are only a very small percentage."

"But they get people fired up the most."

"Hype sells."

Zephyr leaned his head against Atticus' shoulder, smelled his vintage t-shirt. Dexter acted on this signal immediately and put his hand on Zephyr's left knee, which made Atticus put his hand on Zephyr's right thigh, slipping a finger through the hole in his jeans. The reflection of the sun on their pale hands was almost blinding; their painted nails shined like a beetle's back. This wasn't the time to get frisky, although Zephyr liked the thought of being in the middle. Then Dexter's attention was brought back to the street.

"What is it?" Atticus said.

"When nobody's around, I'll show you," Dexter's eyes were darting in all directions. "Or else they'll *see*."

"See what?" Atticus' voice hit a higher octave than normal.

Zephyr looked about the playground. It was now dotted with children and mothers hypnotized by cell phones. Dexter pointed to an area about two-thirds up the block, a CitiBike station that was in massive disrepair; many of the docks had been ripped from the ground, so when a violent wind tunnel came their way all Zephyr smelled was dirt. But Dexter would not stop staring in its direction; the afternoon sunlight rode along the edges of his eyeglasses. Zephyr had a sudden urge to smack them off his face.

"There's a lot more than meets the eye," Dexter said.

"What do you mean?"

"Do you ever think about how these skyscrapers don't just fall over?"

"Not really."

"It's because they dig far into the ground to keep them steady."

"Makes perfect sense to me," Atticus said.

"As in . . . massive holes dug deep into the bedrock."

"What about it?"

Once the families dispersed, Dexter jetted toward the bikes. Beneath one of the crushed stations was a hole big enough to fit an adult. Zephyr almost couldn't believe his eyes, but there was a ladder and rope that would allow anyone to easily penetrate that weird darkness. Atticus looked bemused, an almost stupid facial expression, like when a guy orgasms without touching himself. Dexter didn't waste any time. First to go down, he then reached his hand up and pulled at Atticus' and Zephyr's legs.

"Remember the Mole People?"

Zephyr looked down, saw nothing other than Dexter's purple eyes.

"They made this all possible."

Atticus went down first. Zephyr followed. Night fell the moment he put his foot into the hole. There was an unexplainable shift around him, as if he'd gone through a passageway to another dimension. The ladder was smooth and polished as bone; the rope hung as would an intestine pulled from the gut.

"Where're we going?" Zephyr said.

The descent was a psilocybin nightmare. Fear of entering this void and not coming back the same person. Fear of transmogrification, of melding with the particles down here and turning into a new being. Senses became suspended; thoughts betrayed the mind. Zephyr was forced to navigate by some involuntary process, smooth muscle movement and parasympathetic response. Each step was a fondling of one's own madness, weaknesses cradled in the palm of an imaginary hand, lunacies stroked, and desires pervaded.

Zephyr heard intense echoes, soft chants. He smelled altars. He saw otherworldly markings on the steps of the ladder, runes and hexes and sordid cosmic languages. When he looked away, he saw the swirly and bright visions you get from staring at nightclub lights after taking too much MDMA. He didn't know if he was even halfway down by now, but a great pressure weighed on his head. Then there were stars, or maybe only what he thought to be stars;

the kind that burst in the corners of your eyes when your blood pressure drops too fast.

When his foot finally reached what should have been ground level, the sponginess threw him off balance. Light down here was incandescent, and it seemed to thrive on Zephyr's pale skin. Upon closer inspection, he saw gas lamps and smelled kerosene. The exposed rock was painted a matte black that gave the space a warm feeling. Down at his feet was glistening red grass, and at eye-level were tables that displayed various dead things, tree branches and truncated metal.

"This is where the magic happens," Dexter said.

"What is this place?"

"We can be whoever we want to be, down here."

"How did you find it?" Atticus was perplexed but fascinated.

"Quarantine allowed me to make this happen."

"Took some liberties, I'd say."

"Never underestimate desperate and unemployed artists."

"You mean there're people down here?"

"Sort of."

Dexter motioned for them both to follow. As they transferred into a new room, their feet sideswiped a manner of many things Zephyr didn't look down to see. He had a bad feeling that they were going too deep, that gravity could get so strong down here they'd never see the sun again. Atticus grabbed his hand, which gave him the courage to see him through whatever Dexter was going to throw at them next. And it was nothing he ever could have imagined.

"Unused train tunnels," Dexter whispered. "They're abundant."

"Is that why I hear—"

"So long as the trains run on the other side of these walls, you'll hear a roar."

Dexter opened a door that creaked melodically. A sound that put images into the head of what to expect if that ancient darkness would unfold. Anything was possible. Zephyr braced himself, covered his mouth with his hand. He could feel Atticus' breath slowly rising from behind, wetting the back of his neck. Atticus was the superstitious type, had a massive respect for myths, legends and lore.

"Behold," Dexter said.

The archway extended into the dark, which then fully dissipated as Zephyr walked straight into it. Revealed was an area that expanded too far for the naked eye to see and receded all the same. With each step his own shadow threatened to bolt. For one agonizing moment he saw it standing there, wriggling and bent, then slatted and squeezed as an accordion, as if it had been crushed by the great pressure of the underground.

"Go." Dexter's eyes were purple vortexes.

Into the Gleam.

The area looked like a giant wasp nest fashioned out of dark gemstone. Maybe just plain old bedrock, but the exquisite craftsmanship could not be denied, and it was positively haunting. Every cell was filled with dim light and sweet smoke. Every path was covered in neon grass, night flowers and lightning bugs. When he turned around, Zephyr saw a skyline rise out of the darkness, one of spires, steel and carved stone. Atticus put his hand over his mouth. They'd never seen anything like this in their life.

"A city beneath the city."

5

The next day, Dexter texted our group chat asking to take Zephyr and myself on a quick road trip. *Somewhere special*, he had said. *So you get to know me better.* His only request was that we go at night, which came as no surprise to any of us. We all much preferred to do our biddings at night, whether that meant getting drunk, high, creating art, or stirring up controversy on social media.

"Are you sure you want to come?" I asked Zephyr.

"What else do I have going on?"

"Just checking."

We hadn't really talked about what we'd seen, and it was a growing nuisance between us. Zephyr had been short with me since that day, but I assumed it was just jealousy, not that he was actually thinking about what Dexter had shown us. No matter what bothered Zephyr, I was going to disregard a new friend just because he was all up in his feelings, especially knowing that Dexter liked him too.

"I do think he's a bit strange," Zephyr added as he slipped on his Doc Martens.

"And we're not?" I said, applying ChapStick and a dash of eyeliner.

Meeting Dexter was a spiritual awakening. It allowed me to explore sections of my mind I never knew I could go. It allowed me to see past my inhibitions and live free. I wondered, given how fast we clicked, how much would Dexter challenge me? How would he bring to new heights? And how long would it be until we were sickeningly in love?

"That place he showed us . . . you aren't thinking about it?"

"I don't dwell on things like you do, if that's what you're insinuating."

"No need for that kind of reply."

Zephyr and I rushed downstairs at eleven p.m. Even at this hour I could smell simmering tomato sauce and frying meat pour out of the doors from the Italian families that had been living in this building for what seemed like forever. Ventilation in these old tenements was almost next to none, so it didn't surprise me that whenever I went outside I could still smell meatballs and cigarettes on my clothes, and in my hair.

Our neighbors were always friendly, even if they pried into my business too much for my taste. But I always looked forward to their hospitality and home-cooked meals. There was always enough food to go around, and anytime they caught me walking up and down the stairs they'd invite me over to feast with them. Strangely enough, they didn't judge me for my tattoos and piercings. I think they found me exotic.

When we got outside, Dexter was on the corner of Mulberry and Canal in a filthy two-seater convertible with just enough room for Zephyr to squeeze in the back, despite beer bottles and random pieces of clothing piled there. Dexter's car was interesting, if not straight up weird. It filled Mulberry Street with a dark presence and way too much exhaust. It didn't help that he was blasting Black Sabbath's "Hole in the Sky" so that anyone walking by turned their head in disdain.

We didn't bring facemasks, no need at this hour, and no need being we were outside. However, I felt a twinge of guilt for not doing so. The pandemic had me well trained. But the minute I saw Dexter I lost all thought and jumped into the front seat, eyeing the ghost-green light of the dashboard.

"It's a CD," Dexter said, looking in the rearview mirror.

"How old do you think I am?" Zephyr replied.

"Twenty-five?"

"Try thirty-three. So yes, I know what CDs are."

"Really, Zeph? Could have fooled me for Gen Z."

"Touché. But don't call me that, I hate nicknames."

"Anyway, there's no Bluetooth in this car, so that's why I said it was a CD."

Dexter was wearing a pair of black RayBan sunglasses, which I thought was weird at this hour, and his hair was somehow a shade lighter, like when one sits in the sun week after week in the summer months, and it fell over his brow in delightful little curls. Through the shades I saw the strange purple hue of his eyes that was vexation and sexual attraction all at once. After he applied a bright color lipstick and lit a smoke, his wingtipped foot hit the gas pedal and we sped out of Manhattan.

"Skip proof?" I asked to break the tension.

"Of course. Can't drive without it."

"Whose car is this anyway?"

"My mother's."

The nightwind was warm and permeated with the smell of rain. It felt wonderful flowing through my hair, across the skin of my face like a massage. There were hardly any cars on the road, and so I let my hands glide in tandem with the wind as if I owned a great pair of wings. I kept looking back at Zephyr in the rearview mirror, watching his blue hair fly all over the place, then over at Dexter to see his cunning smile and wild features. I was the luckiest person to have two interesting guys by my side.

"We're going to the cemetery," Dexter said as he slipped a finger through a hole in my jeans.

"Which one?"

"You'll see."

Many towns, little cities and tunnels passed us by. At first it seemed that we were exploring just to kill time, bolting through Queens as if it was some small piece of land one could cover in less than a day. But I knew that wasn't true. Queens was humongous, and depending on which part you wanted to see, you could be abruptly overtaken by a swamp just as easily as air pollution.

From my viewpoint the surrounding buildings swarmed taller than I remembered, lights in the windows flickering like mating season for fireflies. I hadn't been to this side in quite some time, not since childhood. I remember my mother calling this area disgusting. I knew the buildings here were old, overcrowded and so decrepit that running water was constantly an issue. I knew this even as I kept my eyes closed, no need for any visuals. Dexter was driving too fast to let me take it all in anyway.

"*Can you change the music,*" Zephyr yelled. "*I found this back here.*"

"*Can't hear you,*" Dexter replied.

Zephyr tapped Dexter's shoulder with the other CD in hand, and now Black Sabbath was traded for Evanescence. The operatic power of Amy Lee's voice sung me into a welcomed oblivion. I closed my eyes again and thought about that place Dexter showed us the day before. I'd kept it willfully blocked from my brain as it all felt so surreal to me. But I remained fascinated . . . and afraid, which only stroked my curiosity further.

A half hour later, Dexter was winding us through clean little avenues and quiet side streets, to which I saw the cemetery banked on our left, protected by huge gothic gates donned with spires, spikes and barbed wire. The neighborhood itself was generally sparse, looked very safe and was just way too quiet for Dexter's loud car. The only possible sign of life was a florist across the street that must have ignored the shutdowns in order to serve flowers to the grieving.

We parked on a dark block that could not have been more alarming to us queer city folk. I got out of the car and was astonished by how loud my Converses sounded here. There were more houses than I remembered; it amazed me that anyone would want to live so close to a cemetery. Whatever happened to superstition? Perhaps it died when the pandemic hit. Death had become way too commonplace as hundreds a day were perishing. A desensitization to demise was only natural.

Catholic idols donned a few of the front lawns I passed. Mother Mary opened her arms and Padre Pio remained stoic in his brown robes. Zephyr pointed to window displays filled with the flavor of autumn, but Dexter pulled us away, down a narrow road that hadn't seen a car in quite some time, easy to tell given how clean it was and devoid of potholes.

"We have to hop the gate," Dexter said. "Shit's like Fort Knox after five p.m."

"There's no way we're getting in," Zephyr said.

"This coming from a boy who used to break into a warehouse and climb fire escapes. Remember that?"

"I was braver back then."

"Trust, that person is still inside you."

Zephyr didn't reply. Dexter swiftly led us past a very large entryway that had been padlocked, which was two blocks from where we parked. I looked at the oxidized green of these gates, a sign of good iron. My hands wrapped about the intricate engravings and the spiked heads that were meant to discourage intruders who would disturb these people's final resting place. But Dexter was too smart for these rudimentary safeguards.

With his right foot, Dexter kicked one of the hinges until it snapped. The gate made an awful noise, which made me turn and make sure nobody was peering out their window. Then I watched Dexter in disbelief; Zephyr seemed oddly interested as Dexter held the gate a certain way so that Zephyr and I could squeeze through without injury. After Dexter made his way in behind us, he balanced the gate to look as if the hinge wasn't broken off. This would help get us back to the car without trouble, I supposed.

"Where do we go?"

"This way," Dexter pointed to the left.

The cemetery was bright with moonlight. It had myriad little pathways to choose from that bisected this huge sprawl of land. Gravestones seemed to spit right up from the ground, at many different angles so that they appeared like a bad smile. Some were covered with brush and others so weathered it was impossible to read the names. There were trees so big that their branches bent from sheer weight, almost as if they were in mourning for those below us.

I took a bunch of pictures with my phone, half of me hoping I'd see something supernatural when I looked at them later, the other half just simply addicted in that I couldn't imagine my day without using social media. I bent over to look at a few of the stones, touched the sandblasted surfaces. Up close they filled me with dread, knowing that one day I would be forced underground and there was nothing I could do about it. Death is so criminally final.

"It's this way," Dexter said from up ahead.

"Right or left?" I asked.

"Up there, by the mausoleum."

We had to trudge uphill to get there. My legs complained immediately, as did Zephyr's, but I didn't hear any sort of complaint come from Dexter. He pressed forward with confidence, as if he'd done this trek so many times he could do it with his eyes closed. When we got to the top I noticed that the landscape started to change, as if by the work of magic . . . or failing eyesight. It was getting darker, and I had no clue if it was due to the with the bump of ketamine I'd just snorted. No, it couldn't be that.

The moon was now behind a massive mountain of clouds, and the stars felt more dispersed, as if they'd started to retreat away from the very place Dexter was taking us. There were a lot more stones on this side, but less trees, and a cornucopia of flowers. I saw countless Italian surnames and tacky gravestone decor of gold and silver. I knew Zephyr's collectors' eye was bewitched by these gaudy gifts for the dead.

Just as the mausoleum came into sight, out of breath but still smoking a cigarette, I read one of the signs: **VIETATO I FIORI.** *Flowers prohibited.* Then we turned down the hill to the other side, a part of the cemetery that felt isolated from all pathways. We had to step over muck, fallen branches and piles of fresh dirt to get there. Here, the tombs were all above ground, but shabbier than those I had just seen above. Stonework crumbled and names were almost wiped clean from their engravings. I saw no flowers or footprints or signs that anyone had come to visit their dearly departed. Sad, just powerfully sad.

"You see that one there?" Dexter had a green laser pointer and pointed it on the ground.

"It's barely visible from here," I said.

"Just keep looking, you'll see it."

Zephyr was leaning on me now, chin resting on my shoulder. I squinted to get a better look, craned my head as much as I could before I tipped. Then Dexter took my hand, and Zephyr my arm, and we walked closer as a trio. No idea what I was supposed to be seeing, too dark to really tell what was a gravestone, what was a simple pile of dirt, and what was just leaves. Dexter hadn't even removed his sunglasses, which I found interesting; it made Zephyr sneer a bit. Maybe Dexter was just too spooky for his taste.

And then something on the ground fluttered briefly in the breeze.

I heard a sound like a great sigh.

When my eyes adjusted, I saw exactly what Dexter had been pointing at. Immediately nervous, I could hear blood pumping into my ears. It was hair, long and black, flowing about as if it was still on the head of a living person. But that person was no longer alive because they were just a pile of discarded bones; perhaps they'd floated to the surface from lack of care from the staff. Maybe someone dug them up. I saw gnarled fingers and missing teeth, and . . . a skull that had been bashed in cruelly; its cheekbones were shattered, the dome split in two.

"What the hell," Zephyr said. "Is that real?"

Dexter didn't do anything but breathe deeply.

"Who is that?" I said over and over.

Dexter flicked the lit cigarette behind his head.

"My mother."

Zephyr could not believe what he was seeing, or even doing for that matter. But there it was at his feet, an actual pile of bones. He lifted a few of them with the toe of his red Doc Martens until they fell over and clattered into a separate pile. Now it seemed like there were so many more just sitting there at his feet, piled as if the person they belonged to was either ripped apart limb by limb, or crushed by something heavy. Real bones that he'd never seen outside of a movie, so it was a lot to take in.

"Why're they not buried?" Zephyr said.

"Why should they be?" Dexter kneeled and picked up one of the hands, waved it until Zephyr saw a rusted ring fall off. "Are either of your mothers alive?"

"What a question."

"Don't know," Atticus said, and then Zephyr nodded at the same time.

"I had a weird feeling you'd both say that. It's the reason why I wanted to bring you here. I knew you'd get it."

"Get what?"

"The loneliness."

"I don't feel too lonely," Zephyr said. "I've always been an independent person."

"Well . . . I get lonely," Atticus admitted. "Even when I'm too proud to say it."

"I think the pandemic has made loneliness worse."

"Did your mothers raise you?" Dexter asked innocently.

"Barely," Atticus said. "As bad as our childhoods were, we've come to understand as adults that our mothers did the best they could."

"Ancestral trauma is real."

"I never had a mother." Dexter's tone was sad and empty. "I come here to connect with her."

"But why is she not in the ground?" Atticus asked as if this was the topic of normal conversation. However, the reality was quite jarring.

"Don't know."

Zephyr caught the flash of Dexter's pale belly, saw a crow fading into a blue backdrop from the spooky crop top he wore. It was a magnificent, if not sickly skin color. But that made him even more alluring. Atticus proceeded to place a black bandana on his forehead, which pushed his hair back and accentuated his sharp features. It was a look sported by ravers, and Atticus was far from a raver, but he could fit into that aesthetic if he so chose. Dexter followed suit, and then Atticus gave Zephyr a bandana as well.

"It's so hot out, don't want sweat in my eyes," Atticus said.

"These are better fashion statements than facemasks," Dexter said. "But wholly useless these days."

"Why do you need to come here to connect with your mother?" Zephyr asked.

"I just do."

"Don't know what that means."

"Since I never had a mother, I come here to pretend I do."

"Did she die when you were a kid?"

"Don't know."

And that was the end of Zephyr's curiosity for now. Dexter had proven he was not just generally awkward, but that maybe he was on the spectrum. What kind of a person would bring two new friends to a graveyard to look at real bones without knowing them well enough? Not only that, to have them sit vigil before a pile that he proclaimed was his own flesh and blood. The fact that he didn't even know who the woman was left Zephyr with the most questions. What in the world was he doing here? Zephyr just wanted to leave.

"Can we go now?"

"I have more to show you, Zeph."

"I asked you not to call me that."

"You see that over there?"

Dexter used his green laser pointer to show Zephyr a huge white marble tomb, way back on top of the hill, covered by the branches of an oak tree and interlacing green vines. Zephyr didn't know how to take in what he saw, but through the shadows and through the thin slab of moonlight, something twinkled. He perceived it to be jewelry, or keys; maybe gold teeth. His collectors' spirit was intrigued.

"I opened it for you," Dexter said.

"You desecrated a grave for me?"

"No, silly. I just made it easier for you to see the treasures inside."

"I'm not in the business of robbing graves. Save that for HP Lovecraft."

"But don't you at least want to see?"

Atticus tapped Zephyr to signal him to stop being rude.

"Guess it couldn't hurt."

Atticus began walking toward it before Zephyr even said he would. They got to the top of the hill, winded but triumphant. Looking down, the bones of Dexter's mother were now in perfect alignment with the tomb up here. Dexter motioned for Zephyr to proceed, opening the heavy door with his bare hands, even though Zephyr had no idea how one single person could have opened it without help. But with Atticus out of sight, Zephyr simply obliged.

Inside, the tomb was no bigger than a New York City closet. There was no family name, not one that he recognized anyway, and for some reason that ignorance gave Zephyr the courage to step fully in without even asking Atticus to join. He felt an immediate sense of claustrophobia, but brushed it off as Dexter walked in behind him.

"Pretty cool, huh?"

"I'd say so."

The tomb was not well lit. Zephyr smelled dust and the oddly sweet stench of rot; it reminded him of the way organic things decompose. To his right he saw that it was only a stack of lilies, freshly wilted and black; they must have been in here for weeks. With his phone light, Zephyr could see many handwritten notes of mourning in Italian and in English From family members that stepped off a boat, and from those who were born and raised here.

"I'd love to be on molly in a place like this. You wanna do some?"

Dexter sneezed. "No. I can't handle the comedown."

"When's the last time you took it?"

"Don't really remember. All I know is that I don't like it."

Dexter exited abruptly, leaving Zephyr some time to get a better look. The walls were plain, and the floor was streaked in dirt. It felt hotter in here than it did outside, but without ventilation that made sense. All around him he could feel the presence of Catholicism, and somehow, somewhere, he heard the deep sobs of sadness, and the lonely melody of the people whose final resting place this was. It all felt rather violating—what the hell was he even doing here?

Zephyr stepped in further, following the rainbow hue of what must have been a stained-glass reflection, but when he looked down it wasn't that at all. There were jewels and coins and trinkets from a time he could not pinpoint all laid about on a very small altar. The items were fascinating. He wanted them all. But this was certainly not his style. He was not going to steal, no matter how tempting it was. Just as he turned to walk back outside, he saw a flash of purple, followed by the heavy door closing shut on him.

"Where's Zephyr?"

Dexter and I were alone at the bottom of the hill. There was a fine mist swirling about my shoes and the sweet sound of crickets filled my ears, something we rarely hear in Manhattan. Dexter sat cross legged and leaned his head toward his mother's bones. Now that I had gotten a good look at them, I couldn't help but sympathize with Dexter's loneliness.

"I have nobody," Dexter said. "I'm utterly alone."

"You have us now." I put my hand on his shoulder.

"I've never really fit in anywhere. Do you know how that feels?"

"Absolutely."

"It's why I love social media. I can just post, and people want to talk to me."

"That's definitely one of the major upsides."

"You can do it too."

"But I still feel so alone."

"Well, I hate to say this, but if you're taking all your new friends here after just meeting them, then I can understand why some people might not want to associate with you."

"But you didn't bat an eye. I knew you wouldn't. It's been a long time since I met someone like you."

And that much was true. He must have seen something in me that he hadn't in anyone else. Flattering, to say the least. However, even I had my limitations. I knew this boy was weird, but now he'd taken the term to abysmal levels. I touched his shoulder again, noticing that my crotch was brushing up against the side of his head. That's when he stood, grabbed my face and kissed me, right there on top of his mother's makeshift grave. I heard bones rattle beneath my feet, smelled the old dirt that covered them. But none of that mattered with Dexter's sweet lips pressed into my own, his smoky tongue slithering into the back of my throat.

"Mary Shelly did it," Dexter said, breathing heavily into my mouth.

"Did what?"

"Lost her virginity on her mother's grave."

"You gotta be kidding me."

"She's the *mother of horror*, after all."

Now we were on the ground. Dexter's hands were beneath my shirt; his fingernails scratched my torso, but it was a welcoming pain. He was just so soft and alluring; I couldn't bring myself to say no. I grabbed his hair, pulled it until his neck was exposed, licking the juncture near his clavicle. I could not decipher the flavor of Dexter, but he smelled faintly of flowers and the dust of altars. When we locked eyes, a purple haze swelled inside my skull. I felt it, I became it. I wanted more and more of it.

And then my phone started ringing.

Zephyr.

Dexter swiped it out of my hand and proceeded to unbutton my jeans. My cock had swelled to the point where I knew if I didn't let it out to play, I'd be grumpy until I got off. So, I let Dexter blow me, right there in the graveyard, before the bones of his mother, with her bashed eyes watching me and wicked black hair fanned about. The minute my orgasm hit Dexter's mouth I heard him release a great sigh. It was from his own orgasm, as I saw a slimy white gob perched on one of his mother's fingers.

"That was hot," Dexter said.

"I want more of that."

My phone was ringing again. When I grabbed it, I was too late. I saw the messages. *I'm stuck!* Zephyr wrote. *Where the fuck are you?* My heart sank into my stomach, and as Dexter leaned over to read the texts, he didn't even blink. I ran up the hill and slowly heard Zephyr's wailing get louder and louder. I got to the door of that tomb and pushed with all my might, but it would not budge. I screamed for Dexter to help, but he took his sweet ass time to get to the top. Once there, he simply placed his hand on the door, and it opened as if it was made of paper. My jaw dropped.

"You motherfucker."

Zephyr was a juggernaut. He wound his fist back and clocked Dexter in the side of the head. I saw him fall face-first into the dirt, and I had no idea what to do or who I should have helped first. All I knew was that I had to keep both of them calm. I picked Dexter up and used my body as a blockade between them, held Zephyr back with my left arm and Dexter with my right. After a minute, Zephyr calmed down.

"He locked me in there!"

"Why did you hit me?"

"You deaf?"

"I did no such thing," Dexter smirked. "I gave you a gift."

"Oh, a gift you say? What kind?"

"Any antique of your choice."

"You're definitely fucking deaf or choosing to ignore me. I said that I'm not in the business of robbing graves, you fucking freak!"

"Freak? Watch what you say, that's not very nice."

"Atticus, are you going to just sit there and let him do that to me?" Zephyr stomped the ground.

"I didn't see him lock you in there."

"Un-fucking-believable. I wanna go home. *Now.*"

Zephyr headed in the direction of the car. There was nothing I could have done to change his mind. Dexter grabbed my arm, held me back for a moment. His eye socket was starting to swell, and I felt awful for not being able to stop Zephyr from hitting him. But there must have been a justified reason, right?

"I needed that," Dexter said. "I've always wanted to reenact what Mary Shelly did."

"What do you mean?"

"She lost her virginity on top of her mother's grave."

"Are you telling me you're a virgin?"

"Far from it."

"And how did your mother die? You never told us."

Dexter looked into my eyes deeply, sadly, madly.

"I killed her."

Part 2

Shadow into Shadow

*"A truth that's told with bad intent
beats all the lies you can invent."*

—William Blake

6

Hellacious rotation of the day, and Halloween's rare blue moon was perched furiously in the sky. A lunar rarity that hasn't appeared on this date since the second world war. I watched it lurk behind the sawtooth outline of New York, wondering if the relationship I had with it was unique. Full moons usher in mental rejuvenation. They offer the chance for us to bid adieu to one chapter and welcome another. I recognized this as something was changing within me.

In the weeks leading up to Halloween, Dexter and I spent a lot of time together. More than Zephyr knew, more than I thought we ever would. There was no talk about his mother's bones or the fact that Zephyr accused Dexter of locking him in that tomb. It was best laughed off, sort of like how I laughed off the way Dexter told us about his mother's supposed demise. One would think all this talk of mother's would get me thinking about my own, but the last time I saw the woman, I swore her off—physically and mentally.

With the last of summer still holding out, heat present even in the middle of the night, Dexter and I took many long walks together. Liquor was consumed and drugs were dabbled in. Nothing hard like Molly or Ecstasy (Dexter made it seem like he was afraid of the stuff) so we kept it lowkey with ketamine and some GHB. Not much else to do when the city was still shut down.

We perused parks and abandoned office buildings. We took photographs of empty avenues and dusty side streets. To see the city so devoid of people was both culture shock and inspiring. We found new freedoms in this freedom of loneliness, together. All of this was posted to our socials, sometimes together and sometimes not. We fed off the energy that the comments gave us.

Then days would go by without any communication. I thought this was normal at first, at least it was back when people were busy, had social lives and were distracted by the multitude of options New York City had to offer. But with all of that off the table, it left me thinking too much. It locked me in an emotional prison, and the only way to get out was through social media.

I would look for Dexter's stories and posts, and watch his Twitter feed like a hawk. Seriously, I had hours to dedicate to this. It was my way of cutting off texts to ensure Dexter didn't think I was too pushy and give Zephyr a break from accusing me of seeing him too much. I had to take these careful steps or else I would risk upsetting—or setting off—one or the other. My new life was shaping up in an interesting fashion.

When I wasn't staring into my phone I stared at the sky and phantasmal constellations, musing myself with their meanings. I asked the universe if it had any plans for me, because I had my moments of weakness. Sometimes I felt lost, at other times unimportant. While I thought I'd left angst behind in my twenties, I was feeling it—with much remorse—again in my thirties. I tried to make amends with all that I couldn't change or control and got myself ready to seize what I could.

The first sign of serious attraction is doubt. You become so consumed by the thought of losing the opportunity to learn about this person that you find yourself drowning in frivolous worry rather than hopeful consequence. I wasted a lot of hours arguing with myself about this. I watched time whittle away at my fingertips. Time goes cruelly fast when you don't want it to. I find that it leaves me lost in an incurable anger rather than being thankful that I still have a chance to be alive and breathing.

"He's weird."

Zephyr was peering over my shoulder; I could feel the heat of his eyes, which made me shut my phone off. I turned around to see that he had a cup of black coffee near his lips, the steam crawling across his face until it formed little beads of sweat. I was in my underwear, felt eerily skinny, my tattoos and piercings suddenly ugly. Zephyr, on the other hand, looked well-rested and polished, blue hair slicked back, skin positively glowing and eyebrows like two check marks upon the pale canvas from which they were drawn.

"Dexter's no different than you or me."

"Then why are you pacing?"

Zephyr saw right through me; he knew me better than I knew myself. I stared at him, blank-faced with a cigarette burning uselessly between my lips. I was falling in love with someone else and he called me out on it without saying the exact words. I wondered when Zephyr would come to understand. Time would see this through for me. We'd never agreed on a suitable third before, but I thought to myself that Dexter might be *the one*.

"He never apologized for what he did."

"You were on K and panicked."

"No, he locked me in there."

"How do you really know?"

"I saw him close the door."

I didn't reply.

"You gonna say anything?"

"No."

I turned away, slid back into the chaotic comfort of my studio. At my worktable there was no organization, no chance at determining the path I needed to propel my craft. I'm not a planner; I much preferably work in the world of pantsing. Element of surprise, learn as I go. But what I'd done to my workspace was unforgivable. Cigarette butts and drifting mountains of ash; crushed beer cans and clouds of ketamine. It was the habitat of a filthy drug addict, though I was far from that.

"Why not?" Zephyr entered without knocking.

"Because I don't feel like it."

"He's your new bestie now, huh? Your new *oomfie*?"

OOMF is a Twitter acronym for "one of my friends" and Zephyr was doing a great job mocking that culture.

"Stop that."

"You two spend so much time together, it's as if you don't want me around."

"That's not true at all."

"Yes, it is. He's never asked me to hang out."

"But I have, many times."

"I'd feel much better if it came from him."

"Can't you see I'm working?" I said it with a tone of finality.

In this grand experimentation of quarantine and new love, I'd achieved existential laziness. Clutter was my new way of life; the more shit in my studio, the more chances I had at destroying it and putting it back together in some dark and evolved way. I melted toys, pulled synthetic hair from various dolls in every color of the spectrum. I had a stack of roof shingles, sticks and concrete powder that I used for textural purposes. Chicken wire, barbed wire and wired baskets all at my disposal to reshape, rebind . . . rebirth. Anything could be used for sculpting if you put your mind to it.

"I have eyes."

"You're asking a lot from a person who barely knows you," I said as Zephyr walked away. "You've never complained about any of my friends before."

"This ain't just a *friend*."

"Huh?"

"You've never had a 'friend' you didn't want to fuck, which is just toxic. But Dexter's different. You *want* to keep him around."

"And what's wrong with that? He's a brilliant mind, a brilliant creator."

"You really are letting it fly over your head, ain't you?"

I hit my work desk. "Just say what's on your mind."

"Let's start with . . . oh how about that sculpture? Just weirdly shows up after ten years?"

"That means nothing."

"And the bones he took us to?" Zephyr brushed blue bangs away from his one green eye. "You still going to tell me that wasn't weird at all. They looked alive; I saw where its hair was ripped out by the roots on the skull."

"Was probably eaten by rats."

"Rats don't eat hair and bones. Do you take me for a fool?"

"No," I sighed.

"And you're still convinced he didn't take me to that tomb on purpose?"

"Do you respond to his stories or tweets?" I said that to deflect.

"You're impossible," Zephyr sighed, not taking my bait.

"Some people need to break the ice that way. He's lonely; you can reach out to him too, ya know."

"Already defending him? Riddle me this: When will you start calling him your boyfriend? When're you gunna think with your actual head instead of the little one between your legs?"

"It ain't small," I laughed. "And you know it."

"You're *my* boyfriend. Remember that next time you defend him."

I was quiet for a minute, unsure of what to say. "Don't overthink it."

"I see the way that you two post," Zephyr snapped. "So cringe."

I'd no rebuttal for that one. Dug my own grave, that's what I did. Truth is that when you meet someone new and there's an immediate connection, we feel this internal pressure to show them off to our digital audience. Dexter knew it had to be done as well. Needing this sort of attention/validation is beyond my own millennial morals, but we both easily fell prey to posts and selfies and engaging with comments, good or bad. It's the new rush, the new drug.

"You know what's the best part? I don't even need to ask what you two do, since you're constantly one-upping the other with your posts."

"All I have is one friend and you're going crazy."

"I'm not going crazy; I'm being careful. I have a bad feeling—"

"I'll talk to him, ok? Now go."

I had to cut Zephyr off or else my head would've exploded. But it was my first real lie. I knew that I'd never bring this subject up for fear of awkwardness. I wasn't about to risk my relationship with one of the most interesting people I'd ever met to quell Zephyr's insecurity. My connection with Dexter was almost unwholesome, but that made me like it. And why should I not explore it?

I began to spiral. A man my age is best suited doing anything other than giving into dread and self-loathing, but here I was licking the old boot of doubt and fury. However, I was also a man hardened by the clock. Experience thickened my skin. If growing older meant that I was now ankle-deep in the eventual grave, it also meant that I was supposed to be free from the chains of insecurity.

In this moment of weakness, I decided that I wanted to date Dexter. He may have been a lunatic led by passion, but he was an interesting enough risk; he barely had to lift a finger to captivate me. Also, the idea that beneath my very feet was some kind of city, or hell, intrigued me. I couldn't erase, nor deny, the images of that place.

Dexter would send me pictures of it on Instagram every now and again, which made me question it more. Every single one of them was different from the next. Nothing seemed right down there. Things changed even if you didn't want them to. How that could even be was beyond my understanding. But that was part of the fun.

There's no sun or moon. No rules. We avoid the light.

Dexter wrote that to me in a direct message after I responded to one of his stories, a dark selfie with a wicked new creation lurking in the back. He told me that he hadn't seen the sun in over a week, which was why we hadn't talked. I knew then that he had a bond with that darkness, a bond I wasn't ready to make sense of. It was no wonder the boy was so pale. He was a night creature.

We see things others cannot
See what?

The cruelty of the world!

You don't need to be down there in order to see that. I added an emoji with a tongue sticking out just to be cute.

It's just a diff experience below ground. This place was made for people like us.

Us?

The people that the real world doesn't want. Queers, artists, thinkers, believers, skeptics.

Scares me to think about that, I admitted to him. *What if I really like it down there?*

Why's that scary? Dexter typed back right away. *You embrace the dark but now want to run from it?*

I left Dexter on *read* for an hour, then replied.

My life is settled. I don't want to change it that much.

By associating with me, Atticus, you know that's not true. I'd never hurt you. I only want to find out more about you.

It's more of a feeling I have, Dexter. There's something primeval down there. It's not a safe place.

WOULD YOU HAVE IT ANY OTHER WAY?

I didn't respond to that.

Don't you want to create? Isn't that your dream?

I create art! You're creating madness.

Madness is art . . . art is madness. We're at war, Atticus. Work must be done!

I slid my finger angrily across the keyboard of my phone, cracking the screen even further.

There's something in your own work that you don't see. Dexter garnished this sentence with a Devil emoji. *But I see it. Isn't that every artist's dream?*

"Do you want to tell me anything?"

I was sitting in a chair at a local café that had just reopened, though we were not allowed to do such. Our culture had turned into grab-and-go, but at least it got the city moving again. Empty shelves and a very bland pattern of wallpaper that was almost too insulting to look at took over my line of sight. There was one sad-eyed employee, but she let me sit without issue, so long as I would get up if asked.

The sun pounded through the storefront window, which made my lips sweat and my cloth facemask stick annoyingly to my face. Dexter was facing my direction, also awash with afternoon light, cross-legged and spooky facemask just as wet as my own. His skin was whiter than I remembered, and there were weird looking marks on both his arms, like someone had twisted to the point of rug burn, someone with claws.

"What are those marks?"

"Got hurt on the job."

"On the job?"

"A sculpture fell on me."

That seemed a suitable enough answer for now. My only worry was that he was either hurting himself or that someone was hurting him. I checked my phone, saw a few texts from Zephyr, nothing angry or resentful. He was in much better spirits today. I replied back to him, chipper in my own way, didn't want him to think I was ignoring him or doing something he wouldn't approve of.

On the table between us, a bunch of photos fanned out. The old-fashioned Polaroid kind, but much smaller. Dozens of dark images contrasted against the ugly table. It had been so long since I'd seen, or even held, an actual photograph. I had no idea that these were still even being made, but I was filled with much needed nostalgia.

"Instax Mini," Dexter said.

"What?"

"That's what they're calling them now. Instant photos."

"Like a Polaroid?"

"Sort of, yeah."

He handed over the small camera, simple silver and black with an even simpler interface. Very limited options: just snap the picture and go. I admit this made my technological heart stammer; it was like time had rewound and we were suddenly back to the simple life. No filters, no FaceTune, just the real world printed on this special square. I took my facemask off, despite the rules of the carry-and-go café, and leaned close to Dexter to snap a selfie of us. I grabbed his cheek and brought it close to my tongue. He smelled devilishly good. *My* eventual devil.

"Save that for the archives," Dexter said.

I put the photo in my pocket before I watched it develop.

"Zephyr still mad at me?"

"Sort of." The lie tasted terrible, but I had to.

"About what now?"

I sighed. "He says you locked him in the tomb."

"We're still on that?" Dexter clicked a red thumbnail on his lower teeth.

"I can't force him to not be upset."

"But I didn't lock him in there. I swear it." Dexter's face flushed a deep maroon. "I don't want to fight with him. I like Zephyr."

"I know you do."

I went back to the photos on the table. Dexter had been arranging them slow and steady, either creating some kind of narrative or completing a puzzle. If someone were to peer, they wouldn't see much other than some blots of darkness and bright gashes. But I saw something deeper, more sinister. He was piecing together a makeshift portrait, and each photo connected to the other brilliantly, surreptitiously. Another one of his hidden creative talents.

"Does he want me to apologize?" Dexter didn't look up.

"Yes."

"Well, I'm not going to. Because then I'd have to admit I did something I didn't."

"Did you do anything?"

Dexter continued arranging the photos, even carefully placing some of them between the light and shadow cast upon the table. It was a marvel to watch him work. Then something else caught my eye. Not quite at first, but after twenty minutes the pictures started to look like something out of a Charles Fort nightmare. I saw darkness twist and turn, as if it was a living, pliable thing. The gashes were not a reflection of the flash, but teeth. Or maybe eyes . . . eyes as big as my own head.

"I've seen this before," I said.

"Yes, you have."

Dexter sucked his too-white teeth. Perhaps he wasn't sure if I was seeing exactly what he wanted me to. But I knew the color of that place, could still smell the sulfur and wet dirt that permeated the air down there. It was the kind that stuck to your skin for days, much like my neighbors' cooking. And then Dexter motioned for me to look down again, made my eye follow two of his fingers until they were pointing at something that I most likely would have looked over if not for his help. It felt very much as if Dexter was implanting these images into my head.

"When you were down there with me . . . I thought you didn't notice."

It was one of the greatest sculptures I'd ever seen. A huge thing made of wings and talons, some prehistoric behemoth that made no sense. A crenelated horn of gold sprouted out of its huge forehead, and below it were three menacing eyes the color of no-color; you couldn't tell if its heavy glare was for you, or that it was watching something else. Its stance was both agitated and relaxed at the same time. The craftsmanship was unmatched. This was Dexter's signature style: an amalgam of two cryptids, or more, into one.

"What's it called?"

"*Animus.*"

We sat in silence for a few minutes. The café had served a few customers during this time but was now completely empty, save for the bad-attitude employee. I wanted to slap some sense into her; she had her job back, and not many others could say that. Instead, I slid my hand in and out of the sun, sipped my black coffee after noticing that the sun had colored a portion of the skin on my thigh. Then I entwined my foot with Dexter's. We didn't talk, didn't need to We were becoming that close.

But the photos were now starting to bother me. I felt that sick urge to whip out my phone and tell people what I was doing with my day, but I backed away from temptation and focused my attention on the moment. If I moved my eyes in one direction, I could swear one of the great wings flapped, and then if I moved them in another direction all three depthless eyes followed my gaze. Whatever kind of trick this was, it sure entertained Dexter. The biggest smile stretched his sharp features from ear to ear.

"Who's it for?" I asked carefully, not trying to pry too much.

"Don't know yet."

"I know that feeling."

"I'm sick of having some kind of 'purpose,' I've done all that. I'm more into winging it these days."

"I think a lot of us are."

"What about you? Are you working on anything?"

"Always, but I feel like my attention span is fucked."

Dexter looked down at my phone. "Gee, I wonder why?"

It was going off again. More texts from Zephyr and a few DMs. I peaked at some of the DMs—just a bunch of thirsty boys—then went back to find a newly annoyed Zephyr in his messages. He told me that he was going out, that his phone was low on battery and he would be back. I only knew one place he'd run to when upset. The warehouse where we met almost eleven years ago.

"Anyway, I just wanted to show you this," Dexter said, breaking my trance. "I'm off to do more work. Text me later."

Dexter put the photos back into his bookbag and slipped out the door in a way that made it seem like he vanished into thin air.

The first time Dexter and I had sex could only be described as lock and key. I can still feel the phantom strength of his hands on my body, the delicious flavor of his mouth. There was never a moment of hesitation or damnation. We didn't let our egos get in the way. It was about the exploration of the flesh, and dare I say it, the conquest of the heart.

Dexter's candy-colored eyes intensified in my mind, undressing my inhibitions without saying a word. I noticed my hands were beginning to ache daily from unconsciously clenching them into fists. Dexter made me this way, tense and feral. His testosterone was always through the roof. I noticed it from the protruding veins in his skin, to the huge gobs of come that slithered out of his penis.

Rose petals, he once told me. *You taste like rose petals.* I had no words in the English language to describe his flavor. Until one day I blurted it out. *Shadow*, I said, licking my lips clean of his glossy spit. *You taste like shadow.*

He brought me back to feelings of virginity. The way my throat ached, how my pulse increased, drying my mouth until my tongue was sandpaper. I could swear I was sixteen years old again. When his body covered my own, all angled and sharp but still impossibly soft, it sent my bones into an uncontrollable quiver. It was as if my cells and his cells exchanged a code that unlocked the secrets of attraction not nature never intended to reveal.

The position never mattered (many gay men obsess over top and bottom roles, but Dexter didn't believe in any of that). Without voicing it, we learned the intimate pleasures of one another's body; drank every sinister slime our orifices produced. The endorphins released upon kissing was a shared addiction.

Dexter quickly became my muse. This made me draw endlessly. Nothing to take note of, not at first; the comely outline of a beautiful boy donning glasses, sharp nose and vampire's smile; skin like the underside of a pearl. All of that quickly shapeshifted into the outline of a different boy with blue hair and an impish grin about his soft mouth, and the most innocent disposition. Then there was a third boy; skeleton grin and wide eyes veiled by thick hair, a touch of mania in his face.

I began to see a wretched pattern. These boys were driven by darkness, sowed in onerous desire. They kissed in one drawing with forked tongues, then regressed into rage, clawing at one another until there was nothing but tawdry lines and endless circles, the pages left black and gleaming. It was a wicked mirror pushed into my face, cracked and brittle as cobweb. I broke through it with my mind's fist, ripped the pages apart. The next night, I found them as if someone had stitched them back together.

"I finally texted him," Zephyr said to me a week later. "No answer."

"Try his socials."

"Did that too." Zephyr eyed me like I was a bad child.

"He's down *there*," I emphasized, pointing my finger at the ground, swirling it.

"In hell?" We stared at one another for a solid minute. "He sure is doing a great job at building a relationship with me." Zephyr's dark sarcasm singed my nerves.

"What's with the pettiness?"

"How would you feel if the shoe were on the other foot?"

"Interested," I said flatly.

"You're only after him for social clout."

"I have more followers than him, thank you very much."

"Then it's because he's hot *and* insane."

"Don't forget creative."

I thought about the correlation between insanity and creativity. Artists are branded as "different" very early on in life. It's seen in their interactions with other children, manifested in the way that they take the lead. This creates a psychological label that divides them from others, but is also the sharpest tool in their personal arsenal for years to come.

"Don't forget I'm here too."

"Please stop." I was resorting to begging now. "This is not a good look on you."

"I don't know what's happening, but it's driving me crazy."

That was the end of groveling for the next three weeks. And now I was once again left alone to be my own madman. Every night that came and went, I dreamed of that dingy underground circus, thus my craft took a twisted turn. I found ways to meld metal and plastic and acrylic paint. Taxidermy would become a wimpy thing of the past compared to what I was conceiving. Wet clay in my hands, violence in my heart, sex on the soul. Profuse deviance. I had to match what Dexter was doing.

That's when one of the bastard things started moving.

I named it *HeadCase*. Bald and brazen and wholly mutated; lips the color of death, eyes wet and alive as my own. It was the kind of thing that slid out of your nightmares and stared at you while you were asleep. I could swear it bared sharp little teeth when I wasn't looking, veiny wings flapping against my rationality. I told Zephyr about it first, but he dismissed it as a trick of the studio light, or the flickering of my candles. I knew he was wrong.

"Do it again," I said to it. "*Move.*"

It lay cold and clammy in my grip, which was odd as this little doll was erected from plush materials and resin. I smoothed it over with sandpaper, so it still had an acrylic feel to it. Yet it was moist in my hand as would be a jellyfish. When I put the ghoulie back on the shelf with all my other miscreations, it looked very out of place. *Garden Gob* flanked it on the right, all green and tentacled; it could swallow this new one whole. On its left was a stone fae with cloven hoof hands, black tears on its cheeks, and horns where its eyes should have been.

need you

I smacked the shelf. When they didn't flinch, I smashed a liquor bottle and threatened to cut them, then myself. Once again, they did nothing. Four cigarettes later, the walls inside my studio finally showing the yellow scars of tobacco smoke and spilled IPA, I scoured the internet for mindless entertainment but found myself filled with envy at the work of other sculptors, especially Dexter.

hate you

I could hear them. But could anyone else? I took some pics and uploaded them to my online portfolio. First on Instagram, then on my website MiniMonstrosities.com, and then Twitter. I noticed the funniest thing. *HeadCase* appeared a bit bent in the photo, its jaw slack, as if it was opening to scream, or eat. Maybe it was in my nature to freak myself out, but it garnered some audience appeal. The post got seventeen hundred likes within a few hours on Instagram and went almost instantly viral on Twitter. It even got some attention from Electric Orchid's official account, a local band I was quite fond of. But I wasn't very fond of the comments.

Looks like something out of a Grimm Fairy Tale, one user commented

Gives me the creeps, said another

If I didn't know any better, I would say that thing is real

Attention is the prerequisite for an ego boost. Yet there is something very hurtful about social media that all of us partake in. We've come to a point where we value ourselves in how many likes a post can get rather than being secure in our own authenticity. Satisfaction is derived from a random stranger's double tapping. How did we get to this point? Why do we let ourselves get tangled in that mess when at the end of the day, the audience always moves on? Attention spans are about as big as a grain of sand. You're forgotten as soon as you're noticed.

never forget

My ear started to bleed. I knew that voice—but I chose to ignore it. I checked my message requests, decided to entertain myself with stupidity for the next hour. There weren't as many as usual, and the account that had sent me that weird message was gone. I felt sad, and alone. The social-media web had trapped me. I could feel a pout forming on my lips, until a solitary email landed in my inbox. *DoN't YoU KnOw WhAt YoU WiLL dO?* The sender was unknown. When I replied to the email, I got a message back in what felt like a blink of the eye.

The Eventual Devil is Dangerous.

I shut my phone off, subsequently shutting out the digital world.

7

Zephyr waltzed through a sodium arc spill of streetlights before slipping back into the dark, his old trickster of a friend. It was a tumultuous, albeit productive walk. Feelings ebbed and hormones flowed as repressed emotions began to show their face. Trying to overcome them was pointless. It left Zephyr in mad-like state in which the skin and soul acted as spectators in awe of one another.

The warehouses welcomed him as they always had, squat, rusted, and somehow calming. Zephyr scaled the fire escape, metal scraping metal, paint chips clashing to the ground, wallet chain clanking like chimes. As he wriggled his way onto the main grate, Zephyr noticed that the support screws were threatening to pull free. Two seconds too long and he could be sent back to the cement, heavy steel crushing his body, intestines squeezed out of every orifice like silly string.

Inside, a New Moon party was being held, so said the silver and black banner that fell like tentacles from the ceiling. Zephyr immediately smelled cigarettes and incense, so potent he knew it would stick to his clothes and skin for a long time. The crowd brimmed wall to wall, relatively young, somewhere between Gen Z and millennial, and a sprinkling of Gen X. Three generations divided, but they all had one common purpose here: to party.

A DJ was raised upon a dark dais, spinning a weird mix of industrial, heavy metal and a dash of house disco; beats dropped like a guillotine into the soul. The sound system was so good it was almost surreal given the DIY atmosphere, but anything was possible in this new world of quarantine and bored people. Somewhere deep within the music, the voice of Stevie Nicks and Amy Lee echoed.

What bothered Zephyr the most was that everyone was in such close contact with each other when they were supposed to be at least six feet apart. He knew it would only be a matter of time before some cultural terrorist would post about this on social media to inflate another cancel war. Until then, everyone's hands were in the air, feeling the music as if times were normal, as if people weren't being offed daily by the virus.

But even with as many people as there were here, Zephyr felt utterly alone. He was in his head again, and with Mars in retrograde, he wondered what vicious plans were in store for him. He lit a cigarette and looked at its red glow, as if he was smoking a speck of Mars dust. His was just one little prick of fire amongst a sea of bright little coronas, smoke glowing upon exhalation.

He let the music take control. Every trek of treble was like pins and needles in his feet; every bashing beat of bass crawled up his extremities, ending in sparks. He knew that once he started dancing, everything would be alright. The night was young, as were the hands that possessed popular club drugs. Ketamine, molly, GHB and chocolate psilocybin mushrooms would surely be floating around.

To disintegrate one's haunting insecurities, neutralizing thoughts was key, which is why these drugs were so popular. Zephyr swallowed an encapsulated molly and snorted a bump of K. In no time his mind unsheathed like an old skin. He found himself enjoying the moment. A dozen mouths found his; some were soft, some were sticky, and some were dry as bone. He tasted lipstick, cigarettes, daubs of coke. None of these mouths belonged to Atticus, so there was no special ferociousness.

Images swirled before his eyes and the world slowed to a single blinking light. He could lose himself in this hole or pull himself free. All he needed was a sign. That's when he saw Atticus' face, and his hand reaching out—but when Zephyr grabbed hold, the face he saw was Dexter's, skin the color of rot, melting until there was nothing but a grinning skull. Zephyr disregarded the hallucinations and squeezed himself into the crowd.

Multi-pierced ears and vacant movements shrouded him. They all wore facemasks, which limited conversations to darkly lined eyes and muffled speech. Toward the other end of the warehouse was a stage, black wood and black fixtures, matte as far as Zephyr could tell, and mounds of black glitter. A crew was unraveling wires and chords that led eyes to the sight of movie-like stage props; every horror trope, cliché and iconic monster rolled into one.

That's when he smelled Jägermeister and spicy green smoke, the token scent of a band whose music had been haunting New York's underbelly ever since their debut album *Shadow Stories* tore a hole into the metal scene. Electric Orchid's sound was the offspring of Nine Inch Nails and Black Sabbath, born in an age where technology was lightyears ahead of their predecessors, which uniquely juxtaposed their advanced sound and antiquated goth getups.

At the lip of the stage, Electric Orchid's color scheme of black, red and green could be seen. Neon bats were drawn on every amp, a tiny hex on every chord. This filled Zephyr with a primal charge, like the feeling you get when on high alert, of being torn out of a bad dream only to find that you've been transported into a worse one. But then he noticed why.

To his right a pair of eyes was locked onto him, and even though half the face was hidden behind a black and red mask, Zephyr knew it was one not to be reckoned with. High cheekbones, dark eyes and artist's choice of clothing: distorted white tank top speckled with glitter, paint, and a flowering smudge that looked like ink. A scrollwork of tattoos illuminated on moonlight skin, hair pulled into a tight ponytail, shining like a crow's wing.

And this person wasn't alone.

With him was an equally exhilarating individual, but one who didn't live in shadow as much as the former. This one was taller, impossibly lankier, but the energy encircling him was preternaturally dark. Hair past the shoulders, all black except the bangs which hung like silver string. Dracula eyebrows and nightmarish irises, the kind that saw things others could not.

His getup was as powerfully stated as the first boy's: green crop top and *NEW YORK FUCKING CITY* graphitized across; a slew of rings and piercings that caught the club lights, as well as an intricate line of tattoos and white Doc Martens on his feet. They looked like a fashionable couple that loved to spook each other.

After a few minutes of staring, the boys drew themselves back into the crowd, but their sharp little faces remained imprinted in Zephyr's vision. It was as if he was being forced to recognize them, and it took a few more minutes to realize that he had just been in the presence of Dorian Wilde and Sebastian Ricciuti, famed underground painter and New York's reigning macabre drag queen, the Hydra.

Part of the strangeness of this small artistic community is that you are bound to see the same people at the same parties; remember their faces but not their names, remember their art but not its meaning, remember their book without ever reading a single word. Dorian and Sebastian were a prime example of this culture that polluted New York's creative circles. It didn't matter if they interacted with you or not, everyone knew who they were. Then a hand grabbed his shoulder.

"Gotta watch yourself." The voice was deep and dark and assertive.

"These folks have a thing for eating their own kind." The other voice was higher in pitch, but equal in force. "Got a light?"

"I do," Zephyr said.

"This is Sebastian. You might know him as the—"

"*Hydra.*"

The two boys removed their masks, revealing naturally red lips. An incredible silence ensued as they all took in the moment; Zephyr recalled the many drag shows where he'd seen the Hydra perform, and the plethora of galleries where Dorian had presented his paintings as if they were not meant to be kept on a wall.

"I've been to many of your shows . . . if that's what they're calling them these days."

"It's been so long that I almost forgot what it was like to be on stage."

"This pandemic has destroyed so much," Dorian said.

"I also have a few of your paintings."

Dorian's eyebrows wriggled and Sebastian's went into a mad V shape. Zephyr saw droplets of sweat perched on the edge of their mouths, which gave him the sudden urge to kiss them. They were both objectively good looking, and subjectively sexy, at least by Zephyr's standards. For a moment the room went still, despite the music continuing to worm itself into Zephyr's ears, growing inside his head like a huge flower.

"Only a few?" Dorian clicked his black pinky nail against very white teeth. "How do you expect me to eat?"

Zephyr said nothing.

"I'm kidding. But I'm shocked you haven't thrown them away."

Dorian turned. A girl with ratty hair approached him from behind, emanating a curmudgeon's demeanor. Beside her was a cute boy who had a bandana wrapped about the top of his head in the fashion of New York party boys. His hair was sandy brown, and very thick; his eyes just as black as Dorian's.

"Why would I throw them away?"

"They do weird things, I'm told."

"Just like my boyfriend's art."

"*Boyfriend.*" Sebastian stepped closer and lit his own cigarette. "What kind of art?"

"He's a sculptor. Are you telling me you don't follow *MiniMonstrosities*?"

"I can't say that I do," Dorian said shakily.

"He would be shocked to hear it."

"Artists are so sensitive."

"*Men . . .* are sensitive," Zephyr quickly responded. "And you look so different out of drag."

Sebastian didn't reply to that comment.

"Sorry, I know that sounds dumb."

"But am I still cute?"

Sebastian took out his cell phone and started taking selfies. That's when the lights changed color, red sluicing across the crowd, as if someone had thrown bloody water at them. All eyes turned toward the stage as Electric Orchid crept onto it. *Delilah*, the crowd howled. *Make them Rise!* It had been a long time since Zephyr had seen a live show; the last time it involved a different type of warehouse and a mysterious death that was best not revisited.

Delilah took center stage, a tiny girl drizzled in pink and black, her dreadlocks as snaky and notorious as she'd always kept them. Her sapphire eyes and assured presence blockaded all other energies. She took up a lot of space for being so small . . . cosmically and figuratively. Behind her, and off to the right, was an androgynous person whose skin was brighter than starlight; his eyes pierced through the smoke, which gave way to a face that would make Lestat de Lioncourt freeze up. Zephyr knew that this person was Alex, the synth master, a staple in the queer/questioning/nonbinary crowd.

Alex's spider fingers crawled across the keys of a synthesizer. The guitarist's black nails picked at the strings of a BC Rich Warlock; an equally disturbing bass guitar shook the foundation; double bass pedals struck madly and in time with cymbals and cowbells. And finally, pink and black nails slid across the microphone, ushering in vocals that almost taunted the synthesizer to battle.

The first power chord ripped through the room. There was no respect for transition, verse or chorus. Electric Orchid jumped right into a blazing industrial abyss that severed musical veins. The band had a powerful grip on the crowd. They all went stiff, as if absorbing the warbling music, and it made Zephyr want to knock into them like bowling pins, as most had fried their brains from drugs anyway.

Delilah swung her mic stand at the crowd, hitting the people in front with chains, lace and leather. Then the floor opened into an old school circle pit, and before it swallowed him, Zephyr got out of the madness by latching himself onto the periphery and pushing bodies back into it. Dorian and Sebastian did the same. While mosh pits were all the rage in one's teenage years, when you're over thirty they become dangerous. But the band didn't care how old you were, all they asked of you was your rage.

Delilah's voice was muscular as much as it was mercurial. It slid into every ear and wrapped energy about Zephyr's body like a noose. It was as if he had headphones on, the music felt so intimate. But when a rogue elbow cracked him in the chin, Zephyr woke from the trance. Bodies flew in every direction as if thrown by some secret force. Heads collided, eyes shed blood tears. Piercings were torn from various orifices and hair was pulled screaming from its roots. Those who didn't pay attention were crushed and swept away.

Oddly, Dorian's eyes were closed, as if he was meditating. Sebastian moved in front of him to ward off any stray bodies. It was amazing to see Sebastian's strength; how it came from such a lanky body was beyond Zephyr, but he was able to thwart off people twice his weight and many inches above his head.

Then the heaviness of the music was exchanged for an extremely relaxed bridge of clean guitar and echoing bass. Delilah's voice was now citing poetry, and then she growled so deeply Zephyr almost lost his mind. That's when Dorian's eyes opened, brush in his hand as pointed and sharp as a butcher's knife. He quickly painted a circle on the floor.

"Time to go," Dorian said. "She's about to raise hell."

Sebastian pulled Zephyr away from the dancefloor, but Zephyr wriggled his arm free.

"Don't you want to come with us?"

"To where?"

"A safe space before the madness begins."

"I've *seen* madness," Zephyr said with his jaw clenched.

"Not like this."

A preternatural energy filled the room. That's when an e-boy fell through Dorian's drawing with horrifying ease. Zephyr saw the body disappear, like the way one does when falling into a huge body of water. Then a girl with explosively colored hair jumped in, no fear in her eyes, just feral curiosity. And the music kept churning, yearning; a needy and greedy thing that would suffocate and suppurate until it got what it wanted. Delilah's eyes burned a hole into the smokescreen. The crowd loved it. Heathens know no bounds, but more importantly they had no reason to.

"I've seen worse," Zephyr said. "It was you, Sebastian, who left your own skin piled on top of a stage."

"Trick of the lights."

"You think I'm that gullible?"

Sebastian didn't say anything back.

"And it was your painting, Dorian, that ate someone. I saw it with my own eyes, the night your poet friend killed herself. What was her name?"

"Tyria. My lover."

"Aren't you gay?"

Dorian's face went grim. "Sexual assignment wasn't a factor when it came to how we felt about one another."

"All I'm saying is I've seen these antics before. Zealots don't frighten me. Neither do art cults."

"Then what *does* scare you?" Dorian asked.

"Follow me."

As they distanced themselves from the main warehouse, Electric Orchid's music began to wane, until it was but a cinder that Zephyr could put out under his boot. Not that he didn't want to hear the music, he just didn't want to be bothered by the imagery anymore. The swirly glowing worms and hallucinogenic aftermath left him with a huge headache, as if Delilah had shoved a knitting needle up his nose and popped his brain.

They went through door after door like a Russian doll; each one emptier than the next. Nobody said a word. Each room was dust-scented and so terrifyingly dark that one's shadow would be afraid to enter it. Secret city beneath the city. Zephyr hadn't realized it before, not until Dexter had changed his viewpoint. When they got to the final room, the floor was wood instead of concrete. Three pairs of feet creaked across, awakening rodents and cats and hell knows what else, so said the feeble gleam of eyes.

Despite it appearing a dead end, there was only one way to go: down. Zephyr rapped his fist on the sheet rock, empty at first, until his knuckles finally slapped against something solid. A glass door. It was secured by a heavy-duty padlock and rusted chain. He had to keep it this way. People were crazy in this part of town, but not even the most desperate fiend would be able to get through the four-inch glass, nor the infuriating chain without hurting themselves. The only key was with Zephyr; he'd learned long ago to never make a copy, and would happily swallow it on his deathbed, just so nobody could touch his stuff.

"Feels like another world," Dorian said.

"I only know of one other place like this," Zephyr whispered. "That's what scares me. So there, I answered your question."

A cold finger ran up Zephyr's spine. What he saw in Dexter's labyrinth came back to haunt him. That horrible black city and its buildings so tall, he had no idea how far below ground he'd gone. Emptiness suddenly surrounded him as he remembered the dark streets, confusing as much as they were intriguing, giving way to the even darker force that weighed down his soul. It made the most dangerous parts of Queens feel like paradise.

"Smells like mold." Dorian coughed into his hand.

"Tastes like it too."

"There's more to go," Zephyr said. "Lower, I mean. We're going lower."

"Oh great, suffocate me." Dorian lit a cigarette that gave off colored smoke.

"That smell, by the way, is rat shit. I bet you never thought you'd smell it," Zephyr chuckled.

"You sure it's not just water rot?" Sebastian was holding his nose with one hand and his hair up with the other.

"Nah, there's a difference. I've smelled death, I've smelled rot. This is just rat shit."

They slipped into the dark entrance. Narrow stairs forced them to descend fast; dewy walls didn't help with balance. A mass of ancient cobwebs coated the air down here. Dorian and Sebastian held onto one another like children lost in a forest, exposing their growing shadows in the harsh brilliance of Zephyr's cell phone light. If he listened closely, past the sound of dripping water, Zephyr could still catch small vibrations of the music, feel it travel through the stone and endless muck.

When they hit ground level, Zephyr's ears popped. They always did down here, and it wasn't something Dorian or Sebastian expected. They had a strange look on their face. But this is what darkness does to your mind; plays tricks, sucks you into its wild world unwillingly. Things felt immediately different at this level, like the world, or just this room, didn't obey the commonplace laws of physical science. It left a stale taste on the palate.

Zephyr felt up the filthy wall in search of the light switch, and when he found it there came the sound of a snap and crackle, followed by halogen lamps sizzling to life one after the other in a domino effect. The room was as big as any studio apartment in New York City, but it was in so much disrepair Zephyr sometimes wondered why he kept his precious stuff in it. The floor sagged under the weight of the three bodies, threatening to collapse at any second, and the ceiling flowered with rust-colored shapes; wood turned to mush down here, allowing for a myriad of creatures to thrive.

"Are we not on concrete?" Dorian said.

Zephyr pointed down. "The floor's weak because the rats eat it."

"Rats eat concrete?"

"I don't think there's anything more disgusting than rats," Sebastian gagged.

"They'll chew through anything to get what they want. Concrete, steel, glass. Bone."

"It'll be the rats and the roaches when the world ends."

"And Cher." Zephyr winked.

Turning into the light, seeing it beam off Sebastian's hair and soak into Dorian's horrible black eyes, Zephyr found himself once again oddly and intensely interested—one of those weird moments where you see something in someone that you didn't see before, like the way Atticus became interested in Dexter so quickly. Zephyr was hounded by horny thoughts of these two skinny artists nipping his neck, smoke-scented tongues worming about the back of his throat.

His mouth became dry, pants tightened; a great pressure seized his testicles. It had been a few days since he'd orgasmed, and he was certain all it would take was the right touch by one of these boys to make him burst. Hormones, no matter how dangerous or devastating the consequence, would make the decision for him.

"I wonder if this place connects to it?" Sebastian said.

"Connects to what?"

"That thing you're afraid of," Dorian said fast.

"What do you know about it?"

Dorian came between them, shined his phone light at a broken piece of wall. "Looks like it does lead somewhere. I just can't tell where."

"That hole is new," Zephyr said.

Only now did the intense blackness of the basement begin to dissipate, revealing all the color that was covered by the dark. Ghosts of red, hues of blue, fountains of yellow. A rainbow warzone. You had to blink a few times to make sure the eyes weren't damaged, give your rods and cones a moment to adjust, settle the darkness and allow yourself to see through it. But it wasn't so. This place was just another anomaly.

"My life's work."

There were three large tables put together like an isosceles triangle. Things were randomly—if not awkwardly—arranged on them, as if Zephyr was a hoarder rather than an antique collector. He could see the confusion rape Dorian's face, and the bewilderment take over Sebastian's. Perhaps it was the profuse pleasures and treasures that were spilled atop; gold medallions, teeth and goblets. Perhaps it was the taxidermy that tended to move ever so slightly in one's peripheral vision.

But this didn't put a damper on Dorian and Sebastian's curiosity; somehow it was enhanced. Dorian picked up a haggard doll and shook it until dust hit his face. Sebastian eyed haunted artifacts that told stories one was better off not knowing. Then Dorian fingered a multicolored string light of orange, purple and green, eyes traveling toward a ghostly ticking grandfather clock.

Sebastian fingered a shiny black bust, its features mummified, elongated face and yawning mouth seeming to reenact a desperate scream. Once he'd amused himself enough with that, Sebastian picked up a glass rectangular box that housed a ghost cicada, *Ayuthia spectabile*, its wingspan the same length and color as his entire hand. Maybe he wanted to see it come to life; maybe he was fixated on the halcyon hallucination.

"It's all fascinating," Dorian said.

"Is there a story to tell?" Sebastian eyed Zephyr.

"Always."

Zephyr took out some items from his backpack that he'd purchased from a closing sale and scattered them into the mountain of stuff. To fit them into this current story of morbidity and antiquity was going to take some time, but he knew he'd get it done. Another day, another week. What did it matter? For now, he wanted his new friends to enjoy the ride.

Dorian turned back to the pile, suddenly jarred. His hand had reached deep into it, as if something called out to him. Zephyr watched him carefully as he pulled out a small canvas, still wet, which made the painting feel alive. It was one of Dorian's own. Its colors wavered and swirled, a subtle trick Dorian used in his work to make people believe they were seeing things when there was not much there.

"I've been looking for this."

"I found it a long time ago," Zephyr said.

Now Zephyr saw a hurricane with an actual eye in its center, and beside it a fiery serpent queen made up of dragon scales: nails the burning color of comets, eyes of onyx stone. The Hydra danced, entrancing her audience, challenging the stereotype that every other drag queen set before her. She was not a performer of glamor and opulence, but of rage and poison.

"I was there when you found it."

The sultry voice echoed, polluting the room like subtle smoke. It grabbed Zephyr's ear and pulled toward the sound. In the pale light there was an even paler, yet radiating corona. A small girl, early thirties, maybe younger, her porcelain face hidden behind snaky dreadlocks and the pink and black fashions of yesteryear's Hot Topic. Adjacent were two other bodies, androgynous and quiet, perhaps only there to do this girl's bidding—or protect her.

"Delilah," Dorian said.

"Happy to see me?"

"Always."

Dorian hugged the girl in a way that real friends do.

"What did you think of the show?" Delilah said with her hands on Dorian's skinny torso.

"Always innovative."

"Um, excuse me," Zephyr said. "How did you get down here?"

"You left the door open."

"It shuts and locks—"

"Don't worry," Delilah cut him off. "I won't be long."

Her eyes went straight for the painting in Dorian's hands. What once was a smooth black surface had now riled itself into something as sticky and warm as tar. Zephyr could feel heat emanating, as if it didn't like Delilah, as if it couldn't bear the thought of someone calling it out for what it was: an anomaly of science and art. When it started to shake, Dorian pressed his finger into the matrix and it abruptly stopped.

"A monstrosity," Delilah said with conviction. "It should be destroyed."

"No."

Delilah ignited a zippo lighter, but before she could put the flame to the painting Dorian held it in the air as if he would hit her with it. That's when the two silhouettes behind Delilah stepped out of the dark and exposed themselves to the light. Zephyr recognized one of them as Electric Orchid's keyboardist; the other looked identical to Delilah. They didn't mean any harm, and Dorian knew this too. He began to laugh, hugging them both. Apparently, it had been a while since they'd seen one another.

"Hi Rez. Hi Alex," Dorian said.

They all talked for a few minutes, playing catch-up. After that, Delilah opened her hand, where a strange piece of shrapnel shined. Dorian's eyebrows immediately furrowed, rich and dark and decisive. Sebastian took two steps back, finding balance on a table until it toppled over. He didn't even mutter an apology, just kept walking back. It looked like one of Dexter's twisted metal sculptures.

"I know that style," Zephyr said.

"I bet you do." Delilah looked him right in the face.

Zephyr felt like he was drowning in her shadow. "You know him?"

"*The Eventual Devil*," Delilah said. "It's the only thing true about him."

"Yeah, he's way too prevalent on social media."

"And much more beyond that."

"What do you mean?"

Sebastian came rushing out of the dark. "Delilah's *always* sticking her nose in someone else's business."

"How do you know Dexter?"

Delilah's face cringed at the name. "I'll tell you another time."

"And how do *you* know that I know him?"

Delilah sighed. "This is exactly how he gets you."

"I'm not saying I like him. I'm just asking how you even know?"

The sculpture made strange sounds. *It's somehow alive,* Delilah said as it began to pullulate in her hand. Zephyr put on his phone light to see it better, but Rez and Alex glided in his direction, somehow forming into one solid shape. It was as if they were creating a wall around Delilah so the light wouldn't penetrate the sculpture's features.

"We all know one another in this community, somehow . . . someway."

"From being at the same parties?"

"Mostly from social media," Delilah said.

"Well, that's the culture of today," Zephyr said. "We make connections via apps first, because we've lost the courage to meet people in person and strike up a conversation. That's how Dexter knew about Atticus."

"He isn't who or what you think it is," Delilah's tone was serious.

"It?"

"Dexter."

"I barely know him."

"Good then we still have time."

Delilah raced her eyes up and down Zephyr's body, as did Rez and Alex. Zephyr could feel all three of them undressing him with their imagination, peering through his clothing and past the piercings and tattoos; slipping beneath his skin down to fascia, bone and into the marrow, then even further inward to the billions of DNA helixes and innumerous codes that are the building blocks of life.

"He's not marked," Delilah said.

Zephyr raised his hands in frustration, then dropped them hard on his hip.

"Not *what?*"

"You haven't told him?" Delilah pointed to Dorian and Sebastian. Zephyr heard their throats click loudly, faces going all shades of red and gray.

Sebastian turned. "We planned to, but your impatient ass always does this."

"Rez and Alex should be the ones explaining this anyway."

"A master manipulator," the boy with emerald eyes said. "Hi, I'm Rez, and this is my boyfriend, Alex." Both nodded their heads. "We were once—"

"We were lovers," Alex interrupted. "A throuple. Ever heard of that?"

"Yes, we're all queers here aren't we?" Zephyr said.

"Not Delilah." Rez winked. "Straight as an arrow."

"Lifelong ally."

"Anyway," Rez continued, "Dexter is specifically into couples."

"You mean like it's his kink?"

"I guess you can say that."

"He's definitely kept saying how lonely he is."

"Dexter destroys relationships. He's the type of toxic you have to get rid of immediately."

"Do you know the old adage *misery loves company*?" Alex asked.

"Yes, but what you're telling me sounds no different than any gay boy in this city."

"Meaning?"

"Gays in general are toxic. They always want what they can't have. For example, as I've seen time and time again, when someone is in a relationship they become more appealing to the gays rather than when they were single."

"Ain't that the damn truth," Dorian added.

"The thing about Dexter is that he's *really hot*," Zephyr added. "Too hot, really. Barring all the strangeness."

"Have you fucked him already?"

"No."

"Thank the gods!"

"But I'm sure my boyfriend has."

Everyone stopped talking. The only sound that could be heard was a faint dripping.

"I'm sorry, but he's a goner." Delilah's voice was as deep and cold as graveyard dirt.

"What do you mean?"

"Soon he'll become obsessed . . . your boyfriend. Soon his whole existence will revolve around Dexter."

Zephyr thought for a moment before he spoke. "Atticus has always been a bit of an obsessed person. How else do you think he sculpts? It's one of his tools, helps him focus." Zephyr couldn't tell if he was talking logic or showing the early signs of denial.

"I'm sorry, but he's a goner," Delilah said again.

Nobody said anything specific after that. They exchanged numbers and socials, then went back to being quiet for a few minutes.

"Has Dexter shown you his 'art'?" Rez used air quotes.

"The sculptures?"

"Have you touched them? Seen them?"

"I have. They're very weird."

"Did they touch you back?" Alex closed in on Zephyr.

"No, but they definitely touched Atticus."

"He's marked."

Rez and Alex put their faces on either side of Zephyr's, so close he could smell their menthol breath and hair dye. They were so heartbreakingly gorgeous that he wanted to turn both of their faces in his direction for a three-way kiss. What the hell, everyone was doing it these days. But Zephyr didn't move. He waited for them to speak in the pin-drop quiet, the longest pause of his life.

"*The change*, they both said. "We gotta go."

8

As the light of the morning sun began to seal his eyes shut, the boy attempted to sleep. He buried his face into the black lethe of his sheets, but the sheer emptiness of his bed injected itself into his consciousness like a blast of caffeine. Being alone was a rude awakening, though it was good for him when he was working. But at the end of the day, or night, he craved the body of another to join him.

He reached for his cell phone, browsed social media to take his mind off the rage of another lonely dawn, but quickly bored himself. A few minutes later, he jumped onto aching feet and walked over to the full-length mirror. His body was pale and scrawny, white scarecrow jutting out of this room's darkness, still in the same clothes from the night before: Pantera crop top, black jean shorts, and white high-top socks.

To his right, a desk was swarmed with notepads that had one name written all over them: Atticus. His handwriting swooped across like the wings of a bat, a black cursive that was now going the way of the dinosaur. He looked at the name, felt a mini fire building inside of his body. He hadn't been this infatuated with someone in quite some time. Boys come and go, heartbreak forces desensitization of emotions . . . and just when you think that you'd never allow someone into your life again, the universe shows you otherwise.

About ten feet away, there was a single dangling lightbulb that swayed whenever he walked past it. A new sculpture he was working on lived half in the bulb's iridescence and half in the place the light never touched. He called it *The Witness*, and it was intended to be a gift for Atticus. The boy slid his fingers into the area where the light didn't touch, cool dark depths so familiar, yet so foreign. As a feverish chill ran up to the crook of his elbow, the boy pulled back and raked a hand through the curls atop his head, then put on his glasses. It was time to work. He pushed the lightbulb in the direction of his sculpture, which unveiled its true form.

Gargoyle benediction and little hands that asked to be held. Reincarnated in acrylic, metal, and resin, superiorly detailed down to the grotesque nails and lines across its knuckles. Its mouth was a hole ringed in jagged metal, and the face scowled so negatively he couldn't bring himself to accept it. He didn't bother himself with the how and the why. He was simply in awe of his own craft.

With its eyes meticulously gouged from their sockets, this caused the cheeks to appear sunken. Its paunch was twisted in metallic mummification, where he'd driven a sharp piece of steel through so that the entire thing was raised on the small glass dais as if in the act of throbbing. And carved into the bottom right corner of the glass was his signature, *The Eventual Devil*, which made Dexter smile.

It almost felt like the work of someone else, seeing it now after having stepped away from it for a few days. Sometimes one artist can influence another profoundly, but somehow you still make it your own. If the boy stared at it long enough, he thought he could *hear The Witness* . . . not speak, not make a sound, but just hear it, deep in his mind. The boy yawned again, fighting exhaustion. He was tempted to text Atticus but knew better than to come off too desperate. If he appeared as someone who always had too much free time, it would remove the allure of Atticus getting to know him.

However, anyone who owned a cell phone could use it as a means of passive-aggressive communication, more so now in the midst of this pandemic and crippling quarantine. One could send subtle signals via subtweets and vague posts to those whose attention they wanted to catch. The magic of curating your online life was all rooted in illusion, and it enhanced the reduction of face-to-face interaction, implanting fantasy in the heads of anyone who followed your account.

And Dexter did just that. He fixed his oily hair, made sure his glasses were straight on his nose, then snapped a selfie with *The Witness* in the background. But it was no good; he looked tired, nearly haggard, and he knew the unspoken rule: if you don't look perfect, you don't garner a response. He tried again, and when he didn't like the result, he took what felt like endless selfies until the picture was as perfect as the lighting against his face, with *The Witness* hauntingly angled a few inches behind his heavily pierced ear.

The hope was that Atticus would view his story first, but that would be a long shot. He wouldn't dare check; he simply needed to post and let it be. If anyone responded—If any of those people were not Atticus—he would just leave them on *read*, which would thwart the narrative that Dexter was posting for attention, another joy of this current cultural craze.

After a while his phone began to buzz. Messages were coming in, but he hadn't a clue who half the accounts were. His following had grown tremendously after being tagged in photos with Atticus and Zephyr, which was never a bad thing, but it had its downside. The endorphins people feel from outside validation has become what defines us. He'd seen it happen to many artists, their egos completely removed from creativity and poured fully into becoming Instafamous or going viral on Twitter.

An hour slipped by, then two. A heavy yellow wall of light was trying to break through the blackout curtains he'd nailed over the makeshift window. On the wall closest to him was a shelf of many of his half-finished projects, and that's the only part of the room natural light could touch. Specifically, there were two heads, one with a black and gaping maw, lower lip nailed to a piece of cheap wood. The other's lips were stitched shut with actual needle and thread. One forever screaming, the other forced into silence.

Sometimes he surprised himself. Every grisly detail from cheek flesh to eye color was almost overwhelming. The skin about their faces was moist and lifelike, but a few more lines of paint and good chiseling would have these ghouls looking like they belonged on a movie set. Maybe he'd have to sleep on it. But sleep is for those who need to reevaluate their dreams, not those who know exactly who they are.

They say when you go to bed, you wake up the next day a new person, biologically and metaphorically. The old skin sheds, blood cells divide, die and are reborn. Old is tossed out for new; the morbid poetry of yesterday is transcended by what we learned from it. We are washed clean of the past and made pure again, so that we can rush into today and become a better version of ourselves.

Dexter knew some of that statement was true, but he had no desire to sleep any part of himself away. Every decision would be uniquely his own. Even if hate sometimes guided his way, he wasn't about to let that stop him. Sometimes the delicious elucidation of simply being alive takes us places we don't want to go, emotionally . . . physically, but that's part of the human story, and it's better to embrace the moment rather than beat ourselves up for it.

Even if one feels like they're at an end.

And there's no way out.

His phone buzzed again. A direct message that wanted trouble. *I Know What You Are.* It was a screenshot of a handwritten note on black construction paper in white ink. But Dexter wasn't about to let some internet troll hijack his day. It was time to go. He grabbed *The Witness* and put it in his backpack. One of the many buttons that polluted the pack's surface snapped off, *Resting Book Face.*

Half a smoke later, he was scurrying through the early morning streets of New York City. Morning fog had blotted out the tops of buildings and veiled his line of sight on ground level. The pandemic made it so a thoroughfare brightened by natural light was now a haunting sight. And at this cumbersome hour, the quiet was almost unnatural; to be in a metropolis but able to hear a pin drop felt wild.

But the leaves were beginning to change, and they were falling off trees like orange and red snowflakes. A few stragglers judged Dexter silently, most likely because he wasn't wearing a mask. It was almost too much to handle, this new reality, this new way of life. Everything a person did risked the consequence of being judged or outed on social media. So he sped fast through a throng of bums that lay up ahead, people so filthy it looked as if they were part of the asphalt.

CaN Ya hElP a PerSon iN NeEd? read a soggy sign, followed by an even soggier cup that had a few coins inside. After walking a span of four blocks and one avenue, he hadn't enough fingers and toes to count the number of vacant businesses that the shutdown had created. Nobody was making money; stocks were tanking; restaurants and retail closed indefinitely. It further fed everyone's anger.

He sent a text to Atticus, wondering if he would be up this early. *U up?* And just like that he saw that Atticus read the message. *Couldn't sleep*, Atticus wrote back. *Me either. You wanna meet up? I'm bored.* Atticus sent a thumbs up emoji and Dexter sent him the place he wanted to meet. Now his mind could finally be at ease because he was about to see the guy who interested him more than anything in the world.

And then he saw another cardboard sign propped against the brick corner of an alley. His heart skipped and he almost tripped over his own shoe. *I kNoW wHaT u ArE!* was scrawled across the old beer box a dozen times. He took out his phone to snap a photo of the sign, but a hand snaked out of the darkness and swatted it away. Dexter dropped to his knees and picked it up, was almost tempted to throw a rock into the alleyway from which the hand came. But right when he got the courage to do so, he saw that the sign had changed to a different plea. *NEED MONEY FOR DRUGS—JUST BEING HONEST.*

A brisk wind sped him along. Delancey Street, formerly known as one of the busiest avenues in Manhattan, was now a human dust bowl. Dexter took a hit off his vape pen, swirling sweet and spicy smoke into the fog. He sat on the corner and waited to see the sun peak.

Brighter days were ahead, which meant umbrage was on the other side.

"Looks like you've been busy."

The effects of partying were clear on Zephyr's face. Heavy bags beneath the eyes, fine lines of exhaustion pressed into his dehydrated skin. One of his multi-pierced ears was red with frustration and a half smoked cigarette hung from his mouth. I knew he hadn't slept; I could smell beer and boy sweat on his skin, which automatically pinged my jealous alarm. But I knew if I acted on it, he'd have called me a hypocrite, so I just let that feeling go.

"I did molly in the warehouse."

"Your pupils are so dilated I can't see the color of your eyes."

"New moon *party*." Zephyr emphasized that last part. "Felt like old times."

"You're lucky you're not canceled right now."

We'd taken a walk north through the twisting tenement streets of Little Italy, up onto the Bowery, until we reached Nolita. Night was a great time to do this, especially these days when there were barely any people. The once glassy thoroughfare was now a warzone of loneliness. Its cobblestone streets were filthy, and its edifices were caked in black exhaust. Zephyr held my hand as if he'd never done so before. I made sure to hold his back just as tightly.

We went three blocks without talking, read all the lamenting signs on the closed stores that said they would be back in business as soon as they could be. It was like looking at a photograph, but in real life. I could see that once the shutdowns took effect, these businesses had no choice but to evacuate. I saw clothes and shoes scattered on shelves, boutiques with their doors ajar as if they'd been freshly looted. It all reminded me of a movie, or maybe just a bad dream. There was no telling when we all would wake up from this.

"How many more times are your notifications going to go off?"

I wasn't paying attention to my phone, surprisingly. When I pulled it out of my pocket, I immediately saw that Zephyr wasn't wrong. There were more notifications than I wanted to deal with. My Instagram was blowing up. And my last Twitter post was going viral. I dared not check my texts, as I knew they'd all be from Dexter. Zephyr did his best not to look at my phone, but I saw a wandering brown eye drift down to catch as much as he could in his peripheral vision.

"Did you talk to Dexter?"

I noticed that Zephyr's eyeliner was smudged, as if he'd been crying.

"About?"

"You know."

"Don't you think you're overreacting a bit?"

Another notification, which made me put my phone on vibrate. I wasn't sure if it was the connections I'd developed over time or that people were more bored than ever and liking anything they saw. Either that, or it was my shirtless post, which is what all gay men want to see—but whatever the reasons, it was out of control. I didn't want to spend half my day looking at my phone, though there was no denying that I loved the attention.

"Another pic with one of your little monsters." Zephyr was staring into his phone. "Body is on-point though."

"I'm calling it *HeadCase*."

"Yeah, you certainly are." Zephyr's lips shriveled into his mouth. "I never realized you were such an attention whore."

I looked up, saw a red dot in the sky. Mars was in retrograde. I truly believed that the planet of war had a filthy red grip on both our souls Its celestial hand had a leash about my neck specifically, as all Aries are guided by that rusty smudge of light. It burrowed into the weakest of us, energizing our curiosity and empowering our wills, oftentimes with potent consequences—for better or worse.

"I never felt like I was until recently. The pandemic's changed everyone."

"It's changed *you*."

This catty version of Zephyr was irksome to say the least. Maybe he'd left the warehouse unfulfilled. The insecurity was clear. It used to be that he'd go out to the warehouses to reset, but ever since Dexter came around, Zephyr had been on the offensive. He took the cigarette he always kept behind his ear, lit it with his plasma arc Zippo. I watched him smoke it fast, inhaling so deeply it looked as if the smoke could drown him. We were silent for a few minutes, both of us needed to decompress.

"Do you know who Delilah Dellinger is?"

"The singer for Electric Orchid?"

"Yes."

"What about her?"

Zephyr turned to me. Moonlight washed his face in dull light, filled the crevices of his blue hair. He looked more than just a little worried. He looked scared.

"She and a few of her friends know Dexter."

I felt something snap in my head. "So?"

"They had nothing good to say. It made me feel a bit vindicated."

Now my heart was in my throat. "What do you mean?"

"That he's not the person you think he is."

"And how would they know?"

"Apparently he dated Delilah's brother and his boyfriend."

"At the same time?"

"As far as I know, yes."

I asked to hear no more as we walked back to our apartment, quickly withdrawing myself into the studio, once again ignited by fury. Things took a turn for the worst. My drawing hand had become a thing of its own. I saw my fingers go gray with exhaustion, small bones aching. But I kept putting pencil to paper, even if I pushed so hard it broke through. The things I created were horrible, and even my own eyes didn't want to see them.

The area where Dexter's sculpture nipped me had begun to tingle. But there was no wound, not even a mark. I was psyching myself out, somehow seeing necrosis stitch itself into a bright pink mouth. It was the work of witchery. A few hours later, something like tentacles appeared on my forearm. They went from my wrist to the crook of my elbow. I'd never seen anything like it, as if the blood in that area was black, but nowhere else. I didn't dare tell Zephyr about this hallucination, given his flare for the dramatics.

Lately I did nothing right. Sneeze and he'd blame Dexter. Cough and he'd say Dexter gave me Covid. I was walking on eggshells but not terribly upset to be doing so, being I'd made this choice. Hours slipped into days, then into weeks. We drifted apart, slightly, using the time away from one another to simply do our own thing. Sometimes space is necessary. We basically only saw one another when it was time for bed, despite us both lying awake but talking very little. There was much wariness in Zephyr's face, and I suppose there must have been some in my own as well.

Our minds were elsewhere. Maybe the flame that had brought us together was going out. I never knew such coldness between us, or lack of synergy but we were both too afraid to talk about it. So we just kept ourselves busy as the torturous burning of always wanting what one can never have bloomed within my entire body. I was horny beyond control, found myself having wet dreams as if I was fourteen years old again. The pulsating pleasure of orgasm had become a secondary hobby. I lost interest in hookup apps and sex with random strangers. This portended my next move. I'd have to break the awkward silence.

I wanted to have sex with Zephyr and Dexter at the same time.

As twilight ended, every window, door and walkway was laved in glossy plum light; paths and portals for people to enter life's routine, and close off the mysteries of ones they don't want to know. The colors asked things of us, to carve out silence, relinquish our cell phones and social media; to disconnect from the glittering internet; to light a Road Opener candle for those who are no longer here, and most of all, to pay attention to the future—both the one you want to create and the one with which you're destined to collide.

When Zephyr returned home, there was some sweat on his upper lip, and l licked it off without even saying hello; bee venom chapstick stung my tongue. I'd been drinking Hopitcal Illusion IPA, so he didn't want to kiss me back, but his cigarette breath and lemony armpits made my hormones blaze. I used my imagination to undress him as he stood before me; petite, delicious and exhausted from hanging out all night.

The black pants he wore were ripped in the style of e-boys, and I saw his soft inner thigh exposed, the skin freshly shaved and pearlescent. When he turned to take off his backpack, I took notice of his moony ass, knowing very well what the sweet pink center tasted and smelled like. His essence was a melody in which I knew every single note.

By the time he'd gotten down to taking off his Doc Martens, the sight of his checkerboard high-top socks had put rocket fuel in my cock. I could never find myself getting sick of Zephyr sexually. He was reliable magic. I often caught myself still having moments as if I was touching or kissing him for the first time, butterflies transmutating into lust zombies. And this was one of those moments. The way his neck sloped, how his tattoos glowed against that snowy skin. Our bodies knew what to do.

I grabbed his chin and latched our mouths together, pulled him closer until he collapsed into my grip. Bone to bone, four sharp hips bruising the thin skin that covered them. I put my hand beneath his multicolored tank top, fingers traversing the soft beads of spine, the flat curve of his sacrum. His skin was moist, and his sweat had the faint notes of alcohol and truck exhaust.

"Stop." Zephyr put his hand on my shoulder, thumb ring biting through my shirt. "I haven't showered."

"Were you with someone else?" I had no idea why I asked this.

"No. But you were." Zephyr zipped toward our bedroom, posters flying off the walls and settling by my feet.

I chased after him. "What does that mean?"

"You know." Zephyr lifted his hands. "My gods, it's like you don't even know who I am anymore."

"That's not true."

"He's just a *friend*, right?"

"Yes."

"*Nothing more?*"

I paused to think about my reply. "You're my number one man."

"So then why do I feel this way?"

"You don't have to. I'm not going anywhere."

Relief washed across Zephyr's features. I buried my face into his neck, slowly licked all the way up to his chin, then to the back of his ear. Zephyr's hair stunk of smoke and dye and that special oil only his body could produce, a kind of sage-marijuana-frankincense that I'd never smelled on anyone else. Then our tongues went to war. We both were dominant kissers. Sometimes I imagined our lips becoming tied into a meaty knot the way we pecked and slobbered each time we introduced our mouths to one another.

Zephyr broke away for a moment, and before I could thrust him back into my arms, I saw it was only to pull his pants down. The smell of his shaft wafted. It filled me with diluted insanity and thwarted arousal. He had no hair from the hip down, and neither did I. We both couldn't bear the thought of something like body hair to come in the way of our sex. Hair creates barriers. Skin to skin was, and has been, our sexual dogma.

My right hand found the waistband of his neon jockstrap, danced along the edges before cupping Zephyr's ass and fully erect penis. His skin was velvetier than I remembered, paler. I saw the black nails of my hand scurry like insects, caught the veins throbbing darkly in time with my own pulse. He undressed me now, shirt off so that our tattoos danced with each other's. But his had changed. All of him was a bit different, as if I was in the presence of a future Zephyr and not the one of right now.

Purple eyes glinted.

I could smell the dankness on his skin, a secret darkness. Then he took my new haunted hand in his, guided us through the light of votive candles that illuminated the eyes of various rock stars I had stapled to the walls. I followed my boy as he asked of me, door creaking open and then turning into a hellish sound that could only have come from one place. The sound of a city fissured deep beneath New York. We were no longer in our bedroom. Before I could speak, Zephyr's lips were against my own, only this time they didn't taste like him. It was the flavor of no flavor.

Shadow

"Isn't this what you wanted?" Zephyr's soft lips moved, but the voice had lost its innocent cadence.

"I don't know."

Yes, you do, I thought. *You want to experience the heights of new flesh and drown in its bottomless pleasures. You want to go insane, drive yourself into a boy frenzy. You want to peer over the ledge of tainted love and jump. You want to test the limits of your own desires. You know exactly what you're doing, Atticus.*

"Isn't this what you had in mind all along?"

We floated into night. Naked and unafraid, I wasn't certain whose body was with me. It was a mere shell, only a black thing beneath it. But I found myself too lost in the sweet taste of the moment to care. Disheveled hair, dark bags that looked like tiny blowfish beneath his eyes. It was like seeing a skull appear in real time, as if he was slowly withering away.

Zephyr broke our kiss and did a Vitruvian man on the bed. His body looked like a chalk outline at a murder scene. Then he put his knees up to his small nipples, legs as wide as a wishbone, exposing a hole as red and volatile as Mars. It puckered against my tongue, sliming my lips as I kissed it. I used no lube to enter that fiery kingdom; it budded like a lotus and chose me.

"Too bad," the voice said. "Because this is what you're getting."

9

Delilah had sent Zephyr a deluge of text messages. Apparently, the woman was not going to stop until she got what she wanted. Dorian had warned Zephyr about her being pushy, if not completely stubborn and equally annoying. So, to abate her insanity, Zephyr agreed to meet with her again, but this time he only asked her to not be so vague and downright overbearing. She dropped her side of the bargain the moment she showed up.

"Why're you inserting yourself into my life?"

Zephyr's annoyance was clear in the downturn of his eyes, the way his hand covered half his face, blue hair slouching. A headache had claimed him, sending hot pain all the way to his neck and into his clenched jaw. *A bad come down*, he thought. The group sat quietly around, glancing every now and again at Zephyr as if he was a sideshow freak on display. Perhaps he was, given the smokey eye makeup and glittery nail polish, as those fashions had died out in the late eighties. But these people were no different.

"What took you so long?"

"Haven't even told you the whole story," Alex said.

"I won't listen to it." Zephyr absentmindedly gazed into his phone.

"If you keep looking at his social media—"

"I can look at Atticus' socials all I want."

"Then why are you on Dexter's?"

Caught red-handed, despite lowering the screen brightness. It seemed Rez and Alex could sniff Dexter out whether it was online or in person. But that didn't change their biased views, no matter the story or legend they wanted to tell. Zephyr didn't want to hear it. He was paranoid enough already. He also believed in clean slates and second chances, even if his intuition told him not to. Dexter had locked him in that tomb. Dexter was pushing him away from Atticus. This much he knew.

"Fine. You got me. Happy?"

"You like him." Rez grabbed Zephyr's kneecap with clammy little fingers. "But you won't admit it."

Rez's hand felt nice, but he didn't want to be distracted, not just yet. Zephyr didn't care for cancel culture and felt best making decisions by judging a person's current actions rather than their past faults. If this group allowed the past to dictate the present, that was their problem. But he could feel how heartbroken Rez and Alex were; they had it out for Dexter for personal reasons.

"Not in that way."

Zephyr mumbled into his hands, but the words were weighted as if made of stone, never meant to land on the ear. Frustrated, he got to his feet, almost forgetting he was on the E train heading into Manhattan. It was expectedly empty; not many people used the trains these days for fear of catching the virus. Each window glowed like a hospital hallway, and every twist and turn of metal was felt in Zephyr's bones. It was a different feeling with all this abandonment.

"What else can it be?"

Rez handed Zephyr a lukewarm coffee as they'd been up all night and he wanted him to stay awake. Little did they know insomnia was his friend. Zephyr lit a clove cigarette and stepped between the train doors, hoping for a moment of serenity via the screech and howl of metal upon metal. It wasn't as soothing as it used to be. Coming off amphetamines was not a pleasant experience without a Xanax. Zephyr was jittery, both emotionally and physically, and could not sit still even if he tried.

"It can be many things," Zephyr explained. "Curiosity. Neurotic fascination. A dash of sexual attraction."

"Ah, there's the kicker."

The dark underground swelled around him; it was in the black wind and the smell of sparks, in the rancid taste on his lips: *We want you to join us.* Dexter's suave voice was in his head. Zephyr imagined pathways and doors and portals, places to enter and exit that he knew shouldn't be there; imagined things that lived deeper than New York's infamous Mole People. What if he were to take Dexter's offer? What if he were to live down here instead of up there? Would life be a series of upside-down events? Or would it continue as per usual, but with an eternal black cloud hovering?

"Why's that so shocking?"

"Dexter works fast on people. Trust that we know."

Zephyr sent a text to Atticus. *Where are you?* Five minutes went by, no answer. *People here trying to tell me Dexter is bad news.* The second he sent that text, Atticus replied. *Why do you care what they say? You should trust me.* When Zephyr told him that it was yet again Delilah, Atticus replied, *get me an autograph LOL.* Zephyr sighed and put his phone away, not shocked by how willfully blind Atticus had become.

"You believe us now?" Alex was leaning over Zephyr's shoulder.

"No."

The train screeched to a stop. Zephyr flicked the clove, followed the tiny orange light down, waiting to see if it landed somewhere. But it seemed to keep burning, or falling, he couldn't tell. Down, down, and further down as if the underground wanted to show him something, open its endless maw and carrion arms. Motion sickness creeped around his gut, so slow and steady he felt every particle of bile form before it all rocketed out of his mouth. He closed his eyes to recenter himself, but all he saw was the image of Dexter eating the image of Atticus.

"Let's go."

Delilah pulled Zephyr back into the train, then out the shuttering doors and into the night. East 14th Street was dead as dead can be; didn't need a doctor to confirm it. Just as dark as the train tunnels, and Zephyr felt like he hadn't shaken himself free of that place. It was all around him, every time he closed his eyes, every time he licked his lips. He eyed the empty and squat buildings, intermittent windows dotted with light, chains chiming and keys jangling in the distance. The sidewalks were eerily empty, aside from overflowing garbage cans.

"I think I'm sleep deprived," Zephyr said. "Been having really weird dreams."

"That's how it starts," Alex said.

"I'm seeing shit that isn't there . . . even now."

"You really should stop walking so fast." Delilah darted ahead of Zephyr and put her little hand out. "Let me talk."

Zephyr twisted himself away, avoiding her. "There's nothing to say. I like to figure things out on my own."

"Okay, tough guy."

"What's wrong with choosing for myself?"

Zephyr was too focused on what he'd just seen, or thought he'd seen, to let Delilah get under his skin. That big black world beneath him was now fondling his careful curiosity. The idea of going back down there, knowing very well Atticus was already doing it behind his back, was enraging. Yet the idea sucked at him like a metaphorical leech. How much was it going to take before he'd crack? In time he knew that he'd go back, third wheel or not, to witness that black majesty.

"Why did you agree to meet us again if you're creating such a stink?"

"Boredom."

"Wrong," Rez had just put his lips on a flask, so his comment sounded paralyzed. "He's into Dexter. He wants to know."

"How do you know who I'm into and who I'm not?"

"We *know* how this works."

Zephyr wished Dorian and Sebastian were here with him; he needed their voices of reason. *Getting it on*, Delilah mentioned. *They're in love and don't even know it.* If that was the case, then he was happy for them. But as soon as he thought about a lover,

Atticus came to mind; Zephyr wanted Atticus to stand with him, but was too proud to admit that. For now, it was time to iron out the wrinkles between these people and Dexter.

"Let's drink," Alex said.

"Nowhere Bar is close."

"It's not open."

"When's that ever stopped us?" Delilah chuckled.

A few more empty blocks, their boots scraping across concrete with a sound so intense it sliced through the gracious silence. Zephyr looked at every dark doorway, every crack in the blacktop and sewer with a new clarity. Everything we can't see is a door leading to somewhere, and every opening we do see is a door as well, if you believed in it hard enough. That's what made it real for Dexter. Had all of this been here the entire time? Or had the pandemic created a new kind of monster?

Zephyr was now ready for a drink himself. Nowhere Bar popped up out of *nowhere*, but was set so deep into the sidewalk he could barely see it. No bouncer at the door, no lights, just a hole in the wall covered in glass. Rez descended the stairs first to make sure the coast was clear; Alex remained on street level to do the same. It seemed the three of them had practiced this one too many times. Four thumbs up meant they were good to go.

"Ready?"

Delilah slipped a hand into her pocket, withdrew a bright green blade. Zephyr saw the thing shimmer as she whipped it around her fingers a few times. Noting Zephyr's questionable look, she proceeded to perform a trick that made the blade appear as if it could fly right out of her hands. She stopped, smirked with all the arrogance of a trained assassin, then jimmied the front door open.

"Sorry, not sorry."

"Coming in?" Rez said as he passed by.

Zephyr turned his face toward the moon, closed his eyes and felt the cold light beat into his skin. He knew he was making his first mistake, alcohol mixed with heightened emotion. If anything was going to trigger him it was going to be his own feelings, and without any inhibition to stop him, he knew it would bring out the worst. Too late to turn back.

He entered the bar. It was quiet but astonishingly alive, as if it'd been frozen in time since the city had closed down and enforced social distancing. The smell was crisp with smoke and beer vapor; red lights flooded the ceiling and floor, illuminating the long bar and its wondrous taps. Delilah went right to them and served some warm beer.

"I'm not gunna play telephone with you people." Zephyr's voice was filled with finality, but also despair.

"You people?" Delilah said. "Who do you think we are?"

"No idea, but please have some pity."

"Pity?" Delilah raised her voice. "My entire existence, at this point, is based on pity. Why do you think I went out of my way to contact you?"

"That's not the same."

"You mean have some *empathy*," Alex interjected. "It's almost the same thing."

"No, pity is when you know how to feel bad for someone else's pain. Empathy is the ability to *share* it."

Delilah turned back to Zephyr, removed her black denim jacket and then headed to the pool table. After downing her beer, she inserted quarters and played a game all to herself. The bar was so quiet that the sound of the billiard balls was like a metronome. The only other audible sounds were of breathing and feet bouncing against bar stools. If it wasn't for the fact that he'd already met these people, Zephyr would have felt very awkward.

"You probably already told him something," Delilah said from afar. "Or else you wouldn't be hanging with us."

"Atticus?"

"Who else?"

Zephyr felt his face get hot. "I've been trying."

"And he didn't want to listen?"

"How did you know?"

"Because that's what boyfriends do."

Zephyr was tight-lipped, silent.

"I'll tell him myself if I have to," Delilah said, frothy mustache on her upper lip. "Even if it's by alt means."

"Alt means?"

Alex cut in. "For someone with such a social media presence, Atticus isn't actually a social person."

"That's how it goes for a lot of people."

"When's the last time you ran into a big personality on social media, and they were actually a big personality *in person*?"

"Not often. But we're veering away from the point," Rez said.

"I still don't get what you all want."

"Wow . . . you must be an Aries. So stubborn."

"You think I'm stubborn?"

"Absolutely."

"Maybe you're just not considering my feelings."

"Listen!" Delilah slammed her glass on the bar top. "We all could benefit from being better listeners and better empaths, but there's no one better at that job than me."

"What's your point, girly?"

"Girly? You're lucky I don't smack that smirk off your face."

"It was a joke."

"Your humor sucks. When I go out of my way to tell somebody something, it's for an important reason."

"If you think I'm resisting, wait until you meet Atticus."

"Another Aries, I assume."

"Dexter is a Scorpio," Alex chuckled. "Fire and water ain't an astrological match."

"Wrong!" Zephyr said it so loud he heard his voice echo. "You haven't seen them together. It's such a match that it's cringe."

"So you're telling me that Aries and Scorpio are emotionally and intellectually compatible." Alex grit his teeth.

"What do I care about emotions?" Zephyr clapped back.

This crowd saw through Zephyr's lie; he knew it by the way they arched their black eyebrows, how their mouths turned down to reveal teeth stained the same color as their dark glittery lipstick. Zephyr had always been a bad liar. His ears wiggled when he did it, and his face immediately turned red. They undoubtedly noticed this. Empaths possess a wicked intuition, allowing them to easily pick up on vibes. It was usually impossible to hide things from them long term.

"Anyway, if you got anything to say, he should be the one to talk to, given his obsession and all."

"It starts with you . . . the rational one," Delilah said. "Atticus is already a goner."

"Gone?"

"Marked . . . lost . . . whatever you wanna call it." Delilah's tone was deep and meaningful. "All I'm trying to say is that we make choices every day, and those choices dictate the reality around us. Be careful of the choices you make, Zephyr. You never know when they'll bite you in the ass, and not in the way I know you like."

"I haven't felt this much parenting in my life."

"Helping you out is hardly parenting."

Just as quick as these three had haunted his peripheral vision, they began to dissipate from it. Zephyr was relieved to see them go, but knew they'd be back. All he wanted was to find Atticus. But before doing that, he would have to confront Dexter. Zephyr exited the bar and ran in the direction of Little Italy but stopped when he saw a sewer cap shaking in the middle of the street. Three dead-looking fingers clambered near the lip for a moment, then snaked back in as if they knew Zephyr was staring.

When he finally reached the graffiti haven of Essex Street, Dexter began to calm down. A crimson throng of Chinese characters glowed into his eyes, as if Antares itself had descended to swoop him into a flaming paradise. Timeworn facades blazed and ramshackle tenements glowered. But he knew this place too well to let his imagination run free. After months of perusing its streets, shopping in its delis and smoking on its corners, one becomes part of a neighborhood without living there. Atticus would have thought no different. He was the one who found the place.

The building was abandoned; long windows crusted shut, beer can carpet, dead shrubs and cracked edifice. A few lines of freshly painted poetry caught Dexter's eye: *COVID-19 KILLED ME* and *MASK IT OR CASKET!* The door was made of wicker and gave off a nasty sound when one used it, as if to announce to the resident ghosts that something alive was about to invade their home. A juxtaposition of the dying world and the one that was already dead.

One long hallway led to another, bleak with no pictures, holes in every wall. Above, wires hung like rubber nooses. Bank left, and the darkness unveiled railroad-style living quarters. Bank right, and the sheer emptiness would have one question the special depths of this place. Dexter was both amused and horrified as these types of apartments made him think of intricate mazes that spiraled into geometric shapes, where one could never find their way out.

But there was always a way out. For every abandoned building and junkyard above ground, there was a winding tunnel below. For every window and door there is a mirroring one beneath. You just had to know where to look; how to feel the shift in air temperature at the crevice of a certain entryway. Everything was connected, even if people didn't realize it.

Since the pandemic sent people out of New York City in droves, it made a run-down hellhole such as this feel even lonelier. It amazed Dexter that even in a city as busy, dirty, and industrialized as New York, as soon as the human population dwindles, nature finds its way. He saw this in the vines that were growing across the windowpanes, and the dandelions that quivered at his feet. Pigeons had already made a home here, stalagmite nests as high as his head and distant cooing weaseling into his ears.

Dexter lit a joint, let the fragrant marijuana smoke encircle him. As he walked around, he noticed that whatever light made it through the slatted windows wasn't enough to help him truly see. It was dim inside this place, almost as freaky-dark as the blackness that lives behind the eyes. Anything could reach its way in via wayward physics and snatch him. A monster, a lover, a repugnant ex-boyfriend (or two). Manifestation was a powerful tool of the mind if one believed in it.

"I was wondering if you got lost."

The voice set his hormones ablaze. Atticus was tucked into a huge loveseat at the other end of the room, cross-legged and ripped black pants showing off his pale legs. A single drop of light sparkled in the dark mop of his hair, caught the lenses of his aviator sunglasses. The shabby boots on his feet looked as if they'd seen better days. But the man was as radiant as ever. Blinding, even. Dexter was stupidly in love with him.

"Never lost when I'm looking for you."

The weed sent Dexter's mind reeling, almost as if his blood moved too fast in his veins. It was hard to catch his breath, hard to resist the temptation that was Atticus' pheromones as their lips gently touched, tongues searching one another's mouth for secrets and lore of the saliva. It was a long and deep soul-kiss.

"You always taste so good."

Atticus' hand sailed beneath Dexter's t-shirt, caressing his sternum and taut nipples. The touch of his hand was wildly different. There was a special static charge from Atticus' fingertips that Dexter's skin immediately accepted. He couldn't remember anyone's touch doing this for him. When you connect with someone, your desire for them grows exponentially. The feelings engulf everything else.

"Isn't that sweet." Atticus wiped dust off his Stevie Nicks crop top. "Share it, won't ya?"

Dexter handed him the joint. When their fingers clasped, Dexter's heart ricocheted. Why he felt so helpless in Atticus' presence was beyond him. But we can't control how love makes us feel, in fact our rational brain never has a say. It's all gut instinct once you are locked onto *the one.* He watched Atticus lip the burning joint, suck in the smoke and then blow it out of his mouth and into a hole in the wall behind his head, causing the black sash covering it to drift.

"How long were you sitting there?"

"Long enough to watch you do your thing."

"Okay, stalker."

Atticus got up and moved swiftly towards the wall closest to him; it was sheetrock, easy to tell by the hollow sound as he wrapped his knuckles against it. Dexter wasn't sure what he was looking for, and when nothing happened, Atticus shrugged, almost as if to dismiss any possibility that there could be a pathway behind the wall. Not only that, it was also as if he was challenging Dexter's theory about how the world above was interlaced with the world below.

"I want to show you something."

"In here?" Atticus' tone was somewhat surprised.

"Yes," Dexter said. "Because this place isn't what it seems."

"It's as empty and abandoned as it always was."

"On the surface, it seems that way."

Dexter walked to the other side of the room, boots and wallet chain chiming as would an alarm. The only sign of past human habitation was the sight of scattered books, paint brushes and a colorful mountain of dried paint that was reminiscent of a murder scene. Melted candles warped the cheap countertops, pizza boxes were mounted on the plastic furniture. Smelly rags and a broken mop were the only signs that any cleaning may have actually occurred.

"Have you ever thought about what's between the walls?" Dexter said.

"Why do you think I'm knocking?"

"There're doors and windows and entryways. But nobody's gunna come answering. It doesn't work that way."

"Then how does it?"

"I'd have to show you."

"Do it now then."

Dexter put his finger on his lips to motion Atticus to stop talking. He pointed to the floor, watched as Atticus' one brown and one green eye followed. He tapped the wood, showing Atticus how hollow it really was. He seemed surprised, but Dexter knew that he had to do this too. His hand found a floorboard and lifted it out, which then allowed him to start removing more as if they were the same weight as confetti.

In no time there was a hole big enough for both of them to fit into. Dexter investigated it, saw virtually nothing. But he knew that slimy smell, it was that of the underground. Then he shined his phone light down. At first it was unable to penetrate the blackness, but after a few minutes of Dexter concentrating a ladder appeared at lip of the hole, which now looked wet and alive as a human intestine.

"Now do you see how it's all connected?"

"I never used to think about these things."

"Why not?"

"I believe my eyes only."

"You don't think stuff like this is possible?"

"What?"

"That these walls . . . these floors," Dexter pointed to the hole, "are all like huge arteries that connect throughout the city. You just don't want to see it."

"We got fairytales for that."

"If you wanna mock me, that's fine. Been dealing with that my whole life."

"I'm not mocking you, just playing devil's advocate."

"So you know I'm not lying," Dexter said.

"You're not lying to me."

"Got no reason to, Atticus."

"Because you already showed me the heart of darkness, right?"

Atticus walked in Dexter's direction and kissed his lips again; this time the warmth of them was exponentially greater.

"It just frightens me, is all," Atticus said as he broke away.

"What does?"

"The idea of a physical hell."

Atticus slipped his finger into a crack in one of the walls until it completely disappeared. Dexter watched Atticus' face flood with vexation. Perhaps something reached out, like the possibility that a void could take him to an entirely new place, and was as real as the hand in front of him. If only Atticus knew how many doors there were. If only Atticus would just say the word, so they could disappear together . . . forever.

"So, you said they all connect?"

"Indeed."

"They just keep going down?"

"Yup."

"Is this what you mean?" Atticus again put his hand into the hole and it completely disappeared. "Is there a door here leading somewhere as well?"

"Could be."

"Will I ever master this knowledge?"

"It has more to do with manifesting . . . than reality."

"Do you change reality with your thoughts?"

"I just know what's there and what's not there."

"I don't get what you mean."

"Come, let me show you."

Dexter took Atticus' hand and guided them into the vacuum, nothing to stand in their way, no walls or stairs or any temperature that human skin could recognize. The science our species has come to trust was thrown out the window; just dark, not even the absence of light, but an informal process of motion. So much black that the rods and cones of the eyes could not adjust to even pretend illumination was up ahead, behind, above or below. Black like the shadow that creeps behind whatever light touches.

Released from gravity's reign, free to simply slide down into the mouth of madness. Spiraling together, as if they were locked inside a twin dream. Walked as much as they floated, ran as much as they fell. Dexter was amused by Atticus' reaction; to finally see that he was understanding how easy it was to just let go of inhibition and try something new, even if all one wanted to do was reject the fact that it was possible. It's in our human nature, a protective, evolutionary mindset.

"Why does it look so different?"

Atticus started to take some videos. *For the socials*, he whispered. Dexter smirked as they moved along. This hallway could go on forever, if they wanted it to. Every now and again Dexter would direct Atticus' phone light, but it barely illuminated an inch in front of them. As expected, this didn't jar Atticus from snapping selfies and posting them right away. The notifications came almost instantly, then suddenly stopped.

"Shit. No more signal."

"What were the messages saying?"

"I dunno. Weird things."

"Like?"

"Something about doctoring the photos. That someone was behind me, but also in front of me at the same time. It makes no sense because you're right next to me."

"Anything else?"

"Just weird comments and responses. Maybe they're pulling my leg, cuz I don't see anything like that in the pics."

"Sometimes people see things you can't. Reality is as slippery as any dream."

"You have a way with words most don't have, which is refreshing."

And then they were ascending back to the real world, or the world they thought was the real one. Through the endless void that was neither hot nor cold, damp nor dry. It was just a pathway, a process, to propel one from the edge of an infinite nothing to the static safety of atomic mass and physical science. Dexter led them back through the same hole in the wall, helped Atticus in with his hand.

"That was wild," Atticus said.

"I can show you a lot more, if you let me."

"I'd like to see more." Atticus went right back to his phone.

"You will." Dexter was silent for a moment. "Your social following has grown so much. *MiniMonstrosities* is as popular as Electric Orchid and that drag queen the Hydra."

"I'm honestly growing sick of social media slavery. It's so fleeting. If you don't post daily, they forget about you. It's all fake."

"Fake, yet necessary."

Atticus sat in the dusty chair and busied himself. The light of his phone bled down his face, filled the hollows of his eyes. Dexter pulled up Instagram and watched Atticus' stories. Nothing seemed right, nothing represented the place where they'd just been. Dexter saw lights in the sky and blank faces that were never there. He wondered how many others saw what he saw, felt what he felt.

"So," Atticus lowered his voice, changing the subject. "What's going on with you and Zephyr?"

A horrible pang of jealousy blossomed in Dexter's chest. Why this happened was beyond him. His only competition when it came to Atticus, but it wasn't as if he hadn't known about Zephyr from the start. He simply hated that Zephyr was always on Atticus' mind.

"I dunno." There came Dexter's first lie, one of many he knew would come.

"Zephyr told me you don't reach out to him, that you don't try."

"It's not about Zephyr right now."

"He *is* my boyfriend. But I'd like you to be too."

Again, Dexter thought.

"What exactly does Zephyr know about us?" Dexter bit his tongue.

Atticus was silent at first. "I guess it depends. He's not exactly being kept in the dark."

"If he's not into me, how can this work?"

"I think he's very into you. That's why you two should talk."

The idea sank fast in Dexter's gut, deepening his unexplainable hurt. But he knew that he had to shake it off to continue the conversation. He made his body rigid, he fixed the muscles in his face that only wanted to frown, forced them to neutralize. Atticus noticed this because he began to caress Dexter's face with his hand.

"What I'm trying to say is, I want you both."

"Why not just me?"

Atticus removed his hand. "Are you serious?"

"We have so much more in common—"

"Let me stop you right there." Atticus' eyebrows skyrocketed into his hairline. "That's not an option."

"*What if I make it happen?*" Dexter's whisper sliced through the air.

"What did you just say?"

Dexter turned his face away. "I'll reach out to Zephyr. We're overdue for some quality time."

"I appreciate that. And listen, things like this take time." Atticus moved Dexter's face in his direction. "If there's no spark at the start, sometimes people need to kindle one."

A minute of silence went by.

"But . . . there's *something* there. I guess we just aren't seeing eye to eye."

"And that can change." Atticus smiled.

"I have something for you," Dexter said, extricating himself from Atticus' lovely presence.

He pulled *The Witness* out of his backpack, trying his best to display it in a good light. The countertop was too cruddy, and the floor was no place for it. But Atticus didn't need any light to see the thing for what it was. He had that special eye that saw beyond superficial darkness, and Dexter could see this plainly as Atticus' face morphed into that hollow, speculative glare that sometimes seizes the countenance of a person who is in deep concentration. Dexter braced himself for the worst.

"Oh—"

"It's shit," Dexter sighed.

"No, it's quite good. Never really seen anything like it."

"It's garbage."

"I said it's *good*."

"Are you sure?"

"When I look at stuff like this, I realize there's so much talent in the world. And how much I still haven't discovered."

"A lot of people have a hard time understanding art. They see no value in it."

"There're pockets of people out there who do."

"But I want more of that."

"Don't we all?"

Atticus shifted his body, brought himself into the few bars of light in the room. He removed the black fingerless gloves from both his hands, exposing two surgical steel rings about his pinky and thumb, then lit a candle and set it atop the counter. In the warm incandescence, Atticus pointed to a few black lines on his arm, but they were not dark enough to be tattoo ink, and they ebbed and flowed as if blown by wind.

"Your handiwork," Atticus said.

Dexter reached his hand out and touched the black lines. His head instantly swelled with a hundred emotions and manifestations. *Your sculpture*, he heard Atticus say. Dexter had almost forgotten that day, because he'd been spending every waking moment since sucking face with Atticus. Maybe he'd blocked it out on purpose. His brain was funny that way. It could think up scenarios, all that worked in Dexter's favor, almost as if he had no control of it. At the same time it could also erase anything he wanted.

"Does it hurt?"

"No."

"Then why are you showing it to me?"

He'd waited all his life for a moment like this. Targets locked: Atticus, the famed underground sculptor, and his boyfriend Zephyr, collector of the macabre. It was reminiscent of what had happened between him, Alex and Rez—until that snake-haired bitch Delilah started questioning Dexter. Everything went straight to hell from there. But he hadn't seen them in over three years, a long time in the generation of cell phones, short attention spans, and social media.

"Something's changed . . . in the things I draw. And the decisions I make."

"How so?"

"It shouldn't be this intricate, nor this deep."

"What do you mean?"

"Everything's different now. My art, my life . . . but somehow this feels . . . right." Atticus caressed the spidery black appendages slowly traveling up his arm. "But I feel like I've turned into someone else."

10

It was a red sunset. All of New York City was the color of blood.

Zephyr sat poised and still as a gargoyle, knees to chest and arms at his sides, half in the shadow of the oncoming night and half in the fading day. The rooftop was six stories high, but the streets seemed further away. He dreamed of wings sprouting from his back, leathery ticket to the skies, away from the shallow problems of this planet.

Not too long ago, someone had jumped from this very spot, impaling themselves on the gate below. Suicide always bothered Zephyr. What makes a person decide that this already short life needs to be even shorter? They say to call a hotline, or a friend. Don't make that final choice, because once you do there's no going back. The thought made the hairs on Zephyr's arm stand up. Every day was an opportunity for reinvention—but only if you stuck around long enough to realize it.

And the sun sank deeper. Shadows on the rooftop lengthened.

In less than an hour, the big black carpet of night would unravel and cloak the city. While the calendar said December, the temperature had yet to drop. Weather patterns were becoming more and more unhinged in New York; summers were lasting through November, spreading heat easily into December.

The music in his headphones was too loud, Chevelle's "Hunter Eats Hunter," and the cigarette butt was wet between his lips. A bottle of Jägermeister sat at his side—a parting gift from Delilah. The Jäger was intrusively cold and its syrupy brown burn twisted his insides, but it had to be drank that way to avoid it tasting like cough medicine. He took another sip, which warmed his face instantly. Once the buzz kicked in, Zephyr gave into boredom.

He browsed Instagram, scrolling past posts and stories he cared nothing for, all of them lamenting about lockdown; some accounts were partying in other countries that had minimal quarantine laws, in which he saw them get called out out for their irresponsibility by popular accounts that shared their social media handles, full names and places of employment. It was ultimately shocking as much as it was necessary.

Then he came across a close friend's story from Dexter's account. Atticus was hunched over a desk he didn't recognize, scribbling madly, spine arched so that it almost looked like a V. Dexter had written a caption, *IYKYK*, which made Zephyr squirm; more inside jokes he didn't get. A quick bout of jealousy took over his mind, so he shut it off before the video could reveal to him anything more that was going to ruin his night.

Social media is key to comfort as much as it is a key to envy.

It was time to unplug and enjoy this moment alone. Put the phone down . . . let go. So many people lacked the attention span to just sit back and take it all in. The addiction to screen time has only increased. Capturing every waking moment on a phone and posting it was the new way to express self-importance, though people have failed to recognize how their lives are being reduced to a single lens.

It was a life Zephyr was guilty of partaking in. Sometimes he rejected it, other times it was easier to jump on the gravy train. Social media had become the premier platform to connect with anyone. A post had the power to set people off as much as it could uplift them. The pandemic had only exacerbated the power of the screen. Without it, you might as well be gum under someone's shoe. With it, you had the ability to satisfy that need for human contact—start a mindless fight, a friendship, a romance, a new trend—and do it at what we perceive to be a safe distance.

Maybe that's what Dexter was doing, starting a trend of his own by barging his way into already established relationships. *He manifests*, Delilah's silvery voice repeated over and over in his head. *Not the kind of ghost you're used to.* That part he was starting to believe. It takes a special type of human to create that kind of entity. Someone who isn't afraid to show the animal that lives beneath their skin. Someone that isn't ashamed of getting what they want, no matter the cost.

Are you saying he's a ghost?

"Hi Zephyr."

The voice made him cringe, but the Jäger had warmed his soul just enough to deal with it. He flicked his cigarette off the roof and watched it burn out before hitting the ground. The smoke he exhaled was overtaken by a smell that trailed with the voice: frankincense and leather. It brought about the images of vintage clothing stores and book shoppes, a roaring twenties jazz club that Fitzgerald and Stein would frequent. It brought about a darkness that was deeply rooted into the earth, and more importantly, into the fiber of the voice's being.

"Hello, Dexter."

Zephyr didn't turn around to see the alluring creature; he felt Dexter's dark energy before he even made a sound. *Puts things in your mind*, Rez had said. Zephyr shook his head. *Be careful of the power of a chaotically tight body and beautiful face.* Was Dexter putting things into his head right now? Had the work already begun?

"Nice headphones."

Zephyr took them off his ears. "How'd you get up here?"

"These old tenements aren't hard to maneuver."

"How did you know where I was?"

Dexter stared blankly. "You realize I follow you on Instagram, right?"

Zephyr had posted a story of the sunset from up here. But the fact that Dexter knew the exact rooftop was still strange. He turned, saw Dexter sway between the same shadow as himself.

Somehow his portion felt a lot cooler as the boy glinted in the last few minutes of dusk, face half in the light, barring the fact that he already looked like he belonged to the dark, a fungus growing from its soundless depths. Still, he was irresistible in his white Converse sneakers and black high-top socks, ripped shorts and Evanescence t-shirt that gripped his skin like a vice.

"I guess I forgot," Zephyr lied.

"You're not a good liar," Dexter sighed. "Your ears wiggle."

"Caught me red handed," Zephyr said with an attitude.

"May I sit?" Dexter was lascivious; the cigarette balanced between his pale lips reminded Zephyr of the lollipops that boys suck on when they take Molly.

"Sure."

Dexter sat down, delicious smell encroaching, purple eyes going dark. It wouldn't shock Zephyr if this boy pulled the shadow over them both like a blanket and trapped them forever. Dexter could quite possibly be not of this reality, just another fashionable art-freak who lived by passion instead of the rule of society. At this point Zephyr didn't care. But then that would mean Delilah was right.

"They just let anybody stroll in these days, don't they?"

Zephyr crossed his arms over his chest, squeezing the Tool tshirt he cut into a crop top like an accordion.

"Not my building."

"Then how did I get in?"

"You have your ways."

"I guess I do."

Zephyr swerved his body to keep a few inches distance between him and this supposed poltergeist. His mind raced; his pulse beat against the side of his throat and the warmth in his face became increasingly worrisome. He had no idea why Dexter made him feel this way. The last thing he wanted was to look scared and skittish. It meant Dexter would have the upper hand, or that he was seriously horny and trying to hook up. Sister sentiments of confusion.

"Especially with Atticus."

Dexter looked at Zephyr. "Why? Because we're friends?"

"Not just friends."

"What else could it be?" Dexter sighed. "You're very melodramatic, you know that?"

Zephyr remained silent, angled his face toward uptown, a brightly spiked portrait that polluted the sky with too much light.

"What's it to you? After what you did to me—"

"Here." Dexter offered Zephyr a small blue object.

"Your vape?"

"Yeah. It's weed. Smoke some to calm down."

After a few tokes, Zephyr began to feel relaxed. That's when he noticed that the rooftop was a wreck. Crushed beer cans created a fermented ring around him; there was a soggy mound of cigarette butts and gum wrappers flying around. Grease vapors from the restaurants below left a coruscating trail of slime that dripped down the side of the building. It was the first time Zephyr found himself thinking that New York City was too dirty and too old to ever become modern.

"Tastes good."

"A hybrid blend."

Zephyr handed back the vape. "Now tell me, how did you get in?"

"You know." Dexter's voice was slightly elevated.

"The same way you closed that door on me."

"Now why are you still on that topic?"

"Because you've yet to apologize."

Dexter looked away. "I'm not apologizing for something I didn't do. It's all in your head."

"Maybe you put that into my head," Zephyr said sharply.

From this angle, the symmetry of Dexter's face—sharp cheek bones and busty lips, the fashionable glasses and pallor—was something Zephyr found slightly mesmerizing. He quickly grabbed his phone to make sure he wasn't being set up, but found no messages from Atticus, so there was no actual reason why Dexter should be here. They didn't have the type of relationship where one can just pop up without warning and expect a warm welcome.

"My building has been Italian-guarded since the forties. Our apartment is the only non-family unit. Atticus only got it because the owner's son likes his sculptures."

"Even the old Italian strongholds have limitations."

"Why do you gotta be so spooky about everything?"

"I'm just being me."

"You sure are *different*." Zephyr formed air quotes with his fingers.

Dexter playfully laughed that part off, stuck his hand into his pocket and came back with a vial of ketamine. He snorted a bump off the small spoon and offered Zephyr some. He could never say no to a bump of K, even with fentanyl on the rise and no test kits in sight. But a little dissociation wouldn't be so bad, so he took a large bump up his nose and waited for the sweet serenity of anesthesia to see him through.

"I wanted to talk to you about something."

Zephyr's ears got hot. "Go ahead."

"About Atticus and . . . *our* relationship," Dexter said.

"Spit it out."

"He's very special to me."

"And to me," Zephyr said quickly.

Dexter sighed. "What I'm trying to say is that . . . I want to do whatever is right by him. He loves you and doesn't want me to get in the way."

Zephyr's chest burned. "But does he *actually* love you?"

"Yes, he does," Dexter hissed. "I'm not just some shiny new toy."

"How do you really know that?"

Dexter didn't answer. Rather, he caressed Zephyr's hair, then drew one finger slowly down Zephyr's face with just enough softness to make Zephyr feel his hormones come alive. As infinitesimal and ubiquitous as a simple touch is, most people don't consider the implications behind it. We touch to greet one another, to hug, to fight, to inspect, to kiss; to balance and to alleviate pain. It's all taken for granted in the grand scheme. But Dexter's touch was something not to be taken lightly. It was part redemption, part indelible seduction. And it turned Zephyr's mind into goo.

"You put things in Atticus' head," Zephyr said.

"Is that what Delilah told you?"

The tone in Dexter's voice made Zephyr's body freeze. How had he known about Delilah? Was he weaseling his way into every social circle? His mind began reeling, and that's when his phone started getting notifications. Zephyr saw that his Instagram was flooded with direct messages from Delilah, Dorian, and Sebastian. He turned it off, not wanting Dexter to see. But it was too late with his peripheral vision he saw Dexter's face go sour.

"Not exactly." Zephyr cleared his throat.

"You think I don't know what she's up to?"

"I don't know what you know."

"How are Rez and Alex doing?" Dexter said that with a mocking tone. "They must really miss me to go out of their way like this."

Zephyr shrugged. "I only just met them."

"What are they after?"

"I don't know." Zephyr's throat clicked dryly, so he took another sip of the Jäger. "And why the fuck am I explaining anything to you?"

"You're right, you don't owe me shit. However, you've known me for some time now."

"I barely know you."

"Then get to know me!"

"I don't know how."

"We'll both learn how. But just trust when I tell you that Rez and Alex are dangerous, jealous little babies. Whenever they see someone happy, they want to fuck it up."

"Funny, that's what they say about you."

"Do you believe them?

"I never said that I believed anything they told me."

"The social circles in this city can be . . . petty."

"Ya think? I run in a few."

"And the creative circles are even worse."

"That's why I wanted to be alone tonight. I'm tired of them all."

Zephyr now found himself reaching back, slowly caressing the top of Dexter's hand in the way good friends do when they need support. But that quickly fell to the throes of lust. The want to discover someone else's skin, trace the tree-like rings of their fingerprint, caress the folds in the palm of their hands. New touch, new smells, new lover. It was very easy to just give into it. Atticus had been doing it, so why couldn't he?

"I like it when you touch me like that."

Once he realized that the hand he was holding wasn't Atticus', no matter the heat that emanated from both of their bodies, Zephyr knew that he was being tricked. Dexter was putting this into his head; he was here for trouble. That's what people usually want when they show up unannounced. He knew now that Dexter was not normal in any sense of the word—the fact that he lacked social cues, the fact that he believed he could just insert himself into people's lives without consequences—and so Zephyr did not want to give into that kind of manipulation.

"Why did you come here, Dexter?"

"I wanted to see you."

"Stop lying."

Compulsion controlled him now, the comfort of another was irresistible. Zephyr grabbed Dexter's neck and yanked until their lips touched. An electrical discharge somehow was transferred, repelling them like two magnets of the same polarity. But that did not stop Zephyr from wanting to try again, and this time he cupped Dexter's face, removed his glasses and traversed the inside of his warm mouth with his tongue, tasting all the things he now knew were driving Atticus mad. Unexplainable flavors and sensations, which unexplainably made him want more. But Dexter pulled himself away.

"I didn't mean to do that."

"I wouldn't say no if you did it again."

"But Delilah—"

"A habitual liar and a drunk." Dexter kicked a beer can over. "Scum."

Zephyr was quiet, then said, "Her circle is quite secretive."

"Circle jerk."

Before Zephyr could respond, it seemed as if the earth no longer tilted on its axis. There came an abrupt stop of sight and sound, nothing but a pinhole of light and the echoes of small stones slapping against windowpanes. In the heaviness of the void, three silhouettes came into view, and the way they touched one another was the way decent lovers would. There were other shadows, like moving pieces of art, creature-features that put ammonite and cephalopod nightmares into his head.

"Stop it, Dexter."

"Stop what?"

"You're making me see things."

The muscles in Dexter's face went soft. "I thought you'd like it."

"You don't think that's creepy?"

"No."

"You don't think it's wrong to control what others see?"

"Consider it my creative freedom."

If creative freedom meant that Zephyr and Atticus would be influenced by some outside force rather than a true connection, then Zephyr was going to have a hard time believing anything that Dexter said. Regardless, he was nearly impossible to resist.

"Is that what you do to people? You trap them?"

"Trap who?"

"Let's start with those people you're hiding below ground."

"They're there by choice."

"What kind of a choice did you give them?"

"It's not a cult. I see it as more of a collaboration."

"Of what?"

"Whatever we feel like." Dexter flicked his Zippo lighter, just sparks and no flame. "We're creating worlds, altering realities. Enhancing them. Defiling them."

"How?"

"With our *minds*."

"Then what do you need me and Atticus for?"

"Without an audience, artists only talk to themselves."

"Why not just use social media?"

"I need real people. I need people close to me."

"That doesn't make much sense."

"You know what it's like to be rejected. You know it's hard out there for people like us, the ones who live on the fringe."

"I'm well aware," Zephyr replied, cold as stone.

"So . . . then you'll do it?"

Dexter's eyes were periwinkle disasters. Zephyr walked to the southside of the roof, took a seat and dangled his feet. Dexter did the same. This would be the perfect scenario for Dexter to push him off, send him plummeting until he became impaled on the spiked gate below. Zephyr knew Dexter was capable of such violence; and it would be the quickest way to get rid of the person that was holding Atticus back from giving his full attention to Dexter. But no such thing happened. In fact, Dexter was rather gentle, and empathetic to Zephyr's rage, which only made him more attractive.

"I wanna figure this out with you."

"That starts with Atticus." Zephyr felt himself getting irritated, so he took another swig of the Jäger.

"Don't drown your thoughts with that drink."

Dexter touched Zephyr's leg with his own, the skin of their calves gently meeting. They were hairless and heavily tattooed; an intricate landscape of symbols, ambigrams and insignias of various meanings lived on him. His skin was also warmer than the average person, but like Dexter said, he was anything but average. And now Delilah was in his head again, warning Zephyr that Dexter equaled chaos. But if chaos meant that he'd get his rocks off, then so be it.

Zephyr's loneliness and curiosity was in charge now, and the alcohol was already creeping down into his balls, exposing the incriminating ache of horniness. The sky was fully dark by this point, but the moon had yet to rise, so there was a light sprinkling of stars, as well as a vibrant Jupiter and Saturn. Dexter pointed them out, talked about rare occurrences and fate.

"Destiny is a joke," he said. "Fate is . . . what we make."

"Like in the movie."

The conversation was escape from reality, and they allowed one another to take turns talking, learning about the other. It felt like a first date beneath the ghostly stars and rich candyscape of twinkling buildings until Zephyr felt a weight in his feet, and it seemed Dexter felt the same. Something pulled at their limbs, beckoned them to look down.

From this angle all that was visible were the small spaces between the alleyways, spiraling darkness that would take someone forever to hit bottom. Maybe it was the underground asking them to look beyond the broken facades and disintegrating cornerstones, beyond the pavement and the concrete and the sewer caps. Deeper than the sewers and subway tunnels. But the thought wasn't his own, he knew. It felt foreign and forced.

"Embrace this moment."

He's been marked, echoed Delilah's words in Zephyr's mind.

"Riddle me this," Zephyr said. "Why are Rez and Alex coming back for you after all this time?"

"Maybe they're still in love."

"Do they mean anything to you?"

"They're from my past. I never think about them. We all have a past, don't we?"

"Yes, we do."

Dexter swooped closer. "What they don't realize is that the person they thought they once knew is dead and gone. Reborn . . . *changed*."

"Maybe you should show me," Zephyr said.

They didn't need to talk any further. The language of the body was the only form of communication left between them. Sometimes it's better to just let nature take its course. Dexter began by caressing the back of Zephyr's neck; this time just the touch of his hand changed Zephyr's mind about the boy. Signals were exchanged; the chemicals between them were an immediate fit. Maybe it had something to do with the planetary event, that it had been nearly four hundred years since Saturn and Jupiter passed this close to each other, and nearly eight hundred years since the alignment occurred at night.

Special things happen during special moments. And this had to be one of them.

In the New York City gay scene, hookup culture can take over your life. Not only are men hypersexual, but the idea that you live in a city with an endless selection of people to choose from—people from all parts of the globe—only exacerbates a person's curiosity, and the need to quell the mystery of the flesh. But sometimes a hookup can rot before blooming; sometimes two people's pheromones just don't match, or something is missing in the kiss; sometimes a person shows up at your door looking entirely different from the pictures you've been staring at for months on social media.

But with Dexter this was nothing of the sort. There was an odd sexual magnetization, and it sounded alarms inside Zephyr's head. Maybe this is what Atticus felt, the dance in this new land of exciting beginnings while at the same time ignoring all that you've built over the last ten years. The past only brought its annoying weight with it. And so, Zephyr took the bait, caving into selfish needs for sex, fun and diversion.

The taste of Dexter's mouth was once again nothing he expected. There was no word for it, no feeling capable of describing the utter deliciousness, or how powerful Dexter's tongue was. In fact, everything Dexter did was not without physical power. The way he pulled Zephyr's body into his, the way he tore his shirt off, the way he kissed from neck to navel. Zephyr felt horribly helpless in his grasp, but it was the exact kind of sexual experience that Zephyr had been craving: a man to take charge and have his way with his body, no questions asked.

They tumbled into the garbage. A fast-food wrapper landed on Dexter's face, and a can of beer wet Zephyr's back. One by one they removed an article of clothing, but in such a sensual way Zephyr's skin shivered. He'd never hooked up on a rooftop before, and the thought nearly jarred him, as did the thought of Atticus finding out about this. He grabbed Dexter's head, licked the sweat from the side of his face.

As their mouths met again, their newly naked bodies became two wiry things beneath the pale moon. Dexter's hands seized Zephyr's waist, leaving a small red crescent in his hip bone. There was an immediate burn the moment his fingers released him, but that only fueled Zephyr's need to have this boy. Two slick hands parted his legs slowly, fingers caressing down the inner thigh, zigzagging through tattoo ink until they reached the groin. Dexter cupped the delicate sag of Zephyr's scrotum.

"I want to be inside you," Dexter whispered.

Zephyr lifted his knees to his chest so that Dexter could kiss the soft pink entranceway of his fevered cavity. Lips to wet lips. Zephyr felt the incredible urge to moan, but Dexter's tongue was already creeping up his torso, once again ending at Zephyr's lips so that they could exchange the secret language of the tongue. That's when Zephyr spread his legs further, inviting Dexter in. He thrust himself into Zephyr, searing and silken, and with a cock that was pleasantly bigger than expected. They became on single being lost in the moment, deliciously ignorant to the past, present and future.

Then something flashed between Zephyr's eyes. It was as if his own head had been split open, and he could only assume that the warbling blob shifting past him was his brain. The rooftop was replaced by an endless honeycomb scourged deep in the earth, deep inside someone's mind, a lost place. And Dexter was taking him down there, while at the same pumping his ass full of darkness. That's when Zephyr knew that Dexter wasn't going to let him go, that he'd be descending until the end of time.

11

Social media is the root of all evil. Not just the root; it is the foundation, the edifice, the veil. Seed and sow; addiction and vice; rot, entropy and the perfect drug. It is salvation wrapped in the suit of damnation. Calm before the storm. Cure to loneliness and key to suicide. Social media is the real pandemic.

I'm just one of the innumerable numbskulls enslaved by it.

While social media has opened the door to momentous lovers and every freak, geek and circus act you can imagine, it has also been a source of much discomfort and self-loathing. It was never a shock to receive strange messages, a threat or two from some internet troll, or even nude pictures from boys that I've been talking to. Yet nothing prepared me for today's set of events.

It all started when I saw Dexter posting stories with Zephyr. What should have been an immediate sense of comfort—romance?—was bulldozed by jealousy. Where was my invite to pose as they did on that ratty rooftop? Where was my invite to bathe in the dark, let moonlight fill my eyes and wash over my skin? I decided not to text either of them or engage with their posts. Instead, I went for a walk.

The weather was quite somber, much like the city since the pandemic hit. It wasn't too cold out, nor was it too warm, just another confused meteorological pattern. It had been this way for a week. Everyday I'd look up and wish for the little clots of metal-colored clouds to part, show me that dazzling blue and amazing nighttime circus of stars, the great red eye of Jupiter and scintillating sights of galaxies far, far away.

I hit the streets in black Converses, ripped jeans and a Guns n' Roses muscle shirt. The assortment of rings on my fingers winked in the daylight, as did the lightning bolt pendant about my neck. The city was a phosphorescent and tinsel nightmare of silver, red and gold, signaling that we'd finally arrived at the ass-end of another year. If I listened close enough, I heard Christmas music chiming from inside the myriad of apartments. But there was not much cheer in the air.

Crowds no longer surged at the typical holiday tourist destinations. It was a new way of life, one that I considered creepy in a big city. The overwrought holiday display that plagued Fifth Avenue was now a showcase of ghosts, and the kaleidoscopic Christmas lights of Rockefeller Center sparkled for nobody. The ice-skating rink of Bryant Park's Winter Village was at twenty percent capacity, creating an eerie echo in a city that was supposed to never sleep, but now had to follow new curfew laws.

When you can hear a pin drop in Manhattan, you don't want to be on the streets by that point. Night after night I found myself becoming more and more saddened by these sights, perusing avenues and corners, trying to use all the powers in my mind to fill it with tourists so that some of New York's life would rise from the dead. I had no such luck, nor such powers.

But back to today's events. I headed uptown to something important. I was a wanted guest, so said the message from Electric Orchid's official Instagram account. It was one of those things where I had to blink my eyes twice, laugh nervously, and then scramble to find the official blue check mark. Two cigarettes down and a glass of Montepulciano later, I was confirmed to personally meet one of New York's heaviest and most mysterious underground bands—not to mention one that I was a very big fan of.

The Museum of Natural History was our destination. Little did they know that it was one of my favorite places in all of New York City. I knew all twenty-six of the interconnected buildings, its plethora of exhibits, the planetarium, the library and its exorbitant gift shops. Two million square feet of fossils, minerals, plants, animals, rocks, meteorites, gemstones, bones, cultural artifacts and more.

Sunset was the time of the meet, and I was requested to be at the Theodore Roosevelt Statue that sat in the center of the museum's grand staircase. But I ran on what we call "gay time" and made it out of Little Italy *after* sunset. There was something about the crimson light of dusk bleeding slowly through my window, warming the tops of my hands and the capillaries of my face, that bombarded me with a rare call of the muse (I normally work best late night or very early morning), and so I made the dire choice to ride that feeling until the end of the black rainbow.

I worked without thinking, let my hands do what they wanted. A monstrosity of acrylic and bone was born, something that I'd been thinking about creating since the moment I met Dexter. Vertebrate stem rising out of a gravelly grave; two aching bodies infused to one set of wings made from pleather and razor wire. Sunken eye sockets spiraled into darkness; filmy hands clasped, fingers twining impossibly into the other, twisted and taut as a rope. Oversized heads balanced upon one another, jaws blossoming rows and rows of carrion teeth. This was how our souls communicated, I knew: bound by the guise of flesh.

It would be a wonderful companion to *The Witness*.

I felt a rare moment of completion. I stood next to the sculpture and took a shirtless selfie, remembering how I once wanted to prove that one could be an artist *and* have a good body at the same time. Now it all just felt dumb. My drawing hand threw a pair of devil's horns, and I stuck out my tongue as well, captioning it *LoVeSiCk*. After posting, I realized that I was still in such a ritual high I'd not even noticed that the squid ink on my right forearm was gone. After fifteen minutes, the picture was becoming one of the top photos on all my social accounts. Then I received another message.

where are you?
omw! I wrote back.

Out the door and back onto the orange-slicked streets. In the times of the coronavirus, we must suffer newfound horrors of the subway system. What used to be a subterranean refuge has now become an ominous jungle of emptiness and mold. I found myself becoming more and more hesitant to take the train; not for fear of contracting the virus, but for fear of the unknown down there. The underground was alive, it was hungry, and there wasn't anything being done about it.

Dexter single-handedly made me question every crack, crevice, and pool of darkness, for I knew the depths were limitless, intent unimaginable and the hunger . . . fathomless. Crime had tripled. Groping, pickpockets and brawls were now commonplace. People were getting pushed in front of trains and hobo hostels seemed to pop up everywhere . . . the subway was now a literal monster. So before entering its maw, I prepared myself to be gnawed.

I got on an uptown train at about eight pm, used my cell phone to enter the turnstile now that they were slowly doing away with metro cards. The stations near Canal Street reeked of the 2020 perfume of mildew, bleach, and homeless urine. A far cry from the original rot and vomit. Water drizzled across fungus-laced tiles; paint stripped from myriad pillars, and a steady rumbling wiggled into my ears. I held my nose the entire time, wondering if/when an underground phenomenon was going to come my way.

As the train squabbled into the station, my anticipation was quelled. A subsequent wind pushed horrible odors straight into my mouth. I felt immediately filthy, but the train was cleaner than expected, and wholly abandoned in terms of typical New York ridership. One delivery guy, a maskless bag lady and a snoring wino. Objectively, I was quite fond of the lack of people; but I also knew that taking the train with fewer riders was dangerous.

Throughout my years I've been spit at and coughed on, choked, have been in a few fist fights—and was once mugged—on these forsaken tin cans on wheels. But nothing really prepared me for the reality of what could happen down here without a crowd to bear witness. Every horrible movie scenario played in my head as the stations scurried by. Murder. Rape. Werewolves. Zombies. Vampires. Poltergeists. Cults. Anything was possible.

I sat down and caught a glimpse of my reflection under the harsh fluorescence. Warbling hair, dark bags shrouding my dual-colored eyes; facemask grinning wildly, more gum than teeth. It almost looked like a sketch, or a sculpture half undone. I knew it was something Dexter would appreciate. If he were here with me, I'm certain he'd whip out his pencil and sketch pad, capture me as I was in this moment, since we all know those are fleeting and we never experience the same one twice.

Oddly, sleep took me fast. Must have been the wine.

My ethereal body peeled away from earthly flesh like an old scab. I waded through time, space and geography in such a way that it would make anyone's head spin to try and think about it. Gliding as if the earth had suddenly dissolved and left victim to a parabolic darkness.

The further we delve into the necessity of sleep, the more our brain can show its true potential: the out-of-body experience This can either be a one-way ticket to euphoria, or a nosedive into despair. It really depends on the person. But in this instance, I felt more like I was in a torturous zone between awake and not-awake.

The train rumbled beneath my bones; lights flashed over my face. I smelled moth balls, dirty feet and bleach, heard nails clicking against phone screens, but I was not conscious enough to actually say that I could move my body. I was vulnerable to absolutely anything. The underground could swallow me whole, pickpockets could pick me dry, molesters could have their way.

Something told me to take any direction, as if it even mattered. So I did: straight through the train doors and into the dusty tunnel until it looked as if I was leaving footprints in black snow. I walked for what felt like days. My new eyes could see things that they normally couldn't. Above my head, through the barricade of old concrete, labyrinth of pipes and decay, I saw cars and people; I saw lights in the sky, smelled the classic New York aromas of pretzels, candied peanuts and the tangy water of hot dogs.

But then I saw the city at its worst. Gang fights and civilian gunfire; rape, murder and larceny. Midtown shimmered in flame. Planes crashed into buildings, incinerating them upon impact. I saw the poor eating the poor, and the rich ripping off the working class as history has replayed since the beginning. I saw New York become watered down by gentrification and big business.

After what felt like a terrible movie on repeat, I arrived at a dead end and lost sight of the train. In fact, all trains became a distant echo this far into the tunnel. Rats bolted out of every crevice in the walls, their eyes scintillating as they passed. At my feet was the remains of a party: beer cans and bottles, random garbage. I thought about the Mole People, then about Dexter's underground circus. I couldn't tell the two apart.

But amongst this disgusting display of existential laziness, I heard a delicious cadence. A melody that violated every particle of my being. Each rising and dying note punctured holes in the air, spit black glitter into my face that was reminiscent of Lana Del Rey and Amy Lee, but one that could growl as hellishly as Otep and Angela Gossow. I knew that I would follow this sound until something haunted and hopeless found me. There was just no other way in this place.

That's when it broke through me. A bright ball of incandescence so cold it was hot, or so hot it was cold. When you reach such temperatures on either scale, you can't tell the difference. A wonderful odor surrounded me in the aftermath, one of clove cigarettes, licorice and esoteric incense. Yet it was gone as quick as it came, leaving behind what looked like a few strands of pink and black hair and a white shape on the wall in front of me that I could only describe as the inverse shadow of a woman.

Somehow, I knew the only way out was through. My hand breached the concrete wall, broke it apart as easily as cobweb. On the other side was the mouth of madness. I saw the glimmer of a white thing from the corner of my eye, followed the trail of spicy vanilla smoke until the surrounding shadows melted away.

"I knew you'd be late."

It was a woman, and one that filled me with more fear than wonder, more insanity than relief. She stood about as tall as Zephyr, despite the busted-up boots that gave her an extra two inches of height. Her skin was the same color of that white shadow on the wall, exquisitely marked up by tattoos and a heavy assortment of piercings in various orifices. Her hair was a brittle spider swirled pink and black, and her eyes were like emerald flame. Delilah Dellinger.

"How'd you know I'd be down here?"

"This is my dream," Delilah said.

"Actually, it's mine."

"No." Delilah turned toward me sharply. "This is *my dream*."

"Fine," I said, lifting a cigarette to my lips. "I heard you were a stubborn girl."

"Girl?"

"Sorry, woman."

"And what makes you think we are where you say we are?" Delilah tilted her head questionably.

"I know my power."

"As I know mine."

I thought about that. "So then . . . am I awake or am I dreaming?"

"It doesn't really matter."

I spent the next few minutes wondering if all the things I'd heard about Delilah, and even seen with my own eyes, were true. Was she a witch? Did she possess the power to raise the dead with her voice? Was she able to slip into other people's dreams? The gossip about her was extensive. It was on the lips of everyone in my social circle, both online and in person, and in not so many ways was it flattering. *Delilah's a bitch*, one junky had said to me. *She'll eat your heart*, blabbed a fleeting queer of nineteen, *and she'll smile while doing it.*

"Are you the one who's been messaging me?" I had no idea why I finally realized this.

Delilah's shoulders tensed, mesh crop top wrinkling between her shoulder blades. "Yes."

"Why?"

"I had to be discreet." Delilah didn't meet my gaze.

"Discreet is code for shady."

"Or . . . it's my way of not allowing that bastard to find me."

"Dexter?"

"Wow, you're intuitive," Delilah smirked. "Anyway, I can't be shady anymore. It's gotten me nowhere."

"What do you want from me?"

"You'll find out soon."

"Why not now?"

"In time."

The way Delilah peered into my eyes was as if she was lock-picking my brain. Searching for answers? Searching for anything. She wasn't going to get it out of me. I'd never once heard the name *Delilah* leave Dexter's lips, so all of this was rather strange. I was privy to some of his past relationships, but nothing in major detail. What's done is done, I always say. I had no reason to pry into Dexter's past life. I was interested in the boy he was right now, not the boy he used to be. Too many people I know obsess over the past, which bars them from joining the present or entering the future.

"I don't have that kind of time."

"You've nothing more than time, Atticus."

"You're the one who came to me . . . who wanted to tell me something. But now you won't? You better check yourself."

Delilah sighed. "I've been tracking *it* for years."

I paused, no idea what she meant. "It?"

"*The Eventual Devil*." Delilah spit when she said it.

"Dexter?"

"What a stupid handle." Her voice lost its softness, and I could see her fingers trembling.

"What about him?"

"He's not what you think he is."

"How did I know you were going to say that? Zephyr already spilled."

"You're a wise-ass." Delilah's tone had a childish inflection. "Before he was your boyfriend, before he really was *The Eventual Devil*, he was in a throuple with my brother and best friend."

"So what? Gays do that all the time."

"Slow ya roll, Atticus. You didn't let me finish."

I remained quiet.

"Thank you. Point is that it went to shit . . . fast."

"Ask me why I should care?"

"Because he's doing it again," Delilah said quickly.

I stamped my foot. "You're telling me nothing."

"He's horrible."

"Maybe you're horrible," I said mockingly. "People get into shitty relationships all the time without realizing it. They're different every time."

"Not like this."

"Sometimes relationships fall apart . . . amicably or not. Sometimes they last a decade, sometimes for life. But does that mean people can't try again?"

"A relationship with that *thing* is anything but. I wish it were that simple."

"It actually is."

"Have you noticed how off you and Zephyr are?"

"Shut up about him!" I yelled.

"See, you're getting loud because you feel guilty. But it's not your fault. This is what Dexter does."

"You're coming off like some jealous ex. And it didn't even involve you."

"I protect the ones I love. You don't know what that monster is capable of."

The word *monster* triggered me. The moment those words left her lips, something blazed throughout my ribcage. It was either primal rage or desperate realization. Dexter was a monster indeed . . . a monster talent, a monster lover, a monster mystery.

The last part is what kept me coming back. But a monster in the traditional sense? Delilah was grasping at straws.

"I can hear you," Delilah said. "You think I can't?"

"That's a violation of my private thoughts."

"Not when you're in *my dream*."

"So then tell me, what exactly did Dexter do to his ex-lovers?"

"It's not for me to say."

Delilah looked me dead in the face. All of dreamland throbbed and moaned in time with her growing woe. The ennui had worn her down, both physically and mentally; it made me more nervous than I wanted to be, especially in the presence of someone I respected so highly. The art and the artist can sometimes be two entirely different creatures. Because of this, I felt indifference grow inside me. I'd never questioned Dexter about anything. How we met—*why* we met. How he could talk his way through any strange situation by making light of it and, of course, how he never failed to heighten my feelings for him.

"He doesn't deserve you or Zephyr."

"And you're the judge of that?"

She reached out and put her hand on mine. Normally I'd back away from anyone trying to touch me without permission, a simple reflex people born and raised in this city develop. But I found myself wanting her to touch me, infiltrate my DNA with that special magic she possessed. If there's a will, there's a way. As soon as our skin made contact, I thought I felt her heartbeat through her fingertips; thunder cracked between my ears, lightning coruscated before my very eyes. I heard the sweet seduction of Electric Orchid's music and rode the spiraling sound into oblivion.

When lights stopped drifting across my vision, I saw Dexter, but a completely different Dexter. He was younger, skinnier, and had less tattoos than now. I couldn't tell the year but judging by the size of the cell phone I knew it was a long time ago. With him were two other pale boys. Every time I blinked, something insane would crawl across my vision, enough to send my sanity to war.

Blink. Terrifying screams. *Blink.* The hot sting of tears. *Blink.* Diaphanous swirl of blood.

Blink. An animal roars. *Blink.* A knife is drawn. *Blink.* A noose tightens.

Blink. Tears fill the corner of black eyes. *Blink.*

"What is this?" I said at the top of my voice.

"His handy work." Delilah's grip on me intensified, heat rising.

Blink. Hot rain falls. *Blink.* Hearts are broken. *Blink.* Funeral pyre.

"STOP!"

My vocal cords wrenched, reaching such a high octave that I felt the little flaps tear. After what felt like an hour of pleading, Delilah released me so that we were back to square one.

"This isn't about some rando who jumps from relationship to relationship . . . some lost soul. Dexter might as well not even be a *person*."

Her voice slipped into the realm of uncertainty when she said that last word, as if it was not supposed to be said.

"Is he a ghost?" I uttered that with such insincerity I almost wanted to say it again.

"He's not like us, that's for certain. And he's got his nasty little claws in you."

"Nobody's got their claws *in* me."

"I can see his signature work."

She lowered her eyes toward my hand. In that moment it looked irregular, as if it had its own source of a pulse. The tiny wound was slimed the deep color of bacterial mucus. *You can't stop him once he's got you hooked*, she said assumingly. *He'll never stop.* A great black web grew up my arm, pushing Delilah's voice straight into my head this time. Being a true New Yorker, I swatted at the sound in self-defense.

"This can't be happening."

"Well . . . believe it." She shrugged.

"I've heard the rumors about you."

"And what are those?" Delilah turned, face as sharp and bright as the apex of a canine tooth. "That I'm a witch?"

"No. Just that you aren't . . . normal."

"What else?"

"That you do things with your music. You *hurt* people—"

"I've never done anything of the sort."

"Are you sure?"

Delilah stepped closer, black lipstick smeared on her weirdly white teeth. "I've never hurt anyone that didn't deserve it."

A spark went off in my head. "So you admit you're dangerous?"

"That's not what I said."

"What if I told you that I've seen it with my own eyes."

"Then I'd say you were drunk, or you made it up."

"I've been to your shows. I've seen what happens there."

Delilah was silent, then said, "Why do you think they keep coming back? It's never my intention to create havoc. But if my music has that effect on people, then so be it."

There was a slight crack in her voice, a childish hindrance that made me realize she was in fact human. Delilah had a soul, she felt things. One thing the notorious rumors agreed on was that she was a deep thinker, an empath beyond her years. Maybe I was being too hard on her. After all, she was the driving force behind one of my favorite underground bands, and I had no right to be rude to her. She was trying to help—I just didn't want to deal with it. Dexter was too precious to me. There was no real reason why I should keep going on about this. Lovers, new or old, tell each other everything, eventually. That's how Zephyr and I lasted this long.

"I'm sorry. Didn't mean to offend you."

"Have you ever been in love, Delilah?"

"A long time ago," she said coldly.

"Then you know what it feels like . . . that uncontrollable joy, that warmth . . . the—"

"The constant need, the pain of being too happy. The fear of it all being taken away."

"You *do* get it."

"I'm human, aren't I?"

My lips tightened, teeth clenched. "I won't stop seeing him."

"I knew you'd say that," she sighed.

"Read my mind again, didn't you? You're quite crass for a supposed empath."

"I'm realistic."

"Nah, you're just a straight-up bitch."

Delilah chuckled. "But if I were a man, you'd call me a rockstar, right? I'd be worshiped as a tough guy. But the fact that I'm female . . . makes me a *bitch*."

"That's not what I was getting at."

"I know, but you don't see how that stuff is ingrained into our DNA."

"I'm sorry I said *bitch*. Maybe I should've said *insane*."

I remembered all the things I'd seen when Delilah hit the stage like a piece of dark matter torn out of the furthest portions of space. I felt myself getting amped up, I suddenly wanted to argue, wanted to see her crumble. Who was she trying to be telling me that Dexter had his claws in me? I never had a mother, and I wasn't looking for one now. I had enough friends to last me a few lifetimes, and I had two lovers that I trusted more than I ever could the average person.

"Sometimes I wonder if the things I shed light on, the things that are already there lurking in the dark before us all, are worth my effort. Charles Fort knew this. I *know* it. People like you just choose not to see it."

"It's not a choice. I'm literally in love. And you expect me to just drop him."

"That's not my intention."

"Then tell me what it is. Do you not see the wrong in penetrating my dream?"

"You're in my world. I called you here."

"This is my fucking dream, not yours."

"Do you know what astral projection is?"

"Yes, it's when you leave your body in a dream–"

Delilah put her hand up. "Okay, you know what it is."

"Aren't you the one who sang the lyric, *those who live the hardest, dream the hardest*?"

"'Gilded Nightmare.' I know my own song."

"What's that even mean?"

Delilah took a drag of a cigarette, blew black smoke in my face. "I'm not the only one who can do it."

She began walking in the opposite direction. I had no sense of left, right or center, and so all I could do was follow her trail of smoke and spice. With every step this dream world changed. The first scene of that sad looking place with all the drawings and notes on the walls disintegrated into a shadow the shape of Dexter, which I only knew by the height and size of the head. Delilah's voice rang out again, gripped me like an embrace. I could stay locked up in that lovely sound forever, it was so soothing.

"Do you know that he killed his mother?"

We kept moving. Before I knew it the train tracks were at my feet, and there I became astounded at the fact that I could stand upon the third rail and not feel my skin sizzle like bacon grease. Delilah didn't seem as amused, nor was she in any sort of mood to play, so said her very stern face. We glided away from the train station, and only a few paces in did I see myself as a wild-eyed child, unbeknownst to myself that a creator was about to be unleashed.

"Supposedly."

Then I saw myself as I am today, without regard to how insane this entire experience was. As soon as I reached out, the image flipped away like turning pages in a book. Once that dust settled, I saw Zephyr alone on a rooftop. It was raining, and very cold, and he only had on his torn leather jacket and a pair of Converses. Behind him lurked a presence with glowing purple eyes. I had no idea what this meant, just that I needed to find him.

"What is this?" I asked Delilah.

"I can't see what you see," she said, her eyes the ghost-green of neon lights. "Otherwise, you'd never find your own way."

We arrived at the rock show. The audience was angry, their heavily ornamented fists held high, smoke swirling about them. Delilah ascended the stage like a tiny goddess of melody and mayhem. The music rang out, and I caught sight of the band members, specifically the synth player, which I somehow knew was one of the boys Dexter used to date. But my attention was being asked for by someone else. Delilah's voice flooded my ears again, rich and hot as spilled blood.

In the back of the room Dexter and Zephyr were hand in hand. When the song came to a crushing close, Zephyr vanished.

Dexter's lugubrious grin spread wider than my facemask.

Part 3

Speculative Reckoning

"Like patience, passion comes from the same Latin root: pati. It does not mean to flow with exuberance. It means to suffer."

—*House of Leaves*, **Mark Z. Danielewski**

12

Another month of pandemic pandemonium, first true chill of the season. Everything shivered, skyscrapers and rusted playgrounds, sentinel city trying to rid itself of the invisible disease. With social distancing now law of the land, social media had become the dominant form of communication, ensuring hugs, handshakes and anything that connected humans through physical touch became a thing of the past.

By nightfall, Brooklyn was aglow in sodium arc light. Bodies wandered like ghosts and masks continued to cover half the countenance. Through the warehouse window, Red Hook's streets were bereft of traffic, apartment buildings devoid of tenants. Winter certified that not only would New York City remain shut down, but also shut in with the new twist that people had to do it in solitude.

Sebastian's lipstick created a candy-colored halo on his face. In the reflection of his work mirror, Dorian saw himself lurking, skeletal and sharp, esoteric facemask accentuating his haunting features as he eyed Sebastian like a snack. Strikingly beautiful, both as a boy and as a drag queen; his Mediterranean genetics made him appear much younger than his thirty-three years.

"They envy you," Dorian said.

"Take that ridiculous mask off."

Dorian pulled the mask off his face and slid it onto his wrist. "Did you hear what I said?"

"Yes, but I don't believe you."

"When was the last time you checked the comments on your posts?"

"I'm not fragile enough to do that."

"You're a bad liar, beautiful boy."

"Puh-lease. Is this how you flirt? You're so bad at it."

Sebastian turned around and typed furiously on his phone. From what Dorian could see it was yet another social media black-hole argument, Instagram and Twitter the finest platforms to foment internet feuds. Why Sebastian fell so easily into those traps, Dorian would never know. He didn't exist on social media, which meant he just simply didn't exist. Dorian hadn't the patience nor the time to devote to it. Judging by how random lunatics got under Sebastian's skin, Dorian knew he was better off not having it.

"I know what it's like to *not* have genetics like you. I'll be a prune very soon and you'll still be young and beautiful."

"Not the young part. Get some Botox."

Dorian didn't say anything

"Just being honest." Sebastian looked at his phone again as two more notifications came in.

"Little cock sucking toad!"

Dorian strained his eyes to see what Sebastian was typing. PHONY and FAGGOT were capitalized on the screen. Sebastian hit his knee against the underside of the table, which sent fake nails and tubes of eyeliner flying. Annoyance quickly reshaped into tears. Sebastian sighed deeply, and when he calmed down, a slew of positive affirmations fell from his lips; he apologized for letting himself get so worked up over a nonsense argument. Then he put some music on, "Particles" by Nothing But Thieves, and turned back to the mirror to apply eyeshadow.

"You alright?"

Sebastian sighed. "You think I'd be used to these trolls by now."

"They're keyboard warriors. I'm surprised they don't get banned for the homophobic comments."

"When they do it from fake accounts, what do they care?"

"People need to get back to work. The boredom is clear."

Sebastian clicked his dark fingernails against the worktable then released his dual-colored hair from the manbun he'd tied it up into. Black and silver brushed ever so softly across Sebastian's Dracula eyebrows and tattooed shoulders. The maroon tank top Sebastian wore looked like it had been made for females, despite fitting his twiggy body marvelously. Dorian inhaled deeply, threw a cigarette between his teeth lest he walk straight up to the boy and take a handful of his hair, put their faces together and swirl their mouths into a fleshy candy cane.

"You're delicious," Dorian whispered.

"One hookup and still on my case."

"I know a connection when I feel one. No boy has gotten to me like this since Leland."

"Trust, that shit will fade."

"So negative!"

"How is Leland doing these days?"

Dorian didn't want to talk about his ex, so he walked away, twirling bare toes through the trippy carpet at his feet. Sebastian called this place Whyrlwynd, an apt match for his unhinged yet creative mind. The current state of disarray was all one needed to see to understand that this place was more a temporary home for the rejected and disconnected, rather than a pious workspace. It had become all too common to see a queer smoking crystal meth or snorting bumps of Ketamine; smell the spoon and lighter of a dope fiend and glimpse a hypodermic flower with blood.

Transients bring their vices and make everyone endure them.

"How much longer are you going to let these people destroy this place?"

"They can't help themselves. I let them do what they want since it's safe here."

It was more than Dorian could say he did in terms of community effort. When outcasts think they have no place to go, Sebastian shows up and shows them that people still care. It was as if he exuded a queer bat signal, and that astounded Dorian to no end. Heart of gold beneath a spiked shell. Sebastian pointed toward limited-edition tour posters of various metal and industrial bands hanging loosely on the wall, but Dorian had no idea why.

All around the room there were stacks of books where the ghosts of antisocial readers once cornered themselves, sketch pads for inspired artists, tubes of acrylic for the painters, and long sections of bare wood floors for the performance artists to practice. Whyrlwynd was not just a home, but a space to transform oneself. At Dorian's feet was a warzone of lipstick, primer and glue-on nails; powder trailed like a cocaine spill, glitter and fringe fanned out in a shimmery array. Costume jewelry, wigs, lashes and sashes were laid out and on top of every drawer and armoire. This made him realize how much he missed going to shows and putting on shows himself. Of all the things the pandemic took away, that hurt the most.

"It feels like an eternity since I've seen a performance," Dorian said.

"To people like us, it has been that long."

"I really hate this pandemic. It's killing art."

Sebastian nodded. "I miss that special magic the crowd creates."

"They feed off us as much as we feed off them."

"I remember you once painted a hole in the ground, and people fell into it."

"Trick of the hand."

"You sure about that?" Sebastian grinned.

"Don't you miss being New York's Queen of the Night?"

"I still am," Sebastian said with widening eyes. "Just don't say her name."

"... *Hydra* ..."

Sebastian put his hand over Dorian's mouth. "She doesn't need any attention. I have her right where I want her these days."

"A very important part of us is gone," Dorian said. "Without performance, who even are we?"

"One day we'll get it back."

"You got any beer?" Dorian said. "I'm thirsty."

Sebastian threw a bottle of Dark Wing IPA into Dorian's open hands. The black beer hissed open; frothy malt and stinging hops danced within Dorian's olfactories. It was the smell of freedom, accented with bits of coffee and pine. Having grown up on the piss taste of lagers, an IPA was something holy. When Sebastian cracked open his beer, they clinked their bottles so that they could share the moment together.

"To art." Sebastian smiled darkly.

"To the memory of performance." Dorian drank deeply.

Delilah was heavily asleep on one of the scrungy couches. The only way they knew she was still breathing was by her intermittent snoring, otherwise she looked dead with her body half-eaten by the smelly cushions. Stevie Nicks hung above this specific couch, as well as some drag queens—most notably the queen of Halloween herself, Sharon Needles—and Maynard James Keenan in notorious blue body paint from Tool's Ænima tour. Out of the corner of his eye, Dorian could swear the posters moved on their own; a twirl from Stevie, a menacing laugh from Sharon, a ritual dance from Maynard.

"No escape," Delilah wailed.

The sound was so loud it jarred Sebastian. His beer made a *thud!* on the work desk, erupting foam. One of the lightbulbs that crowned the mirror fell to a glittery crunch. A memory eclipsed Dorian, things he was better off forgetting: dance clubs and mania, paintings that came to life. Peyote Nightmares. Swirling ouroboros. Life feeds on life. The cycle never ends. It was this place that asked him to come out of hiding all those years ago; it was this place that made him want to draw again. Sebastian brought that out in people, all the things you thought were gone but were just hiding somewhere else in your brain.

"Is she talking in her sleep?" Dorian asked.

"Like you never have?"

Delilah uttered something: *I know what they want.* Then the couch rocketed towards Dorian, crashing into the back of his knees and forcing them to buckle. Before his body had the chance to fall on top of Delilah, the couch hurtled itself toward Sebastian, but he was fast on the defense and jumped over it. A vinyl record shattered against the wall and a tube of lipstick began drawing on its own. The first letter was D and the last letter was H. The rest was left blank as if it wanted to play a game of hangman.

"Death," Sebastian said.

"You alright?" Dorian was on his feet, dazed and confused.

"Her dreams really *are* dangerous. I had no idea they could manifest this way."

"You thought Tyria was the only one?"

"I was talking about myself, but now that you mention it, yes."

Delilah shrieked. Another lightbulb burst, followed by a stack of books tumbling onto Dorian. There was a pounding at the front door. Sebastian's ears pulled toward the sound, almost as if his body was controlled by it. *Finally.* He grit his teeth. But before Sebastian could get his hand on the knob, the heavy metal door flung open. Two black shadows slid into the room, followed by a refreshing cold breeze that smelled of new snow and clove cigarettes. They sailed past Dorian and hovered over Delilah until her eyes bolted open.

"Is she up?" Sebastian said.

"Almost," Rez said.

Delilah yawned loudly. "What's the matter?"

Alex lifted Delilah's legs, then draped them across his lap. "Had to get some things done for the band." He tapped his long white fingers on Delilah's fishnetted calves. "Guess what I'm doing?"

"Don't make me guess." Delilah's brow was beaded in nightmare sweat. "I got a headache."

"New music has come."

"I'm not feeling very creative right now."

"Oh, but *I am.* Ever since I saw him, I can't stop writing melodies."

"I'm starting to think he's the *actual* devil," Delilah said. "When did all of this start?"

"Not when we saw him at the antique shoppe, I assure you. I wasn't ready then. This started the other day."

"Just the other day?"

"I was in Little Italy, hoping to bump into Zephyr. You know, the old-fashioned way. Just as I was about to turn on Mott to get to Zephyr's building . . . there he was . . . staring into the sky. I literally froze. His hair is still that same soft, curly nightmare, eyes so bright and chaotic that they turned the lenses of his glasses purple. He hadn't changed one bit. The only difference was that he'd dyed his hair white as snow."

"And you waited until now to tell us? Ever heard of a text?"

"I couldn't help myself. He hypnotized me . . . I lost my focus."

"Sounds like Dexter," Rez said.

"I thought I felt him reach out to me . . . I really did. Like something out of *Star Wars*. You know . . . the force? I was completely frozen."

Delilah lifted her hand. "So now he's inspiring you again?"

"Not exactly." Alex suddenly looked confused. "Wasn't this couch on the other side of the room?"

"Yes, it was. Now it's here." Delilah grabbed Alex's hand. "Please just explain."

"You know not to grab this hand."

Alex removed the fingerless black gloves he wore slowly. With each menacing tick of the clock, Delilah's impatience and exasperation was growing. Finally, after what felt like the slowest five minutes ever, Alex's right hand was exposed, and in the dim light Dorian saw the rope-like scar of pink and white that wrapped about his palm, all the way to the top of his wrist. It looked as if he'd been burned by a hot metal wire.

"I don't remember what he did," Delilah said.

"That's because you weren't there. And it doesn't matter anymore."

Dorian caught Rez wincing, almost guiltily.

"Now where was I? Oh yeah. I thought I was broken inside when Dexter left. Not just that. Like, I felt . . . dead."

"Truly," Delilah sighed.

"It was the same for Rez, obvi. Even though we had one another, we both felt so alone. He couldn't write any new stories. I couldn't write music. But now? We're filling up books. There isn't enough time in the day to enjoy it."

Alex's enlightenment made Dorian happy. He knew how good it felt when creativity and the muse worked together. But the smile shaped Alex's face wrongly—the way his lips tightened, the way his small teeth flashed—as if it shouldn't be there. He went back to tapping the new melody he was writing on Delilah's leg, traced a few of her tattoos and the lines of the fishnet stockings before she nudged him to stop. Rez temporarily zoned out, but his green eyes remained brilliant. Dorian couldn't help but to stare at them out of his own bemusement. After a minute Rez shook his head and collected himself.

"What does that mean?"

"Dexter doesn't have his claws in us anymore."

"Because they're in Atticus," Rez said.

"And Zephyr soon enough."

Dorian and Sebastian grabbed one another by the hand, the way people do when they are afraid and look to another person for protection. Dorian felt many a great thing as their fingers clasped. Sparks and electrical imbalances for starters, then a truck load of dopamine, the signal the body sends when it wants more of whatever you're feeding it. This is how he knew he was falling in love, and that there was no stopping it. The look in Sebastian's dark eyes said the same thing: too many feelings being transmitted—but worth the risk one needs to take in order to experience love.

"Well then, let's shine some sunlight on his vampire-wannabe ass. Did you bring it?" Rez said.

Delilah had her eyes closed, but Dorian could see they were rolling around madly behind the lids. Rez was biting his nails ferociously, so much so Dorian thought he could smell the blood suffusing his cuticles. The music stopped and the room became silent.

"Yes. And it's alive."

Zephyr woke with an unfamiliar pain in his stomach. It felt as if he'd swallowed rocks, given how his intestines pressed so forcefully upon the bone of his pelvis. The sun was beating down on his face, warming it until he broke a sweat. Then a cool breeze swarmed his body, and when he came to he realized that he'd never made it back downstairs after hooking up. He was naked as the day he was born; Dexter was nowhere to be found.

The rooftop was messier now that his clothes were scattered everywhere. Zephyr sat up, put his hand up against the sun that was now starting to blind him. Then the weird pain in his stomach began to feel as if the rocks had turned to liquid, maybe gas since the pain was causing him to belch uncontrollably. He began to dry heave. Never had a hangover been this bad; never had he no control of his bodily functions.

Zephyr looked for his phone, but it was nowhere to be found. He frantically searched the pocket of his jeans and his black denim jacket, then his Converses and balled-up socks. But it was gone. This sent Zephyr into panic mode. These days, when a person loses their cell phone, it feels more like losing an appendage. Phones have become such an integral part of the human identity that many could argue a vital part of us disappears if we were ever to conduct our lives without one.

The bottle of Jägermeister that he'd drank was smashed. Green glass glittered in his peripheral vision and the smell of licorice made him gag. But nothing sickened him more than the things he now saw lying around. Three rats and two pigeons that had been beheaded, but not by the clean slice of a blade. They'd been mangled; it looked as if the heads were twisted off by bare hands.

Gore winked and blood dripped into little black pools. Zephyr caught the sickly-sweet odor of decomposition settling in. Soon there would be flies, then a huge white blanket of maggots; it would make no noise other than squirming sounds as they fed off these diseased animals. The thought made Zephyr sicker. In a quick bout of bravery, he picked up the rats by their tails, the pigeons by their wings, and flung them off the rooftop, but didn't watch them land; didn't want to see their guts spatter or hear people scream.

Zephyr slowly put his clothes back on and spent the next hour, or what felt like an hour, scanning the rooftop for his phone. Worry made his mouth dry, unlocking a taste that he was very unfamiliar with. His tongue felt like sandpaper, and his lips were so chapped that when he licked them, they burned. He soon gave up looking for his phone and headed back to his apartment.

Before he went down, he caught sight of Manhattan in a weird moment of serenity. The skyline north of here looked crisp and brilliant. So many new structures of glass and steel squeezed between the older buildings that were comprised of mostly stone and fascinating engravings. He was bearing witness, ever so slowly, to the new world swallowing the old, little by little. It was basically a metaphor about his life.

Down the stairs, no banister and a broken fire alarm, and Zephyr found that the door to his apartment was slightly ajar. Before he opened it, he smelled something deep, wet and endless. He thought it could have been his neighbor's cooking, perhaps they'd burned something in the oven. But it was none of that. He pushed the door open and found that his apartment was covered in a soot-like substance. It was heavy stuff, almost like liquid, but not a liquid he knew or had ever seen.

Zephyr entered, and as soon as the door closed, he knew something was wrong. It was that flaring pain again, then it was realizing that his apartment was no longer recognizable. He touched the wall, and his hand broke through it like tissue paper. He saw a tunnel now, winding deep and fast into the earth. Not just a tunnel, but huge throughways the color of no color, and where they lead he had no idea. All he knew was that it was down.

He stuck his head in. There was no suction or any real reason that his senses should be on such high alert. No sound unless silence is considered a sound. And then there was movement, a flash of purple, which brought him back to the memory of that tomb. Claustrophobia so intense he might have hallucinated, considering he saw a skeleton rise from its stony final resting place, attempting to lock him in forever.

Now his stomach was in knots, which slowly turned into nausea. He needed water, fast. But the sink was coated in soot, as was the glass he took out of the cabinet. The faucet would not turn on, and he hit it three times with his hand until a gelatinous substance plopped into the cup. It reminded him of black tadpoles, billions of them swimming in a small cup that made them crash and meld into the other. No, not tadpoles. Sperm.

Somewhere in the apartment, he heard a phone vibrating. Zephyr swiped the glass onto the floor, saw the black sperm flop about like fish out of water. He walked into the living room; everything was gone except for the couch, which had always been a cheap piece of shit, but was now even more unappealing. There were no cushions, just the black liners placed unevenly on top of it. The phone vibrated again, and this time he saw the light from between the spring cushion and the side of the armrest with just enough space to fit his fingers in, but when he went to grab it, something touched him in a way he didn't expect.

I'm inside you

The nausea forced something up his esophagus. Zephyr's jaw pried open but nothing came out, even as his entire thorax burned. Then his jaw opened wider, tongue flopping, and this time a loud wet belch erupted from the back of his throat. Then another dry heave until a swirling black cloud wrapped about Zephyr's face, clinging to his eyes and cheeks as would sputum. He felt the stuff crawl slowly out of the orifices of his nose, eyes and mouth. It was like he was bleeding it out.

He grabbed his phone again, tried to call Atticus but his fingers wouldn't let him. The pain was too confusing, the blackness too thick. It filled the room, darkening it to appear as if nightfall had come. The closer Zephyr looked, the more he realized that the underground was somehow sprouting above, opening its maw to show him a land of dark treasures and pleasures. But it was a land he didn't want to know.

There were a great many things sailing past his line of sight. Gravestones and huge winged animals; talons and cloven hooves. He smelled sulfur and rot as a purple gleam sizzled beside him. Then the burning slid down to his anus, the sanctuary that Dexter had recently laid his seed. Did they use lube? Zephyr couldn't remember.

"What are you doing?"

The voice jarred him. Zephyr was not able to recognize it. Then there were hands, lips against his ear. He knew them. Atticus and Dexter, the only two humans he wanted to help him. But he could not open his eyes, the pain was too crippling. He let out another belch, as if that was going to free him from all this darkness; instead, it only kept him prisoner. The black substance spread fast, pushing into the window panes until they made a horrific cracking sound.

"You were talking in your sleep."

Zephyr opened his eyes. He saw Atticus looking a little spooked; the muscles in his face were taut with worry, lips pulled tight. Somehow Zephyr was back on the rooftop. Had he ever left? Dexter was next to him, and sticking out of a pocket was a phone, Zephyr's own, which he recognized instantly from the green gel case. He hadn't lost it. Maybe Dexter had stolen it. But the visions, the roads of darkness, they felt as real as the sun on his face, as real as Atticus' lips touching his own, even if they were infected with a bit of jealousy.

"Hope you two had fun," Atticus said.

"We did." Dexter's voice sounded very far away, but his eyes proved he was not.

"Isn't this what you wanted?" It was all Zephyr could manage to say.

Atticus lit two cigarettes, handed one to Zephyr. "Well, yes and no. I didn't think I wouldn't be invited if you two were hanging out."

"We needed to talk," Dexter said. "Here." Dexter handed Zephyr his phone. "Didn't want anyone to take it. You knocked out."

"Must've been the alcohol."

Atticus's eyebrow raised. "That's new for you. You a lightweight now?"

Zephyr got to his feet. He was fully clothed and the sun was almost too hot now, despite the cool breeze. He checked his phone for any weird messages but didn't see any. Same stuff, some delayed responses from Delilah and a few random people commenting on his stories. He took a drag of the menthol cigarette, feeling a headache slowly starting to creep into his skull. He needed coffee, and fast.

They made their way down, out into the chilly streets where there was barely a business open or a person in sight. It was only eight o'clock in the morning, so that was about the only thing that made sense. And then things started to take a turn for the worst. Atticus and Dexter were up ahead, holding hands playfully, but the way their fingers entwined spoke of romance.

It wasn't just that. The higher the sun rose into the sky, the weirder their shadows became. Atticus' was elongated but shaped perfectly like the dark twin that should have been. It was Dexter's shadow that made Zephyr do a double take. It was not in the shape of a human, but something far more confusing, as it constantly shifted into something winged, with chitinous legs and horns. The shadow moved by its own accord, was not a carbon copy of the object from which it was cast. Zephyr decided to not say a thing. Too many illusions had plagued him already.

"I wanna stop in here."

It was a bakery, *Ferrara*, so said the glitzy sign. It only took Zephyr a few minutes to figure out what he wanted. A cup of coffee and two cannoli. He devoured the first in a single bite and slurped down the black coffee as if he would never have a cup of it again. Powdered sugar daubed Zephyr's upper lip, but Atticus wiped it away with his thumb. Dexter stayed out front, and through the store's window Zephyr eyed his movements, how he secretly looked at his phone, almost skeleton-like with the sun beating against his pallid complexion.

"You gunna get me one?" Atticus said.

"Nah, you never liked them."

"Guess that's true."

They exited the cafe to a now windy street. Paper plates and takeout cartons flew over their shoes. Starting on this block, Chinatown clashed with Little Italy, but both neighborhoods would eventually be swallowed by Big Business, which was spreading faster. Each day a new boutique hotel and designer shoppe popped up. It was a sight to see, but not uncommon.

"You must be starving," Dexter said as he watched Zephyr wolf down the cannoli. "Where we going?"

"I wanted to go back home, but I realize that I don't now. I had a bad dream."

"I did too," Dexter added. "But I feel happy today."

"You both should," Atticus said.

"Do you wanna talk about it?"

"About what?"

"The dream. Duh."

No, he did not want to talk about that. He was embarrassed enough. But now that he thought about it, he wondered if Dexter had wanted him to be found like that, alone and sad on the rooftop. Once Zephyr was betrayed, he wasn't the type to forgive and forget. But he knew he was better off not saying anything just yet. Keeping the peace was most important.

"By the way." Dexter had stopped in the middle of the sidewalk, motioned for the two of them to follow, then started walking southeast. "I know she's contacted you both."

"Huh?"

"That snake-haired singer."

Atticus quickly paled. "I didn't tell her anything."

"I'm just curious what she said about me."

"She doesn't like you," Zephyr said. "That much I know."

"The girl knows nothing about me."

"She claims she does."

Dexter's face reddened and his features twisted into a terrible scowl. He pulled at his hair recklessly and spit uncontrollably. Zephyr had never seen the boy be so expressive, and it was almost too awkward to watch. It was apparent that Delilah was a trigger for him, so Zephyr didn't want to press the situation any further due to Dexter virtually possessing zero social cues. "Alright . . . calm down, Dexter." Atticus put his hand around Dexter's shoulders as if he'd seen him have an outburst before. "Let's just keep walking. You two have a lot to tell me anyway."

The walk took them southeast, and they approached the Williamsburg Bridge faster than expected. Its bony shadow loomed, as did the shadows of the buildings. For a split second, as they all stepped through, Zephyr thought he saw part of Dexter vanish into the shadow itself—not just vanish, but become part of it. Once he blinked, the illusion was gone.

"I know where we can go to relax," Dexter said. "I mean . . . before I take you both back to my real home."

13

Rez put Delilah's head in his lap; Alex had her legs draped across his upper thigh. The three of them scrunched together was reminiscent of a goth-rock album cover, maybe something The Cure would have done in 1987: sharp faces, overly dyed hair, and black clothing. How they kept their authenticity against modern culture was beyond the scope of Sebastian's thinking.

It was clear that they were all very close. It made Sebastian slightly envious, but also curious. He could not recall the last time he was close with another person. Perhaps Lilith, but she was gone now, doing her own thing. Then there was Dorian, his new man of interest. But he was still unable to find a way to trust people, which was becoming more of the norm in a world that was knee-deep in toxic social media.

Sebastian couldn't imagine the hate that poured through Electric Orchid's socials. People go to great lengths to make sure their negativity falls into your lap. Sebastian spent a lot of time trying to ignore this archetype of ingrate human, but social platforms give them a voice, and not just that, they give them *power*.

"How long's it been since you last felt creative?" Sebastian asked.

He'd been listening to Electric Orchid's music since they came to New York City. More than that, it interested him to know what propelled and inspired the band; what made them tick, what made them create such sounds of havoc, as well as sounds of comfort. The band was an anomaly of strange time signatures and lyrical poetry that fit together like a sacred equation rather than heavy music.

"A long time," Alex said.

"More than a year?"

"Feels like a lifetime."

"I know that kind of pain. The emptiness, the loss of identity."

"It's been sixteen months . . . almost to the day." Rez opened a heavily embroidered cigarette case with stars and planets, exposing little white sticks that smelled like incense. "Salvia, anybody?"

Sebastian instinctively put his hands into the pockets of his jeans. Drugs were something he was always weary of. He could drink the house down, could sip on cough syrup like it was water from Ponce de Leon's Fountain of Youth, but there was something about mind-altering substances that did him wrong. These "fun drugs" (as people in his circle called them) didn't mix well with the psychotropics he had to take in order to keep his mental health in check. Sometimes the fun drugs literally set his mind on fire, and often there was no coming back from that madness for what felt like days on end.

"Who the hell did you cop from?" Dorian took one of the joints. "Nobody's selling right now."

"You know." Rez winked.

"Is Adelaide seriously still dealing?" Dorian bit his lower lip until he drew a bead of blood.

"You ladies reunited last year," Sebastian said.

"That's hardly what we did. And I haven't talked to her since Adrian—"

"Shh." Sebastian put his finger across Dorian's lips. "We don't talk about him."

Dorian was outwardly annoyed that Alex had done a drug deal with the one woman he hated, and Sebastian was fully triggered at the drop of Adrian's name. He hadn't thought about him for a long time. Part heartbreak, part betrayal, all venom. Adrian wasn't some fly-by-night friend brought into Sebastian's life. Adrian was a now a scab on his conscience, caused by the physical hardships of constantly butting heads with the one person you loved the most.

The friendship turned sour the day that Adrian began a romantic pursual of Sebastian. And when Adrian was met with a series of no's, Sebastian was then invited to a dilapidated runway drag battle against Adrian, which turned out to be unlike anything any audience had ever seen. The protege, now turned season queen, wanted nothing more than to take the drag throne for himself. Delilah and Dorian were there, and the two of them saw things that the other did not. This shared hallucination was felt throughout the performance warehouse, all the way to Adrian's sudden disappearance once the show ended.

Macabre drag queens don't enjoy the same notoriety as the fabulous ones, so they must work twice as hard to awe their audience. But after that night, the Hydra was the source of much gossip. This solidified Sebastian's place in the underground drag world: its reigning Queen of the Night. Consequently, Adrian had become a stain upon his existence, because without him, Sebastian would not be where he was today.

"So then?"

Delilah and Dorian were staring at him now. Their eyes looked possessed, as if they wanted him to fall prisoner to his memories and release the pain of it all, to recall the magic and mayhem, the hole in the floor that Dorian created with just a few strokes of paint; how it swirled into a cyclone at the sound of Delilah's delectable voice. Somehow this sent Adrian soaring into the air, but not to fly, only to fall into the black vacuum, leaving behind nothing but a wispy silver shawl, the signature color of Hera Wynn, his drag persona.

"I know people will want to cancel me for going out there and doing my thing," Alex said. "But Addy has supply and I want drugs."

"What does she deal?"

"She's like one of those delivery services. Send a text and she shows up with a fancy pouch filled with your chosen escape from reality."

"Does she test it for fentanyl?"

"Addy doesn't cut her drugs with that stuff."

"What about her suppliers?"

"I've been buying from her for years. Don't worry."

"She's not a junkie anymore," Rez chimed in.

"What's that got to do with dealing?"

"Been sober since the day Tyria—"

"Let's not get into that," Dorian interrupted. "All I'm saying is judging from the last time I saw her . . . she looked like shit . . . like she was still using."

"That's what depression does to people," Sebastian said. "I fight it every day."

"As if I ain't depressed myself. I think everyone here's a little depressed."

Dorian fired up the joint. The first toke came in a bit too strong. As much as he tried to fight the cough for fear of appearing as a lightweight, it was too much to hold back. He expunged a huge cloud from his mouth and nose that looked as if he was exorcizing a ghost. Sebastian saw his eyes get bloodshot and skin go gray. Apparently, one should never take a hit of salvia like you do marijuana; even the most seasoned smokers don't do it.

"Looks like *Dangerous Dorian* ain't so dangerous after all," Delilah teased. She toked her joint at a slower pace, allowing the smoke to escape her mouth and slither up her nose. "You can't handle it."

"It's been a while. Sarcasm is not needed."

"You forgot about your old friend now that you fell in love with ketamine."

Dorian chuckled. "K is certainly my love."

"Ketamine is my enemy," Sebastian said. "That stuff *sends* me."

"Good thing I keep a stash in my pocket." Dorian took out a small cylindrical vial, undid the cap and daubed powder out near his thumb, then sniffed it up.

"It's eleven in the morning. Why're we doing drugs this early?"

"Because we can," Dorian said.

"Ketamine and off-brand sage?"

Alex stood and got in Sebastian's face. "You got somewhere better to be?"

"Have you ever tried it?" Rez was almost offended.

"Of course. I don't like the visions."

"Salvia visions do hit different."

"Like nothing else out there."

"How so?"

"Take a hit," Alex said. "You'll see."

Sebastian took the lit joint from Dorian, wrapped his lips around it and inhaled. It was so quiet he could hear the tiny embers crackling, a lovely cadence that ended as soon as the herbal flavors exploded over his tongue. Salvia does not enter your cells like weed; it has a punch to it, the smoke somehow thicker and more robust, latching to your throat and sliding heavily into the lungs. Sebastian noted this immediately, and there was even a slight numbness to his lips and tongue.

Dorian offered him a bump of ketamine so he could relax and enjoy. Sebastian snorted the singeing powder, pleasantly waiting for the bitter trickle in his throat. Suddenly there was an immediate, mute shift in the atmosphere followed by waves of psychedelic imagery. This was the reason Sebastian didn't want to smoke salvia in the first place: it would just unlock his bottomless imagination, stir trouble when trouble wasn't needed. But Sebastian had never tried salvia with K, so he hoped it would calm some of the effects.

"Fuck, I feel it already," Dorian said.

"Me too."

Then it happened. Delilah's eyes went comically wide, as did Dorian's. This made paranoia fan out from Sebastian's loins, all the way to his shivering extremities. He turned his head toward a voice he didn't recognize and saw nobody there. *Not again*, he thought. *Stay put.* Then there was a gentle knock at the door, and the sound of plastic bags rumbling. He forgot that he'd ordered pizza.

. . . love you . . .

Sebastian flicked his head. The voice was gone. Delilah began to laugh, which led him to believe she was the one who had said it, even if the voice was fiercer and more sybaritic than hers could ever be. Instead of investigating, it was time to dole out pizza. The distraction was needed. Sebastian laid the pies down on one of the spare circular tables at the far end of the workspace. Hot cheese and tomato sauce blossomed in his nose; he flicked the crispy crust with his nail, true New York style. Everyone took a slice. Alex poured red pepper flakes on his; Rez overdid the oregano. Oil ran down Dorian's chin; a small piece of green bell pepper became entangled in Delilah's magnanimous hair. They all cracked open an IPA and lazed on their respective sides of the room.

"If I drink, will it make it worse?" Dorian said while tipping a bottle into his mouth.

"If anything, it'll calm you," Alex mumbled.

"Chew with your mouth closed," Rez said. "I hate the sound of lips smacking."

"Then how will I bird-feed you?" Alex kissed Rez's face with crumby lips.

"You two literally nauseate me," Delilah said.

Rez and Alex had *that* kind of relationship. Despite being together for so long they still flirted with one another in weird ways. It takes a lot of effort to stay above the waters of temptation, change and new needs. But they managed it. The two of them laughed so hard their faces flushed red, but that was probably an effect of the salvia. Delilah got to her feet, almost angrily, and stood above them with a death stare and arms entangled like a pretzel. The two of them went from playful to adolescent fear as she snapped her fingers, and then put out her small white hand.

"It's time," Delilah said. "Give it to me."

Rez opened his heavily pinned and patched backpack, then pulled out a statuette. The thing gave Sebastian the sense that it was not from this dimension. Something about it was just wrong. It was oblong—or appeared to be—and black, as if charred in a recent fire. And slightly bent, too, but not actually bent—you just knew it shouldn't be bent. It was somehow reflective, as if made of gemstone or glass, had a wide paunch and a few free forming proboscises, followed by a dark spine that stuck out of the reflective skin. It was also pliable, so said the way it moved in Delilah's hand, which was impossible if it was made from glass. And the face was worm-like, seemed to be all mouth. No eyes, no nose, but there was a sharp tongue and razor-wire teeth.

"The fuck is that?" Sebastian said.

"It's Dexter's."

"But what *is it*?"

"A wrong thing."

Delilah cupped the wrong thing in her hands as if it was a baby bird. Alex was behind her, shadow into shadow with a cell phone in one hand and a cigarette in the other. *Watch*, Delilah whispered as she set the sculpture on the floor. From a faraway source, Electric Orchid's music growled. *It hates our music*, she whispered again.

"Now," Delilah said.

In came music. A track she purposely chose called "Secret Scream" from Electric Orchid's new record. The song quickly climbed in volume, but also persistence with each passing note. Calm synth and cymbals created a conduit of sonic sound for the eventual buildup of bridge, verse and chorus, filling the room with a muscular force. Then it led to a shift in tempo, haunting synthesizer and guitar as loud as a volcano forcing itself into the ears of its listeners.

All eyes locked onto the wrong thing. Its dark beaded spine vibrated and the proboscis scintillated in time with the power chords and deleterious vocal melodies. The music was so intense that it was as if ions were plucked from the air, dancing electric along the senses. Delilah took out a vial of pink powder from her pocket and sprinkled it atop the wrong thing.

"It's 2C-B," she said. "To wake it up."

"Why would you waste that on a piece of shit glass statue?"

"Shut the fuck up and look."

Dorian didn't know if it was a trick of the salvia or if Delilah was playing a game, but his vision tunneled, as did his auditory sense. The entire universe focused all its energy into that thing as it began to change before his eyes. There was a violent reaction, chaotic flailing of arms; its red-wet mouth uttered indistinguishably; beguiling lips yearned for a kiss. Bony processes ripped free from the glassy paunch, spitting shiny particles all over the floor. Pincers and a scorpion-like tail sprouted, the sharp crescent beaded in venom. And then it made a harrowing noise, one so terrorizing it could only be heard by those who dared to listen. It reminded Dorian of the raw sound of suffering.

"The skin is porous." Delilah laughed through little white teeth. "You wouldn't know it by looking at it though."

"Porous?" Dorian's tone verged on being frightened. "How would you even know?"

"I just do. I also know that it doesn't like the drug . . . much like its creator."

"Are you saying they're connected?"

"No, I'm saying this is Gizmo and water."

"Enough with the jokes."

A guitar solo detonated in Dorian's ears, freeing his mind from earthly consciousness. Then a whammy bar squealed, forcing him back into reality. This was one of the effects that Electric Orchid's music had. It was like a drug without the drug. He saw Delilah dancing maniacally, arms flailing and hair whipping in the same fashion as the tiny idol. Alex was doing the same thing, long trench coat overtaking his skinny frame, fists whipping about in his own personal mosh pit, all without losing focus of the task at hand: to record the moment.

"Don't stop the music," Alex said.

"It's almost time."

Everyone took a step back. Pinch harmonics and wailing vibrato shivered into everyone's bones. The sounds elongated into a single scream that ran steadily up and down the neck of the guitar. Then a drum and bass line that defied normal time signatures ignited, which in turn created a tornado of sound. The wrong thing was now wavering, the room growing darker. Rez stood behind it, smoking a long black cigarette, sad eyes and curled lower lip. And then he saw Sebastian, belly tucked in, back curling, teeth bared and fully dilated eyes, much like how a threatened street cat would look.

"What am I seeing?"

Sebastian's face interchanged between glee and shock, and Dorian could feel his own face molding into the same sentiments. As much shit as he'd seen over the years, as many horrors as he'd been involved with by his own accord, the afflictions artists endure to make their work come alive—literally and figuratively—always flabbergasted him. Then Sebastian grabbed Dorian's hand, thumb ring biting into skin as the wrong thing became more sinister in its strange prance and harmful vocalizations.

"That sounds like Delilah's voice."

"It *is* my voice, you moron."

"You're doing too much." Sebastian's tone was threatening.

"Don't stop the music," Delilah said. "I'm warning you."

A hiss escaped the wrong thing's tiny, toothed mouth, followed by a maddened clicking sound as its arachnid legs dashed across the hardwood floor. It ran in many directions, the way a cockroach rockets passed you when you try to swat it. The music intensified, building power and static that left the taste of electric in Dorian's mouth. He watched the wrong thing continue its race to nowhere, glass body reflecting his own eyes that somehow seemed to get darker as the salvia tipped the scale into hallucination.

"Welcome to Electric Orchid's circus," Alex said like a news anchor into his phone. "Chaos brought to you by *The Eventual Devil*."

Dorian saw that he had gone live on Instagram, and that hundreds of people were tuning in. Then an invisible force wrapped itself about Dorian's body, cold and ugly, squeezing air out of him. At the same time, Delilah's voice swelled, haunting every part of the room as if Whyrlwynd had gone the way of a monastery. All things began a peristaltic movement, temporarily turning the foundation to rubber. Dorian went on a mission to understand where the music was coming from, until Delilah stepped in his way, frozen in place, eyes closed and lips going a mile a minute, but no words falling from between them.

"This is what he does. He gets into you. And he never leaves." Alex kept the phone near his lips. "Everyone needs to see this. They need to know what he's made of."

"You're putting this out there for the public to see?"

"It's the only way Dexter will pay attention."

That's when Sebastian dropped to the floor, shirt torn along the spine, horrific growl belching out of his mouth. Dorian saw the muscles of his back pulsing in a strange arrhythmia, impossibly growing, spine inverting, lips stained bloody, until he was on his hands and knees like a wolf. *Not again*, he thought. The last thing Dorian saw was the flash of serpent eyes and glistening scales before Sebastian became a white spider gamboling up the wall.

"Don't touch it!" Delilah yelled.

"It'll mark you," Rez said, chasing behind Sebastian.

"It can't," Dorian said without even realizing what he was saying.

Sebastian was now crawling across the ceiling, smashing the fluorescent lights to powder and dusting everyone below. The wrong thing clacked down the adjacent wall, but Sebastian kept following, mouth gaped and a long forked tongue darting. For one sickening second the two entities sized up one another, bleeding lips and slimed tongues, a forest of hands and teeth. Then the music stopped. Everything returned to homeostasis.

"Why did you do that?" Delilah yelled.

"Stop recording."

The only sound was irregular breathing, and the pull of cigarettes. Nobody looked at anybody. Sebastian was at their feet with his eyes closed, and the wrong thing somehow symbiotically attached to his lips, two very different forms of flesh wrongly knotted into the other. He was humming the rest of the song. Dorian couldn't tell if the red smear on the black glassy body of the wrong thing was blood or Sebastian's lipstick.

"Get it off him," Dorian demanded.

Delilah's anger melted into sympathy as she helped Sebastian to his feet, clothes now hanging off his body like old rags. Alex draped his trench coat about Sebastian's shoulders. Then Delilah put her hands on the sculpture, almost weightlessly, but also with such a vigor that it somehow unlocked the bond between Sebastian and the wrong thing. The only evidence anything had happened was his chapped lips and a small bruise on his cheek. Dorian cradled Sebastian. His black eyes locked with Dorian's for a full questionable moment before collapsing into Dorian's arms.

"It doesn't like him," Delilah said.

"I told you he can't be marked." Dorian was serious. "He's already taken."

A light went off behind Delilah's eyes. "What do you mean *taken*?"

"By the *Hydra*," Sebastian said.

"You mean she's back?"

"I don't think she ever went away."

It seemed Delilah had forgotten about the thing that lived inside of Sebastian. Judging by the enlightened look on her face, she'd never forget it now. Delilah took a moment to collect herself, using the blade of her butterfly knife to pry some gum off her boot.

Then she was on her phone, clicking and swiping so madly it was impossible to tell what she was trying to do.

"How many people joined?" Delilah said.

"At least three thousand."

"Perfect."

"What is it you're trying to achieve?" Dorian was curious.

"What I *need* is to show people what *it* really is. A tick. A Leech. A vampire. Whatever."

"People will question what they saw. Just because it's on video doesn't mean it's real. There's technology out there right now imposing people's faces in videos. It's fucking scary."

"This is the only way for people to see the real Dexter, and what he can do with his toys. Doesn't matter if they believe it."

"You only made him more famous. Everyone's going to follow him now."

"That's exactly what should happen. The more distractions the better."

"Then no time is better than now to share our side of the story."

Alex swished a cigarette through his skinny fingers, sucked his teeth and pushed his red and black hair away from his eyes. Rez clipped the one he was smoking with a small knife and took the wrong thing out of Delilah's hands. He walked over to Alex; they looked each other in the eyes, nodded, then kissed. Envy and jealousy flared inside of Dorian. He wanted the same type of relationship with Sebastian. But then Delilah zipped back into view like a locust, giving the final cue so that Rez and Alex could tell their dark love story.

14

Dexter shot up from our comfortable slumber. Newly dyed white hair but still black at the roots, remnants of it under his fingernails. His weird eyes jetted from cell phone to skinny body, dirty finger tracing random tattoos, as if he'd forgotten consciousness was trapped inside his own skin. He was not focused on me, or Zephyr. It was the phone in his hand and the social media war that was unraveling.

"Twitter is not real life," I said.

"I know that," Dexter hissed. "It's ruined my concentration and exacerbated my ADD."

"You have ADD?"

"At least I think I do. Fuckers!"

Dexter hit the bed with his fist. Loose sheets of paper rained across us like confetti, papers scrawled with random poetry and zigzagging art. I'd been drawing while everyone else was asleep. It felt good to be creative, though I was unsure of the stuff that my hand wanted to show me, so I just let it do its thing. Being we all had made amends—the wrinkles we once could not iron out now flattened—I felt a weird form of elation consume me.

"What is it?"

Zephyr barely had his eyes open, and his sky-blue hair was showing some roots as well. This look had sieged many alt gay boys of New York City, which was headed by none other than macabre influencer Sebastian Ricciuti, aka the Hydra, New York's scariest drag queen. She had an Instagram following of over a hundred thousand and growing. Many of the boys who looked up to

Sebastian ripped off his style. Zephyr and Dexter had taken a thing or two from his book, even if they would never admit it.

"Is this real?"

Dexter put his phone in front of my face. Someone had inboxed him a screen recording of Electric Orchid's Instagram live. I saw Delilah's stupid snaky hair, the infamous Sebastian with his vampire eyebrows and skunk-colored hair, and then I saw a few other shadowy people. But it was the sight of a little statue walking on its own two legs, followed by a huge serpentine thing blotting out the rest of the video, that jarred me the most.

"I have no idea if this is real."

"She kept saying my social handle. The Eventual Devil. With that horrible song playing."

"I like their music," Zephyr added with a yawn.

"Tacky at best. I got six hundred and sixty-six new followers!"

"No pun intended?" I said, running my fingers through Dexter's sleep-sweat hair, tiny pale corkscrews reflecting as bright as the piercings in his ears and lip.

"Some of the dye is on the pillow, I can smell it."

"I told you it had to set a lot longer." Zephyr sat up. "You didn't listen."

Though it had only been three days and three nights since we became a throuple, it felt like we'd been together for an eternity. With jealousy quelled and desire satiated, curiosity was now being explored. No more he-said-he-said. No more juvenile quips. Left only was the freedom to build this relationship and find ways to make it work in a world where not only were homosexuals still being stoned, but polygamists were thought of as evil creatures worthy of eradication. The word itself was ugly. *Polygamist.* Say it three times fast, you'll see what I mean.

But I was stupidly giddy, stupidly fulfilled. I thought about how much misinformation we are taught about what love is supposed to look like. The template of one man and one woman is shoved into our faces as soon as we come out of the womb, but as we grow up, we find out quickly that it's not always such. It can be so much more than one man and one woman. It could be two men, or two women. It can be three men, if that's what people choose.

I used to believe that we are all born as halves in constant search for a single partner to make us whole. But could it be that we are born as thirds, innocently wading through the terrors of romance and the treasures of heartache as we subconsciously put our vulnerable selves out there for a second mate? Anything was possible. The world was a changed place. The pandemic had taken so much from us; people were breaking away from tradition and reshaping social culture.

Given the fact that my reality shapeshifted the moment I met Dexter, I felt this a valid moment to just go with the flow. Gut instinct or Venus flytrap, take your pick. Dexter was the organic connection, that *real love*, that everyone raved about. The kind of love that changes the chemical composition of the body; makes the heart beat faster, lungs breathe deeper, vital organs quiver. Our brains turn to mush and our rational mind is thrown into the gutter.

This unsheathed a primordial, almost biological need to make sure I got to know Dexter in the deepest and most uncomfortable of ways. If that meant I was once again forced to navigate the mysteries of human nature, bear the tortures of lust and go to war with my own emotions, then so be it. Instincts are to be trusted, that's why we have them.

"What're we going to do about it?" Dexter was angry. A bright tear welled in one of his eyes.

"Nothing. Ignore her. She wants to get a rise out of you."

"You're with me now. You're mine now, and you choose to do nothing?"

"She's not worth the fight," I said.

"That's because you like her shitty music."

"I just don't see any harm in what she did."

"Embarrassed me, for starters."

"How so? You a ton of new followers. You should be happy."

"I don't want her scum existence touching my socials."

"Then go private."

"She'd love that too much."

"Eventually, they all would've found you. The more content you post, the more people will want to follow."

"Are you the social media culture committee now?"

"It's just common sense." I kissed Dexter's cheek, which was red hot.

"What about my post that you shared?" Dexter was looking right at me. "People follow your lead."

"You mean his body." Zephyr winked.

"I'm not that influential."

"Don't underestimate your followers."

"All seventy-five thousand of them?"

Dexter mouthed *wow* and raised his eyebrows. He was clearly impressed. I laid my head back down and attempted to nap, but Dexter started a song through the portable UE Boom speaker at the other side of the room. Heavy synth and metallic bass snaked over our bodies, "Sludge Factory" by Alice in Chains. Then he sparked up the rest of his joint, wake-and-bake kind of morning. I nudged Zephyr, signaling for some cuddle time, and he curled his back into my torso. Dexter blew spicy smoke over us, and then laid back down with his face to Zephyr, reaching his arm over and pulling us both into him.

"Got any Black Sabbath on that phone? Tool, The Cure?"

"Spotify has anything you want," Dexter said.

"I prefer Apple Music," I said. "Better layout."

"You must have OCD given Apple is much better at arranging release dates in chronological order."

"Doesn't that make sense?"

Dexter laughed. "I like the chaos of Spotify. Plus, it has better recs and an easier platform to create your own lists."

Then it got quiet again. I listened to the sound of two beautiful boys breathing beside me. Took it all in. I looked about the space we inhabited. What we considered livable quarters others would call absolute destitution. Crumbling fort of limestone and stained glass, at one time or another a house of worship, then a bank, and finally a husk of failed condos that ran out of cash thanks to the pandemic.

Abstract art polluted the walls, as did three bookcases of classic horror novels. A portable microphone, amplifier and guitar was scattered to my left; black lights for mood, strobe lights for fun, second-hand furniture, a proper refrigerator and exposed brick which was the key to my interior design heart. Places like this in Manhattan, especially ones this size, were few and far between, even though I knew that the outside world would soon have its way and vanquish it.

"I like it." Dexter stuck out his tongue. "Even if you argued with me nonstop about it."

The way we communicated had begun to feel as if we'd been doing it for years. It was decided that if we were going to start a relationship we should also start with a fresh dwelling. Be it to hide from the pandemic, the ghosts in our heads, or just to chill, we felt that a neutral spot would be best for everyone's mental health. With murder, suicide and petty crime on the rise, we were no longer living in safe times. Desperation transmogrified into a newfangled pandemonium, one that drove people to do things they never would have done before. Jobless, ravenous, and filled with alacrity. Nobody was rational.

It seemed my dreams followed this trend. What are dreams in the first place? When a person has so many of them, you can't help but to overthink their purpose. Cryptic messages. A gateway between our reality and imagination. Dreams can be a straight narrative or disjointed and mysterious. They can set the tone for the day ahead or make one afraid to even close their eyes. Freud defined dreams as a window to our subconscious, thus revealing our true thoughts, desires and motivations. My dreams kept coming, and I fell headlong into them without any concerned effort to escape.

The same paralytic story. I saw myself being taken to places that offered me subtle answers to riddles I didn't even know I was supposed to answer. Delilah's silhouette would come like hot lightning in the deepest recess of my mind, but I quickly canceled her out. There were bigger things happening. My dominant hand—the hand that Dexter's sculpture had bitten—was doing things I never thought it could. Little by little I drew the freakish nature of my dreams and built surreal sculptures with a precision that exceeded my actual talent.

What is an artist when they can't control their dominant hand? It made me feel inauthentic, being I'd never experience something so otherworldly. Shape the base of a spooky paunch, crush the bones of some inanimate thing and reshape it into a completely foreign and impossible work of art. Two shadows in furious tandem, in the shape of Dexter and Zephyr. I couldn't mistake them, no matter how devoid of detail they were. I knew my boys well enough. Then I'd wake up screaming, only to see my boys safely asleep beside me.

Many things that Delilah said were beginning to irk me. The end of the beginning and the beginning of the end. Dexter posing as a human, but all phantom within. I thought about all the things Dorian, Sebastian and Delilah had told Zephyr. I dared not share any of this with Dexter. I couldn't risk losing him or helping him go insane. I didn't want to start this journey with a fight about something Dexter may or may not have done in the past. I barely had the facts straight. I didn't even care.

In the days that slagged, all three of us endured the bitter reality of boredom. The clock ticked but life felt frozen. I thumbed through a copy of *Interzone* by William S. Burroughs, a rare author who inspired me to emulate his words via sculpture. I cleared my headspace, cleared my physical space, falling into Burroughs' universe. Zephyr had found me an original copy, knowing very well of my admiration for him. Words were his weapon, and they transported my mind through every wormhole of the universe and back again as if I'd taken an illicit substance.

Dexter made art every which way he could. Even when he didn't have proper tools, a stool to sit on or table to work at, he was chipping away at some grotesquery. He created quality in half the time I did. Sometimes that filled me with envy, at other times shock. He was truly gifted, enough so that I thought his sculptures moved between each blink. This reminded me of Dorian Wilde's paintings. If you looked at the things he drew—all the inanimate horrors and wild sex organs—they would do something on the canvas that you couldn't explain. Wink, whisper, and stink. I drove myself mad just thinking about it.

"Now look at my inbox."

We'd been locked inside for three days. The weather was awful and there were no social gatherings happening. Dexter's boredom reached new heights, as now I was looking at an entire direct message brawl between him and Delilah. It made me physically ill to see it, and she'd not even reached out to give me the respect that she was now taunting him. I turned around and saw Zephyr staring at me with one eyebrow raised. *Told you*, he mouthed silently to me.

"I'll talk to her."

"Nah, fuck it," Dexter said. "When the time comes, she'll find me."

I gazed into my phone, toying with the idea of sending Delilah some nasty text messages, but my attention shifted quickly. Instagram showed me how the rules of the pandemic were being broken. Vacations and smiles as if there was no serious virus going around. So I convinced Dexter and Zephyr to create our own shenanigans. We cared not about catching Covid or passing it on to others. If they were doing it, then we were going to do it too. Tit for tat, despite the crucial consequences. After being shut in and told to stay put for nearly a year, these critically craven choices felt like a normal rebellion.

We didn't worry about the baubles of science or social media police and their hashtags. In the crowds we socialized with, you could never get a picture clear enough to post for public shame. We all hid behind makeup and the black light of some random warehouse. The majority of these people lacked proper day jobs, had no formal education or anything tying them to the real world; there was no threat severe enough to make them stop. They didn't fear cancel culture because there was literally nothing to lose.

Out of the three of us, Zephyr was the most careful. But even he sometimes needed to just get fucked up and see people. All I wanted was to find alternate ways to learn about Dexter and get reacquainted with Zephyr. You might think you know everything about someone after being together so long, but I always believed there was more to learn, more to share, more to destroy.

After exhausting myself with Delilah's drama, I began inquiring about Dexter's underground world. *Take me there again*, I said, suddenly feeling Zephyr's eyes behind me. *Us*, I corrected. Zephyr didn't like the idea of going back, and he'd alluded that some outside force was guiding him away from Dexter. Must have been Delilah. But I wanted to do what I wanted to do, stubborn as any Aries you'll ever meet.

Down there it seemed the world didn't exist. You could literally be who you wanted to be, free of every disease, mental disorder and physical disarray that would normally get a person shunned. No facemasks, even when we'd become conditioned to always carry one. Listening to Dexter's stories got my brain going. The people down there really weren't that much different than any niche artist in Bushwick, Williamsburg or the Lower East Side. It's just that now they'd receded to their "safe place" and didn't plan to emerge until they were good and ready.

Gentrification had stolen their cheap rent, and the pandemic had erased their opportunity to put on shows. They were angry and stubborn and felt no qualms about abandoning the world that had already abandoned them. I'd seen this brand of rage once. It was back in 2019 when people could still go out and socialize. The club was halfway between Eleventh and Twelfth Avenues. I was led by a pack of vacant bodies with only one mission in mind: to see a show. It was a battle of macabre drag queens, two best friends competing for New York's black diamond crown. It wouldn't surprise me if the same people that gazed stupidly at the drag queens transcending performance art were the same ones that lived in Dexter's city beneath the city.

"Do they ever come up for air?" Zephyr asked.

"They don't need it," Dexter said.

"Ya gotta be kidding me."

"If they did, don't you think they'd go get it?"

"You know," I interjected. "This is all going to end soon. The vaccine is on its way."

"If you knew anything about viruses, they're master manipulators. Variants will arise. This'll all happen again, as it's happened before."

"And just like viruses, people manipulate as well. They get sick of the rules. Sick of being held down."

"Anti-maskers?" I said jocosely.

There was a momentous flutter of darkness in Dexter's eyes, but it quickly died. "We're not *that* stupid. We respect science, but have our reasons for doing what we do."

"And what are your reasons?"

"To make art."

"Never heard that before," Zephyr said.

"But have you ever seen it *come alive*?"

My sculptures came to mind. I'd confided in Dexter about them, so I was a little shocked he was talking this way.

"You mean the manifestations?"

Dexter's face lit up. "We make art to survive, both emotionally and physically. We just can't do it at the same pace these days."

"The internet and solitude and social media pretty much proves you wrong."

Dexter turned my way fiercely. "Focus is dead. But more importantly, we lost actual *audiences*."

That part stuck with me the most. What the pandemic took away from artists was something only a world *without* an air-borne virus could provide: people gathered under one roof to enjoy a show. While Twitter and Instagram had kept me busy, I'd overlooked the fact that I'd been denied my human-to-human interaction time. That was something I took for granted, being I was naturally anti-social.

I immediately went back to work, as did Dexter. We filled notebooks with prose and drawings by candlelight; the callouses on our hands roughened from molding, carving and painting every painstaking color to perfection. New macabre sculptures, a healthy dose of competition, and then some collaboration to create even more magnificent grotesqueries. I posted the before-and-afters to Instagram and Twitter, always tagging Dexter. It was my duty to satisfy a few of the Ws (who, what, when) for my nosiest followers.

We showed off our work in a way that we knew would get us attention, tongue-to-tongue in a strange sexual pose, clay rubbed beneath our eyes like football players; hickies on our necks and eyebrows raised for a spooky effect. We donned facemasks to keep up with pandemic fashions, while at the same time showed off our too-white teeth, even though we smoked and drank like there was no tomorrow.

We browsed antique shoppes, even if they were closed. Dexter knew his way around with a lock pick. Zephyr lived for that kind of rush, though he was respectful enough to never take anything without laying a few dollars on the counter before we left. Our relationship was strengthening. Romance bonded us, but more importantly, we were chained by copulation.

Sex hypnotized the three of us. It snapped, crackled and popped. Random sex is one thing, but when a connection is made between souls, the sexual experience is heightened. It's a rare occurrence for two people to find this, let alone three. We all shared the same animalistic drive, laced with a desire to please the other, while at the same time yearning for all the delectable fluids the human body had to offer. The slimes that leak from your lover's orifice hits you differently. The taste and smell is not repulsive as it would be from some random person, but more aphrodisiacal, almost sinful in knowing you shouldn't be enjoying it that much.

When I first saw Zephyr and Dexter kiss, my heart shattered and my penis swelled. It was one of the most erotic sights I'd ever come across. I knew in that moment things were different. I could no longer trudge through life chewing on other people's rhetoric. This set me apart. This set us apart. These two boys who owned my soul, becoming one through the power of a kiss. Not one moment felt wrong, not one moment was I riddled with rage or jealousy. I was a spectator to my own future.

I listened to the rhythm of my body. The whispering of blood; heightened hormonal chorus; circuitous vessels, lungs pulling in air and the electric snap of my synapses. The body itself is a song, so why not enjoy its melody? Now it was my time to bring my true self to my two lovers.

My face was wetted with their twisted strings of saliva. Zephyr's lips pressed into mine so that I could smell Dexter's tobacco-laced spit, and then Dexter's lips on my own so that I could taste Zephyr's bee venom chapstick. Dexter's hair was flaxen and heartbreakingly soft as it brushed across my face. Zephyr's hair was more robust, the kind you could tug. Then the three of us kissed, spiraling tongues and alcohol infused breath. The energy between us, the smell of their mouths, sent my hormones into overdrive.

Dexter took the lead, having had experience with this sort of thing. We all removed our clothes and headed to the bed. Zephyr was the obvious choice of middleman given his versatility and boyish beauty. Who wouldn't want to lick the skin of a pale god, caress the tense muscles, nibble at the neck? His legs were a meaty wishbone to crack, welcoming me into his hairless heaven.

Zephyr upended himself, now on all fours. I took the helm and Dexter the moony ass. Zephyr licked the head of my dick, spiraling his tongue down the shaft as Dexter kissed every single bead of Zephyr's spine before spitting on his hand and penetrating him. Zephyr moaned heavily, pushing his face into my groin as if overcome with too much pleasure, and then got back to work on me. I leaned over and kissed Dexter, as Zephyr sucked me and

Dexter fucked Zephyr, unknowingly creating an invisible chain that would bond us forever.

It was as fresh and selfish as the orgasm that was coming to existence in both my and Dexter's balls. Once our eyes locked, something was exchanged between us that transcended love. *Don't stop*, Zephyr said. All three bodies ebbed and flowed. I grabbed Zephyr's head as his mouth seemed to get warmer, then Dexter's hand, interlocking our fingers so that I could feel their heartbeats as a perfectly synchronized orgasm exploded out of all three of us.

"You boys are beautiful," Dexter said, his head resting upon my limp hand.

"As are you."

We were bunched upon the king-sized mattress, our bodies covered with a black blanket. Zephyr was sandwiched between Dexter and I, blue straggle of hair splayed across my shoulder, bony body mostly curled into mine, but still somehow leaning against Dexter's. I watched Dexter run his hand through Zephyr's hair, working his fingers down the curved dome of skull that held all the chaotic thoughts that shaped him, then slowly crawl them across my chest to show that he loved us both. I loved them more in this moment, if that were emotionally possible.

"I feel like a bum," Zephyr said. "Need a shower."

Dexter's sharp face was half in the sunlight now, veiled in billions of dust particles. "You smell good as is."

Zephyr yawned, stretched until his hands reached into the bars of light streaming in from the early morning sun and got on his phone. We'd been up the entire night and didn't plan on sleeping anytime soon. I saw many notifications flash across his screen, a slew of text messages from names I didn't recognize. He quickly glanced through them but didn't really pay them any mind. Me on the other hand, I wanted to know why his phone was so busy and mine wasn't.

"Anything good?" I asked.

"Nah."

One of Zephyr's small pale feet was intertwined with Dexter's, and one with my own. Their toenails were painted all sorts of colors, and their cryptic ankle bracelets jangled every time one of them moved or attempted to knot their heavily tattooed legs together. It was the cutest sight I had seen in a long time. I leaned over and kissed Dexter's cheek, sliding my tongue toward his lips. Then I did the same to Zephyr, but he pulled away.

"Feels like something bit me."

"Where?"

"My side."

Zephyr pulled the sheets down. After staring at his perfectly round and hairless ass, I noticed the mark on his right hip. A necrotic crescent that smelled of rot and his pheromones. I shined my phone light on it, saw that the blackness was slowly fanning out as if that small part of his body was already dead, leaking and creeping and spreading.

"What is that?"

"A little rough play," Dexter said passively.

"You bit him?"

Dexter sucked his teeth and got to his feet. "I don't remember. It was all in the moment. You guys hungry?"

"No."

Zephyr and I said that in unison. We never ate this early in the morning, mostly for fear of gaining weight. I do not know a single gay man in New York City that doesn't skip a meal or two every now and again to keep control of their physique, since being overweight is a one-way trip to being ignored sexually. Zephyr laid back down and went to his phone, his face doing all the normal motions of boredom and elation, but quickly shifted to shock and awe.

Dexter headed into the kitchen and made a bunch of noise by the refrigerator. When he came back, he had string cheese in his hand and a bottle of cheap beer. I wondered how long we could last here without money. Dexter and Zephyr worked in the restaurant industry before the pandemic, so the shutdowns had put them out of work. I lived off the sales I made on Instagram, but those had pretty much stopped.

"You don't need to worry about money," Dexter said. "I can see it on your face."

I shrugged. "We need money to survive, to buy art supplies . . . drugs. What about good old-fashioned food?"

"If you took my offer, you'd never have to worry about any of those archaic forms of exchange again."

"What exactly is your offer?"

Dexter looked us both in the face sternly. "It's all below our feet."

That made my body tense. I waited for Zephyr to respond.

"Let's do it." Zephyr wobbled on two legs to grab his pants. "I'm bored of this pandemic."

We all got dressed in the colors of neon and darkness. It felt like a prelude of things to come. I sported an Avenged Sevenfold crop top and black jeans shorts I cut from pants. The walk to Hester Street was insanely quiet. Thoroughfares completely devoid of life other than the sight of steel and brick; pathetic poetry of graffiti artists; the reek of hand sanitizer and anxiety, 2020's official scent. Dilapidated tenements gave way to blighted avenues; people stared aimlessly out of their windows, locked inside their walk-up prisons. The Manhattan Bridge looked ugly off to the south, and the Williamsburg Bridge haunted our eastern view. The edifices that surrounded them were painted with Chinese characters and the ghosts of Italian summers.

Dexter wore a facemask of gilt and gray, like something Stevie Nicks would drape across her shoulders. Mine and Zephyr's were fraught with esoteric symbols of the tarot, and sat on our faces more like a bandana. We looked like a trio of witches commanding every avenue in our black getups, wingtip boots and Ray Bans to cover the rest of our mysterious visages. We stampeded over to Hester Street, ready to take on the day.

We approached the spot. Dexter winked; Zephyr took a final drag of his cigarette. The hole hadn't changed since the last time I saw it, but since it snowed the night before it was now a big black mouth ringed in white lipstick. Dexter was halfway down before I made him stop. Zephyr's one green eye judged me. My heartbeat threatened to close off my throat. If only I could have sewed my lips shut, despite my fear of secrets, despite the dread that filled my chest and the ecstasy swirling in my brain . . . as the sound came drizzling out of my mouth. Word vomit.

"Fuck it, I love you."

15

Can a man be a demon? Or a demon a man?
 —you can't stop a feeling once you feel—
 But why do we punish ourselves for it?

Dorian had written these words down in a journal. Poetry wasn't his forte, but he liked what he was reading, even if he wasn't the type of person who analyzed thoughts through prose; drawing took care of that for him. But sometimes he felt the need to jot things down and see where his fingers would take him. He looked at the words again, wondering where the hell they even came from.

In typical Dorian Wilde fashion, the words were surrounded by sketches—a framework—of No. 2 graphite, so said the way it smeared when he rubbed his thumb across it. His forte was orifices and grotesque caricatures that could send a viewer into hell via pencil and sketch pad. Not since Goya, Dali and Bacon had such profound, long-term effects on viewers been noted. Psychosexual shadows bordered the edges; vertiginous pathways spiraled through the center. A moldy penis spit semen across half the page; thorny lips wrapped about the glans and threaded the skin down to mucus.

Dorian studied the tawdry lines and decadent shading, using all the powers of his mind to bring the sights and smells to life. Manifesting was key to his artistic survival, much like Dexter. For one inglorious moment, a thorn pricked his finger and gooey bleach stung his nose. There was no real reason or rhyme as to why he'd drawn that. Best to not question the art when you can't even recall why you created it.

Life had become a blur ever since meeting Sebastian. The boy tore a hole into his soul. The love he felt was now forcing Dorian to dig into his consciousness and face all the negatives he'd been avoiding—loneliness, abandonment, the death of his lover—but it was much more of a process than expected. It seemed creativity always came rushing back in during times of emotional crisis. That's what happened last year when he first laid eyes on Sebastian. The boy was in danger, and dreams of this boy came to Dorian. Now Zephyr and Atticus needed the help.

"What the fuck is that?"

Sebastian and Delilah were hovering over Dorian. It was hard to tell at first as no shadows were cast, even as their corporeal bodies blocked the neon-soaked atmosphere of the nameless dive bar, one that was so dark not even streetlight made it through the dusted windows. With COVID-19 closures more volatile than ever, some businesses chose to keep their doors open illegally. It was like prohibition all over again, but with less secrecy and more alcohol. The reward of some petty cash was worth the risk of being shut down for good. Testament to the need for revenue.

"Haven't figured it out yet," Dorian said, sipping his beer slowly.

"Another Dorian puzzle, yippee."

"This is just how it is."

"Right."

He could tell Delilah's jaw was clenched. She was probably grimacing and grinding her teeth, maybe smearing lipstick on purpose. He didn't need to turn around to find out. When you spend enough time with someone, you unveil their ticks, pet peeves and obsessions rather quickly. But this bonded them more than the average friend group. They all had a sixth sense in terms of what the other was thinking and what they'd want to eventually do. So it was quite alright to just meander, eyes tired and minds chaotically awake, powered by an invisible fuel that was undeniably necessary.

"Can we sit?" Sebastian had his hand on Dorian's shoulder, fingers caressing the collar bone.

"Oh, shit. Please do."

Dorian grabbed the papers and pencils and paperback books, shoved them into his backpack. Sebastian sat across from him, tapping the lip of the cheap table nervously and playing footsie with Dorian. Delilah plopped next to him with a beer in hand and a half-smoked cigarette in the other. They settled into the mood, taking in the music, some sort of indie industrial funk, and then got back to overthinking and overanalyzing.

"He's been messaging me," Delilah said.

"Cat's not surprisingly out of the bag. What did he say?"

"Empty threats, how much he loathes me."

"So that means Atticus and Zephyr know too."

"Bingo."

Delilah was back on her phone, black fingernails clacking against the screen madly. The way she hyper-focused, Dorian felt like he could slap her square in the jaw and she'd not even flinch. Seeing this made him feel a lot better that he stuck to his guns and kept his social media usage to a bare minimum.

"Sounds corny when you say that, Dorian."

"Did they reach out to you?" Sebastian sucked on his vape, blew out a berry smelling cloud.

"Of course not." Delilah was chipping away at a new nail so that her words came out like a mumble. "Those boys are too horny to care."

"That's how new love goes." Dorian looked right at Sebastian. "Don't you agree?"

"With what?" Sebastian's face flushed so red he had to turn it away. "How people never listen when others try to help? How they want to make up their own minds?"

Delilah slapped her leg. "That's why we're trying to get involved."

"Sometimes it's better when people learn by making their own mistakes."

"Not when it can get them killed."

"And where's your proof of all this?"

"Alex and Rez can enlighten you. Text them to come."

The room grew silent. Then: "Delilah, you can't just insert yourself into people's lives. I know you want to save the world, all its fauna and flora, but you can't pressure yourself with such a task. That's way too much stress."

"If I don't step in, who will?" Delilah's anger toppled the tension. "You all just sit back and put your feet up, not giving a fuck about things you can possibly change."

"Right, but it's that exact control that I've given up. I'm in my thirties now."

"As am I."

"We all are," Sebastian said. "Let's not argue like children."

"Look, Delilah, we've been through a lot . . . you and I. You're my friend, but more importantly a brilliant musician. I look up to you. But my life is just too chaotic to get involved in other people's problems."

"Trust, their problems are *your* problems."

They were all in this nightmare together. Stick your nose where it doesn't belong, you get what you get. After a few more minutes of the argument going nowhere, Delilah's phone buzzed, taking her attention span with it. She smirked, wrinkled her brow, then turned away. Dorian eyed Sebastian; their calves touched beneath the table, and it made Dorian insanely horny. He knew how Sebastian's hairless legs smelled and tasted, knew how the tattoos popped on that moonlight skin.

It pained him that Sebastian was closed off to love. What made it worse was that he knew all the right things to say when Dorian needed to hear them, but the second Dorian expressed romantic interest, Sebastian would take it all back. Sure, he'd hook up, down for a cuddle session as well—but to commit was asking a lot. Still, Sebastian was worth fighting for; Dorian knew firsthand about the troubles with Adrian, how psychotic and possessive he became, so all of this caution made sense.

Being that Dorian didn't want to open any wounds Sebastian wasn't ready to face, he was simply stuck with these thoughts. Stuck in this cumbersome mission of breaking people up he barely knew, all because Delilah said so. Friend loyalty might have been Dorian's greatest characteristic, but it was also his greatest weakness. He consulted his journal again; Delilah remained hypnotized by her phone and Sebastian played with a tube of black lipstick

"Twitter and Instagram are blowing up," Delilah said.

"Shocker." Sebastian lifted his beer, then put it to his lips. "Damn, tastes good."

"Yeah, tastes even better knowing we shouldn't be out socializing," Dorian said.

"A vaccine is coming, so stop worrying."

"The world is fucked, with or without the pandemic."

"But it's up to us to slow it down."

"Always up to the little people, never our so-called leaders."

"Guys!" Delilah shot to her feet. "This isn't a drill."

She put her phone in the middle of the table. There was a very intense Twitter thread entitled *Two Twisted Minutes*, in reference to Delilah's dangerous dance with the wrong thing, a dance with the devil indeed. The feed was overloaded with comments and questions and hashtags. It was retweeted and quoted and liked thousands of times. Everyone gagged, sucked their teeth. Hate flowed; curiosity sparkled. The audience didn't question what they saw, rather they craved more. Word was spreading fast, and now people were opening their eyes to the spectacle that was Dexter.

"Got your wish," Delilah.

"Shh. Look at this."

Delilah pulled up the comments from Electric Orchid's live feed. There was no order to them. An astronomical amount of skepticism, envy and apathy polluted the feed. *#NotThis* and *#DelilahIsAtItAgain* were the most popular hashtags. Dorian searched for the desired names, as did Delilah, but they weren't there. Atticus, Zephyr, and especially Dexter, may not have even seen the video when it went live.

"He did this," Delilah said. "I can feel it."

"You a Jedi now?"

"Sith, thank you very much."

Then a new number appeared on Delilah's phone, the area code typical of Queens and Brooklyn. *I'm coming for you, bitch.* Reading that, Dorian could hear it in Freddy Krueger's voice. Delilah smacked the phone off the table and made an angry sound. Dorian picked it up and saw a few other messages. *It's Your Funeral, bitch. I bet you didn't think I'd find out.* Dorian turned the phone off, didn't want to read any further.

"Pissed him off good."

"That's what I wanted."

"What's the plan now?"

"The fuck do you think? We kill him."

"Kill?"

"I'm not going to jail for some nerd."

"He ain't what you think he is. Nobody's going to miss a ghost."

"I don't care."

"He murdered his mother."

"You don't know that for sure."

Then a new presence entered the room. Twin shadows—it seemed they always appeared as shadows—swooping in like bats from a night sky. Dorian felt nightwind sluice over his body, saw it ensconce the table, veil Delilah's bright eyes and Sebastian's dark lips. Rez and Alex sat next to Delilah, out of breath with cigarettes between their lips, and in their hands were cell phones inundated with messages. The cat was out of the bag now, and there was no stopping the gossip war on social media.

"Back, back, back again!" Sebastian said.

"We needed some air." Rez had a journal in his hand, pen ink drizzled across his thumb. "I've been writing now that my mind is less clouded."

"That's usually how it works." Dorian winked. "We can't create unless we're comfortable."

Alex's hand went into his pockets, sinking so deep it gave the illusion he went up to the elbow. *Jnco jeans?* Dorian whispered. Alex didn't reply, though he mouthed the words *Yellow Rat Bastard*, searching so hard Dorian could hear things jangling, until he brought up a vial of ketamine, a small gold shovel, a bag of grass and some pressed pills. Dorian recognized the drugs—molly, ketamine, salvia—and asked for some. *Shut off my brain, please!*

"K makes me paranoid lately. Feels like everybody is after me." Alex raised his thin eyebrows. "I'll do a bump anyway."

"Me too," Rez said.

Alex snorted the K off the shovel, then leaned his head back, resting it on Rez's shoulder. Dorian and a reluctant Sebastian did the same. *No repeats*, Delilah said, implying the insanity they suffered the other day. *Much to be done*, as she got to her feet and did a bump herself. The collected state of mind was now dissociated, pulling all of them to the calmest waters before the storm.

"Sometimes, if I close my eyes . . . he's right there with me," Alex said. "I can see his face. The obscure angles of it, his eyes melting me, stealing my lifeforce. At least that's how I imagine he did it."

"Stole your lifeforce? Like a vampire?"

"Not exactly."

"Maenad?"

"No."

"Then what?"

"It's literally just looking at someone you love . . . and the more you love them the more they take."

"That was the worst poetry I ever heard," Dorian said.

"Well, it wasn't poetry. And I don't fucking care if you get it." Alex turned his back to them.

"This isn't a joke." Rez was getting loud. "Dexter isn't exactly human."

"Then what is he?" Dorian was overtly curious now.

"Ask the Hydra."

"The fuck does that mean?" Sebastian turned his head so fast the manbun came undone. "Ask me what?" hair in his mouth, blotting out his eyes.

"Not *you*," Rez said. "*Her.*"

"I don't know what you mean!"

"It responded to—"

"Look," Delilah interrupted. "This isn't about semantics. Just tell the fucking story. They deserve to know. They've been kind enough to help us this long."

"Alright," Alex said. "Get the popcorn ready, because you won't believe this even if you try."

The sky closed overhead like a light switch. Zephyr found himself being pulled into a downward spiral of poetic nonsense and truths. Caught up in the riddles of life, chance and circumstance. How lucky we are to be here, but how much of a burden it is to be put through all these cosmic tests. We drift alongside phantom moments and streams of hopelessness. Time is precious. Life is fragile. Choice is the glue that keeps it all together.

"Welcome back."

Ahead, Atticus and Dexter were black and white dots that spoke in secret sculpting code and social media runes. Any normal person would be ridden with jealousy and envy seeing how well they clicked, but Zephyr could no longer find those feelings. That part of him was dead, buried six feet beneath an enlightening new feeling: love-lust. It took over his body, trickled like a living thing across his skin, burning all the way to the tip of his dick.

The only other time he felt this was when he first met Atticus. The no-sleep-mind-fuck-no-eat-no-thinking about anything else other than how this one person took over his mind. Falling in love is absolute surrender. The chemicals our bodies secrete during this process dictate every thought and action, even if we later regret them. We can't control it. Feels too good to stop.

"Looks different."

"That's right." Dexter winked and met Zephyr's gaze. "We're in this together."

Something suddenly appeared in front of Zephyr's face. Its edifice was decrepit, and its windows were covered in prison bars. It was a literal building, and from what Zephyr could see it was not a welcoming one; not the kind of thing you expect to see below ground, but it was real, so said the way it felt when Zephyr put his hand on it. Once he could clearly see, a black skyline materialized in the distance. It filled his sight with spires, spikes and odd surfaces that can be seen in any big city when viewed from far away.

Dexter led them through a door that had appeared off to the side. Nothing felt right, nothing seemed right. He didn't know his way around or even why he was here, and now he was second guessing himself because the only person who knew the way was Dexter, who was barely trustworthy. It suddenly hit Zephyr: Perhaps they were in Dexter's dark head rather than a city beneath the city. Perhaps these illusions were his bidding.

Judging by Atticus' giddy movements, he either didn't care or he was too possessed to find any thought of his own. Dexter handed them both a weird looking joint, which smelled of potpourri and spicy green. After, he swiveled them through chamber after empty chamber, creaky door after creaky door. Above, night's darkness somehow leaked down the walls to let them know that they were still part of the world above. Zephyr stopped to light his joint, but the smoke cauterized his throat and crashed into his lungs.

"I still don't know what's going on."

"Watch your step."

Zephyr's face almost slammed into a glass cabinet, but a wink of metal was the warning sign that he needed to stop. Upon closer inspection, he saw sculpting tools and monstrous pieces half undone, paint brushes and even a microphone vector. But Dexter didn't let him stick around for long, grabbed his hand and pulled him into a room filled with gothic architecture and fixtures that made it feel like 1500s Romania. Zephyr went to sit on a stone bench, but quickly realized that it was a tiny sarcophagus. He thought about the bones he saw at the cemetery and the tomb door closing, suddenly claustrophobic.

"Look familiar?" Dexter winked.

"That's not funny," Zephyr snapped.

Led by the sounds of brass knockers and shattered glass, Dexter toured them through several more carnival sights. The way Zephyr's ears popped, the way his chest got heavier, it felt like they were winding down an endless labyrinth. The following room was an architectural nightmare. Zephyr saw cornucopias scratched into the walls, as well as swarms of stars and crescent moons awash with candlelight. Graffiti caught his eye in graceless spirals, and they glowed so that any passerby could read the pain of the year 2020 and its pernicious pandemic. *LeT mE BrEaThe* and *tRumP is a HoRe* were the only words Zephyr could make out. That said it all.

Ahead, small pillars of flame spread their incandescence unto the ceiling. There were glyphs and carvings Zephyr knew nothing about. But what he did notice was many sets of teeth jutting out of the stone, as if they could bite if anyone who rubbed against them. Zephyr touched one of the skulls, the smooth round dome, the sharp cheeks. When he put his hand near the jaw, it clenched shut.

"This some kind of trick?"

Dexter didn't answer, but Zephyr started hearing music, which caught his attention. A delectable, intimate melody, as if it was playing from his own headphones. He knew the song, knew the band. The voice forced the listener in its direction, a voice made of stardust and dark matter. It was Electric Orchid's *My Personal Hell* and Delilah's vocals felt crisper, as if it was a rerecording.

"Who would play that here?" Dexter shook his head.

"Electric Orchid," Atticus said.

"But why?"

"Maybe they followed us."

"Impossible. Delilah doesn't know her ass from her elbow."

"But your exes do."

Dexter's face crinkled. "Perhaps you're right."

He twirled a finger through his shaggy white hair, then proceeded to drag Atticus ahead until their silhouettes blended into one. Upon their disappearance, Zephyr was left with his thoughts and a tremendous amount of fear. He started to understand that the dark was alive, and that there were unexplainable things living within it. Life always finds a way, even if science lacks an answer.

"What if she's trying to tell you something?"

"If she wants to tell me anything, she can tell me herself."

"She's coming," Zephyr said. "There's nothing you can do about it."

"Good. When she does, I'll end the drama."

Zephyr used his phone light in the next room, saw an intriguing display of crooked easels, crooked spoons, shredded papers; files, books and broken instruments. There were macabre portraits and laptops blinking uncontrollably. This was a world of chaos and creation that he knew well, but a world that was now simply different.

Then Zephyr heard something crawl behind him. Fresh earth wafted into his nose, sickly and sweet. It made his mind reel. His head was filling with images like a helium balloon. He didn't want to unveil the images, didn't want to smell these smells, but it was happening so fast there was no way he could have stopped it.

He turned to see a red-white swirl of eyes, followed the outline of something pale and gnarled. The thing was of a non-determinant gender. Its body was thin as sidewalk chalk, and its head was covered in matted black hair. If he didn't know any better, he'd say he was standing before the skeleton of Dexter's mother. *I killed her*, he heard over and over in his head. Zephyr simply froze, as did the thing in front of him, which was when he saw that the hair had been torn from the root, and little red globules now showcased the skull.

"Is that how you did it?" Zephyr said the words before he could cover his mouth.

"Zephyr!" Atticus yelled. "What're you talking about?"

"He's talking about my mother," Dexter said.

"I told you to stop bringing that up."

One door shut and another opened. The spiral wound deeper. Punky masonry besieged Zephyr's peripheral vision, followed by loose floorboards that threatened to snap at any given moment. Zephyr had to do a double take to make sure he wasn't swinging on some loathsome bridge, pendulum to infinite darkness. The air became thick with ozone and sulfur, the stuff of star clusters and imploded planets. This room was overtaken by strange idols that had the signature molds, carvings and color schemes of *The Eventual Devil*.

"Do you like it, Zephyr?"

"Yes."

"Pick one up."

Zephyr found a small gremlin fashioned out of scrap metal. Every careful detail jutted in ways he was not used to seeing. Reflective eyes and barbed wire teeth; malicious little lips. The thing barely had any weight to it, which Zephyr found disturbing. But nothing could have prepared him when it began moving in his hand. Its claws scraped him and its pointed ears began to wilt like a dog does when it's angry. When he let it go, Zephyr didn't even hear the gremlin hit the concrete, just saw it bolt into the darkness.

Then the ground shifted into mud, sucking at Zephyr's Doc Martens with an awful noise. He pointed the light of his phone down to his feet, but it was like trying to investigate a black hole. To his left, a drawing caught his eye. Two goth boys intertwined in a sexual embrace, both seemingly in love . . . or questioning the power of it. Above them, something watched. After a minute of observing, the drawing *moved*, and Zephyr saw it reshape itself into bat wings, goat horns and talons.

"Don't look directly at it."

"Isn't that the point?"

"You're not ready to accept it."

"I'll take a video then."

"You won't see what you want."

Dexter made Zephyr hold a door that left his hand full of splinters. There was a drop upon entering the room, and Zephyr did a pratfall, hitting his head. For a full minute his consciousness danced between reality and dream. The tryst of melatonin and serotonin was a wonderful feeling, like swimming through storm clouds, until warm hands slapped his face. As the fuzziness crawled away from his senses, he felt a few things land on his tongue.

"Swallow those," Atticus whispered.

Zephyr knew the capsules were filled with GHB and the Baby Yoda was ecstasy. It only took about fifteen minutes for the G to kick in, which slowed down Zephyr's breath but gave him a high dose of energy. There came the usual flood of euphoria, giddiness, and sharp concentration. This was the kind of drug you read books on or made art with. But all of that was soon swallowed by anxiety.

"You want?" Atticus asked Zephyr.

"I don't touch molly."

"It's a Tesla," Atticus said.

"Don't matter," Dexter growled.

Zephyr thought it was weird that Dexter was so sensitive when it came to taking euphoric drugs. But he let it go. They slipped into another room where Zephyr's ears popped again, but he was delighted to finally see some people. Every race, gender, and sexual orientation. Below the chin they were donned in pleather, metal and clashes of fabric. Above, they were like furious paintings done by a manic artist.

It was like looking at a technicolor scrimshaw of inner tortures worn on skin, further displayed in wild hairstyles. But the thing was that they didn't move or make a sound. It was as if Zephyr was staring at a huge painting, the kind that changed the closer or further one stood from it. A few minutes later, Zephyr noticed the funniest thing. The more he studied them, the more they refused to make eye contact. When Dexter started tugging him, it only made Zephyr want to inspect them closer, even as Atticus was already on his way into the next room.

Zephyr approached slowly. The closer he came, the more things started to change. First it was their skin, sickly and jaundiced in color. Then it was their hair, which somehow started to appear synthetic. He smelled plastic. As he touched one of them on the shoulder, his hand was met with a weird cool feeling, like grabbing a doll. The next thing he knew, that person's head had rolled off their shoulders.

"They're mannequins."

"I want to keep going," Dexter said.

"I thought you said other people lived down here with you?"

Atticus said nothing and Dexter dismissed the question. For a second Zephyr thought that someone would speak up, but the Baby Yoda had started to peak. It was a present high, and as all the drugs unleashed through his bloodstream, all five senses seemed to radiate outside of his body, which made them exponentially more sensitive. Zephyr topped it off with a bump of Ketamine, which sent him flying into the void.

It seemed that his mind no longer belonged to him. It was now part of this place, as if something opened inside of him; he could suddenly see it all clearly. This place might not even exist, and the things he was seeing were just a bad dream. Zephyr leaned his hand on the wall next to him, and it pushed through without using any weight. On the other side was just another pathway leading into infinity, or perhaps an end.

Electric Orchid's music proceeded to get louder. Dexter did not seem thrilled, but Atticus was enjoying it. He was bobbing his head while looking at some pieces that Dexter had left unfinished with a sordid curiosity. His white hair fell lightly across his eyes, and the way his head tilted reminded Zephyr of a Halloween movie. Atticus was blank-faced and clearly green with envy. Maybe Dexter wanted him that way.

Footsteps now, but so light it sounded more like a broom sweeping across bricks. Dexter was far ahead of Zephyr, could only be seen by the white ink blot of his hair. Atticus was way off to the left and barely moving. So Zephyr put his hands in front of his face, and once again it was as if they were part of the darkness, reaching so far in that he actually *felt* something.

Zephyr pulled it toward him.

The thing was no taller than he, and it once might have been genetically male, but there was no real way of telling as its skin was more like parchment paper rather than a living organ. The face was chaotic, and there was a bright smear of vermilion across its lips. Cheekbones so prominent they made the bags beneath its dead eyes big enough to consume the face. All of this was hidden beneath flaxen hair that reached down to the small of its ridged back, and when Zephyr tried to look between their legs, all he saw was a bony plane.

"Hey!" Dexter turned.

"What is that?" Atticus asked.

The phone in its hand was small, barely bright enough for them all to see, and the screen was cracked in a pattern that made images appear like a kaleidoscope. When Dexter took the phone from its grip, Zephyr saw its skin begin to slip free from the body that housed it, stripping away layer by layer. When it was reduced to bone, Zephyr was once again besieged by flashbacks of the cemetery.

"What's on the phone?" Atticus reached for Dexter's hand.

"I'm trying to find out."

The video played, though it was hard to discern due to the cracked screen. Dorian and Sebastian came into view first, followed by Rez, Delilah and Alex. They were arguing; there were moments of dark and light, moments of complete confusion. There was a tiny sculpture crawling around like a spider, climbing up the wall. But something else followed it, something sinister, fierce, but utterly beautiful in its rage. Zephyr didn't quite know what he was seeing until the video was done, realizing that the tiny thing was Dexter's sculpture.

"I didn't see this part," Dexter said.

"They all look crazy, if you ask me."

"Crazy for recording it." Atticus sucked his teeth.

Dexter cut in. "You think I'm *famous* now?"

"Don't really know."

"What was that other thing?"

Nobody talked until Zephyr said, "The *Hydra*."

"The *what*?"

A few minutes later they left the little black room and headed to Dexter's studio. At the entrance there was a wrought iron torch sconce, and between the crown a dull flame. It smelled of lamp oil and gas, and the noxious odor of burning. Zephyr breathed through his mouth to stop himself from falling over. But the heat of the flame was comforting, its soothing light fanning about his hands, warming his face. *Burial vault*, Zephyr thought. *I'm going to be buried alive down here.*

Horrible sceneries were mounted to the wall, execrable colors that would make the fictitious Pickman do a double take. Zephyr had never seen acrylic so wet yet so dry; never seen a jaw gape until the lips tore into jellied strips of flesh. These were the paintings of Dorian Wilde, and Zephyr had no idea how they got down here.

"Who did this?" Dexter was visibly angry now.

"I told you, she's coming," Zephyr said.

"You mean she's already down here?" Atticus was biting his nails.

"That *bitch* wants to *humiliate* me!"

The music got louder, voice like liquid gold dripping into everyone's ear.

"I hate her." Dexter grabbed a torch and put it close to his angry grimace. "I'll show them all."

The color immediately drained out of Dexter's face, reshaping itself. Vampire cheekbones, round chin and pale skin grimacing for the worst; transmogrified into something bat-like, sharp ears and little black teeth. Zephyr didn't know if it was the drugs going haywire in his brain or his own paranoia taking over as Dexter sizzled away, which made him scream. Atticus put out his hand as if he wanted to be part of the transformation. *Dexter is not a real person.* Delilah's voice was in his head again. *You'll see him soon enough.*

The tarantula shadow grew beneath the torch light

. . . fangs as long as talons latched onto Atticus' hand

—as the darkness fell, blowing the world out in a storm of confetti and bone.

16

Summer 2017, the year Alex turned thirty. A year of change. The same year Saturn comes back around to show you the next phase of your life. Through this introspection, Alex realized he'd been coasting through life without giving any thought that one day it must end. The distractions of music, boys, drugs and art had clouded him. Suddenly, it was all so different. The pressure of time, money and circumstance filled him with dread. Mortality and decadence collided.

The jig was up. He finally believed in God, and its name was Death.

Rez was thirty-one at the time. Having experienced the return of Saturn the year before, he too was feeling the inequity of his soul and heart, wondering which one outweighed the other, and which of the two was the better companion. Was there more out there? Had he settled too early in life? Why was vibrancy suddenly replaced by routine?

He and Alex had gotten together in 2009, and for the millennial generation, that was a *lifetime*. The fact that they had remained monogamous for years was unheard of in the gay community. And most people in their age group didn't know love for more than a few months at a time, let alone a decade, given that the social dynamic was dominated by "no commitment" culture.

Strange it had become to be so close to your partner—closer than any other person in the world—while they both slowly accepted that change was in order. But what kind?

Tonight, as Saturn glistened, feelings were acknowledged. Questions about love, questions about identity and ego. For the first time, it felt as if they'd slammed into a romantic brick wall. Something shifted; established emotions were traded for the shaky essence of temptation. Such is the ride of life. We crave change. But we don't know how to accept it guilt-free.

Electric Orchid had just finished a set at the Pyramid Club, one of New York City's last temples for goths, queers, artists and weirdos. Neon perched itself in every corner of the small bar; the taps glowed as much as the nail polish and lipstick of the band. As usual, the 4 a.m. crowd was sparse, strung out on party favors and sucking down shadow-flavored drinks.

Alex wasn't himself throughout the set; he'd forgotten some parts to staple songs, and in a place this size, the intimacy made his mistakes stand out. The crowd felt it. He knew they were watching him, judging; perhaps they could see the warring emotions on his face? Luckily, Delilah didn't let that get in the way. She made up for his errors by tearing apart the venue with her voice.

By the time they reached their closing number, Delilah was visibly upset, while the rest of the band pretended that Alex wasn't off at all—better to leave it unsaid or a huge fight would erupt. When Delilah hit the last note, she rushed off stage, didn't even look at Alex, which was not like her at all. As best friends and primary songwriters for the band, they started and ended their sets together. But tonight, she was just gone, and the rest of the band packed their stuff and slid out the back door, suffusing into the night like mercury spilled from a test tube.

Rez was at the opposite end of the bar drinking a very frothy stout. One of the wonky black lights from the stage was still on, and it dripped over Rez's body with sinister brightness. From the Doc Martens on his feet to the black denim vest covered in patches and pins, he was a ghostly presence at this angle. But then Alex caught sight of a shape behind Rez, the very reason why his back was turned to the stage. Alex craned his neck, saw nifty glasses, curly black hair and a skin tone that seemed too pale to be human.

The immediate feeling that welled up inside of Alex was curiosity. For some reason, he couldn't find any jealousy. Perhaps the trust was that good. Perhaps after fucking up on stage he was dead enough enough inside to not care. Then came something else, fully unexpected. This new boy's presence was strong. His energy drew Alex in, and with it came the idea of a fresh start, something fun to look forward to, which was just the kind of distraction he needed.

Talking to other boys was common in their scene, kissing them was as well. It was always Rez's doing since Alex had an incurable habit of never telling Rez no. And right now, judging by the intensity of their conversation, Alex knew this boy was a keeper Most boys come and go; Alex had learned that through first-hand experience. Meeting someone special was rare, and one doesn't just let that slide by.

Alex heard playful chuckling—an offshoot of flirting—and caught Rez's hands stroking the boy's arm. Rez's body language was tense, but comfortable. A sure sign he was into this boy. While that should have rung an alarm within Alex, it strangely became a form of comfort. Mostly because Alex had yet to admit to himself that he was interested in exploring another. But how do you come out to your partner of so many years and explain that without hurting them? Perhaps it was best left to chance. And right now, it seemed chance had dropped onto his lap.

Alex telepathically called out to Rez. *Turn around. See me.* Rez was somewhat of a sensitive and could feel things others could not. But of course, there was no way Rez was diverting his attention from this boy. Alex knew he'd be doing the same if he was in Rez's position. And that's when it hit Alex. He was not jealous or even envious that Rez was into this new boy—but he was certainly worried how much this boy was *into* Rez. The alchemy between them was a queer spectacle. It made Alex realize that it had been so long since he'd felt those bubbling, beaming, possessive feelings of being newly into someone.

Now that was about to end.

Whitesnake's "Is This Love?" started playing at a 4 a.m. decibel, low and threatening. Apropos for the moment, the uncanny torture. It was the kind of song that encased itself around a person when they are caught up in their feelings. Alex fell prey to the yearning lyrics and sexy vocal melodies. And so, with all the power he had left in his legs, he brought his body out of the dark and barged into the small pool of black light. He approached Rez on the left, kept his hand steady on the bar top, but stopped short when he saw a small white hand squirrel through Rez's black hair, pulling him in for a kiss. Eyes the color of a heliotrope flower locked onto his own.

"Am I interrupting something?" Alex said.

Rez broke the kiss, turned around in haste. "Alex! This is—" as he turned around to the boy to get his name.

"Dexter," the sibilant voice said.

"This is Alex, my boyfriend." Rez crossed his arms, tattoos alive with goosebumps.

"Sorry about that," Dexter said. "He's too cute to resist."

"It's ok."

"You *are* cute too, though."

Dexter moved toward Alex, put out his hand to shake it. Strange how a first moment of touch can create havoc in one's head. His grip was confident, but not overly so. Its softness spoke of a warmth that Alex never knew he needed, despite the calluses on his phalanges. He also noticed that the boy's nails were beat up, but that he'd painted them with wild colors. It was the result of someone who certainly used their hands for a living. An artist of some sort, that's the only type of person who would walk through these doors.

"I see you staring at my nails."

"You work with your hands?" Alex took a closer look.

"Sculptures."

"Piqued my interest," Rez said. "And he's into horror."

"Guilty," Dexter winked.

The next forty-five minutes consisted of the usual unfurling of information, including mutual interests in music, books, dive bars and how art imitates life but how life can't possibly imitate art, no matter what Oscar Wilde said. They chain smoked until their throats felt raw, knowing very well that once they stepped outside these walls there was a good chance they'd be separating, so they found ways to continue to conversation even when there was nothing left to talk about, buy another round when the bar already made last call, anything to just to keep the new electric feeling alive.

"Sculpting is more than reshaping clay," Dexter said. "It's a dream personified. Be it my own or someone else's."

"Just like how music conveys emotion, be it my own or someone else's." Alex's interest was on fire.

"Much like how story writing encompasses the real world around us, our dreams and nightmares, but fictionalizes it for the sake of adventure."

"*Adventure* is the word I was looking for," Dexter said. "Wanna go on one?"

"At this hour?" Alex felt embarrassed when Dexter looked at him like he was a wimp.

"I got a bag of K and a level of boredom that's not going to let me sleep. Plus, Avenue A is lonely and needs some visitors."

Dexter's eyes were truly delightful, they looked like candy stones. But there was something deep inside of them, beyond the fascinating color, beyond the allure of the darkness the ensconced them. This boy was like a grab bag, reach your hand inside and you don't know what you're going to get. Trouble in Shangri-La. Dexter pulled out an iSnuff bullet, put the tip in his nose and snorted. Alex and Rez did the same, unknowing of the size of bump that they'd just put into their bodies, but the drippy burn at the back of their throats told them it was enough to get them going on any adventure.

They sailed into the predawn streets like three little boats filing down a black river. The East Village was silent at this hour. To the east, the sky was beginning to turn just the faintest tinge of blood orange, but in the west, it was still a sky daubed in darkness. Dexter led them almost too fast, bat out of hell swooping and drooping, maneuvering these streets like they had been built only for him.

"Where you taking us?"

"Don't know yet."

The K warped Alex's brain almost instantly. Sound and sight were horrifically slowed; balance was not too far behind. He reached his hand out for Rez, who had already reached his hand out for Dexter, forming a human chain of tattooed flesh leading one another on a road to nowhere. Somehow they got below ground, noted all the graffiti and cigarette butts; smell of piss and garbage terribly sweet. The train hurtled itself into the decrepit station and swallowed them all whole.

"Adventure, right?" Dexter said.

There was no telling if they were headed south or north, but judging by the deteriorated quality of the passing stations, Alex figured they were headed south. Train stations were usually the most unkempt downtown. And then he fell asleep. Dreams swished in his subconscious like filigree, dark dreams, light dreams; nothing made sense. He could still hear the train, metal on metal frustration, people arguing, homeless begging. Then the world stopped. Alex opened his eyes.

He was nowhere he recognized. The first thing he noticed was the smell. Deep, wet, dark as it can get. The smell of the underground, of mud, sewage and sulfur. Dexter's angular bones were above Alex's head, but somehow under Rez's, and his pointed face was illuminated in soft candlelight. Alex caught the boy's shadow, not hominid in shape, but closer to arachnid in the way pincers sprouted and multitudinous legs danced along the rocky walls. What he could have excused for the sinister K hole was immediately negated as the first shiver trickled down the beads of his spine.

Stuff was laid out all over the place in this horrible excuse for a studio, or rusted warehouse, or underground lair. It reminded Alex of the days when his life was centered around chaos and music, psychoactive substances and trying to make it in a rock n' roll band. But now that life was a decade behind him. An ash of memory. He'd grown into a different Alex, one that was an amalgamation of all the life-changing experiences he'd been through. Older, but wiser.

Dexter talked about his art, the paths he chose to create it. His eloquence, intelligence and inspiring way of speaking was hypnotizing. He took them on a tour of the place, starting with the small glass cabinet where he stored taxidermy that seemed to stare back at you with wet and glowing eyes. There were random bones, human carpals, femurs and tibias, and whole skeletons of rodents. Clay bowls were filled with feathers, ash and incense of white sage and musk; all of this was flanked by flakes of gold, black and snake scales.

The wall closest to Alex was so musty that there were little glistening balls of condensation perched on the shelves. He saw all sorts of macabre toys, gemstones and tarot decks. Rez was at the other wall looking at some very small busts and sculptures. There was a universal theme of glittery black and calming gray colors. All of them were intricately detailed, down to the paint on their eyes, talons, and sharp wings.

Dexter placed a macabre little statue in Rez's hand. From Alex's vantage point, he saw multiple arms do a menacing dance; skeleton teeth chattered irrationally, followed by a snake-like tongue that extended all the way around Rez's pale finger. Alex had seen tricks like these in the past. Delilah set off spooky alarms in anyone's head who heard her sing, but for some reason this time he felt himself freak out. It confirmed his earlier suspicions that something was genuinely wrong down here.

"It bit me," Rez shrieked.

"Lovebite." Dexter winked.

As the dark figurine flew out of his hand, Dexter leaned over and put the small bead of blood to his lips, rubbing until they were cherry red. Alex knew that Rez couldn't see past his sexual attraction to process what Dexter just did. But neither could Alex. All that mattered was this moment. Rez quickly undressed, birdcage torso so pale it was almost blinking, hungry eyes upon Dexter with robotic focus. Alex disrobed as well, settling into a more relaxed mindset.

Rez kissed his cheek, leaving behind a translucent Chapstick outline. Dexter pinched the candle out with his bare fingers, then turned on a strobe light that made the room glow as solemn as a silent film. They didn't need to talk to know what would happen next. Boys will be boys. Dexter was naked, and within the terrible lighting scheme he was like the ghostly outline of a sketch that could never be. White shadow. White spider. White devil.

Then came the incipient kissing. Not one pair of lips to another, but three pairs becoming one. Dexter led the way, blindsiding Alex and entrancing Rez even further, who was too into the moment to foresee the oncoming danger. Rez had recently grown sick and tired of caring about the future, or destiny. It was already written for you, so why spoil the journey on the way there?

Strobe light cascaded over Alex's skin. As their bodies became entangled, only their bones kept them from melding into one another. Dexter's touch was fleshy fire; Rez's was cumulus clouds. Dexter placed himself between the boys, arching his back and spreading his thin pale legs so that he could take Alex from one end and Rez from the other.

Every hormone produced from sex, drugs and rock n' roll swirled in Alex's loins, making him lose control as he smelled Dexter's spit on his upper lip, which shocked him how good it smelled. It pulled his rational brain through his ears and spit it into the trash. All that was left was his little brain, also known as his dick, which had taken charge. Now that he was at the base of Dexter's spine, tongue leaving long gleaming trails of saliva all the way to his hairless puckering asshole, Alex now had the boy where he wanted him.

A flower to deflower.

Rez was at the helm, making out with Dexter crazily, and so Alex stuffed his face right between the twin moons of Dexter's ass. Electric flooded into his mouth, followed by the saltiness of sweat. As he entered Dexter, Alex took a bump of K off one of the beads of Dexter's spine and rode the rest of the wave into insanity. There was a moment of black and cold that sailed across his vision, as if he'd entered a cave, or a corpse. But that was quickly erased as orgasm rushed through his balls and squirmed into Dexter's intestine.

They ran out of steam after that. Rez passed out, leaving Alex to bear witness, alone, the next set of events. He saw the sculptures on the wall moving. Their solemn eyes watched him; little clay maws gaped, tongues dangling and metallic wings flapping with the sound of cans rolling down stairs. Then they moved in the direction of their maker, who was no longer between him and Rez.

Dexter was sprawled naked and bent his body lizard-like. Then he scurried away, methodically and carefully. Alex watched Dexter approach the nearest wall, but had no idea what to expect. A normal person might have either bumped their head or just turned around. But Dexter was the furthest thing from normal. He kept crawling, as if there was no wall to stop him.

One hand and foot in front of the other, climbing until he was on the ceiling doing wicked little head spins. When he got to the center, something had changed. There was now an apocalyptic sky of fire and lightning. There, Dexter danced, white limbs angling in ways the human body was not meant to. His fingers grew into prehistoric talons and his spine arched in the way a dog's hair stands when on the defense; bits of bone breached his skin with a construction-paper rip.

Alex screamed for Rez to wake up, but silence had swallowed all sound, the kind of silence that creates a pitch only you can hear. Then the adrenaline rush started to battle with the ketamine.

Fight-or-flight danced dangerously with dissociation, pulling at his cells with such force he felt like they could break in two. He wanted to run, but he couldn't leave Rez, and he was still stupidly attracted to Dexter.

Now the little creatures had taken flight, a swarm of locusts seven times the normal size. Alex was suddenly nauseous, but the musician in him felt it was right to witness this majesty. He lifted his hands up and broke the silence, multiple rings clanging as they clashed with the wings. This repeated for a good ten minutes before Rez's eyes opened. That's when Dexter dropped from the ceiling and things reverted as if nothing had ever happened.

"What was that?" Alex said.

Dexter had a gold shawl draped about his shoulders and did a twirl. "Do you like this?"

"Rez, did you see it?"

"See what?"

Alex reached into his bag and took out a clove cigarette. "Dexter—"

"What about me?" Dexter interrupted, purple sheen of his eyes too entrancing to continue the argument.

"Never mind."

Alex kept the visions to himself. He didn't want to break the smile that was almost permanent on Rez's face these days. Thus, a weird, intriguing, exciting and invigorating new kind of relationship was born. Dexter had become the spark of new life that the original couple had for some reason lost, but was too scared to tell the other. Traversing the shaky territory of love between three was too much fun, despite warnings from friends, ignoring the *actual*

warning signs in the little things like Dexter's possessiveness over Rez, or his obsession with Alex's music, but not Alex himself.

And then a year melted away, followed by another. Two drippy years that somehow tasted as good as any drug they'd taken. They experimented with many. GHB was Dexter's choice, while Alex remained heavily fascinated by ketamine. Rez enjoyed old-school ecstasy, which now had fancy names like Tesla, Rolls Royce and Red Bull. The drugs opened the boys' hearts further to risk and helped undo the laces in their brains when it came to the definition of love.

Alex went back to writing music and performing with Electric Orchid. Dexter was often found slumped over a desk, wrist-deep in warm clay, pencils everywhere, carving knives and solder irons at his side; stench of dust and metal all about him. Rez was the only one who could not get back into his original vice: prose writing. The hand that had been bitten—his writing hand—had somehow outgrown the arm in which it had originally been attached to. Alex sometimes caught it doing things that Rez would never do, starting with wild gesticulations or scratching into the floorboard of their apartment until a nail ripped off.

It wasn't until autumn 2019 when the effects started to show. Two years had crumbled like a wet tissue in their hands. They'd lived the ups and the downs that all relationships go through, jealous martyrs but too proud to say it as they didn't want to suffer the awkwardness. Their creative connection was just too good. Soon enough Rez and Dexter became inexcusably close, while Alex remained the emotional third wheel.

When Alex finally felt ready to confront Rez about his hand, Dexter disappeared. No text, no call, just gone. Most likely in one of his notorious solitary moods, off to finish some monstrous project in the bowels of his studio. Sometimes he'd film there for his Instagram following, and strange things would happen on camera, but nobody questioned it.

One night, Alex and Rez went for a walk through Central Park, specifically in the Ramble, an area so enveloped with trees and shrubbery that it canceled out the noise of the city and blocked out enough air pollution so all one could smell was fresh dew and falling leaves. It reminded Alex of rural Pennsylvania, the way little animals scattered about. All The Ramble needed was a black bear to make it feel like true nature.

They killed a few hours talking, walked until their legs began to hurt. It felt like old times, when it was just Alex and Rez against the world. Humidity was at a stifling seventy-one percent, so their clothes stuck to them like glue and eyeliner clumped in the corner of their eyes. This kind of weather sent the people of New York into hiding. It was just too hot to enjoy, but Alex and Rez forced themselves on the walk as they always loved the park with less people in it.

Sunset was a wild palette of color, cloudless and impaled with rays of orange and red, which made the sky seem like it was on fire. By nightfall, temperatures remained in the eighties, air so humid it filled their lungs with slime. They smoked a joint and stargazed, one of their shared hobbies, and tonight the visibility made stars glow against the seldom cloud.

"What's with your hand?"

Rez took the fragrant joint with his left hand. "I haven't looked at it."

"You haven't looked at it?"

"I said what I said."

They'd come upon a pond and sat with their Converses almost touching the lip. The water was still as the sky above it, occasionally disturbed by turtles coming up for air, which made the reflection of stars ripple into nothingness. The moon lay close to the horizon and was stained a deep blood red, which Alex took as a bad omen. Rez didn't believe entirely in Alex's esoteric superstitions, only because he had his own ability to see and feel things—entities and ghosts, if you will—more than the average person.

"The skin's changing color."

"Just some makeup."

"You don't have a talent for makeup."

"Dexter does."

Alex knew that was a lie. Every time Rez didn't tell the truth, he refused to look Alex in the face, and his ears wiggled. And right now, they were doing a little dance, piercings glinting against the bloody moon, sapphire eyes staring aimlessly into the water. Alex knew that Rez wanted to say something to Alex . . . something detrimental. He could feel Rez's energy shoot through him, heavy chest, labored breathing; rocks in the pit of his stomach. Nothing good was going to come of tonight's conversation. The recent months had driven a wedge between them, and it was something they both avoided bringing up due to the presence of Dexter.

"I love him," Rez said. "I think you know that."

"I know."

"Still love you too, Alex."

"Same." Alex put his hand between Rez's thighs, caressing the wet skin, and leaned his head on Rez's shoulder.

"What are you getting at?" Rez's tone was serious.

"I know you wanna tell me something."

"I don't know if I do."

"Why are we doing this anymore?" Alex asked as sternly as possible. "It was fun while it lasted."

Rez was quiet for one moment. "I want to get rid of him too, but I can't find the strength."

"Let me do it then."

"No!" Rez grabbed Alex's chin. "It *must* come from me."

Then Rez's finger flicked Alex's face. The skin of it was scabrous and cold. It was no skin Alex recognized, but the weed had his mind singing and his skin tingling. He didn't care any longer, he wanted to know. Alex grabbed Rez's hand, brought it before his face. The nails had all fallen off, and the veins atop it were necrotic. He smelled death, sex, solder and darkness. It was the weirdest odor Alex had ever come across. Rez pulled his hand away.

"Why did you do that?"

"I deserve to see."

Then Rez's hand grabbed Alex by the hair with such a force that follicles tore and his neck popped; a gout of drippy light blinded him. As the blood slithered down his skull, the hand pulled Alex down to the floor, dragging him so that his knees, elbows and hands skinned. Then Alex tasted water, filthy pond water polluted with animal droppings, stagnant algae and rusted coins. He was drowning; Rez was killing him. Perhaps this was how he was supposed to go. And then it all stopped. The hand released him. Alex got his head above the water and took a gulp of much needed air, coughed out the slime he had inhaled.

When his eyes adjusted, Alex saw Dexter and Rez kissing. *I always know where you are*, he heard Dexter say inside his head. That's when Rez's hand split in two, then two again, until little black appendages wavered in the air like smoke and prehistoric tentacles slithered up Rez's arm, encircling his neck to choke. Alex screamed for Rez to open his eyes, but Dexter quickly lifted his foot and slammed it into Alex's jaw, forcing his body to immediately stiffen as he fell to the ground. For a moment he was paralyzed, face turned in Rez's direction, teardrops blurring his vision.

But when Rez realized what had just happened, something changed. The muscles of his face tensed; lips pulled back and teeth bared like a wild animal. *We're through*, he yelled over and over. *I don't want this!* With his shapeshifted hand he bashed an unsuspecting Dexter across the face. Alex felt the ricochet of bone and teeth cracking as much as he was sprayed with it. Dexter howled and lost his balance, body crashing to the concrete face-down. His head had done a complete one-eighty so that Alex could see that Dexter's visage had become an unrecognizable meat hole.

Rez, triggered beyond control, continued the assault. He kicked Dexter's face and chest, filling the park with a horrible crunching sound. *Thwap . . . thump.* Dexter's wailing echoed through the woods and over the pond—surely someone would hear. Alex got to his feet and grabbed Rez's body, pulling him away. By this time,

Dexter was no longer moving; just a floppy pale shape drenched in blood.

"My gods, you killed him," Alex said through the chorus of crickets.

"He can't die!"

Rez lifted his boot and stomped until Dexter's head became a swamp. Bone crackled and cartilage snapped. A black blob squeezed through the crevice of what was left of Dexter's ears; two purple gobs slid slowly out of the broken eye sockets. Dexter made no noise, moved no longer. Rez took a huge, relaxing breath.

"What have I done?"

No matter how far away, you'll still feel me

Light posts flickered as if falling stars. The park grew dark in tandem with the arrhythmic pattern. That's when Dexter's body showed signs of life. One arm raised, hand curled into the shape of a hook, as if some invisible force was in control. The red pit of his face began to knit itself back together. It only took a few minutes to transform organic ruin into bright pink scar tissue. The black blob hurtled itself toward Dexter; the alluring purple gobs swiveled in his direction as well. Animals began to screech.

Alex looked at Rez's hand and saw that it had become normal again, so he grabbed ahold of it and bolted them out of the park, never looking back.

17

Delilah tore through the streets of New York City, silent as light traveling through the universe. She eyed the dark horizon, secretly hoping that the sun would never rise. It was a heinous but freeing thought. Delilah, Rez and Alex never liked mornings; that meant they had to live another day and deal with more problems. Sleep, much like death, bored them. Dorian and Sebastian, however, were quite the opposite; they looked forward to a new day.

Twenty minutes later, ringed in sweat and out of breath, Delilah sat with her back against a park bench. It had been chiseled with bleak ruminations and poetic graffiti. She ran chewed fingernails across the words, hoping to evoke a feeling but nothing happened. After smoking a clove cigarette, the heavy smoke filled the air with vanilla, spice and some things not so nice. She moved her gaze toward dawn, which was opening to a magnificent azure. In just a few minutes the city would be bright with watery red light, the cobblestone seemingly wet with it.

"You walk too fast," Dorian said.

"*You* need to speed up."

Before he could get another word in—and Dorian very much wanted to as per his begrudging look—Alex and Rez came storming from behind. They too were out of breath, outwardly annoyed at Delilah's pace, and sweating so much that their smeared eyeliner made them look like they'd been partying all night. They both lit a joint of some fragrant hybrid flower, its plumes slowly eating the smoke of Delilah's clove cigarette.

"I'm not ready to see him." Alex had his fingers in his mouth.

"But you're the only one who knows where to go down there."

"Not necessarily so."

"Huh?"

"Something happens when you enter that place."

"What do you mean?"

"It's never the same."

"When was the last time you went down there?"

"Way before the pandemic. Once with Dexter . . . and once without."

"Why without?"

"Some feeling . . . inside me. I had to see it on my own."

He took out his phone, but the way his hand was trembling he could barely hold it. Delilah, lacking any form of patience, snatched the phone and opened a photo album that was titled EVIL. A series of dark pictures timestamped 2018 rolled by, with not much going on in the backgrounds besides random glowing objects and a few pale silhouettes. But the photos timestamped 2019 were alive with many different things, and the blackness expanded in each photo, as if curtains rising to show off a completely new world. Delilah understood what Alex meant.

"I see the difference."

"It's got nothing to do with the time that went by. That's just how it is down there."

"I get it now," Delilah sighed.

"So, I honestly *don't know* what it's like down there anymore." Alex bit his nails roughly. "It'll make us see what we don't want."

"That I don't believe," Delilah said.

"Believe what you want. The place has a mind of its own."

"Regardless," Delilah leaned forward, "you still need to show us the way."

"Didn't you already send someone down there, Delilah?" Rez poked her thin shoulder.

"That was for a different purpose. She doesn't give a flying fuck about what we need to do."

A few days ago, Dexter had messaged Electric Orchid's Instagram account. *I'm coming for you.* And then a whole bunch of gibberish after that. Delilah's instinct—being a typical Aries—was to play tit-for-tat. *BRING IT ON BITCH!* She replied. Delilah would be dead before Dexter got close enough to lay a grimy finger on any of her friends. So, Delilah came up with a plan to tease with Dexter in a way he'd never expect. It started with music—*her* music, since he never liked it in the first place.

Delilah knew a girl who didn't care about anything, let alone Electric Orchid, or Atticus and Zephyr. She needed someone with a literal death wish, someone who'd be OK if that fate should come upon them. Infiltrating a private space without an invite could be detrimental to one's safety, especially when it was run by someone as dangerous as Dexter. But this girl was strange enough for the task. If Lydia Deetz and Robert Smith ever had an illegitimate and angry child, her name would be Adelaide.

A ragged, wraith of a human being, Adelaide had been on a self-destructive path for the last five years, one drunken-drugged bender after the other, benders she'd not been able to shake since the day her girlfriend committed suicide on the stage where she performed spoken word poetry. After the suicide, Adelaide served no other purpose but dealing drugs around New York City, and as much as a service that was to her community, Delilah knew this girl needed to be put to a different task.

It wasn't hard to swindle Adelaide. She spent most of her time indoors, especially during the day as she no longer wanted to be seen; she barely showered and had thinned herself to the point of emaciation. Being this task could only be done at night, Adelaide accepted. All she had to do was manipulate the sound system down there so that it played Electric Orchid's music on loop as Dexter, Zephyr and Atticus made their triumphant return. Delilah's goal was to make sure Dexter felt her presence. Get to him before he got to her—when he least expected it—and more importantly, *where* he was least expecting it.

"This is it?" Dorian said.

"What did you think you'd see? A sign? A door?"

Knuckle-deep in poetic madness, Delilah branded the bench in a chaotic scrawl with her butterfly blade. *Beginning of the End*. She blew paint and wood chips off her lap, then walked toward the CitiBike station. It was in tatters; something had ripped the bike stands straight out of the black top so that the smell of fresh dirt rose about. The area was encircled with yellow caution tape to keep bystanders away, but if you looked close enough, if you nudged one of the stands with your foot, you would expose the entrance to Dexter's subterranean getaway.

"Going down?" Sebastian's words were muffled beneath his gaudy facemask of black chain link and gold fabric.

"Take the mask off, we're outside," Delilah said.

"That why you ain't wearing one?"

"So sassy today."

"None of these punks have the gall." Sebastian stuck out his pink tongue. "Besides, I can't go down there. I got a weird feeling."

"You got a weird feeling? The entire world we see is weird, so imagine the world we don't see."

"This is why I don't want to know."

Delilah lit another smoke; the orange corona eclipsed one of her black fingernails. "There's a whole fucking city beneath us, and you don't want to see it?"

"Not under these circumstances."

"Then don't." Delilah spit at the ground. "Everything's already ruined up here. Enjoy it."

"Isn't it well known that New York has a mysterious underground?" Dorian raised a sharp black eyebrow.

"Yeah, *creative* underground. This shit is a big black hole."

"Half of that is mumbo-jumbo . . . shit made up to entice weirdos like us to go looking for it. Most fail, the rest give up trying."

"So then how did Dexter find it?"

"It's not about how he found this place," Dorian said. "It's more about how open his mind is to opportunities. He manifests, he wills. He brings it to life."

"He takes over."

"Everything in this universe, the planets, the stars, the moon, are all remnants, descendants and pieces of the big bang. If one were to figure out how to unlock the ability . . . they could manipulate these particles because they're part of us."

Delilah instinctively grimaced. "You know what I fucking mean."

"If you catch an attitude, I ain't going down there." Sebastian turned away from them.

"And I ain't going if Sebastian isn't," Dorian said.

"*You*," Delilah said manically, "are the *Hydra*. Limitless talent and power. And *you*, Dorian . . . are the only thing standing in Dexter's way."

"What do you mean?"

"We're all aware of what your art can do, and Dexter for some reason can't be around it. This happens when he hears my music as well."

"Maybe he just hates us?"

"Could be. Either way, you're both going down."

"What does the Hydra have to do with any of this?"

Delilah turned. "I need Dexter to shed that fake human skin of his. That's where you come in."

"Meaning?"

"You saw it with your own eyes!"

Dorian paused, then said, "Well, it looks like Rez and Alex don't want to go either."

They had crossed the street and now appeared as little black dots held up by bone-white appendages. Two cans of Diet Coke winked in the sunlight. Delilah once again had to bite her lip to keep cool. She charged, mustering all the powers of patience to not trample them both down for quitting when they were this close.

Instead of screaming, she channeled empathy and sympathy to remind herself how Dexter had put them through hell—and that kind of trauma just doesn't disappear. It lingers like an unwanted ghost. Much like her suicide scars.

"I need you both to come back across the street."

"I feel sick," Rez said. "Alex is taking care of me."

"You talk for him now?" Delilah raised a questionably sharp eyebrow.

"No, he doesn't." Alex put out the joint on the bottom of his Converse. "Give us some space, dammit."

Delilah took a step back. "Better?"

"I can't handle it, D."

"You don't have to explain."

"It's not safe down there." Rez looked her dead in the face, emerald eyes to emerald eyes. "I can feel it."

"We know this already."

"I mean in more ways than *we know*."

"There's only one way to find out."

They walked through traffic, though there were barely any cars. No need for streetlights or looking both ways. Most of the avenue was still shockingly abandoned, and the early morning hour only made it more lonesome. What the pandemic stole from this city in terms of sheer numbers of people, it gave back in sickening silence. Delilah hadn't been around such deafening quiet since she left Pennsylvania a decade ago. New York City was the loudest place on Earth, but now it was just a hushed library with too many holes in the ground.

Delilah kicked one of the destroyed bike stands, exposing the hole in which they needed to go through. The lip of it was gritty, inset with sharp little things that looked like teeth, but reflected as do shards of glass. As she peaked in, a wretched swatch of diesel smoke enclosed about her. She saw nothing but blackness; not even dawn could bleed light down there. But then there was some sign of life, a noise unlike any she'd ever heard. Not music, not chanting, nor any language she knew of; nothing that caused a vibration. Just a noise that made one understand that if they were to enter, bad things would happen.

Delilah went first.

Obscenely hot, like she'd stepped into the dripping jaws of some large creature. The ladder was caked in mildew and dotted with all sorts of critters that bounced darkness off their backs. With each step there was an awful squeak as if to warn her this ladder could collapse. The further she went, at least fifty steps by now, the otherworldly noise greatened, reminding Delilah of the hiss wet wood makes when you burn it. Delilah took this as an omen—perhaps it was Dexter's way of scaring off intruders—until she realized that the sound was her own voice. Somehow her vocals had been isolated from her own music.

... further down the spiral ...

Her Doc Martens met the ground with a squish, as if she'd stepped into wet sand. All around her she felt a presence, and she knew that if she moved in the wrong direction someone or some*thing* would have its way with her. She respected the dark too much to take it for granted, and as she waited for the rods and cones of her eyes to adjust, something caressed her face. Delilah brought her fists up, followed by the metallic flick of her butterfly blade.

"Don't swing that thing at me."

It was Alex, but she could only tell by his ice-blue eyes and Jägermeister breath. A few minutes later, her sight fully adjusted and she could see the rest of the boys behind Alex, their eyes darting to and fro, completely taken back by their surroundings. Delilah wondered what they were seeing. The same wrought iron sculptures? The same torches and votive candles? Did they hear the same music? Judging by their faces, everyone was experiencing something different.

"I didn't hear you come down."

"I told you to get out of the way."

Delilah had no recollection of that moment. Where had her mind gone from the time she stepped foot on that ladder to the moment she landed down here? Anxiety was riding in her veins, but she wasn't about to let that little snot rag Dexter have the last laugh. Delilah pocketed her blade and exchanged it for her cell phone, typed out a text to send to Atticus, but it never went through. No signal down here.

"Uhhh, guys—" Dorian's voice sounded weak and afraid.

When Delilah turned, she saw exactly why Dorian was so spooked. A bunch of tall bodies began sprouting from the ground, sailing upwards until everything went black. After a few minutes, the bodies were still and Delilah was able to move around. She maneuvered through them, using her hands to see because it was so dark again. She felt brick and cement, and something that reminded her of dust. When Delilah looked up, she had to strain her eyes in order to understand what she was now looking at. It was a skyline of crystal and dirt.

"Is everyone seeing what I'm seeing?" Delilah scratched her head.

The structures were so precise and clean, it made no sense that they'd simply upended the earth and came to be. Many of the surfaces were smooth as marble, but cold like dead skin; the colors within them looked trapped being the surface of these huge buildings were the kind of black that absorbed all light rather than reflecting it.

"It's a city."

"Or the bones of one," Delilah said.

Then the sound came back around, pulled her in its direction. It added an uncivilized rhythm to Delilah's step, as if it was forcing her to move ahead. *Is that your voice?* Alex whispered. Delilah felt her body twist, hips widening like childbirth, even as her spine went taut as a tightrope. But it wasn't just a sound anymore, it was a presence, a feeling. The entire scene made the tiny hairs on Delilah's body stand up, including the pink and black dreads atop her head.

"Okay, enough with this dance. Let's go."

Delilah led them in the direction of the sound, suddenly brave. *When I see him*, Alex whispered, *I'll end him*, as he reached back and clasped hands with Rez. He instructed them all to do the same so they didn't lose one another, since there was no telling which way the tunnels would take them. The first alleyway they found looked as it would in any city above ground. But Delilah was aware of what was going on. The things she saw were not real, no matter how real they looked in front of her face. She knew Dexter was doing all of this, controlling the narrative.

"Which way now?"

"Through," Alex said.

The road took them to a door, and that door opened to room after blighted room; not a soul in sight, not even a rat or roach; ears popping and headaches arising from the change of pressure. They were deeper than they knew or wanted to know. They were all forced into quietude, thoughts overtaking their tight lips. Alex halted, his gaze lost upon a wall made of limestone, perhaps looking for another door or entry point. Delilah made sure she was seeing the same wall, confirmed with Alex by the way he gripped her hand as a human shape began to form.

And then it happened.

The shadow extricated itself from the wall, branching into curlicues and spirals so that it formed several intricate webs. A cool breeze drifted across their bodies as Delilah's voice amplified from many parts of this room, which made the shadow dance even more dangerously. Sebastian and Dorian were still fixated on the wall, even as the shadow got bigger without any reason why.

"Run!"

It flew toward Delilah, slamming into her body as if it was a flesh and bone human. The wind was knocked out of her, but she got back to her feet, bolting in the only direction her legs would take her. It was so dark she had no idea if she was moving at all. Behind her, she heard the shadow's footsteps, could almost smell its negative smell. The want to turn around and hit it with her fists was burning her alive on the inside, but she knew if she did that, it would win.

Her legs moved faster than she knew they were capable of. As she rounded a corner toward a small yellow flame, it was as if she'd made a complete circle. Nobody had moved. On the outside, it looked as if Delilah had made the whole thing up. She was now back to square one, looking at that same wall, where a human-shaped carving now took the place of the shadow. Amethyst-colored holes in its head watched her.

"What's happening?"

Dorian dropped to his knees, paint brush clenched between teeth, blood glittering across his chin. The bristles were not soft, rather they seemed to be made of razors and had cut his lip and gums. Delilah and Dorian locked eyes. They both knew what had to be done next. Dorian's hand punched through the dark, and when it came back he was holding a palette and a vat of paint. He dipped the razored brush in the small gout of blood on his lip, then scratched it across the wet palette.

"You're right," Dorian said. "The only way out is through."

He began to paint. Nothing to make sense of, just gobs of acrylic intersecting with every stroke. As the human shape behind Delilah slowly shrunk, another sound swelled like a stampede making its way toward them. Delilah didn't have time to warn any of them as the deluge of skeletal bodies bombarded. Eyes as bright and burning as flame, blood glowing black from their fish-like noses and lips; Delilah was certain that it wasn't blood at all, but shadow. As the room closed in on them, as hands and teeth and fingernails raked at their bodies . . .

—that's when the danger was set free.

Zephyr opened his eyes and saw nothing. Not the hand in front of his face, not even the floor he'd been face-down upon. It was a full twenty minutes before he realized that the twin pressure in his chest and head meant he'd gone so deep into the earth that there'd be no climbing his way out. Stuck down here forever, and by his own will. He grabbed his phone and looked for a signal, but after a few minutes of realizing he'd get none, he used the screen's glow to help him see.

It was a strange sight. The light traveled as if it was viscous instead of massless particles. Everything it touched seemed more like a drizzle, slow and steady photons peeling away the fabric of space and time like an onion skin. Then it all stopped, and what at first appeared to be a two-dimensional world of half undone drawings, vertiginous shapes and empty pathways, started to take shape into something more familiar.

Things began sprouting from the ground. Tall things that went so high there would be no way Zephyr would ever be able to see the top of them. Dust slapped his face and things crawled over his feet, but there was no sound as all of this was happening. The light of his phone ciphered into darkness, which only made his feelings become exponentially worse. But then suddenly and without apparent reason, everything stopped and he was somehow able to see.

It was a city, or rather the bones of one, and it was so colorless that even a black hole would be brighter. Zephyr saw tree leaves dot the ground and the bony branches from which they fell grazed the top of his head. Staircases swarmed upon his left; mounds of discarded shoes, garbage, cans and paper were piled to his right. Little black rodents darted to and fro through the mazes of rubble. The more he shined his light, the more this place revealed itself to him.

The ground was neither rock nor dirt. It felt more like asphalt, and when Zephyr brought his phone close to it, little cracks erupted, hissing smoke in his face that smelled of tar. There was no color to the roads, the buildings or the street signs. Even the light posts shined a dull black. Being his cell phone was the only connection he had to the world above, and with the battery at twenty percent, he would be cut off sooner than he would have liked to be.

But he had no choice. He needed the light to press on. So as the dark pried itself away more and more, he began to see clearly. When he looked up, buildings towered above his head. Skyscrapers made of onyx stone and charcoal shooting into a sky that was neither blue nor black, but a deep purple that matched the color of Dexter's eyes. This hue filled the engravings he saw mark every entranceway, and filled the eyes of the stone gargoyles that looked down at him from above.

At street level there were cars, people and somehow the rumble of a train below him. Zephyr smelled exhaust, grease vapors and cigarettes, then the faint vapors of spilled alcohol. It felt like there was literal life in this great expanse, but it was also as if he was stuck in a black dream. He walked at a pace that was neither fast nor slow; the city had its own wayward tempo, and once Zephyr found it he was able to watch it unfold piece by piece.

A slew of voices berated one of his ears, while in the other he heard a beautiful song. The melody invoked emptiness. The feeling of no feeling, of void; of never knowing you were ever alive, or knowing your life is draining slowly back into the universe. *This is death*, Zephyr thought. *I'm living through death.* Only because everything was so black did death come to mind. And the gravity here was so intense it left him feeling weightless as he dragged himself forward, seeing the intermittent flicker of what he perceived to be the whites of eyes.

Zephyr entered a space, some kind of chamber. The hustle and bustle soon quieted, until he heard the scritch of a flint and sizzle of a match, and a lone candle flame came to life against a nearby wall. In no time the light expanded as if it was a malleable thing that could be pulled and lengthened, brightening the space so that Zephyr saw macabre frescoes, portraits and murals. As the light continued to expand, it opened his eyes to a wall on the other side of the room, shapeshifted into many other forms of shocking imagery and lunacies. It was quickly apparent whose works these were: Dangerous Dorian, and deep within the gloom Zephyr heard them, as if the paintings were calling out to him.

He had no idea what they were saying, and so as the skeletons moved in time with his quickening heart, he began to almost hallucinate. The smell of rot materialized, smell of old blood, smell of the body festering. Zephyr turned away, only to be faced with a new mural; three skinny shadows that could only be told apart by their hair, white, blue and black, and the white-headed shadow was slowly devouring the blue one.

Zephyr pulled a cigarette out of his pocket. The smoke tasted like sex and death; a juxtaposition of the two most iconic things we experience in life. He dropped the cigarette and never saw the orange cinder hit the ground, as candlelight began to change the room, pulling images from the walls into existence.

And then there was a noise. The hiss of a light wind. Zephyr covered his face as if his fingers could reach through the skin, massage all worry and woe out of his brain. The sound brushed across his body, thin and flimsy as shadow, until tiny beams of light began to ripple into existence, a purple hew housing the skinny outline of a body and vampire face.

"Do you know where you are?" Dexter said.

"In your world."

"You don't know anything."

Dexter was ferocious, and he would have startled Zephyr if not for the soundless entrance and dreamy glow of his face. It seemed Dexter had been standing there the entire time, absorbing Zephyr's energy in some weird way. After a quick bout of trepidation, Zephyr remembered that Dexter was somehow always a step ahead, always knew where Zephyr was and what he was thinking. Only now did he feel fear, which took over the rest of his emotions. He suddenly wanted out of this life, but he'd made his bed and now he'd have to lay in it, as they say.

"I know what my eyes see," Zephyr said.

"They see what I show them." Dexter's voice grew deep and sinister.

Zephyr turned around fast. "Then get the fuck out of my head."

"Why should I when you lead them here?"

Dexter turned around, opened a door to one of the buildings. Zephyr followed him inside, which was nothing by a long hallway of sorts, but somehow all around him Zephyr felt familiar presences. Dexter was also very far ahead, and it now appeared that the inside of this building was much bigger than what appeared on the outside. This played with Zephyr's mind the most, knowing that he was being led into an infinite nowhere.

"They're the ones who came to me."

Dexter was now in front of his face. "And you didn't stick up for me."

"I barely knew you at the time."

"But you know me now?"

Zephyr had been backed into a wall, literally and figuratively. The more he leaned, the more he stepped into the painting. One of the skeletons put a hand on his shoulder, which made him wail, even though the sound died quickly. This wasn't because the moment was purely insane, but because the bones were so cold and smooth it made Zephyr believe that death itself had touched him.

"Cornering me doesn't help."

Zephyr reached for Dexter, fingers caressing his face, but he was unable to actually feel him. The boy just stood there, made no attempt to lean into the touch. Zephyr drew his hand away, momentarily embarrassed, then tried it again. This time something caught his thumb, something like teeth, the pain so lucid, yet so quickly absorbed he wasn't sure if anything had happened at all.

"What did you have to gain by talking to them?"

"Nothing."

"Did you give them information about me?"

"Why don't you read my thoughts?" Zephyr's sarcasm freed him from fear.

"That ain't funny."

"Wasn't trying to be."

"So, what do they know?"

"That we're together."

"Because you told them."

"They guessed that on their own."

"How could they have known?"

"Ever hear of a thing called social media?"

"I blocked them."

Dexter took out his phone, browsed through his own posts and sucked his teeth. What may have been an innocent post with Atticus, and even Zephyr, could be easily found when your profile is public. It seemed he'd forgotten that even if you block someone on social media, they can always find you.

"I left that life behind a long time ago. Don't we all have a past?"

"We certainly do."

"Then why are you playing this game?"

"I'm not playing games. They're my friends."

"They're no friends of yours."

"Insecurity is not a cute look. And how would you even know?"

"They're using you to get to me. Them and their shitty music and shitty books they write."

"Their music is awesome, actually."

"It's garbage. And you don't see how you're disrespecting me by being friends with them?"

"I'm allowed to have any friends I choose."

"Not if we're to make this work."

Zephyr felt his body go stiff. Dexter leaned in.

"I said what I said."

"I don't like being told what to do."

"You think I do?" Dexter's eyes gleamed mean.

Zephyr knew it was futile to argue. They were going in circles. But it was impossible to not feel that pride was being tested and ego exhausted. Then it began to sink in, everything that he'd been told, that Dexter would show his true colors eventually, that Dexter was not the person he made himself out to be. Zephyr watched Dexter's face go from confounded to unrepented evil. The immaturity could easily topple into madness. That was what freaked Zephyr out the most, not really knowing Dexter well enough to know what he was capable of.

"Just don't tell me who I can be friends with."

Dexter took a deep breath in. "I've been waiting for you to do this."

"Do what?"

"Betray me."

Dexter turned toward the wall with the paintings. *These aren't mine!* he howled, pushing his hand through the wall and wrapping his finger around the neck of one of the skeletons. He pulled until it came tumbling out of the painting, which then made all the other ones follow one by one. But only one sprouted hair as long and black and dirty as the one Zephyr remembered from the cemetery.

And then it moved.

It's hand rising, then reaching for Dexter. Grabbed hold of his hair, the other running its sharp fingers down his face, tracing a wet and red line from forehead to chin. There was no shriek from pain, no resistance, as Zephyr saw Dexter's skin peel back, flesh delineating. Inside Dexter's skull was a swirling, catastrophic galaxy of worms and darkness. And as the skeletal hand pulled Dexter's face off, eye sockets and nostrils illuminated, it threw the gob of skin at his feet.

Zephyr fell faint with horror.

18

All I heard was wind, so shrill that it woke me from delicious slumber. The sound brought me back to a time when New York bloomed with life. I saw myself swiveling through tourist throngs, homeless hangouts, and local artistic lunacies. A mélange of smells assaulted my senses, burnt pretzels, diesel fumes, sewage steam and ectoplasm. New York City, my sepulchral sanctuary, stretched and gloomy as if an infinite midnight.

But then an actual city rose around me, and it was not one that I knew.

Black and endless; somehow stitched, cemented and stapled together, as if a composite of any city I'd seen over my lifetime. I saw every run-down section and seedy neighborhood rolled into one. Graffiti squirmed and smashed windows gleamed like monstrous smiles; posters peeled back from rotted telephone poles, and cantankerous shadows seemed to follow my every step.

I felt my body rise—as if gravity no longer bound me to the earth—through the stony structures and scratchy clouds, free-falling upwards into a sky the color of a smashed eyeball. The way my arms and legs flailed reminded me of a person drowning. I grabbed hold of a gargoyle perched against a spire made of black steel, but when I turned to look at its face, the eyes were purple and appeared to be human.

And then I descended. My body swiveled like a feather falling from a high altitude, unable to control the place in which it would land. The loss of my limbs was exhilarating as much as it was a test of my own phobias, as someone else was in the driver's seat now. I wasn't sure how fast I was going, but upon landing I was not hurt, nor was the breath knocked out of me.

I was overcome with a hot excitement, mostly from my surroundings. Everything had begun appearing as normal as any city, except that many things were out of place in the way they jutted, or remained squat and brooding, or were awkwardly shaped. All at once I began to see what was wrong with the color scheme and the actual layout. The dimensions were like a comic book drawing left undone.

But the more I walked, the more I saw. I realized that I was in fact wandering in some mad blueprint. There was no possible way to navigate as there were entire areas that were simply blank, devoid of color and space/time. I could see that everything had a height and width, but for some reason there was no depth; it was as if I was looking at everything through the screen of a cell phone.

Then all sound stopped. Suddenly my human sensations were siphoned from my body, replaced by nothing. My footsteps made no noise, and I barely understood if they were even moving at all. The sidewalks I ventured upon were empty, and the streets had no cars on them. Flowers had been ripped from the ground and trees were toppled over. Any splash of color that I saw felt wrong. Even my own hands were the color of no color, my nails hidden from plain sight.

I opened the camera on my phone, took a selfie and saw a silhouette of the man that I was, a man I might never be again. This woke me up enough to think clearly. While this city was not threatening, at least not from first glance, I knew it was a dangerous place. I was born and raised in a place like this, so I knew I'd be able to take whatever it would throw at me. However, to an outsider, this was easily the seventh level of hell.

I understood the ways in which one could get lost in the doorways that opened into nothingness, the windows that watched me pass with glassy eyes, the staircases that unraveled like long tongues ready to eat. I had learned from Dexter that there are entrances and exits in places that I was not trained to see. But maybe the world below is not so different from the world above it. Just a mirror turned upside down.

The more I walked, the more I began to recognize the carnage, even the black chaos. Perhaps it began to recognize me. Skyscrapers rose so high they broke the stars into pieces. Bright beads of light trickled over my skin, but they did not burn nor blind me. Perhaps this light was that of a dead star, one that had already burned out before reaching the earth.

When the deep purple sky unsheathed itself and began draping across the great gaseous city like velvet, I instinctively reached for my phone, hoping to capture this moment. The digital age had enslaved me after all, and the social media gods demanded this of us. As the saying goes, "If you don't put it on the 'Gram, did it ever really happen?" But the simple lens of the phone camera distorted reality, never quite finding a good angle or even decent lighting. The darkness might have been too alive to be imprisoned via digital images.

Elements flew through me as do the ghost particles that dominate space. New pathways were unveiled, now bright as daybreak, as if to finally connect both the above and the below. But I was in a completely different area now. An oil lamp shed light unto clay statues. Scraggly bodies and yawning mouths welcomed me into their sculpted nightmare; I knew that I could look at them forever, pleasantly trapped in their creative web.

My consciousness began to play tricks. Neon skeletons singed the backs of my eyes; spiral galaxies twinkled like deep-water fish. I heard the jangled music of dueling rock concerts; the static explosions of blown amps and vocal melodies that didn't belong to this world. There was the ticking of a grandfather clock, a manipulated synthesizer, and the hurricane clatter of construction projects.

Like the Big Bang—or even the Big Rip—I saw a point of light implode into nuclear fusion. Then a huge veil of dust enveloped my body, crystallized over my skin until it broke apart like fool's gold. I remembered that I'd taken a molly. Perhaps I was in some kind of fever dream, riding fast to the deepest, darkest portions of my own subconscious. I closed my eyes and collected myself; wished that someone would find me.

"So, we meet again."

I recognized the voice instantly. The melody of it danced in my ear. For a few minutes a wonderful cadence came about, registering in my brain, or so be it, the mind. I felt the sensation of sound itself, like how music begins by arranging sequences of tones into rhythm and scales.

"I wasn't expecting you."

Delilah whisked herself into existence, more inkblot than actual person. I watched as she extricated from the darkness, as if she was climbing out of a makeshift hole, emerald eyes gleaming through me, lips shaped into an ugly frown. She chewed gum loudly and the sound burrowed into my head. When she was fully materialized, I noted her usual rage and determination. Nothing was going to stop her.

"Well . . . here I am."

"How did you find me?"

She told me about how she climbed down into the City with her friends, and more importantly, found out where I was. The level of her understanding of this place shocked me. She'd navigated random doors and solved random riddles in order to get closer to me; braved endless hallways, seedy alleyways and junkyards just to be able to meet me here. Delilah was a determined individual, and as much as I respected that, I also feared it.

"Things just happen in places like this," Delilah said.

"Are you in my dream again?"

"I wish I was, but we're not dreaming. We're in *his* head."

Delilah was fiercer than ever. She was not going to relent until she had me understand just what Dexter was.

"So . . . you really are down here," I said.

"Yes. Again, yes! How many ways do I need to say it?"

"Dexter knows you're after him."

"Of course he does. He can read your mind."

The invasion of my thoughts must have been something I took for granted. I had no idea people could do this. Now that I knew it to be true, I felt violated, betrayed. The one thing I'm entitled to is the tiny voice inside my head. That's not for anyone to talk to, hear, or even listen in on. But what Delilah also didn't realize was that Dexter was part of me, inside of me; he was my reason for taking in air, the sunlight and gravitational satellite that gave my life a reason to carry on.

"He heard your music and flipped out, by the way."

"Then my plan worked."

"And what do you plan to do now . . . find him and fight?"

"Not exactly."

"You going to play astral projection?"

"I can't down here."

"Why?"

"Again, we're in *his* head."

"Is that why my phone doesn't work?"

"Maybe he's in your phone right now. He's gone through it plenty of times."

I didn't know how I truly felt about that. Another privacy issue. Zephyr and I never looked at one another's phones. What was the point when you'd only find things you didn't want to see? There are never any good intentions when it comes to snooping.

"He doesn't have my passcode or Face ID."

Delilah laughed in my face. "You still have much to learn."

"Okay, Yoda. You going to tell me he's my father as well?"

"You'll find out when we meet in the flesh."

"What are we now?"

Delilah lit what I perceived to be a cigarette, but the flame erupted from her thumb nail and was luminescent as a rainbow. Smoke hung about her face like the ice vapors of a comet coming close to a star. We sat in silence. I looked around for any sign of Dexter or Zephyr, but all I could see were black clouds passing by, shaped oddly like wings, and one of them even appeared to be as wet and mysterious as a vital organ. Delilah saw this as well but purposely ignored it.

"You also went to Zephyr."

"We met in person. I don't need to find him any other way."

"Why's that?"

"He's more receptive than you are."

I hated her momentously. "Maybe I'm not as naïve as him."

"Naïve is a man who won't open his mind to another's point of view."

"I've way too much integrity for this." I had no choice but to stomp my foot.

Delilah looked me up and down with disdain. "Really? That pride will cost you soon enough."

"What I don't get is that if you hate Dexter so much, why not confront him yourself? Go into his dreams and haunt him."

"Much too *vulgar display of power*, as they say in that movie."

"Or is it that you can't do it?"

"I certainly can."

"Then you're afraid."

Delilah tilted her spidery head of hair. "Trust, I'm not."

"Is that why you dragged him live?"

"I did that to get his attention."

"Clearly!"

"When Alex, Rez and Dexter broke up, he just disappeared as if the scars he left would heal on their own. Newsflash, they don't! I can't let him do that to you and Zephyr as well."

"You only made him more popular."

"On the surface, yes. He'll get fame, but no fortune. He'll get some spooky followers; he'll convince them to come down here and perhaps never find their way out. But what he doesn't know is that I've uncovered his greatest weakness."

"Which is?"

"You'll find out soon enough," Delilah said as she began to fade away.

"Wait!"

... You'll find out ...

She was gone. I maundered for a few minutes (if time was even a thing), cussed beneath my ghostly breath. The fact that so many earthly nuisances consumed me was very weird. I needn't listen to her, not if I didn't want to, but the inflection in her voice was inside my head like a game of badminton. A bout of depression swam up from my gut, then something I could only attune to worry, or disbelief, forced my lips to pout. Everything she said was a stake through the heart of trust, a razor opening the flowery vein of love.

I veered off the dark path she left me in, led by a sound that had drifted my way. But it was one I could not explain by a human tongue, yet it felt so familiar that a deluge of memories came to me. I wound myself through the path, sinuous and soundless as shadow, as if I knew what direction I was going. I used my ears to control my legs, the sound growing deeper inside my head, unfurling images of mud, quicksand and steaming stalagmites

My shoes stalled, as if I'd walked straight into the lip of a curb. But this was much softer than cement, almost identical to the texture of drying clay. The sound wrapped around my leg, crawled up until I was forced to look down. Not much to see beyond some meandering glow, the pallid outline of a human. I knew the shape of that body, all 5'8" of it; birdcage torso wrapped tightly in parchment skin, ornate selection of tattoos, multiple piercings in multiple orifices; extremities as smooth and white as bone itself. I choked back my scream.

Zephyr's eyes were open, as if he was hideously aware of his own death. I kneeled to get a better look, pressed a finger into the sharp cheekbone, which left behind a shallow indent. His sky-blue hair was strung about the lifeless body like party streamers, and when I looked at his scalp, I saw red wet dots in the places where hair had been torn out. And his lips, oh those fabulously soft lips, had been peeled off the face, thread by gooey thread like a red scrim.

I tried to stand, felt something glide beneath my foot. I looked inside Zephyr's gaping jaw, saw that his tongue had been pulled cleanly out, and dared not look under my shoe. A pitiful sound escaped my throat, but my mouth was too catatonic to form words. The concatenation snowballed into a pointless babble. I attempted to wake myself up as anyone does in lucid dreams. I bit my hand, scratched my neck and chest until the skin went raw; there was a cinder block not too far from Zephyr's head and I slammed it down on my foot.

Alas, nothing.

That's when I smelled an odor so malicious it reached a gnarled hand into my gut and squeezed. An unknown source of light came to be, dazzling across Zephyr's body to unveil the rest of the catastrophe at my feet. Zephyr had been clawed open, sternum to groin, his jellied insides exposed so that I could see coiled intestine, the frost-rimmed tinge of bone that used to be his ribcage, and globules of dried blood.

Something swished past me with an animal-like precision. I heard multiple legs, saw an arachnid-like prance. And then it was in the air, silent as the membranous wings of a bat, shooting warm wind into my face. I put my hands on my head instinctively, waiting to be attacked, but nothing happened. Then there came a giant crash on the floor, a gentle hiss and something crawling lizard-like in the direction of Zephyr. My first instinct was to kick, and upon doing so I was dragged down to the floor which was covered in foamy blood.

My eyes were level with Zephyr's torso. Specifically, I could see a tiny red remnant of his nipple, but the silver hoop that used to run through it was nowhere to be found. I caught a whiff of his deodorant and cigarettes between the disgusting odor of decay. If my heart were able to skip a beat, it must have done so in this moment. I saw a pair of great wings hurtle toward me, followed by the sight of chitinous legs as if this thing was a cross between bat and spider. The face was familiar, despite being awash with blood, as it dived back into Zephyr's hollowed body. I knew the curves of those special bones, the deepness of the eyes, the Rorschach insanity of his lips. Guilt sieged my moribund soul.

  ... Dexter ...

I expected sunlight to drizzle golden and slow as honey into the back of my brain. Instead, there was darkness. I'd no depth perception or awareness of atmosphere. I could have been locked in a coffin six feet below ground for all I knew. I straightened my arms until the joints made a little pop. My legs kicked up, stretching my lower back enough to send a hot wire down my side.

But I'd managed to get on my feet, grabbed the cigarette behind my ear and lit it with my zippo. The smoke was stale but calmed my nerves. Something sparkled in my peripheral vision, and when I turned my head to meet its brilliance, I made out the glowing gash of graffiti. I traced my fingers across the words, attempting to make sense of their meaning as each syllable penetrated my skin. *Mea eSt AniMa tua* and *Serpens AuTem sciBbaNt erAm* was all I saw.

Below me was a ritual circle of red and gold glitter. I followed the spiral from the inside out, like Dorothy tracing her steps on the yellow brick road. My Converses popped and squelched, as if I was stepping on cockroaches. There was no certain direction the glittery spiral was taking me, in fact it felt like I just kept spiraling in and out of its center of gravity. It left me feeling numb, dumb and completely out of touch with reality.

I was "cracked out" from the amphetamines; had to sit down and gather my thoughts. Delilah was weighing my head down, but she was no longer what I wanted to think about. Zephyr was all that mattered. I was sick with worry. We were symbiotes after all, and if I was hurting that meant he was hurting, and I didn't want Zephyr to feel any pain.

I found myself enveloped in anger, saw into the searing core of my mistake. Never have my thoughts pierced the veil of narcissism, or even ego. But I'd been subconsciously deceived since the moment Dexter came into my life. I hadn't thought about Zephyr's needs; I didn't even ask his opinion on anything that was going on. That proved that I was lovesick. It used to be that no matter what went on in my head—malignant obsessions, endless addictions, hemorrhaging hormones—Zephyr was always my primary concern. This was the first time I'd written him off, per se.

"Open your eyes."

Dexter's voice was a calming beacon, the kind that gave me the strength to suffer another day in this sad, mad world. I walked in his direction. The still of the City wrapped about my body, coursing through my blood as would Covid-19 had I contracted it. A virus is such a smart little bug. Its tenacity is laudable in the way it evades our "superior" biological defenses—raping careful mechanisms, slipping through cellular fault lines, and proceeding to chew away at the foundations of life until it breaks a person down so badly death is the only way out. Love is very much the same virus.

"You knocked out."

His fingers caressed my face. I could smell his sickly-sweet pheromones, feel the softness of his skin. He proceeded to open my eyelids. I'd had my eyes closed the entire time! My guess was that the MDMA and the Ketamine caused these life-like visions. I brought my drawing hand up, felt the thumb with the other, as a sick need to magnetize toward Dexter came over me. I wondered why I was doing this to myself; how did I let it get this far? Why was I so convinced that I couldn't survive without Dexter by my side?

Ruin you

I felt Delilah's voice this time, as if she was still by my side. The fact that I realized now how she'd gone through so much trouble to reach me, and I spent that entire time ignoring her, left me rather maudlin. So, I looked about the room, recognized mildly that I had been pulled away from the smog of the city and just now awoken in some kind of studio.

"I think I had a weird dream," I said.

"I know." Dexter leaned in close, lips grazing my outer ear, tongue running down until I smelled the cigarettes on his breath "If she thinks I can't see her every move, she's sadly mistaken."

His words hit me like a punch in the gut. But for some reason my eyes were fixated on all the art that surrounded me. Ubiquitous and madly placed, every shelf was lined with horrific clay sculptures and monsters carved from gemstone. Books were piled in every corner and dust bunnies the size of my fist rolled about the floor. This was the room of a person who didn't know what organization was.

"I saw the City." My words sounded strange, even to me. "Smelled it, tasted it."

"I told you, there's a city beneath the city. You can see it so long as you wish."

Dexter leaned in, purple eyes like flying saucers, hair sultrily touching the side of my cheek. For one impossible moment I saw his ears turn into apexes, teeth become fangs, and wings replace his arms. But then our lips collided, melted into one another. His mouth was sweet and his tongue tasted like embers. I lost myself in his kiss, forgetting everything. Dexter was my virus. He evaded every facet of my defenses and rational thinking, all the way down to my dick, which was hardening as each second went by.

"What're you going to do about Delilah?"

"Nothing."

"You don't want to tell me?"

"Not yet."

"Are you what she says you are?"

"You think she's smart, don't you?" Dexter's lips and teeth went comically wide.

"I just want to know what happened."

"With what?"

"Your former relationship. You never told me about it."

"The past is dead."

"I get that. But you left behind a trail. That's why she's after you."

"We call that obsession."

"What do you mean?"

"Maybe because I never paid her any attention. Delilah hates men but she's a weak little bitch when she doesn't get their attention."

I was quiet for a moment. "Where's Zephyr? I wanna talk to him."

"How am I supposed to know?"

Dexter grabbed me, but I quickly removed myself from his grip and grabbed my phone, saw that all my socials were flooded with messages. Somehow I'd gotten a signal again, but I didn't dare open any of them after remembering what Delilah had done, given my association with Dexter via socials. All I wanted to do was call Zephyr.

"You brought us down here."

"Why do you always ask about him?" Dexter spit the words out coldly.

"Because I love him."

"And what about me?"

"Loving him doesn't mean I can't love you too."

"How can you be sure?"

"Are you so insecure you can't take my word?"

"He called me that word too."

I heard something move behind me. *I'm here*, came the whisper. Zephyr was in a haggard state. His eyes had lost the glow I once admired, now just an awful dull gray. It looked like he'd seen a ghost, though seeing one would have been an actual treat in our culture. There were creases in his brow I didn't recognize, new folds in his cheeks; shriveled strips of flesh were now his lips. I grabbed him by the hand, in which I felt little bones rattle beneath the parchment skin and held him close to me.

"What happened?" I said, pulling him close to me. "I'm here now."

"I got so lost."

"Me too."

"There's an actual city down here."

"A dead one."

Then Zephyr let go of me and bee-lined toward Dexter. I saw his fingers curl into hooks, bony arms trembling with anger. But Zephyr never grabbed hold of Dexter's actual skin—rather, he got hold of his stylish clothes, and the entire scene couldn't be computed by my eyes. Dexter just stood there, enduring the swings and slaps, the ripping of his clothes, tearing away at flesh that just wasn't there.

"You see!" Zephyr wailed. "He isn't real."

"Have you eaten?" Dexter said. "You're sick, that's all."

"Don't talk to him like that."

Dexter's skin changed color and his dyed hair went white-hot. He was almost doll-like, as if someone had carved and painted his features with insane precision. It was something I could never do with my own hands. The worst of it all was his eyes. They seemed dead, yet electrified by some crazy form of desire . . . hunger.

"Why can he talk to me like that?"

"Because he's hurt, can't you see?"

"I don't know what I see," Dexter spat.

"You know exactly what's happening. It all makes sense now."

My phone went off again. The texts and direct messages were piling up. But I knew if I opened them, I was allowing all hell to break loose into my life. The drama between Dexter and Electric Orchid had reached dangerous heights. They were now public with their need to take him down, and I was caught in the crossfire. For the first time in my life, I feared cancel culture. The fact that they used Instagram Live was even more frightening, for there was truly no explaining how that *thing* sprung up and crawled around, no explaining how the Hydra was able to *challenge* it.

"What *are* you?" Zephyr coughed into his hand.

"I don't know what you're talking about."

"This place . . . your mind . . . is a labyrinth."

Zephyr ripped at his nails until his teeth were rimmed red, beautiful lips stained in gore.

"Something's down here. Something we can't imagine."

"You're killing yourself by sticking around," Dexter said. "Go up if you want to live."

"Not without Atticus."

"He leaves when I say."

"What the fuck does that mean?" I interjected.

Zephyr pointed his bloody finger at Dexter. "I'm glad you finally admit it. Delilah was right."

"Are you two seriously going to let that bitch get in the way of what's to become?"

"Atticus," Zephyr said with conviction. "It's me or him. You need to choose. *Now*."

Dexter's anger could be felt through the air. Something about it was raw and unhinged. My hand began to burn. This time, I saw something I didn't want to. Jagged lines crisscrossing from wrist to elbow, like some sort of map or blueprint; maybe it was the answer to this place. Then the lights blew out and the floor vibrated. Now I remembered exactly what happened in the moment before arriving here, but it only came to me in ugly inkblots.

As I was processing this, a thick black substance overcame me, so dense and substantial that I could have manipulated it with my hands as I would my art.

We've gotten so close, I heard Dexter say.

Soon . . .

–it'll just be us

19

The stress-inducing hour between sunrise and moonfall; sleep would not find them. There was no time. Sebastian hit the night air of the outside world as if it was a wall, knocking the wind out of him, but the taste of freedom was rich and metallic as blood; Dorian retched when he pulled himself free from the underground. Adrenaline sizzled in their cells, lungs barely able to keep up with the accelerated heart rates.

"Did you see the city?" Sebastian asked.

Dorian cleared his throat; a red wad of phlegm dangled from his chin. "Yes. But I don't want to remember it."

However, there was no way to erase that shimmering crystal city, swarming for what seemed like miles, as if the underground was dozens of times larger than that of the world surrounding it. And the skyline went on forever, a candyscape that appeared as a portrait from a certain angle, wanting to be touched, to be savored. Everything had a glimmer and gleam about it, like the sun reflecting off huge mirrors.

But how was that physically possible? How could he have seen skyscrapers so tall they pierced the stony sky and made it rain little shards of light? How could he have seen the roads that went on forever, begging for someone to walk on them, while at the same time not seeing on the streets? How was it so weirdly bright for such a dark place? Sebastian didn't want to think about it anymore, and Dorian had other plans anyway.

Now that they were back above ground, the protective skin of reality felt like it had been breached. Every avenue and sidewalk stretched before their eyes, as if fashioned from some pliable substance. Sebastian's facial muscles tensed into a frown. In the northern view, skyscrapers stood as sentinels, their lights flickering intermittently—but it was a rather dull skyline compared to what he'd just seen. On street level, condemnation and abandonment was rampant. But they were back in the real world now, to once again suffer the pandemic and how it'd rewound time, so that merely walking the streets was a fight for one's safety.

They passed mute neon bars and corrugated metal shutters, a spectrum of protest graffiti. Here and there a business thrived, hole-in-the-wall kitchens that smelled of grease vapors, dollar pizza and thrift shops. And it was only a matter of time before it all crumbled. The thought of collapse brought Sebastian's mind back to his friends. How long would it take before they were never seen again? It made his feet move faster.

Dorian popped a piece of gum in his mouth, lit two Pall Malls and smoked until his walk became a wobble. His Doc Martens looked like they were weighted down with stones, even though he maintained balance with a modicum of grace. Sebastian grabbed Dorian's hand to keep him on the same trajectory, intertwining their fingers, palms sweaty and soft but cold with fear. Sebastian wanted to be mouth-to-drippy-mouth with him beneath the opaque moonlight.

But, as much as Sebastian vied to take this moment to enjoy Dorian's presence, it would only distract him from helping his friends. Now he wanted a cigarette of his own; just one puff of smoke could make this all go away, even though he was old enough now to realize that no matter the drug, no matter the drink, reality doesn't just fizzle away like it did when he was a teenager.

"You want a pull?"

"Huh?"

"I can see you staring."

The orange cinder of Dorian's cigarette was a dull star. As enticing as that was, Sebastian had switched to vaping months back, took a pull of sweet strawberry lemonade instead, and felt happy he did not give in to old temptation. But the vape made his head somehow heavy, blossoming a strange pain in his neck that radiated down to the middle of his back. Maybe it was all the stress, which plays a key role in the way your body processes pain.

"How about a hit of this instead?" Sebastian offered Dorian the vape.

"No thanks. It's filled with heavy metals."

"At this point what's the difference?"

"Taste. Addiction. Quite a lot."

They both got quiet. While Dorian was veiled by the smoke, moonlight had also fallen atop his skin, giving it a weird hue. Sebastian was unsure of what he wanted to say, but he knew that it couldn't be anything stupid. He already had this sick need to impress Dorian, and that sickness was only going to get worse as time went on. Right now, he needed to go back home, not his literal home, but the one that was always there when he needed it.

"Let's go."

They descended into the subway, stepping over two catatonic transients with hypodermics plunged into non-existent veins. Foul twin puddles leaked past their knees, and the warm reek of it polluted the air from the stairs all the way down to the platform itself. The last thing Sebastian saw was dead eyes and slack jaws. Dorian held his nose in disdain, but Sebastian felt his heart stammer in the wake of his sorrow. Just another sad display of wasted youth.

The platform was empty, as expected. It gave them both time to overthink. There could be any type of lurker, dead or alive, waiting for an ignoramus to stumble down here so they could have their way with them. There were secret doors and entrances that the general public was not aware of in the tunnels. Perhaps a whole city could erupt from the ground here, a scintillating and sizzling nightmare that was not meant to be.

Sebastian now saw that Dorian was on high alert, which meant he must have been thinking the same thing; that reality was no longer a safe space. Anything could shift it, anything could pierce the thin veil and screw up everything you once knew. Sebastian checked his phone, fully expecting to see messages from Delilah, but nothing was there. It instilled a new type of worry in him; the reality that they were truly in trouble.

"Put your mask on," Sebastian said.

The oncoming train sounded like a building had collapsed instead of its usual encumbering rumble. Dorian slipped on an esoteric cloth mask, while Sebastian's was a creepy skeletal grin made of silk. They found a seat, let the dark and rocking silence soothe their nerves. Sebastian eyed his reflection in the sticker-scarred windows, skeletal but vibrant with just the right amount of eye makeup; the lips on the mask looked glossed, and his tousled hair was kept under control by a rubber band. He didn't look like someone who was under a tremendous amount of stress, though he was breaking down on the inside.

He tried to steady his thoughts, but his trembling mind easily took over. Not only were his nerves fried, but he was worried about the thing inside of him coming back. A dormant gene unlocked by the simple theatric of Dexter's art. Maybe that was what it was like for Dorian. A few years ago he went into hiding and cast himself out from the scene, only to have the muse rise through him after Sebastian came to him in his dreams; gateway drug to re-open his artistic eye. There was no returning from that. An artist follows the muse when it calls.

Sebastian would one day have to *become* her again. But for once in his life, Sebastian didn't have to suffer it alone. After the debauchery and villainous love that Adrian had subjected him to, he thought he'd never have the urge to be with a man again. Lovers can be fun, sometimes they can fulfill you, but mostly they are a distraction from a person's true calling. Unless you find a lover that's simply different.

He recalled Dorian's deliquescent kiss, soft but assertive. New love sparks new reasoning, naturally, and it also serves as a conduit to self-reflection. To open your insecure self can be the hardest challenge of all. You change for this person; you find yourself doing things you swore you'd never do, just to keep this person around. Sometimes, when you love someone so much, you forget about yourself. Love can be blinding.

But Dorian was relief and inspiration all in one. Though they'd been taking things slow for over a year, they were now deeply attracted to one another, moving past the butterfly stage, and falling fast in love. Sebastian didn't quite understand how he connected to Dorian so fast. It almost felt like a surrender of his own identity.

There was something special about Dorian's hypnotic face, his parchment skin and strong features; how the hair on his head shined like onyx, and the unending spiral of his blacker than black eyes. The dark smile made Dorian appear as the cliched art-type, but Sebastian knew there was more to him than that superficial definition; there was a galaxy of knowledge and passion between his ears, endless wormholes of creativity.

And he knew the feeling was mutual. Dorian expressed it enough, though he hadn't been interested in anyone romantically for a long time. Five years ago, the first love of his life broke up with Dorian, which left him so closed off to romance it was impossible to imagine he'd ever find love again. But he must have seen something in Sebastian to pursue him so fiercely. Despite the explicit flirting and corny pickup lines, the attraction was very much there.

Dorian was careful, almost calculated. He knew the two of them feared being ripped apart by the pain that love can bring. They'd both lived it before. But Sebastian remained intrigued by Dorian's persistence and almost pugnacious demeanor, so the opportunity could not be passed up; all the impossible things that could come of these strange stars aligning would be worth the trouble.

Sebastian gave into Dorian's advances, realizing how lonely life can be even when you're a self-described loner.

"Should we call the cops?" Dorian's stare was deadpan, voice muffled beneath the mask.

"You think they'd believe anything we say?"

"I guess not."

"Cops don't know about the cities beneath New York City."

"Cities?"

"If we saw one, there's got to be more."

The train howled and its lights flickered. Sebastian watched as a bum slid across the seat, and the old-school radio in his hand propelled a ghostly, genderless voice, followed by a maddening ticker noise. It was a news report about the Covid-19 Vaccine, and then one about how the crime rates of New York City had risen exponentially. Then there was a report about how the MTA was crying broke, yet again.

"If they raise the rates I'm gunna scream," Dorian said.

"Scream away, because they don't give a fuck."

They turned from the other. Sebastian looked out the window behind him, just cold blackness out there, pinpricked by a speck of light from the sparks below. He used his imagination to take his eyes on a new journey, somewhere deep within the core of New York City, then even beyond that—through the spiderweb tunnels and pathways, through black holes that cannot be seen by the naked eye. He moved his sense of sight through all of this, much like how neutrinos pass through atomic matter every second of every day.

"How long until we get to Brooklyn?" Dorian said. "We can't leave them down there for too long."

"I don't plan to."

"Why are we going back to Brooklyn?"

"Because I left something there."

Red Hook was a smudge of darkness upon exiting the station. There was a storm brewing in the west, Sebastian could smell it in the air, humidity with a hint of electric. They rushed through shaded avenues and chewed-up streets; construction projects filled the air with concrete dust and paint shavings. No lights emanated from the surrounding warehouses, and the crumbling apartment complexes were too dark to see them fully.

On the corner of Wolcott and Ferris, Whyrlwynd sat like a hole torn into space, dead red brick drenched in graffiti, lightless warehouse windows scrawled in lipstick. Anyone who got close enough was lulled to its dark charm by the force of gravity. Sebastian punched in a code to unlock its only door, steel he'd scavenged from an old junkyard, soldered and bolted and drilled into the foundation. The code machine glowed green and squealed, then the deadbolts lifted.

"Remember when you broke in?" Sebastian said.

"Yup," Dorian said.

"Hence my new security system." Sebastian winked. "Can't let lunatics like you get in *that* easily."

Geometric chandeliers hung above every window and even the front door. Each one was either emerald or amethyst, their light bleeding down the wall brightly. They were in the shape of serpents, flowers, dragons and hexes, all created from stained glass and metal. Dorian reached up and touched one shaped like a rose, but Sebastian quickly pulled his hand away.

"Don't use your drawing hand to touch those."

"Why?"

"They'll burn you. Plus, those are cameras."

Once inside, Sebastian turned on the lights. Each bulb was shaped like a teardrop and filled with bright wire filaments that shed a soft orange glow unto the entire room. In the month that passed, not much had changed. Squatter remnants were everywhere. Clothes, tarot cards, melted candles, liquor bottles and a variety of books, shoes and jewelry. But no drugs. Never that. They'd sooner lose a limb than give away their euphoria.

"This is why I don't want them here anymore," Sebastian said.

"I thought you had *that* removed."

Dorian pointed to a glowing ouroboros that he'd painted on the foyer's wall over a year ago. At this hour, the palest watercolor light passed through the warehouse windows, turning the still painting into a living illusion. Then there came a bright flash, filling the space with so much light it pushed both Dorian and Sebastian backwards, as if light could occupy a room. It was followed by a rumble that shook Whyrlwynd's foundation. It's many cabinets whipped open, spilling makeup, toys, beer bottles, books and a variety of other art-related trinkets.

"The fuck was that?"

"Sounded like a bomb," Dorian said.

They rushed to the window, veering toward Manhattan's lower skyline. At first nothing out of the ordinary, financial district glittering but somehow reticent beneath the oncoming storm. But then they saw an alien light ascend with such speed that it tore a hole into the morning sky, revealing a patch of darkness that could not have looked more wrong. The strange light had no beginning or end, as if all colors mixed into one, shooting up in bars of intensity as thick as the smoke left behind from a rocket.

"What the—"

"Terrorist attack?"

Sebastian brought a finger to his mouth and started chewing. "I don't think it's the kind of terrorists we're thinking of."

Dorian glowered. "Shit's like something out of *Ghostbusters*."

Sebastian nodded. "Delilah warned us."

"Let's just do what we need to and get back."

They both moved away from the window. Dorian looked at his phone, waiting for social media to alert him of what was happening. Sebastian waited in silence, but after a few minutes of browsing, Dorian came up with nothing, pocketed his phone, swiped the garbage off the nearby couch and leaned one knee against it with a Pall Mall lit between his lips. Due to his frayed nerves, Sebastian took a pull to calm himself down, reveling in the horrid flavor of the traditional smoke, but somehow finding peace within the memories of his former addiction.

"Come on, Sammy, we don't have much time."

"Let me think."

Sebastian closed his eyes. He began to will his muscles, organs and mind to relax. Fiber by fiber, atom by atom, down to the almost metaphysical particles that sparked out of nowhere to create the universe. He put himself into a meditational state, allowing his mind to traverse the honeycomb darkness that lived inside his body. He would do this from time to time: unsheathe the many personalities that lived inside of him.

Over the years he'd lost touch with some of the distinct identities. Through creative therapy and the art of drag, he was able to drive most of them away. But one of them remained, namesake of his nightlife persona, the Hydra. She was a constant reminder that not even today's social sciences could control the beast within. For the past year she'd gone quiet, but ever since he saw Dexter's sculpture come to life, she began creeping around inside of him again, a new encroaching shadow.

He rode the black spiral. It rooted deep into cavernous pathways, through endless dark doorways; routes to nothingness, forks in nameless roads, mental dead ends. Roads to nowhere. Soon enough, he knew, his brain would liquify and his organs would go the way of a slow cooking stew. Only then could he break free and remember all there ever was, all that could have been, and all that ever will be.

Even though Sebastian controlled his inner madness, he knew that if he ventured far enough, opened his mind and body like a budding flower, she'd be there waiting, full of venom. That is, if he allowed himself. This time, things were different. And so, these same endless pathways, these same black roads to nowhere, this same abyss, now came to him like beacons.

Beneath his own feet, just a few towns over, there was a hidden gem only accessible by manhole. It was called the Atlantic Avenue Tunnel, which is known as New York City's oldest subway. From Boerum Place to Columbia Street, the tunnel stretches for a haunting half mile. Sebastian and Dorian had once gone on an official tour and thought nothing of how many of these secret cities and tunnels had been here breeding lunacy and darkness and demons all this time.

Now it was all Sebastian could think about. How many secrets were below his feet? How many industries and thriving economies lived below the bedrock? Was it aliens? Was it magic? How could there be entire cities under all of New York? And why didn't ordinary people think about these things? People have a way of becoming so wrapped up in their jobs, routine and exhaustion that modern marvels feel almost like fiction. Even if there are a broad spectrum of miracles out there, sometimes it's easier to just not know about them.

It's the same question scientists pose about the universe and our existence—why are we here, what is our purpose, and where did we come from?

As for the cities beneath the streets of New York, one just needs to know where to look. It's not that hard to find them if you really think about it. New York is the world's hub for a reason. It's the place where all dreams can come true. How many more of these lost tunnels and secret cities and unfinished projects could there be in New York City? Was it truly impossible to think that there was something in the underground beyond the city's water system, subways, railroads and cable lines? Sebastian knew it was true now, and it had been right beneath his nose the entire time.

miss you

The voice crackled inside of Sebastian's head. He knew it like he knew his own face in front of a mirror. You don't forget something as wicked as this. He felt himself clench as there came a sudden sensation of his skin becoming too tight for his muscles. *Love You*. He knew it by the scent of sulfur and funeral pyre. Beauty and rage would once again be given a voice through the body that was formerly Sebastian's. It was pointless to fight.

"Get out. Now!"

Construction paper rip, and no it wasn't the real thing. Skin, stretched to its limits, threaded in red and blue, brilliant fibers, fascia and drippy adipose. Until it wasn't skin any longer but something reptilian, scales or scutes not of this realm. And then the stench of sulfur, so thick it clogged the nostrils; putrid odor as noxious as the thing Sebastian was turning into. Dorian took a step back, heeded no warning.

Isn't this what you wanted? The Hydra telepathically said to Dorian. *Bring back Sebastian*, Dorian demanded. *I know you.* Fungus colored nails, blue lips and a tempting warmth emanated from Sebastian's body. The Hydra was here now, and she could see through Dorian, get to his insides if she wanted. But Dorian had met her before, so he wasn't afraid.

"If you don't bring him back, I'll go in and get him."

"You will *try.*"

Dorian lunged. All hands and a forest of teeth. The insane need to get his boy back was all he needed to fight. But the Hydra caught Dorian by the neck mid-flight, attached her burning lips to his and sent her tongue down his throat and into his digestive tract. There was a moment where Dorian's abdomen began fluttering as if he was a mother-to-be.

Dorian was oddly turned on. The Hydra felt his blood speed up, hormones harassing his rational thinking. *You taste so good*, Dorian whispered. When the Hydra pulled her tongue out, Dorian was red with rage and demanded that she kiss him again. Their lips met like warring titans, teeth breaking the barrier of flesh. This all made no sense, but the pain translated into something more like seduction. Always soft, always sexy.

Dorian used the power of his mind and reached his hand *inside* of the Hydra. Straight through her jellyfish hair, through the dome of the skull, into the tangle of her brain, reached as far as he could go until his fingers snagged something. Sebastian. Now that Dorian had come full circle in his beliefs and his power, the Hydra was no longer a monster that would get in his way, but a vessel for him to use for his own bidding.

And then Dorian's other hand came up, his drawing hand. One of his nails was bleeding and he used it to draw. It was the only thing he knew how to do under immense pressure. He drew on the Hydra's body, bare breasts, her serpentine face, even drew across her lips. Spirals and tendrils and circles, all of the infinite dreams that haunt him. In this moment, he summoned his greatest gift, something like the shining, but more sinister.

The Hydra howled as the images began to singe her. Dorian could do this with his own thoughts, and the Hydra had no defense against it. Then Dorian blinked, bringing a shaky ouroboros to life, so that it spun and spun until all the light that lives inside of a black hole came rushing out, gamma ray burst impossible to see, but the red brilliance too magnificent to turn away from. The blast left a scourge in the hardwood floor of Whyrlwynd and pushed the two bodies to the opposite side of the workspace. Dorian got to his feet, teeth and lips greased in crimson.

Now the walls were alive with drawings, all kinds of runes and maps. Dorian stuck his head inside of the drawings, and when he pulled his face out it was tattooed with a weird looking blueprint. But his hands wouldn't stop; no brushes, no pens, just fingers heating up the paint on the walls to make swirls into spirals, black holes into white holes. An hour flew by, then two. His drawing hand was rubbed raw, the nails chipped away, but his fingers kept going. Skylines and tunnels, various cities beneath the city; glistening red pathways that all met at the same cloud of chaos: Dexter.

"I know what to do," Dorian said.

20

How Zephyr only realized it now, that there are entire cities beneath New York City, left him with a city-sized hole in his brain. What he feared most down here was the darkness. Not the kind he was used to. It was pliable, thick; somehow it could metamorphose. But it was more than that. This darkness was becoming part of him. He was inherently afraid to leave it, as if he was not meant to be anywhere else.

Stuck down here . . . forever.

His body began to feel weightless, stripped of the matter that once kept him grounded, blood cells slipping through the pores of his skin and quickly dissolving into the endless city. There was no real way of defining it; he was made of energy now, of darkness, not the subatomic particles of matter. Zephyr was the stuff of dream.

The wayward streets led him deeper into the city. And the deeper he got, the more confusing it all became. Zephyr started seeing thrush and vegetation. Mountains sprouted in the distance, and a layer of snow was falling atop them. A quick burst of light incinerated his eyes, and when he was able to see again, the sky was as blue as he remembered from childhood, blue as his hair, then was quickly overtaken by a sun as white as Dexter's hair.

Zephyr entered one of the skyscrapers. Its walls and floors were as black and reflective. Ahead, something spindly was cast at his feet, shadow of what appeared to be a tree, or something with many legs. The only sound was his creeping footsteps, which gave him no indication to stay. He stumbled back onto the street and kept walking.

Suddenly roads, buildings and signs were flipped upside down. Even the words written on them were backwards, which only meant to Zephyr that they would lead him nowhere, but there was nowhere to go without Atticus anyway. The determination to find him was all that kept Zephyr going. He fled past huge crystal buildings and onyx tenements, past the black avatars of every bar, club and concert hall he'd ever spent time in, past every warehouse and dilapidated apartment he'd ever partied in or visited. However, inside all of these things was nothing but stillness.

Zephyr fed himself into other random doors and windows, clothes catching on jagged pieces of windowpane, puncturing his skin, but without the agony he knew it should have caused. The only proof was the thin coating of blood left behind. If he had to search every building, walk every road until his feet died on his own body, cross every street and knock on every door until he was reunited with Atticus so he could take him away from Dexter, he would.

And then a small vibration in his pocket, phone suddenly alive with a signal and messages flooding in. He hadn't the patience to go through them all; he'd posted a few stories while down here, and so he figured people were reacting to that. He didn't really want to know what they were seeing, if they were seeing anything at all. The weirdest part about perusing the city down here down here was not being cut off from the world above, it was that he had no phone access. The dependency on that little box almost made him want to throw it away.

Back out on the street and moving away from the buildings that were now as two-dimensional as a window's reflection, Zephyr could see that there was something wrong with everything. The buildings were changing, suddenly fragmented and swaying ever so slightly as they towered above him. It looked as if they were made of random things piled on top of one another, things that looked very familiar. Upon closer inspection, he saw that it was the collectibles he'd amassed over his life, and they were slowly spewing out of the windows and doors, forming a wall of antiques that could crush him.

He jetted back, and what he thought was the main avenue of this place was now gone, and every sign that offered directions had fallen off their posts. The entire thoroughfare was a silent movie filled with all the things a busy metropolis should be filled with, but without noise. The mannequins he'd seen were now placed around all about him as if they were living things. They crowded the sidewalks and infiltrated storefront windows. They had burning cigarettes in their hands and beer foam on their upper lips. They were clothed in the same alt getups of black and denim and ripped t-shirts; they even had tattoos to make them appear more lifelike.

If one were to view this from far away it would be the scene of a mobbed tourist attraction. But as Zephyr walked close to one of the mannequins, which was seated at a table on a street that was open to pedestrian traffic only, he smelled hot glue and melted plastic, which made him realize all of this was fake. He took the lit cigarette for himself, and as he walked away, one of the mannequin's blank sunken eyes turned in his direction, watching him as he fled into the deep night streets. When he turned around, the mannequin began peeling its own face back, revealing a familiar skeleton.

Thoughts corroded Zephyr's mind. How could he have been so stupid? He closed his eyes and retraced all the steps he'd taken to get to this point, ran nervous fingers through his robin-egg hair, noticed that it left the edges of his nails blue. Was it rubbing off? Or just another illusion? Every time he seemed to get control of himself, something changed . . . shapeshifted, same as everything in this place did . . . this unending abyss. Was it staring back at him?

The uncertainty entertained him maliciously. He searched his pockets, found a vile of ketamine, a bottle of GHB and two molly capsules. It seemed that whatever drugs were in his system, this place wanted him to take more. But a faint memory of something

Dexter had said came to mind, that Molly made him become too paranoid, wig out and see things. Perhaps that was the only way he could get rid of Dexter and the rare darkness he exuded.

Whatever feelings Zephyr thought he might have developed for Dexter had died. Understanding that Dexter was pushing him out of Atticus' life changed everything. Delilah had been right all along; he'd wasted so much time trying to make it work with Dexter, time he'd never get back, but he hoped this would one day be a valuable lesson as he continued to try and stay above the choppy waters of life.

Zephyr walked in a direction he thought was the only way to go now, though he could barely see, the darkness so thick that light didn't even pass through it. There was no beginning and there would never be an ending. Then sounds were coming upon him. Footsteps, and something like metal scraping across concrete. There's no worse spook than when something creeps up on a person who can barely see their hands in front of their face.

Slowly, something began to glow. Little by little the pink thing was coming into view. It reminded Zephyr of the visions that come with a great ketamine high. Then the incandescence started to crawl. Two emerald sparks filled his line of sight, as well as the smell of clove cigarettes. Zephyr braced himself for the collision, but instead a small pallid hand reached through the darkness and placed itself softly on his shoulder.

"I've been looking for you."

It was Delilah. She was cast in a strange coronal light, like the outline of a body drawn at a crime scene. All sorts of crazy expressions were worn across her face and there were ornate markings on her skin, more intricate than the scrollwork tattoos and suicide scars. She was slashed and sashed in a weird black substance. Even her eyes were caked with it, which made her appear as a racoon.

"What happened?" Zephyr saw that her arm was bleeding, three crimson furrows that reeked of fresh blood

"He almost got me," Delilah said, out of breath.

"*Dexter.*"

Delilah winced. "He knows we're down here."

"And we're fucking stuck."

"I know. He'll never let us out."

"But even the Devil has weaknesses."

Zephyr had seen many a spook in his day; comes with the territory of making friends with creative people. But nothing compared to all of this. *Do you know what he did?* Delilah was inside his head now, screaming as loud as she could. *He killed his mother!* The words ricocheted as she pulled something toward Zephyr.

It was a table with strange drawings carved into the marble. Tenuous face, gaping jaw; eyes the same purple hue as Dexter's. *That's not all*, Delilah whispered. She thrust her hands into the table, wrist-deep as if it was made of water. She wrestled with something for a full minute before pulling it free. A sculpture of a black heart, maybe a brain, soaked in a drippy tar-like substance.

"It's changed shape."

Zephyr gasped. "That's the thing I saw on your Instagram."

"How long do you think before he comes to get it?"

Delilah put the wrong thing into Zephyr's hands. It was oddly weightless, and bore no specific shape. It kept changing before his eyes, and only when he accepted its presence, Zephyr knew, would he see its true form. Its airlessness and vacuum-temperature was not that of normal clay. This was what Zephyr imagined a black hole would feel like, the anti-feeling of everything, where all matter can slip inside, never to be seen again.

This is what the end of days felt like, Zephyr knew; the end of love, the end of suffering.

"Do you think he has a soul?"

"Yes," Delilah said. "Just not the kind you and I have."

"What do we do with this then?"

"Nothing. I need Dorian and Sebastian to help me."

"Why do you need them?"

"You saw what happened. For some reason this thing doesn't like them."

The table was gone now. A different kind of sound crept about them, or inside of them, whispering as would their own blood. They were now encircled by the mannequins without so much as the echo of a footstep. Zephyr went on his tippy toes and saw that they numbered in the thousands. Blank eyes, mohawks and dyed hair went on forever. There was no telling if they were closing in on them, or if it was their imagination.

"The fuck is this?" Delilah spit.

"I think they heard you."

Zephyr turned toward one of the mannequins, removed a lit cigarette from its cold plastic hand.

"So . . . everything you said was true?"

"Yes. Believe me now?"

Zephyr nodded. "How're we going to get out of here?"

"Push through."

"They're heavier than they look."

"Plastic won't stop me, no matter how creepy they are."

"Wait! What do you think we do so wrong that would make a *thing* like Dexter want to ruin our lives?"

"I don't know," Delilah said. "I want to say something poetic . . . that we don't appreciate the things we have because our focus is always on what we *don't have*."

"And?"

"It's the irony of our nature."

And just like that, the silence cracked open. An elongated scream bled dazzles of light into the air. It sent Zephyr flying backwards as if someone had tugged him with a rope, and Delilah forward as if someone had tackled her from behind. They both crashed into the mannequins, knocking heads and hands into the air. The momentary loss of consciousness brought visions of Dexter and Atticus that in the end melted into the other, until Zephyr opened his eyes to see Delilah's ivory face above his, pink hair veiling her eyes.

"If we don't move, we're done for," Delilah hissed. "They don't want anything standing in the way when they go back above ground."

"I can't go without Atticus."

"Get up, we don't have much time!"

As she finished the words, purple smoke erupted around them.

Dexter

Alex's pulse was in his ears. A jellified stream of makeup had dried on his face. He'd been crying, or screaming, so said the rawness of his throat. He'd seen things that he never thought he'd ever see, at least not while he was mentally sound. Whether he was ready to accept it or not was no longer a consideration. He was at the mercy of memory now, the coldness of Dexter's former kiss and the delirium of his past intent.

He could feel the boy as if he was flesh and blood. The way he touched Alex, from soul to pole, even hole, left him feeling dirty. It was testament to the fact that sometimes when you form a bond with someone, and even if that bond breaks, you can still feel them lingering inside of you. And now that he was back at square one, he had no choice but to face his past so he could finally get on with his future.

On his feet now, bones aching, loins complaining, and some breathless melody swirling in one of his ears, a ghost kiss of dead memory. He took the first road his eyes saw, an arid stretch of land that was like a desert at midnight. The Converses on his feet were so destroyed he might as well have been barefoot; he could feel the hardness of the road, smell the fresh stink of his feet. But he moved, sly and quick, going anywhere as long as he was moving.

The great black city branched in too many directions to understand. How could the buildings fling themselves out of the ground and pollute the skyline with spires, steel and a glass-like material without so much as making a sound? Why were the people, or what he thought were people, frozen like pressing pause on a movie? It was all so difficult to accept, but the only way Alex was going to understand it all was to keep moving.

Into the void. Arms stretched out like poles. He walked defensively, but curiously. He touched everything he saw, felt the pseudo-stone and shimmering black glass; used his nose to take in the smells of this great underground megalopolitan. He knocked into the very still people that suddenly surrounded him, realizing again as a few fell over and burst into pieces that they were mannequins. More reason to justify Dexter's weirdness. Had he been living down here with these the entire time?

Something brushed across his face, a hand but with the weight of a feather. Above, the sky was beginning to pull light down toward him as if it was the web of a great spider. Alex followed the brilliance until it began wrapping around him, forcing his eyes to roll so far back he saw flashes of his own brain. It went like this for what felt like an hour, spinning and weaving until the city began to materialize into something Alex was not ready to see.

It was his childhood home. It had been so long since he'd been here, and he had almost forgotten its name. Seeing Violet Hill now and smelling its anthracite dust, awakened a part of Alex he thought had been cast out after living in New York for a decade. But the memories he made in Violet Hill could never be completely wiped away. He founded his band here, formed his queer identity before it was cool to do such, and most of all learned what a true friend was thanks to Delilah.

He heard piano keys in the distance, the grit and gold of Delilah's voice, but it was overpowered by whatever sounds this place *wanted* him to hear. He found himself flailing through a river of orchids, but these were vastly different flowers, as each petal seemed to be zigzagged with neon veins, or runes. It was some kind of blueprint, and upon closer inspection he saw that it was actually a map. Then the music changed bars to the liquefying squeal of a synthesizer.

The walls were now sticker-scarred and scrawled in teenage poetry that echoed the awkwardness and pain of a life that lacked wisdom and experience; a life guided by spontaneity. The lighting scheme was stroboscopic and dizzying. If he'd been on any mind-altering substance, he'd have fallen to his knees from queasiness. Memories turned like pictures in a book. He rode the starwind in a pickup truck, smoked weed in the woods, and stole beer from the local convenience store.

Then it all stopped. A phantom weight lay atop him, like a blanket with hard edges and sharp fixtures. It reminded him of the bony protrusions of Rez's hips and rib cage. As he wiggled free from this weight, something brushed across his face, and there he caught a flash of red hair dye, green eyes and a maniacal grin. It *was* Rez, and he was slithering his body off of Alex's, but in such a way that Alex barely recognized the movements. The way the bones stretched and the skin threatened to tear—these were not normal or even possible with human anatomy. It was like seeing a human-sized rubber band reach its threshold.

"What are you doing?" Alex said.

Rez said nothing, just kept twisting his extremities, head nearly turned to the other side of his body. Alex heard the awful crack of small bones, snap of blood vessels. The only other thing he could hear was the metronomic sound of dripping. Alex noticed a puddle and put his hand in it. Not rain, but something viscous; the blood of the underground. The blackness coated Rez's eyes and stained his skin as if under the scope of a nightclub's black light.

Now the pressure between Alex's ears was red-hot. The mannequins were moving, step by careful step. Every time he blinked, they had somehow encroached closer. He looked above them, saw nothing but a city becoming more and more crowded with buildings and people. It felt like the place was on the verge of collapse, and the sound it all made—a sweet carnivorous music—had somehow helped Rez snap out of his possession.

Rez, Alex thought as loud as he could. *Hear me*. He pulled Rez's nimble body into his own. *Wake up*. As their lips met, he tasted everything and nothing. But Rez's eyes were wide open, and so blank; what was he even staring at? Maybe the endless skyline, maybe the mannequins. Even Emptiness, perhaps: the thing we're all born from and eventually revert back into. All matter is derived from emptiness and we've no choice but to rejoin it.

"We gotta go," Rez finally said.

Just as Alex summoned the strength, everything began disintegrating.

"Too late."

A purple shadow plummeted.

Dexter

Upon his return, the first thing Dorian noticed was the smell. It reminded him of melted plastic and unsettled dust. But it made no sense, now that the city was rising higher and faster than it had been initially. Each window sparkled darkly, and the edifices interchanged between a gemstone gleam and charcoal smear. The vision was welcoming as much as it created hysteria. There was no telling where Dorian had to go. The only thing he kept reminding himself was that he needed to just walk.

Sebastian was on his right, hypnotized by the rising sights and awful quiet, and he too was simply a silent version of himself. Either taking it in or unable to process the things he saw. All the impossible symmetries of these buildings, the never-ending sky and the doors that opened into an oblivion so bright that it made one think it was dark. Sebastian touched the inside of one of these doorways, fingers parting the light like curtains, only to feel it somehow touch him back, grip him all the way up to the elbow.

Dorian swatted Sebastian's hand, breaking his momentary trance, and then pulled them along. Their eyes could not stop focusing on the buildings, how they wavered and bulged as if they were bending, almost snapping. Spires twisted in metallic agony and gargoyles threatened to take wing. On the ground, detritus was strung about as it would be in any city, a collection of cigarette butts, beer bottles, random strands of colorful hair and plastic hands.

The hands confused Dorian the most. That was literally the only sign of life. If the dark windows and empty doorways were of any indication, no single person and no thing conducted their life down here. And how could they? Most life we know of so far needs light, water and an atmosphere to survive, and this place lacked one or the other, or all three. It would be a long time before anything could last more than a few weeks down here.

"Any idea where we're headed?"

"Your guess is as good as mine."

A new road unfurled, one made of purple stone and glass. Dorian looked down and saw his reflection, bone-white and decayed, perhaps what he would look like after he'd been dead for a few years. But he didn't have time to think about that, because of what he saw when Sebastian stepped into view. Scaled as a dragon and sinister as a serpent, Dorian saw the Hydra in her true form, its tongue darting to and fro, fungus nails parting the veil between its reality and Dorian's.

Dorian put his hand against the reflection. There was a moment when the Hydra's endless eyes locked onto his own, head turning and lips parting to show off its horrible smile. Then a hand snaked out of the darkness and clasped onto his wrist. Dorian could not hold back his scream even if he tried, and the power from the echo shook dust down from the sky.

"What's wrong?" Sebastian said.

"Nothing."

"Nobody screams like that unless something's wrong."

"It's just such a weird place," Dorian coughed into his hand. "Don't think I'll ever get used to it."

"You're right. It's very different from all the places we've seen."

"And we've seen some weird shit, but this really is the weirdest."

A new smell came, invading his windpipe and souring his taste buds. It embraced Dorian; he knew it was all around him even though he could not locate the source. It was the stuff that lives between the walls of old buildings, gateways to other places that were right under his nose this entire time. It was things dying, things burning. It was memory slowly fading away, only to be incarnated as he was thinking it. Each building slowly receding into the earth; the black trees tipping over and the concrete streets turning into gravel.

"What is this?" Sebastian said with his hand over his mouth.

"Hell."

Vast and empty as space itself, at least to the human eye, was all Dorian could see, perhaps what Dexter wanted him to see. Infinite as much as it was finite. There was no sight to behold, no skyline to provide them hope, no glimmer of light to show them that they could perhaps at some point find peace. They were staring into a great pit of nothing: the stuff that was before the Big Bang and would be left after the Big Rip.

Why was it so hard to believe darkness can take shape, reach out and hurt you, just as much as it can show you the way? Why was it so hard to believe that there are things living between shadows, even when there is no light to shine? If space itself could be bent and twisted, what's to stop darkness from doing the same?

"Now what?"

"Watch me."

Dorian kneeled, reached his hand into the void and scrambled it around until he felt something grab him. As soon as it did, he was tugged halfway into the ground, but Sebastian was already pulling him back, hard as he could until Dorian was freed. He was holding onto something. It was an entire arm, but it was stained black; Dorian could see the skin was an ugly artificial hue. It looked like it had once belonged to a mannequin.

"I have to go back in."

"No!"

Dorian had already slipped half of his body into the void. The cold sensation was not as overwhelming as before, but it certainly was not the same. As he slipped further in, as Sebastian begged him not to go, Dorian saw half his body stretch like taffy, while the other half maintained its original proportions. Despite the sight, he felt nothing; perhaps his eyes were betraying him, to see his bones bend and curve as if he was being twisted into some type of sculpture.

There came immerse, singeing heat. He had no choice but to pull back, wriggling his arm free to see that the once tattooed skin was now replaced by first-degree burns. The patterns were not familiar, nor were they even easy to see. Just a bunch of red lines and squiggles that kept bubbling and moving as if they had a mind of their own. When the pain began to equalize, Dorian saw that the lines were the outline of a city.

But Sebastian was running now—away from something or ahead of it, Dorian didn't know. As they collided, it forced them to descend, their bodies contorting into a helix, falling for what felt like forever. When they hit what they perceived to be ground, Dorian noticed that his nose was bleeding. There was only one thing left to do, the reason he even came back. He swiped the blood off his upper lip, then traced his finger on the ground.

The ground was not concrete or grass, it felt more like a canvas. Dorian moved his finger about, allowing the muse to take control and move his hand in ways he didn't even know were possible. The canvas absorbed his blood and repelled it all the same. But he kept drawing until his hand ached, until the bright metallic flavor coated the back of his throat.

The ground began to shift beneath their feet, splitting so fast there was only one way to go. And that was down. Gravity pulled them fast. Rush of blood to the head, red tears from the extreme change in pressure, but as they both swung on the downward spiral there was so much red above them it looked black. Runes, a path . . . a map glimmering in the nightwind until they came to a hard stop, luckily still on their feet as fires of indigo incinerated all around them.

"I've been waiting for you." The voice was hellish, almost sexual. "Now it's time to end this."

Dexter

21

Somehow, I was plummeting. It was as if my body had been hurled into the story sky and I was on the inevitable descent through a hypnotic swirl of dark and light. And then it stopped. I was back on ground, rising to meet Dexter's infinite gaze, his hair still so blindingly white and his eyes as purple as flowers. All around us the endless buildings encroached; it made me feel infinitely small, as we surely are in the expanse of the cosmos.

But I finally believed that there is a city right beneath Manhattan.

I took it all in. The great shabby edifices and ancient windows; the boiling sewers and swimming rodents. Every way I turned there was an empty sidewalk and even emptier housing project. Every corner that was hidden from plain sight, I knew, had the potential to show me horrible things. There were no cars and no trains, but life carried on down here, whether it was pretend or not.

"I won't let them take you from me." Dexter's tone was maleficent.

"Who would ever do that?" I pointed to the mannequins jokingly.

"I'm not playing around, Atticus."

There was something wicked about Dexter's eyes. All this time I'd been possessed by their heated desire, their impossible allure. But I saw something different in them now, and realized that I had to let him go. What could have been the greatest love story ever told was simply over. I felt a twist of pain in my soul; a gray cloud of guilt swelled inside my head. What had I taken part in? What had we all become?

"Where did Zephyr go?" I said without addressing his primary concern.

"Text him," Dexter said dismissively.

"You know that our phones don't work down here."

"I guess no more social media."

"Is that all you care about?"

Dexter shrugged, turned himself away. I felt more afraid than ever, now that Zephyr was not in my line of sight. He could've been anywhere in this horrible metropolis of bone and stone. To imagine a life without Zephyr was to imagine it without air. All would become moot, lost; no reason to gaze at anymore shimmering cities, no reason to question the miracles of stars that sit in the night sky like old-fashioned gas lamps. Dexter knew how true our bond was and did everything he could do to break it. He was selfish.

"I know everything, Dexter. You truly are the Eventual Devil."

"You only know what you think you know."

"And that's the worst part of it all."

"What is?"

"Your lies."

Dexter looked at me as if I was telling a fairytale. The blunt confusion warped his features, and he'd bit his nails so hard it left little red streaks in his hair every time he touched it. That blinding white had become a watery red. But something was off. I knew he was in my head, searching my thoughts and perhaps attempting to control them, just as he'd been doing since the day he met me. Only this time I was sickeningly aware of his little power, and I evaded him by thinking about only one thing: Zephyr.

"I love you," Dexter said. "But it always comes back to him."

"How is it love when you turned Zephyr against me?"

"You did that yourself."

To hear him say that with such callousness filled me with an electric rage. Because it really was all my fault. But there was still time to change course. I was overcome with a need for immediate escape, but the city just kept growing longer, and blacker. The more I thought about leaving, the more the dimensions fanned out, consumed me. There was no way to tell which way I had to take to find Zephyr and bolt.

I perused a random avenue and found that I could have lost myself in its black depths. I heard the squeal of a tricycle and the creak of a seesaw. There was the sound of children's laughter and the angry scowl of parents who sounded too tired to play all day. Cigarette smoke hit my nostrils, as did the freeing yellow scent of beer. I wanted a beer very badly, anything to remove my worry and replace it with liquid courage.

"Do any of the bars have beer down here?"

"Of course they do," Dexter's voice was filled with sarcasm. "Just think about what you want, and it will appear."

And so, I did. Alcohol. I wanted so much of it. But the old-school way, poured from the tap of a dive bar haunted by neon and shadowy people. I wanted to see a life before the pandemic and before Dexter. I kept my thoughts steady and my breath regulated. It would have been so easy to give into my own anxiety—Dexter would love to see that. I closed my eyes, hoped for the best.

When I opened them, I noticed the dark maw of an empty street, which then stretched into a row of bars. Their windows were bright with bleeding neon and their doors lined with rusted barbed wire. Bodies were strewn about the floor; I couldn't tell if they were fake or not but the horrible abscesses told me that they might have been real, and that they were decomposing.

I stepped over them and into the narrow walkways that separated each bar. Now I smelled fermentation and heard a cacophony of voices, the sign of good alcohol to come. Three doors appeared before my eyes, three doors made of ancient wood with foggy little windows cut out at the top that didn't allow me to see in, so my only choice was to just open one of them.

The bar was barren, seemed to be a shrine to dust and negligence. But I didn't care for aesthetics in this moment, I just needed a delicious drink. In the back I saw taps glowing and took it upon myself to pour two glasses of a fragrant IPA. The first one was for me. Suds bubbled over my lips and hops swarmed my palate with bitter flowers. It was a refreshing moment. Just as I was about to pour myself a second glass, my phone somehow had signal, and a text from Zephyr came through.

Put the molly in his glass

And then my signal was gone. But it hit me. Dexter hated the drug, and I'd never seen him use it. It made sense that this would do him dirty, so I laced the bottom of his glass with it. Back outside Dexter was waiting for me. When he saw that I was offering him a glass of beer, he must have thought I'd come to my senses. But the only sense I came to was to block him out of my head so he couldn't read my thoughts.

"What's the occasion?"

"The truth."

"That you finally believe me?"

"Yes."

As weird as that sounded, Dexter seemed to buy it. I closed my eyes. For one last moment I wanted to remember Dexter the way he was, not this thing he'd suddenly become. I couldn't help but still be intrigued by this boy, this mad artist and utter embodiment of brutal seduction. He'd introduced me to so much, opened my mind to things that I don't think I will ever see again in my lifetime, and for that I could never forget him. That made it worse to let him go.

Why is it that we want so much of all the things we shouldn't have?

We're all addicts one way or another, no matter the vice.

"Something about this drink," Dexter said.

"It's an IPA, your favorite."

"I'm not sure we ever talked about what my favorite beer is."

"Educated guess."

I winked at Dexter, then went on the move. Through the black labyrinth but somehow newly charged and ready to take on whatever was thrown at me. I barged through a throng of mannequins, pushed over a cabinet and heard it shatter. I was making any kind of noise so that Zephyr would hear me. If I had any chance to find him, I felt it was this moment of new drunken stupor.

But a mad confusion had come to claim me. I saw my drawing hand rise; neon spun in the air, then down into depths that devoured it whole. I reached for Dexter's face, brought him close enough to kiss . . . to kill. My hand grazed the fault line between reality and nightmare. This made Dexter laugh, perhaps he was already rolling. But my mind was laser-focused on Dexter, the smell of his sweet breath, the impossible glow of his eyes. I locked lips with him, breathed all of him in for the last time . . . before I let myself go. And he had no choice but to fall with me.

As we extricated, Dexter was no longer the white-haired, purple-eyed prince that I fell in love with. His skin had melted off his bones, bones not of this world, but some sort of black and swirling architecture, a clear picture of the darkness that lived beneath a parchment casing. All things moved in a hallucinatory manner, slippery imagery materializing into reality, drip by red drip. Paint gobs, I thought, the wet clay we sculptors yield as weapons.

"Trust is hard to find," I said.

"You've no reason not to trust me."

"No, that's where you're wrong!" I yelled louder than I planned to. "Delilah was right."

The illusion continued. Dexter was now reduced to a screaming mouth that rang out through the blackness around us. But I stood my ground, crazy me, and pulled Dexter closer. He was whole again, entranced by his phone, mouthing over and over that *they* would be here soon. His jaw moved back and forth freakishly, and his pupils had engulfed most of his iris. Dexter was high as a kite. I felt it too.

When I looked down, I saw *The Witness* in all its grotesque glory, blackhole mouth lined in jagged metal, gargoyle sneer like I've never seen before. This time it shrieked, but only inside of my head. Its chitinous pincers clawed at the pole driven through its paunch, while its body slowly raised up on those terrible tarantula legs. Little red eyes locked onto my own with such a force that I felt my knees and elbows bend into benediction. I found myself recording it with my phone. Dexter was as well, his grin as wide and comical as some crazy clown.

I lifted my boot to stomp it, but just before I did a slew of voices, footsteps and screams bamboozled us. Little fires came into my view, slowly spreading into the outlines of various human bodies that smelled of ozone and the blackness of space. It reminded me of the way asteroids go up in flame when they hit our atmosphere. Maybe this was my first trip into dreaming while awake. Maybe this was that corny moment we used to see on TV: *THIS IS YOUR BRAIN ON DRUGS* . . . the dissociative effects finally bordering on permanence.

The bodies swarmed, and as soon as my eyes adjusted, I saw one brown eye and one green, blue hair and bright pink lips: Zephyr. Behind him was the benevolent Cruella De Ville, better known as Delilah Dellinger; the bizarre painter Dangerous Dorian and New York's reigning queen of the night, the Hydra, aka Sebastian Ricciuti. I was now in the presence of safety.

"Atticus!"

Zephyr bolted into my arms. It felt like an eternity since we'd seen one another, and we exchanged no words. We didn't need to; our souls did all the talking. My lips met his, engulfed their familiar softness, tongues quickly gliding to the back of one another's throats. All at once my feelings imploded, everything from guilt to regret, to the calming sensation of *home*. I'd done this poor boy wrong, and here he was like a puppy dog in my arms, just hoping that I would make it all go back to the way it was. And I would. This time I'd not let Dexter bate me with art, and most of all possess me with sex.

"The gang's all here." Emotions waged war on Dexter's face. "Now let's put all this fuss to bed."

"You cocksucking son a bitch," Delilah spit.

"I'm no one's son."

"Because you killed your mother."

Then the last two figures emerged, their hands clasped and white-knuckled, and they didn't need to say anything to make me understand who they were. Judging by the look on Dexter's pale and lifeless visage, he was not ready for the surprise. The two boys, however, were extremely determined, and ready for anything.

"Still up to your old tricks," Rez said.

"I thought you'd have forgotten by now."

"You're a fucking weirdo."

"Not as weird as you stalkers."

"You haven't changed a day," Alex said.

"Even after what you two did to me."

"You really are . . . *something else.*"

"*You* tried to kill me."

"There's no *try* this time."

"I loved you, Rez. Too bad you couldn't ditch that wet rat."

"So, this is what you do?" Dorian stepped forward, wielding a paint brush like a weapon. "You prey on couples, try to break them up?"

"Ah, the famous painter and his tranny boyfriend."

"Not a tranny," Sebastian said.

"The heart wants what it wants." Dexter's eyes were mean and bright. "That can't be helped."

"But cognizance and awareness can be. Seems that's what you lack. If you're even human, that is."

"Who are you, Dorian? The philosopher of the group?"

"No, he's the antagonizer."

Delilah removed one hand from behind her back, exposed a twisted sculpture she called the wrong thing. It trembled in her hand, and as soon as Dexter saw it his face devolved into a frown, all teeth and spit and no control. He swiped, but Delilah was too quick, pulling her body back before Dexter could make contact. Then she defensively lifted her leg and pistoned it into Dexter's gut. A horrible sound fell out of his mouth that made everyone hold their ears.

"You're gunna die, bitch."

Dexter lunged, arms somehow elongating before his body did, terrifying as an unfolding spider. His t-shirt tore from the back, exposing small leathery wings that propelled him faster toward Delilah. But she was ready for him before he knew what was coming. I saw her bite one of the wrong thing's little legs and tear it free from the clay body; black pulp daubed her chin. Dexter stopped dead in the air, then fell to the ground, breaking through the bedrock as if it was made of paper.

A creeping sound slithered below.

Furrows erupted.

Dust and debris blew into my face. I lost my balance, toppled into Zephyr and Delilah, while the rest ran to the other side of the room. I wiped my eyes and soon realized that the screams I heard were not human—they were from the sculptures that were now crawling down from various shelves and display windows. Mantis prance; wings of fallen angels; the broken music of the damned. Just as I got to my feet, I threw Zephyr behind me, saw that my hand was now glowing the strange blue of the deep sea, and Dorian's arm had reached across the fissure, dabbing my wet hand with his brush. He began to paint; Sebastian molted into some sick creature, and Delilah sang us all into the abyss.

It all came crashing down. Like the hissing tail of a shooting star, or the silent geysers on moons we can't see. Like muted screams. This place, this moment, was pulled into a single pinpoint of light—until it burst. The implosion was too intense to actually see, but it sent glittering clusters of phosphorescence into the air. The force pushed Zephyr's body through a nest of neon clouds just as the crippling fingers of MDMA began its crawl from the center of his brain to the tips of his toes.

To be so removed from reality, but also so in touch with it, was a form of vulnerability Zephyr rarely enjoyed. But right now, this was the way. The city was now divided by fault lines that had heated up to the color of molten lava. Many new buildings erupted from these bright depths, and they spit heat into Zephyr's face, enough to dry the sweat in his hair. The rest of the group stumbled around confused but ready to fight, even though there was no sign of Dexter other than the occasional shadow crawling beneath the bedrock.

"This isn't what's supposed to happen," Delilah said.

A raw form of insanity twisted her features. Zephyr watched she stuck her hand into one of the bright fissures, her skin completely aglow as it came up empty handed. *Not here*, she whispered. Then she began scanning the huge city with determined emerald eyes. She shared no words, no warning before she pushed herself through the edifice of one the lava-colored buildings, leaving behind a black outline of her body.

"Now what do we do?" Dorian said.

"We follow."

Zephyr pressed his hand into the fiery fault line at his feet, then let let it sink to the elbow. There was no sensation, and when he pulled it out, there was a black slime on his arm. Then he walked directly into the radiating building. Immediately, it felt like the ground had been ripped out from beneath his feet, earthly body spinning in the void, as if he was riding the great spiral arms of our Milky Way galaxy.

The phosphorescence dripped blue and white behind his eyes. But he pressed forward, guided by the sound of music, Delilah's music, so loud in his ears he thought they'd bleed. Through the flame, Zephyr saw the squiggly pink outline of Delilah's hair, but something had spread out on both sides of her, the great leathery wings of what looked like a dragon. Zephyr called out to Delilah, but she was too far away to hear. He had no choice but to watch.

The wings enshrouded Delilah's body, pulled her into its blackness. As the thing grew larger, making Delilah appear as small as an ant in its presence, Zephyr began to feel its phantom pull. Slowly, his body began to spaghettify. Every limb wiggled like sound waves in the direction of the winged beast. He had no muscle control, no way to stop the gravitational tug. The more he tried to run, the more it took him in like hot quicksand.

The inside of the building was melting all around him. Jellified fire slowly slid down the walls, blocking off the way he had entered. In the distance, the wings were no longer shadow, but forceful hands springing forth, mantis fingers and fungus-colored nails doing an ethereal tarantula dance. They pulled both he and Delilah free from the blaze and back out into the middle of the city.

There, Delilah was levitating in the center of a huge fissure, body wringed in a blue-white light. Her spidery hair lifted, as if it had a mind of its own; one of the pink and black things wrapped about Zephyr's leg, the other Atticus' face. They both screamed as they were pulled by their feet, until they were upside down and slowly being dipped into so much darkness Zephyr thought he saw light.

As the blood rushed to his head, Delilah began to sing. This time, it was in sync with the glyphs that Dorian was painting. He'd climbed up the rocky wall, paintbrush in hand; it was not so much a thing of wood and bristles anymore, but a cosmic weapon that could cut through reality as if a surgeon's scalpel. Zephyr saw the razor-tipped brush slice into the air, peeling back the skin of space and time.

Then something swooshed in the air next to Zephyr, so fast it cracked like a bullet and sprayed yellow ions into his face. The force tore a hole so big he smelled the actual universe, all that electric, X-ray and sulfur. Then it dashed away, this time making the hairs on Zephyr's arms stand up as the imprint of a glistening serpent eating its own tail came into view.

Hydra

She rose from the depths below them, darkness parting like curtains before a show. She was not a thing of this earth, she was something intangible and unimaginable. Beauty wrapped in rage, tied with a bow of blood. Hate personified rising into the sticky black air. With her came the heat of halos and the stench of new death; not the kind that rots deep in the earth and turns to worm food, but the fresh stench of life transferring out of the body and back into the cosmos.

"Behold," Delilah said. "Our key."

A microphone was pressed so close to her mouth that red lipstick stained its silver surface. The melody that left her throat was as succulent and evil as candy, worming into Zephyr's ear so slyly that he felt a tickle in his gag reflex. Dorian was now halfway up one of the buildings; he'd climbed so high Zephyr could barely see the warzone of acrylic and oil he'd painted up there. It was a mountain of wetness, shapes and glyphs of an unknown origin. Waterspouts of paint pushed little particles of neon unto Zephyr and Atticus, which then created a wet corona around the Hydra as she continued to play exquisite corpse with reality and dream.

Zephyr saw her bones bend and snap. She was putting on the show of a lifetime—but it was more than just a show, it was an uprise. She was calling Dexter out. All at once things started rippling into existence, sculptures and doorways and nothingness. There was no stopping it. The forces around them all began to weaken. The earth crumbled.

There may be no coming back

Zephyr grabbed Atticus' hand and dived.

I woke to the sound of Delilah's colossal voice. It filled me with a strength I never knew my body could possess. I could have punched my hand through the bedrock, lifted all the buildings that polluted this city, balanced the world on my shoulders. I was so alarmingly alive. That is, until I saw the wings of a dragon and the legs of a huge spider imprint itself into the molten colored skyscraper.

It was like some surreal cut-out against the supernova brightness, a brightness that pierced my eyes and shot out the back of my head. But the outline was unmistakable. It sent a negative charge through my body; I'd seen it in every dream I'd had since meeting Dexter. I put my hand against the black outline, felt an incredible cold bite it, then grabbed hold. I wanted to pull Dexter out, squash him under my boot like a fly. Instead, some force threw me back; it was Delilah, Zephyr and Dexter tumbling out the flame.

The boy was completely feral. His pupils had overtaken both his eyes so that he looked like there were two pools of ink floating in his head. The shadow cast behind him was exactly how I saw it against the fiery building, huge and impossible. I found myself taking photos of this phenomena–still the social media addict no matter the predicament–even as amphetamines were boiling in my bloodstream. I now knew why crackheads destroyed their lives for this preternatural feeling. It is a state of mind that cannot be adequately described; one of those rare things that must be lived to truly understand. Imagine if we could cuddle hallucination, scoop out the lucid meat in our brains and smear it across the sky; even that could never rightfully explain the chemical sensations.

"I want to feel it," I said to myself.

I stuck my hand into the shadow and parted the delicate membrane of illusion. My consciousness rose into an alternate reality, guided by a tunnel vision that was jarring as much as it was fascinating. I felt myself split like dry wood under a falling axe. With my mortal body left behind in that blighted dark city, I was now free to explore the hills and guttural streets of dreamland.

Everything wavered and waned. Through this dissociation, I was free to become whatever I was to become, free to go wherever I may go. I wandered through this city I could not name. All its lifeless breed of people, shady intersections, and neighborhoods you didn't want to be caught dead in. Graffiti squirmed and featureless faces peered out of broken windows; doorways were blacker than ever.

Every moment of clarity came with an equal maelstrom of insanity. Was I a living being? Was I ever really there? Did the beat of my heart and tick of my brain mean I was still a sentient creature? I thought that this must be what death is, the intangible state of a melodious song, as the soul slipped free from the awful responsibility of life and was transferred into the great unknown.

I'd been to this wasteland before; Delilah had shown me the way, and so I knew that there was no actual path, no end goal. I just needed to move. I saw shadow and light, the stuff between shadow, the stuff that light is made from. Particles too small to see with the naked eye shattered into billions of bright beads, formed geometric shapes, then slowly devolved into caricatures of myself, Zephyr and Dexter.

I felt something cut me before I realized that my hand was in my pocket. It was a sculpting blade slick with blood, as well as a small splitting hammer and pointed chisel. I was holding these holy sculpting tools, yet not holding them at all. I could feel the almost erotic pleasure I get when chipping away at a new project, that magical moment of the small bones of my hand colliding with fresh clay. I used the blade to cut an entrance into time and space, until a dazzling doorway of vacuum yawned before my eyes.

Between the planes of dream and reality, I saw a great serpent-skinned monster shine like onyx stone, eyes as hideous as a low gibbous moon. Her dance was feral, almost sexual in the way her tongue gyrated across blood-red lips, fungus-colored nails sizzling. I knew this creature was the Hydra, a personification of beauty and rage. Her ritual dance was something I've seen in countless clubs and in the faces of people possessed by MDMA, mushrooms and ketamine.

She beckoned me through the curving darkness. That's when I saw the dragon wings again, shiny fangs and the blackest eyes. As I moved into her circle, I was taken by the sight of another being. A skinny man whose face was veiled by a curtain of black hair, pale skin slashed and dashed in neon acrylic. He wielded a paint brush like a weapon rather than a pathway to art.

It was Dorian, and the strange patterns he drew were all somehow coming alive on the canvas. All at once a massive blueprint appeared, as bright and burning as fire itself. The shapes meshed, collided, and I felt the twinge in my hand, felt the pulse beat right into it. The song continued playing, and I knew the voice that flew over the industrial guitar chords, golden and sweet as honey. *Delilah.* That was when the shapes began to form musical notes, and those notes spun until they sucked me down into the vortex of soundless sound.

I saw the outline of a man waiting for me on the other side. We stared at one another for a very long time, as if we had nothing but time. Heliotrope irises locked onto me, and the pupils were as black as dark matter. But that man was no man at all, I realized. He was just a figment of my imagination, craven lust and selfish desires. But I was his as well, the seed that sprouted into an opportunity that he could not stop himself from taking. One's loneliness can drive them to do crazy things. But for me that adventure was over.

"You can't be without me," Dexter said. "No matter how hard you try, I'm in here, Atticus." Dexter pointed to his brain. "I always will be."

Dexter's finger, which was no longer a finger but a small chisel, bore a hole into the side of his head until his temple and cheek were slick with an oily black substance. I touched the stuff, found myself instantly attracted to its poison. But at the same time, for the first time, I felt myself fight temptation. I retracted my hand; he cried out. His human form began to devolve into something so sinister my vision could not decipher what it truly was. A ghastly thing made of time, space and darkness.

But I would not let it go.

"Is it more painful to be in love than never know love at all?" I said.

With the heart he daubed in darkness, I grabbed his head and began to squeeze. Skin delineated and fascia tore; the bone beneath popped like a light bulb. I felt the tiny hairs of his face tickle my fingertips, the wetness of his eyes pour onto my hands. This new neon blood boiled inside of me; it was the only way I was going to make sure this creature would go away and never come back to haunt me, Zephyr, or anyone.

Then I heard Dorian say something like *mangle him*, and the Hydra say something like *get inside*. And so I did. Fingers digging until they pierced the jellied madness cradled within his skull. I saw into his darkness, the depthless hole in his soul; countless cities beneath every city, to a place where light and energy went in, but never out. My other hand recorded it with my phone; perhaps I would show this to the world later on, make Dexter more famous . . . in death.

My anger could not be tamed. I just kept tearing into Dexter until I exposed the empty cavity of his thorax. There, I was able to see all the gelatinous human faults and traumas, his hominid shell, until I reached the dark arc beneath, process of no-process, a place where the infinity of the universe might have started by means we cannot explain.

"I loved you," I said to the newly transmogrified face.

Then I dug deeper.

My artistic hand was wild and free; I had to get inside of him, my gods I had to *feel it*. Gaping jaw, gaping hole in the heart and head, my hand reaching deeper and Dexter screaming louder. Down through the mouth and throat, rattling the small bones of the neck, further than any hand should go; clear a path to a place where just maybe no one has ever been. I lost myself between sight, touch and sound as every sense blended.

All of this to unveil—no, *unzip*—him as if he never had a skin at all, just a sheet of meat housing that had been fashioned in hell. Thread by gooey thread I undid Dexter . . . until he fell apart in my hands, house of cards crumbling, but wet like organs; gob by glistening gob he bubbled away, irises and soft hair, particle by particle he was called back to the city beneath the city, the unnameable darkness that he had daubed upon my heart.

All of this in my hands falling away, not like grains of sand, but dried clay.

NYC born and raised J. Daniel Stone writes urban horror with a queer focus. He sold his first story when he was twenty-two and has since written four novels (*The Absence of Light, Blood Kiss, Stations of Shadow* and *Daubed in Darkness*), as well as a short story collection (*Lovebites & Razorlines*) and a novella (*I Can Taste The Blood*). He writes under a pseudonym to keep the wolves at bay.

Visit him at **www.SolitarySpiral.com**
and all socials **@SolitarySpiral**